Among Us

A Novel By A.J. Mayers

This is a work of fiction. Names, characters, businesses, organizations, places, events, and incidents are the product of the author's imagination or are used fictitiously. Any resemblance to actual persons, living or dead, or actual events is entirely coincidental.

Copyright © 2011 by A.J. Mayers

Edited by Krysten A. Michaels

www.aj-mayers.com/amongus

ISBN 978-1-105-11123-5

To my Mother, Ruth and My Father, Anthony for always supporting and believing in me...

Contents

Chapter One:
The Undisclosed Location

It had been one of the hottest days in the city of Los Angeles. The sun was setting below the mountains on that summer August day. The 101 freeway was bumper to bumper with the usual L.A. traffic of commuters heading home from a long day of work.

Derek Conrad, a professional photographer and entrepreneur, was very successful in his craft. His majority of work was dedicated to "A-Listers" and the high fashion industry. Derek was in his forties, and possessed an attractive, distinguished look. Derek's hair was salt and pepper, and he possessed a sort of confidence that was very attractive.

Derek was zipping in and out of lanes in haste to get home. He drove a black BMW convertible. The top was off and he was enjoying the warm breeze, which was much nicer than the sweltering heat from earlier in the day.

"Tomorrow is going to be another hot one," the DJ on the radio station from Derek's car said, "Definitely going to be in the nineties. Get those swimsuits out and flock to Santa Monica beach or even Malibu! Hell, if you have to work, wear shorts – if they let you!"

"I'm my own boss, so I will," Derek chuckled to himself.

He put on his turn signal and took an exit off the freeway and headed up the canyon to his Hollywood Hills home. He lived alone. He was married to work, and although he dated occasionally, he was more content with the love for his camera and the stills that he produced.

Derek's cell phone rang, and he answered, while speeding up the hills in his BMW, "Hello?"

"Hey it's Candy," said a sultry voice from the other end of his smart phone.

"And to what do I owe for this pleasant surprise," Derek replied with glee.

"Well," Candy began, then paused for a few minutes. "I was wondering if you were in the mood for a few cocktails. Perhaps your house? Tonight?"

"Sure, I'm actually about to pull up to my pad now. What time should I expect you?" Derek responded.

"Give me an hour. Muah." She kissed the receiver.

Derek pulled onto the pavement of his expensive two-story white wooden house, nestled nicely through a gate, on top of a hill. His home overlooked Hollywood with the L.A. skyline in the distance.

He opened his door and was greeted by his two Yorkies barking and hopping with excitement at the view of their owner.

"Hello girls, you hungry?"

After feeding his puppies, he proceeded to his bedroom to dress into something more comfortable. He was wearing a Polo button down shirt and slacks, and even after a long day of stress and photographs, Derek was always tactful with his appearance.

His phone began ringing. The ringtone sounded like a bunch of camera flashes that were coming from a press line or paparazzi shoot. The caller ID said "unknown" so he let it go to voicemail.

He checked his phone minutes later and noticed there was no icon that signaled a voicemail had been left. Instead, the day's date, August 13, was shown. Then, the doorbell rang.

"Coming!" He yelled and he left his phone on his bed and ran to the door to open it. As he did, framed between the doorway was a beautiful woman. She was tall with dirty-blonde hair. She was curvy and had piercing green eyes. Her slender form and flawless face would make one think she had work done. She was in her mid thirties but was trying to look twenty-five.

"Candy! Gorgeous as always," Derek said.

"Derek Conrad, photographer extraordinaire to the stars. How the hell are you? It has been too long. Are you going to invite me in?" Candy persisted.

"Of course. Care for the usual? Gin and Tonic?" Derek asked.

Candy looked at him with a sensual smile. "Yes Mr. Conrad. Make it worth my time."

Derek served himself a whiskey coke from the bar in his luxurious living room. Everything in there was modern and simple. It all was designed very retro-chic. He then poured a gin and tonic and made it stronger than his and gave it to Candy as she sat down on his couch.

"Thanks Derek," She said, "You know that I'm here because I need your services."

"Again doll face? Last month you wore me out," Derek winked.

"Hmm. Mmm. I'm not here to let you down. But what I meant was, I want to do another photo shoot. I want sexy. I need new headshots and, um, chest shots. These... are new. Meet the girls," She said pointing to her breasts.

"Indeed, um, new...they are new! I don't remember them looking so—perfect," Derek blushed.

"The thing is," she went on ignoring his comment, "I'm not getting any younger. I haven't booked a model or acting gig in a year. Well, one that is worth my time. I do need to pay my surgery bills too."

"I thought you were going to work on this big blockbuster superhero film?" Derek said.

"It got recast with some skinny young bitch that looks like she's eighteen but she's really twenty six," Candy said through gritted teeth.

The two continued to drink away and conversed like old friends that had not seen each other in years.

Derek habitually reached for his cell in his pocket only to realize he left it in his bedroom.

"Got to check my cell. I have a call time tomorrow, but waiting for the producer to send me my schedule. Be right back." Derek proceeded to his bedroom.

Candy yelled to him from the living room as he reached for his cell phone on his bed, "You know your place is quite lovely. Why is a handsome man like you still single?"

"Handsome?" Derek yelled back while looking at his phone only to notice there were fifteen missed calls from an "unknown" caller. "Why thank you. You are quite the temptress…"

"It adds character. Just shave it all off. A lot of leading men are doing that. Gets rid of the grays too," Candy said seductively.

Derek did not reply. He was scrolling through the missed call log. There were no voicemails either. Just then it began to ring again.

Derek hesitated and answered, "Hello?"

"Is this Derek Conrad from Derek Conrad Photography?" asked a voice with a southern accent and drill-sergeant type of manner.

"Yes it is. May I ask who this is? I don't take business calls after eight PM, unless it's urgent or with a client," Derek said annoyed.

"This is urgent. Mr. Conrad," the man on the line continued, "we have come across some of your work and it appears that you have camera equipment that is superb for shooting in low-light situations and from great distances. You must have some lenses that zoom in very far. Not many photographers in your field use this type equipment, however you are the closest person to our camp and we request your services at three AM this evening in an undisclosed location. This is not something we are asking, more like ordering—"

"Are you crazy? Who the hell is this and do you know that I have plans this evening that do not allow me t—"

"Mr. Conrad," the man continued in a more urgent voice, "I am with the United States Military. We are contacting you on orders from one of over government organizations. I cannot talk about the name of the organization over the phone but we will explain when we arrive at your residence off of Mulholland Drive."

"How the hell? What the hell?" Derek seemed confused and freaked out by this unknown caller claiming to be from the U.S. Military.

"A group of my men will come for you and fly you to our base camp and give you an orientation for the task ahead. This is all classified information. We will be at your residence in about an hour."

The caller hung up leaving Derek flabbergasted. Candy had walked into the room apparently having eavesdropped but not understanding much more than Derek was able to even process.

"Who was that?" She asked.

"I have no idea. Listen, maybe you should go? Let's do dinner next week once I'm done with the current project I'm on. Are you ok to drive?" Derek asked.

"Really? It's early. You know I wanted to stay later." Candy said put off.

"Candy, I'm not in the mood tonight. Listen, I have lots to attend to right now. Let's reconnect via phone tomorrow and hash out details for a dinner date. I'll even have my publicist friend stage paparazzi at the restaurant so you can be photographed arriving and leaving."

"You know how to get a girl wild. Thanks babe, I'll talk to you tomorrow." Candy left her glass in the living room bar and walked out of his house.

Derek locked the door and closed his blinds. He turned off his TV and walked to his upstairs lofted office. He turned on his iMac and opened his email. He still had not received his shoot schedule for the following day.

Just then his phone rang again, however this time the call was from a familiar name, "Robert Powers."

"Robert!" Derek answered.

"Derek, hey I hope your shoot went well today."

"It did, what's up Rob?" Derek replied.

"Can't a guy call his best bud for the hell of it? I'm coming into town with the wife next week and we want to have dinner at a five-star in Beverly Hills. Can you make that happen?"

"For college buds, of course! I can't wait to see you and Pam. What are you in town for this time?"

"The kids wanted to go to Disneyland this year so we thought we'd do a Hollywood tour as well. We're also going to visit Pam's brother and nephew," Robert said, "You've met them a few times."

"Yes! Your nephew reminds me...of me. He's good at wielding a camera if I recall. Come to think of it, I promised to give him one of my old ones. Remind me about that and keep me posted. I have some business to take care of. We'll talk soon. Sound good?"

"Yeah. Thanks bro!" And Robert hung up.

Derek placed his phone in his pocket and walked over to his front door and looked out through the peephole. There was nobody there. He shrugged, and then walked to his kitchen to fix himself a sandwich.

There were stainless steel appliances in his kitchen. Everything was clean and shiny. It was obvious that the house was new.

Derek began putting mayonnaise on his sandwich, when he heard a loud truck engine outside. He looked through the kitchen window, which gave a small view of his front porch driveway. He noticed that this was no ordinary truck. He had two visitors in military uniforms get out of an army Hummer and head towards his front door. Seconds later, there was a rushed ringing of his doorbell that chimed throughout his home. He ran to the door, heart pounding, and opened it.

There in the doorway stood two tall, fit men. They were in military uniforms, and a United States flag was embroidered at the chest. They seemed like real officers, but Derek could not help but think this was some sort of joke.

"Derek Conrad?" asked the officer with blue eyes. It was the man who had talked to him on the phone earlier.

Derek answered, "Yes. I presume it was you that I spoke with on the phone? What exactly is going on?"

"I'm Lieutenant Carter. I don't have much time to talk, but my colleagues at our base camp will give you more info. I was asked to tell you to bring your lenses and camera gear for low-light situations from far distances. All you need to know right now is that you will be taking high-profile and classified confidential photographs for the United States government for a confidential organization called the Department of NHR."

"What's NHR?" Derek asked completely shocked that the government wanted him to work for them. "And you do know I only photograph celebrities. Is this part of the high-profile aspect of it?"

"Not necessarily sir," the other officer piped in, "I'm Officer Williams. Look, we can't talk more about what we have already told you, but as a civilian you will need to be briefed before the project that will take place at three AM, Pacific Standard Time. Due to the sensitivity of this mission, you will be transported to an undisclosed location."

Lieutenant Carter jumped in. "Mr. Conrad come with us. You will be doing your country a great favor."

Derek was unable to get a word in. Both men, larger and stronger than he was, pushed him from his back and abruptly rushed him to the army vehicle.

Once inside, the two men jumped to the front seats and Lieutenant Carter drove off. As he sped down the narrow Hollywood Hills roads, he looked into the rear-view mirror and spoke to Derek.

"We'll be taking a private plane out of Santa Monica Airport."

"I have to work tomorrow. What time will we be back?" Derek asked defeated, knowing at this point there was no point to argue.

"I'd say seven AM the latest," Officer Williams replied.

"Good. I just won't get any sleep. Perfect." Derek mumbled to himself.

About thirty minutes later, the Hummer pulled into the Santa Monica Airport. Carter and Williams got off and ushered Derek into the terminal where a small private civilian plane was waiting.

"Discreet, eh? Trying not to look out of place?" Derek said looking at the plane, then back at the commodious Hummer he had arrived it.

"Don't miss a trick do you?" Lieutenant Carter said and smiled for the first time since they had met face-to-face.

A group of more military men and two men in black suits were waiting on the tarmac next to the small private plane. Derek was ushered to the men in suits. He gave them one glance and smiled, but their expressions remained stoic.

"Mr. Conrad if you would please head up quickly, we'll be on our way," said one of the suited men. He looked like he was in his mid thirties. He was a very good-looking man and had dark rimmed black eyeglasses. The other man, Hispanic, seemed much older and his dark hair was graying.

Derek began climbing up the steps into the plane. It only seated eight people. The suited men and both Carter and Williams were taking flight with Derek. They all sat in their seats and buckled up. Derek was very intrigued by what was going on. The only thing that came to mind, was perhaps this was some sort of national security defense crisis. Yet, he still was unsure why his photography skills were needed.

"I'm Agent Ramos," said the Hispanic man in a thick accent reaching to shake Derek's hand who obliged politely. Agent Ramos seemed much more relaxed than the military men in his presence and he was rather friendly in nature. He kept staring at Derek in a curious manner.

"I'm Agent Parker," the other man in the suit said. He was seated next to Agent Ramos and they were both facing Derek.

"Nice to meet you. Now is this where you explain why I am here?" Derek asked.

Agent Ramos began, "Yes. We were planning to brief you at the camp when we landed but its much quieter here and the flight should be smooth."

Agent Ramos looked out the window. Just then the plane began to back out onto the runway.

"So," Agent Ramos continued, now directing his attention to Derek, "Agent Parker and I are part of the United Stated Department of Non-Human Relations – NHR."

Derek raised his eyebrows. Up until this point he felt everything was very serious and political in some way, but after hearing "Non-Human Relations" he felt like laughing. However, after a quick glance at Carter and Williams' serious faces, he decided against making a sarcastic remark.

"Mr. Conrad. Derek," Agent Parker began, "This department that Ramos and I are a part of is very, very small."

"Prepare for take off," the pilot's voice came on over the intercom. Just then the plane set forth full speed and a minute later the wheels were off the ground and the jet was airborne over the Pacific Ocean. Derek could see the Santa Monica pier distinguishable by the Ferris wheel lights. It was pitch black towards the endless horizon of the ocean.

Derek looked back at Agent Parker who then began speaking once he and Derek made eye contact, "NHR. Our department name is very specific. We focus on relations with beings that aren't human. I won't go further into this matter because we are already divulging information that took years for Ramos and I to receive. Anything you see or hear today must not be relayed in any way, shape, or form. Not via phone, text, social media, blog, news media, books, etc. I will not make you sign any kind of non-disclosure forms, but you will be taking an oath right before we land."

Derek was still trying to process what he just heard, "So what do you mean by non-human? Are we talking creatures that can interact with humans and have some sort of relation? Aliens?"

"Derek," Ramos spoke up, "You are to make your own assumptions. We cannot by law tell you much about what we do and what—who we deal with per say, but you will get a glimpse. We do not talk about work outside of work. We ask that you do the same. You will be under surveillance and receive counseling sessions for check ups for about three months after this night."

"You cannot," Derek said eyeing them both back and forth, "Be serious? This sounds absurd."

"Derek," Parker said, "We are sorry for the inconvenience. You will be compensated twenty-five thousand dollars for any trouble this has caused. The counseling will be free and it'll be with one of the top psychiatrists entrusted to the government."

Derek was dumbfounded. He decided not to complain. He was actually very interested in what he was going to see.

Outside the window, Derek saw nothing but mountains in the distance. There were no city lights in his range of vision. They were in the desert. He wasn't sure if he was in California or not. They had been airborne for over an hour and were slowly descending.

He moved up his sleeve to check the time. It was already two in the morning. He yawned and though exhausted, his curiosity kept him from falling asleep. He grasped his bag that held his camera equipment out of habit to make sure it was still there. He took another glance at the window and could see lights getting closer. It was so dark, but he figured it was the camp base they were going to land at.

"We are a few minutes from landing. Seatbelts on, everyone." The pilot said.

The landing strip was becoming more and more noticeable. The area of the camp was very secluded. There were no public roads or any buildings he could see for miles.

The intercom started up again, but the cabin could not make out the voice of the pilot. It was very static. Seconds later, the lights went out and it was pitch black.

"What's happening?" Derek said worried.

"We'll be fine. There's a significant amount of activity in the area that causes electronic malfunctions. It's never anything serious," Carter answered.

Derek swallowed hard and looked out of the window towards the ground. The jet was heading straight toward the landing strip. He glanced up in the sky and did a double take. For a second he thought he saw a full moon but he looked out the window on the other side of the plane and saw the moon was on that side and it was not full. He looked back at the white orb he first saw, but it was gone. Were his eyes playing tricks?

The lights came back on just as the wheels touched the ground. It was a smooth landing. He stared at the different hangars surrounding the landing strip. It looked like he was at a movie studio. The buildings looked like large warehouses. In the distance he could see they were in an enclosed facility with walls that must have been thirty feet high.

"Well, we are here. Sector 7," Agent Parker said.

"Is this Area 51?" Derek blurted.

"Ha. No," Agent Ramos replied, "Parker said it's Sector 7. That's all you need to know. Thank you. Now, lets get off this plane."

The officers, agents, and Derek disembarked from the plane to be greeted by several officers with guns at their side. Another man in a suit greeted them. He had a book in one hand that looked like it was a bible.

"Derek Conrad, my name is Agent Green," the man with the bible said, "I am to give you your oath as there was lighting issues before the landing. Can you rest your hand on this bible?"

Derek obliged.

"Do you swear to keep any information you may see or hear in the next few hours, prior to your return to Los Angeles, with yourself until the grave, so help you God?"

Derek looked at Agent Green. This was not a joking situation. He could sense the tension with over twenty officers with guns at their sides. He gulped.

"I will. So help me God."

Agent Green smiled and ushered Derek down the tarmac and straight to an army Jeep that seated four: Derek, Agent Green, who was driving with Agent Parker and Ramos in the backseat.

The Jeep sped down a small path. Sector 7 was well lit for the night. It looked like it could have been daytime. The buildings were all gray and metal looking. They were unmarked. There were no signs. He assumed that if you worked there you knew what was inside and where you were going.

After a few minutes, they reached the entrance to Sector 7.

"We're leaving the camp?" Derek asked.

"Yes, our business for the evening is a few miles out. We are heading up to that mountain," Agent Green said, and he pointed at a dark looming mountain that seemed a good few miles away.

There were a few guards standing near the huge gate that let them out into the dark desert. The high beams of light of the Jeep flipped on, and they proceeded down a narrow dirt path.

The night was cold. It was a stark contrast to the warm LA night he left just a few hours prior. There was complete silence in the jeep. The only sound was the engine and the wheels racing against the beaten dirt path.

Derek kept looking at the sky trying to find the moon, but he could no longer see anything. The sky suddenly appeared nebulous.

"Strange," Derek said, breaking the silence, "There wasn't a cloud in the sky when we were up in the air."

The agents gave each other uncomfortable looks and continued to gaze towards the mountain they were traveling to.

"This is so weird," Derek thought to himself.

The drive seemed to go on forever. They had been driving for half an hour when they began to climb up on this small man-made path on the side of the mountain.

"We're going to be late. It's ten till three." Agent Ramos said.

"I'm hauling it Ramos," Agent Green responded sounding frustrated.

Derek remained silent. The agents kept glancing at the time on the dashboard. There was nothing but darkness on the edge of the mountain. In the distance, he could see the glowing lights of Sector 7 miles away. He saw lights shooting out from it, which he gathered were planes taking off.

"Just over here. We'll park," Agent Green said, "Derek get your camera equipment ready. Parker, toss him a jacket. It's going to be chilly.

Agent Parker pulled a Northface jacket from the trunk and tossed it to Derek in the passenger seat. The Jeep then came to a complete stop, and Agent Green turned off the engine.

"Everyone, off! Stat!" Agent Green ordered.

The party exited the Jeep, and Ramos and Parker beckoned Derek forward to the edge of the mountain cliff. Though they did not go to the mountain's peak, they were high enough to see for miles as if it was daylight.

"You can see Sector 7 over there to the north, but we will be looking just a bit east. It's already three AM. They are late." Agent Ramos said.

"Maybe not," Agent Green blurted pointing up at the sky.

It was in this moment that Derek knew why they didn't give him an abundance of information. If they explained the next few moments to him before arriving there, he would have been confused, maybe even freaked out. This was an event that had to be seen by the human eye not only to believe, but also to understand.

From the surface of the dark clouds, a white, bright light that appeared to be an orb, floated through them. Derek realized this must have been what he saw from the window of the jet an hour before. There was no other light that could be seen for miles.

The agents all looked at Derek's shocked face and nodded towards his camera bag. Without waiting for direction, he took out his camera and put on his night vision lens. He opened the shutters and the light from the orb helped him to see what no human eye could in the darkness.

"This is beyond amazing. This is better than any celebrity I've ever photographed, and I have no idea what the hell I'm looking at," Derek said.

"Just take as many photos of the events." Agent Ramos said. "The details you capture will be very useful."

Derek began snapping away and as he did, a white beam of light shot down to the ground. Derek gasped and began to click his camera furiously. He felt as if he was right there at the site of the light, even though the event occurring was about five miles away.

Derek noticed there were tiny specks of black falling slowly to the ground through the beam of light. They were figures. He could make out arms, legs, and—

"Heads! They have heads. What are these? People?" Derek said, but he did not remove his eye from the viewfinder and kept on clicking away. He tried to zoom closer to see if he could make out faces. In Derek's mind, this had to be something from another world and the figures were not human beings. After all it was the Non-Human Relations agents that had brought him there.

"I've never seen anything like this before. These photos may come out even better than what I'm seeing," Derek said it complete awe.

"That is our hope," Agent Parker responded.

"Can I at least know what they are? Or who?" Derek asked, finally taking his eye off the viewfinder to look at the agents who were gazing at the orb.

Derek figured he would not get an answer, but Agent Green spoke, putting one hand on Derek's shoulder.

"There's so much to learn about our worlds. About them…about us. One day we can probably rewrite history. They live among us as…us."

Agent Parker and Ramos exchanged uncomfortable glances then shook their heads at Agent Green.

Agent Green continued, "Derek, I know we've put you through so much and that you must be exhausted. Just understand that the less you know about tonight and what you are witnessing, the better. You'll be safer. It's dangerous information right now."

Derek did not respond. He took his eyes off the viewfinder again and noticed the agents were gazing deeply at the orb. He pulled out another memory card and attached it to a secondary slot in his camera to allow for each picture to save in two separate memory cards.

"I'm keeping a roll of these photographs for myself," Derek whispered to himself, "There's no way they will let me keep them. They'll never know."

He began to snap even more fiercely, and he zoomed closer to the ground to where the figures had landed. He couldn't tell how many figures there were, but they were moving around. It seemed as if there was some type of interaction, but it was too dark to tell how they looked or what exactly they were doing. It was the creepiest thing Derek had ever witnessed.

Then there was a flash of light that emitted from the orb and in that instant the ground was lit up. Derek snapped away, taking a few more shots. It happened so quickly, but he was sure, with the extra lighting, that he must have been able to capture the figures' faces.

"I think they are about to leave," Agent Parker broke the silence.

"I must have thousands of snapshots," Derek breathed excitedly.

Derek had so many burning questions. If this group called themselves the Non-Human Relations department, does mean they have communicated with them? He did not ask, as he believed they would not respond with an answer.

The figures on the ground began to float back up through the beam and into the orb. Derek was zoomed in so much that he noticed some interesting characteristics.

"It looks as if some of those bodies are shorter than the others. Perhaps they are children and the taller ones are adults?" Derek spoke aloud.

The agents remained silent. Derek's fingers were tired from all the pictures he took. He slipped out the second memory card he inserted for his personal use and tucked it into his boot.

The orb's beam was gone, and all the figures had disappeared into it. It flashed again and within seconds it had moved up into the clouds and was no longer visible. Derek had forgotten how dark the desert was prior to the orb's illumination.

"Can we have the memory card?" Agent Green asked, although it sounded more like an order.

Derek obliged and handed it to him.

"Thank you Derek. We'll drive you back to the base and get you on the jet back to LA," Agent Ramos chimed in.

The agents began to climb into the Jeep. Derek took one glance back at where the orb was, then to the sky, and then to the north where the only light left was Sector 7. He grinned knowing that he had his own copies of the photographs. He would examine them first thing when he arrived back at his home office. His heart raced also realizing that his camera had geo-tagging, so when he uploaded the pictures on his computer, he would be able to tell where the location was of the orb sighting. This meant he would have an idea of where Sector 7 was located.

"Come on!" Agent Green called to Derek.

Derek turned to the agents, climbed into the Jeep, and they were off back towards Sector 7.

"This has been the most interesting experience of my life," Derek told himself as the Jeep made its way down the mountain, "Mental note to self: make sure to keep a journal about my experience."

Chapter Two:
I Want Candy

Five Years Later...

Los Angeles in July was always the time for tourists to pour into the city. The Hollywood Walk of Fame was overcrowded, the beaches were flocked by college students on vacation, and Star Tour buses added to the already ever-growing traffic in the Sunset Boulevard area. It was a month of clear blue skies, temperatures mostly in the seventies, and people tend to wear less clothing.

Malibu was also a nice getaway spot for most locals. While it was still a touristy area, many locals that were well off, had beach houses in the area. This was no exception to the Baker family. Todd and Emily Baker, both doctors in Beverly Hills, owned a beautiful summer beach house on the Pacific coast. However, with their busy working schedules, they didn't utilize it as much as their only son Shane.

Shane Baker, twenty-three, was an athletic brunette with blue eyes. He had freckles and a smile perfect for the camera. However, he preferred to be behind the lens. He was studying business with a minor in photography. Photography was his long-time hobby, and he figured he could have his own photography business like his uncle's best friend once had.

He was one semester away from graduating from Pepperdine, conveniently located in Malibu. His parents let him use the beach house as an apartment for his senior year of college, which was to start in September.

"A little over a month left of summer vacation, and we have yet to throw a killer party here," Shane told his friend Alice, whom he had developed a crush on over the past few years but never had the nerve to tell her.

Alice was a California girl through and through. She had blonde hair, green eyes and was an aspiring actress studying theater and cinema at Pepperdine.

"Yes to the party, but didn't you promise to do some headshots and model shots around the beach for me?" Alice insisted, "Graduation is in December for us and I need to start shopping myself around to agents."

"How very L.A. of you," Shane laughed. "Can't you be more original than being the actor, slash model type? Ha ha!"

"Shut up Shane," Alice smiled and rolled her eyes.

They looked at each other and grinned. Shane looked away with fear that she would see him blush. He never really was smooth with dating. He never had a real girlfriend relationship before and felt he was behind on the dating scene. As much as Shane grew up into the twenty-three year old he was now, he had always been the skinny nerdy kid up until high school. Confidence was always a challenge for him.

"Listen Shane, it's getting late and I have to drive to Venice. I'm having dinner with the girls. Call me when you are ready to schedule that photo shoot," Alice said.

"How about we," Shane began to ask her out, but then flushed red and said, "do it next week? I work the next few days at the camera shop and my aunt, uncle, and cousins are coming in so I got to drive to the 90210 over the weekend to see them."

"Alright. Don't work too hard at the shop," Alice smiled.

"I'll try," Shane replied, "But at least I get discounts off the merchandise and equipment. Win-win."

"So essentially the money you make goes back to the store?" Alice teased.

"Well, yeah." Shane shrugged.

"Ok, well bye. Text me in the next few days with a game plan," and Alice left the beach house to hop into her Volkswagen Beetle and she set off down the Pacific Coast Highway.

"Smooth Shane, real smooth," he mumbled to himself reaching for his camera. It was a recent purchase he made after working at the independent camera shop in Santa Monica, La La Land Camera Co., for a month.

Shane reached for his car keys on the dining table and headed out the door of his lofted beach house. He went to the garage and jumped into his Jeep Wrangler. The top was off and ready to be driven down the PCH with the cool summer breeze blowing through his hair.

Shane pulled out of his garage and headed down the highway. He reached for his cell and punched in a number. It rang.

"Hello?" said the voice on the other line.

"Mike, It's Shane. I'm heading into Santa Monica," he said.

"You working tonight?" Mike asked.

"Yeah. I thought we could grab a few beers at a pub or something before. I need some advice," Shane said, "about Alice."

"Still haven't asked her out? Pathetic!" Mike remarked.

"Well, it's not easy. I've known her for several years. I mean, I think she just sees me as a really good friend," Shane said defeated.

"Or a brother! Ha!" Mike laughed.

"Yeah, maybe so. Well I don't have to go in until noon so a few beers are in order. I can't really go out this weekend anyway, since I'm going to have family in town," Shane continued, "and I have to go hang with the parentals."

"Well man, I guess I'll see you at the 2nd Street Pub?" Mike asked.

"Yeah." Shane answered.

Shane hung up the phone and continued down the PCH, watching the sun set below the Pacific Ocean.

The 2nd Street Pub was a popular spot among local college students. Shane walked in to see a group of familiar faces of fellow students he had classes with, but had never really talked to. It was a small establishment with an Irish theme and tons of beers on tap. Shane walked up to the bar to place his order.

"I'll take the 2nd Street happy hour special please," Shane requested.

The bartender poured him his beer and Shane gave him a tip after paying. He walked to the back of the bar to find his best friend Mike Campbell, who was an African-American guy with short dark hair, and was a few inches shorter than Shane. He wore huge thick black eyeglasses. Shane always had the suspicion they were just for fashion and not really for vision.

"What up homeslice?" Mike jeered.

"Yo," Shane replied, "What are you drinking?"

"Dirty martini," Mike said, "I like it dirty."

"I'm sure you do," Shane teased.

"Well at least that's what Alice told me," Mike teased, "Bam! Ha."

"You ass," Shane responded, "Not funny."

Shane took his seat opposite of Mike and took a huge gulp of his beer and said, "But seriously why is it that you have better luck with the ladies than me?"

"Cause I have a big," Mike went on as Shane shot him a dark look, "Heart." He finished.

"I need to get my mind off her for now. She's in Venice tonight. Sleepover." Shane smiled.

"Oooooooh yeah?" Mike looked as if Christmas had come early. "Does that mean she'll be with other girls dancing around in their underwear?"

"Don't be such a creep, dude," Shane laughed, "Why don't we talk about this mini-vacation we want to take in the beginning of August?"

"Oh right," Mike said still distracted by the thought of college girls sleeping over together. "I was thinking Palm Springs. It's not that far and it'll be hot and toasty."

"Too hot really," Shane went on. "It's the freaking desert and it's August, one of the hottest months in SoCal."

A waitress walked up to the table to take their finished drinks and asked if they wanted another. Shane nodded and Mike said, "Extra dirty." He ended that line with a wink.

"Smooth," Shane breathed.

"Yes she is – I mean thanks," Mike sniggered.

"Why don't we just travel north? Maybe San Francisco?" Shane added.

"San Fran? Hmm. Nah. I'm thinking we do Vegas. Big style!" Mike's eyes lit up. "We can take Alice and her friends. It would be a-ma-zing!"

"You know what," Shane looked excited at the thought, "that sounds brilliant. And you know what they say: What happens in Vegas—"

"—Stays in Vegas!" Mike finished for Shane.

"Exactly." Shane smiled.

"Now you just have to get the balls to ask Alice out or at least try to hook up with her while we are dancing the night away after a long day of gambling." Mike looked over as the waitress brought back their round of drinks.

"You boys look thirsty," The waitress said. She was wearing daisy dukes and a short tank. She had curly blonde hair tied into pigtails.

Mike looked at her and smiled, "I'm very thirsty. I could just put my lips—"

"Uh thanks for the drinks!" Shane barged in to interrupt anything awkward Mike was about to say. He then looked over at him as the waitress walked off, "You are quite ballsy sir."

Mike winked and took a sip of his martini. He swallowed, then looked at Shane, "So Vegas it is. I'm texting Alice now and letting her know she can bring friends. Let's say the first week of August?"

"I'll text her!" Shane said, grabbing his cell and punching in the text: "Vegas. You, me, Mike, and anyone else interested. Week one of Aug. In or out?"

Minutes later his cell phone chimed and the message from Alice showed: "In. Def."

"She said she's in! Hell yes!" Shane said excitedly.

"Great," Mike responded, "It's settled. Now let's play a game of darts at the bar, and we can worry about the details later."

Later that afternoon, Shane pulled up to the parking lot of the camera shop he worked at, La La Land Camera Co. He entered the store and smiled at a few customers looking at the latest camera models that had just shipped in that week. He headed to the back room to clock into work and saw his boss working on receipts at his desk.

"Good day Bob," Shane told his boss.

Bob was a burly man in his fifties with thick glasses and white hair. His age really showed. And he was short and squat.

"Hi Shane. Sorry, this morning was busy and I had this lady attempt to return a camera that clearly had water damage and bits of sand from the beach in it," Bob told Shane.

"Story of our lives, eh?" Shane responded.

Bob just grunted. Shane put on his nametag and headed to the counter to help out some curious customers. A really pretty Asian girl with dark hair and bronze highlights came up to him. She was about Shane's age.

"Excuse me, but I'm looking to purchase a larger memory card for my camera. How many gigabytes would you recommend if I want to store at least one thousand pictures?" She asked.

"Two gigabytes should do. What's your name?" Shane said catching himself off guard at how brave he was to ask the pretty girl's name.

"It's Caroline," She said, and then she looked at his nametag and said, "Nice to meet you Shane."

"Did we have class together? I just realized you look familiar," Shane lied to keep the conversation going.

"Ha. No. I graduated from USC two years ago. I'm a writer for a fashion magazine. My boss needs a new memory card. I swear I'm no longer her assistant but she keeps making me do these mundane tasks because the new assistant just plain sucks." She smiled at Shane as he laughed at her response.

"Well that's cool. I'm about to finish up at Pepperdine myself. Photography. Is your magazine in need of photography interns? Heh." Shane said nonchalantly.

"We are done hiring summer interns, and fall interns won't be hired until later in September. However, we could use freelancers – plus you would get paid! Do you have a portfolio?" Caroline asked.

"I do. It's online on my personal website. I can write down the URL for you," Shane said excitedly. "I mean I don't have much experience in fashion photos, but I've taken lots of scenery pictures and headshots for some of my model slash actor friends."

"Great," Caroline said as she took the piece of paper with Shane's URL written on it, "I'll look into it. My freelancer is not very dependable. He gets gigs on larger magazines and tends to flake on me. I guess they pay more and it looks better for him, but still. I need someone dependable. We lost one of our best photographers two years ago in an accident. Since then, we haven't had as great of results. Plus you are cute."

She winked and Shane turned a bright shade of scarlet. He even accidently kicked the cashier counter too hard, stubbing his toe. He ignored the pain. Caroline noticed his shyness and smiled even more.

"So yeah, thanks for, um, you know offering to show my work. I am definitely down for anything to add to my resume and just to get more experience," Shane said much faster than he wanted to.

"Here's my business card," Caroline passed Shane a card that read: Caroline Lu / Reporter / Fashion Rack Magazine. It also had her e-mail and phone numbers. "And here is my cell phone." She took back the card and wrote it on the back.

"Thanks Caroline," Shane said feeling like he was about to sweat, "I really, really, really appreciate this."

"No problem Shane. Let's chat soon." She winked and then left the store after purchasing her memory card.

On Shane's drive home from work he called Mike to tell him all about getting a number from a really pretty customer.

"Way to go man! Does that mean I can go after Alice? Kidding." Mike sneered.

"Ha, we'll see. Caroline just gave me this flirty look. I think she was digging me," Shane said grinning as he pulled into his beach house.

Shane's phone started beeping.

"Mike, I'll call you back, it's my mom on the other line. Peace," Shane hung up and answered, "Hey mom."

"Honey, it looks like your aunt and uncle will be in a day early. We are planning to have dinner tomorrow night at the house. Your cousins aren't coming after all, since they went to a summer camp last minute. Your aunt and uncle needed a break from the kids," His mom said through the receiver.

"Sure mom. I'll head over after work. Looking forward to it. I haven't seen them in over two years!" Shane said.

"Well you know your uncle travels so much with work. It'll be great to see my sister too. Well I've got to go. Your dad is almost home, and we are going to see a movie tonight." His mom said goodbye and they hung up.

The next morning Shane woke up from an odd dream where he assumed he was a werewolf because he was howling at the moon. That was quickly erased from his mind when he found a text from an unknown number left on his phone overnight: "Got your cell off your website resume. Want to grab coffee and talk about the freelance position? – Caroline Lu."

"Yes!" Shane yelled to himself. He got up and began getting dressed for work.

As he was brushing his teeth with one hand, he used his other to text a response to Caroline's message. "Sure, let's meet at the Beach Cup in Malibu. Tomorrow at 8." He sent it.

Shane arrived at his parents' house later that evening in Beverly Hills. The two-story home was luxurious but much more modest than the giant mansions lined up and down the neighborhood.

"I'm home," Shane called as he entered the front entrance of the house he grew up in.

"Hey dear. I'm in the kitchen!" Called Mrs. Baker

Shane walked into the kitchen and saw his mom stirring a boiling pot of stew. She had curly red hair and brown eyes. Her smile was very motherly, as her eyes fell upon her only son. She ran over and gave Shane a big hug.

When she let go of him, Shane noticed his Uncle Robert and Aunt Pam were seated at the dining table waiting for dinner. Uncle Robert was a very large man that at one point must have been muscular. He seemed to have let himself go a bit, but his chest still stuck out as though he was pumping iron regularly. His wife Pam was petite and also had curly red hair like her sister, Shane's mother Emily. They looked almost alike except that Pam was older and thinner than Emily.

"Getting taller boy," Uncle Robert said as Shane's father Todd walked in. Todd was blonde with brown eyes and a little more on the heavy side but still not as large as Uncle Robert.

"Hello Shane," Mr. Baker said, "How was work at the shop today?"

"Bearable. I'm starved. Good to see you Uncle Robert and Aunt Pam," Shane said heading over to them to give them each an embrace.

"Alright everyone let's take our seats," Mrs. Baker demanded, "The roast beef stew is ready. Shane, get the salad from the fridge. Thanks."

Shane pulled the salad and placed it in the middle of the table. Everyone was seated and conversations began. It was a family catch-up, as Uncle Robert and Aunt Pam had not visited L.A. in so long. They lived in Arizona where Uncle Robert worked for a law firm. The last time Uncle Robert had visited was...

"And the last time we were here Emily–what was it two years ago Robert?" Aunt Pam said while speaking to her sister.

"Yeah," Uncle Robert said, "When my college friend Derek passed away."

"That's right," Pam continued, "We were here for the funeral. This time though, I think we should all spend more quality time."

"Speaking of which," Uncle Robert continued, "Shane, you remember Derek right? Derek Conrad?"

"I do," Shane said thinking back to when he was younger and he first met Derek Conrad through his uncle. Derek was actually the one person that inspired Shane to get into photography. They spent many times practicing and shooting subjects. He once took Shane to the set of a fashion shoot he did with some Victoria's Secret models and to a shoot on a movie set with a well-known actress that was friends with Derek.

"Well," Uncle Robert continued as he swallowed a piece of his bread roll, "he left behind something for you."

"Really?" Shane asked very interested. Derek once promised he was going to give Shane one of his old cameras when he was old enough to take care of it. It was a vintage 35mm camera.

"Yeah. It's not much, just a CD. It either has music or it has files of photos. Not sure. I never opened it. It was left in his home office and had your name on it.

Shane smiled politely, yet he felt defeated that it wasn't a camera.

"I wonder what it could have?" Shane thought out loud.

Uncle Robert pulled the CD out from Aunt Pam's purse and handed it to him. It was a CD that was recordable and burned with some sort of data. There was no label except for "Shane

Baker" written in permanent marker. It seemed like such a personal gift, even though it was not the most fancy inheritance. Shane was close to Derek when he was in his early teens. They shared a common passion for photography. Derek was the inspiration behind Shane's dream to one day own a photography business as well.

"Thanks for passing this along Uncle Robert. He was a good man. He's the reason I want to have my own photography business one day," Shane said smiling.

Uncle Robert smiled back. It seemed like he was fighting back a tear.

"Robert," Mr. Baker broke in to change the somber subject, "Do you want to see my new golf clubs I bought? We should probably hit the country club tomorrow."

After dinner, Shane bid farewell to his parents, aunt, and uncle before heading back to Malibu.

The streets of L.A. had significantly more traffic than usual on Shane's drive. He was frustrated and wanted to get to bed early so he could be well rested for his coffee date with Caroline the next day. He gripped the steering wheel in frustration and looked down at his passenger's seat where the CD from Derek lay.

He picked it up and inserted it into his Jeep's CD player system. It loaded and was read by the system. It was in fact an audio CD. There was only one track.

"Odd," Shane thought, "Why would he give me a track with one song."

The song began to play and he recognized it as a familiar tune. It was "I Want Candy" by The Strangeloves.

"Yeah this is so very random. A camera would have been nicer. Ha!" Shane said to himself as he began to hum the tune for the rest of the drive.

Chapter Three:
The First Date

Shane left work early to avoid traffic down the Pacific Coast Highway back to Malibu so that he would have time to change and shower before his coffee date with Caroline. He was nervous and was over thinking the night that he didn't realize "I Want Candy" was playing on repeat in his car.

He absentmindedly was humming and singing the lyrics over and over has he drove. He lowered the volume and decided to call Mike out of worry he would have a nervous break down.

"I mean is it a first date? She texted me on my cell for coffee…" Shane told Mike over the phone.

Mike paused, then said, "But she wanted to talk about your resume and what not. That doesn't mean it's a date. How about this: why don't you text and ask her if it's a date?"

Just then Shane's phone beeped from a text. It was from Caroline: "How about we ditch coffee and have dinner at Geoffrey's? Actually, I already made a reservation for two."

A car honked as Shane was slowly merging onto the other lane. He snapped back to reality, focusing on the road and said to Mike, "She just said it's now a dinner for two at Geoffrey's."

"I like this girl," Mike said, "She takes control. And that place is nice. I think it is a date."

"I'm going to throw up now, let's talk later," Shane exaggerated, and then hung up.

Shane arrived at the beach house and ran in through the door in haste. He took a quick shower and spent thirty minutes trying on different articles of clothing to wear. He finally decided on dressy jeans, a blue button up shirt that matched his eyes, and a casual black blazer.

He poured himself a glass of wine to calm his nerves. One glass became two, then two became three. Eventually he had six glasses and had use the restroom twice. He was not as nervous anymore as his wine buzz set in.

"Malibu Yellow Cab, this is the operator, what is your location?" a cab operator woman said when Shane called for a taxi.

He felt that it would be safer if he took a cab to the restaurant at that point, as he was feeling slightly tipsy after the six glasses of Merlot he drank.

The cab arrived outside his place, and Shane ran to the door. He struggled for five seconds before sliding the taxi van door open, which he pulled a little too hard.

"Where to?" Said the disgruntled cab driver.

"Geoff-hiccup-rey's," Shane said, wiping his mouth and holding his breath trying to get rid of his hiccups.

Shane began to hum "I Want Candy" a little too loudly on the ride over. The cab driver seemed annoyed.

Geoffrey's was set right on the edge of the water. As it was summertime, the sun was barely setting around eight when Shane arrived. There were torches lit that gave off a very romantic atmosphere. In fact, it appeared as though all the clientele were on dates. There were parties of two mostly seated around the restaurant.

Shane walked up to their table. Caroline was already seated and looking nervously at her iPhone. The location was on the edge of a balcony, so they had a view of the ocean. Caroline realized Shane was there and darted up to give him an awkward handshake that turned into a hug.

"Glad you could make it," Caroline flushed.

"This is so much nicer than coffee," Shane breathed.

"Sorry if it feels much more formal. I just really like this place and I'm rarely ever in Malibu as I live in West L.A.," she responded.

"Totally fine. I've only been here once," Shane gushed, "and it was a family affair."

"Nice. So, I saw your website and résumé. You have some real talent. My boss really liked it. I think I'd like to hire you to be my personal—I mean my freelancer," Caroline blushed and avoided eye contact with Shane.

Shane sensed she was nervous and it made him feel more at ease. He gained back his confidence, which might have had to do with the wine buzz.

"Well you know," Shane started, "I don't mind being your personal anything."

Shane slapped himself and looked at Caroline who was not at all upset by this. She started laughing.

"I mean," Shane continued, "I, um, gosh sorry. Let me be honest. I drank six glasses of wine. I'm borderline drunk. I mean—I'm not drunk, just tipsy."

"You are adorable. Do I make you nervous?" She asked.

"Very," Shane blushed.

"Good," She said and was eyeing the waiter.

The waiter came over and took their food order. Caroline ordered a margarita with her meal. Shane avoided the cocktail and wine list and picked a simple chicken dinner for his meal.

"So were you born in California?" Shane asked.

"Yeah," Caroline said, "But in Northern California. Sacramento to be exact. I moved to L.A. for college of course and landed a gig at Fashion Rack Magazine."

"Not a bad gig at all. That magazine is huge," Shane replied. "My hope is to one day have my own photography business. I want to be as successful as my uncle's old college buddy."

"Does your uncle's buddy work in town?" Caroline asked.

"Worked. He died." Shane replied. His mind wandered on the CD for a moment.

"I'm sorry," She said. "I told you about my former photographer we would hire for freelance, right?

"Yeah, I think you mentioned it at the store," Shane said.

"Well he had a high price tag, but he was huge and very talented. He passed away in a freak accident two years ago. Derek Conrad. Google him."

Shane nearly dropped his glass of water.

"Oh my God!" Shane said out loud, causing a few couples near by to turn. "That's my uncle's friend! He's the one that inspired me to work in the biz!"

"You are freaking kidding me?" Caroline said in surprise.

"Not at all. Jesus, what a small world this is!" Shane said.

"You're telling me," Caroline said still dumbfounded by how quickly they found a common thread.

"Do you know how he died actually? My uncle never really told me," Shane asked.

"Were you close to him?" Caroline asked.

"Well, when I was younger and in my early teen years I'd see him when my uncle was in town. He once took me to a fashion shoot, and now that I think about it, it may have been for Fashion Rack," Shane explained.

"Well," Caroline went on, "I know it's not exactly the most cheerful conversation I was hoping for, but since you knew him and you don't really know what happened, I can tell you what I know. It's very strange actually…"

"Don't worry we can have a happy conversation later," Shane said now fully hanging on to Caroline's every word. It was mainly due to the fact that he had received a CD with one song on it from Derek, and he was still scratching his head as to what it meant.

"Ok," Caroline continued, "I had just started Fashion Rack when I first worked with him. I was maybe two months into the job. He was scheduled to shoot an actress friend of his on the set her film, and it was going to be an exclusive cover. It was a comeback film for her because she had not landed a role in a while. Booking the movie was huge for her, and I was excited to be a part of it. Rumor was that the actress and Derek had a love affair or something of that nature. They were very friendly, so she had requested that our editor hire Derek. That was a no-brainer. Derek had such huge list of credits in this town.

Anyways, we emailed him his schedule and call time the night before, and he responded with a 'thanks.' However, morning of the shoot, he was a no-show. We called and called. Even Candy could not get a hold of him. We had—"

"Candy?" Shane cut her off immediately at the edge of his seat at the coincidence of this name, "Who was Candy?"

"Have you not heard of her?" Caroline said in wonder, "Candy 'Sweetheart' Adams"

"Oh! I know who she is!" Shane said, putting two and two together. "She was 'America's Sweetheart,' which is how she got the 'Sweetheart' nickname. She was big years ago, when we were kids. She was on some sitcom and made a name for herself in motion pictures, right?"

"Exactly," Caroline said.

"I had no idea Derek was seeing her. Good for him, I guess," Shane said, making a mental note to himself to do some research and remembering that he went on a shoot with Derek and her once as a teen.

"So," Caroline continued, "Where was I? Oh yes! So Candy began to get worried. He was very reachable via Blackberry, but an hour passed and we were behind on schedule, so we had to call a back up freelance—the guy I use now that flaked on me recently. His no-show bothered Candy so much that we eventually ended up not shooting with her since she was worried. We lost the cover and she pissed off tons of people. She didn't trust anyone but Derek. To be honest, she was a bit of a diva for this because she had lost her star power and this would have brought her back into the limelight.

Her manager contacted my boss for days trying to get her to be rescheduled but we passed and decided to go with someone else for the cover. My boss Stacy can be a huge bitch, and she took Candy's diva ways personally. She claims she is the reason Candy has no career because eventually she was fired from the film by the director. Stacy believes it was because they lost this huge cover, which was a great press opportunity."

"Wow," Shane said, "that is very intense."

"This town is cut throat. So don't screw us over," Caroline said winking.

"What happened next?" Shane asked, completely unaware the waiter had just served both of their meals.

"Anything else?" The waiter said.

"Um, oh, no thanks," Shane said and he beckoned Caroline to continue.

She continued, "Well, it wasn't made public, but he had actually gone missing. I just heard bits and pieces and hearsay, but I think the only person that really knows what happened was Candy, because she was definitely shaken up. In fact I think she quit the movie and didn't actually get fired. I heard from another photographer we use, that was friends with Derek, that he was in fact alive and he did make contact with Candy. I gathered he was running away from something.

Anyways, it was probably a week after his no-show at the shoot, that we got word he was dead. It was an accident. He drove his BMW off one of winding roads in the Hollywood Hills one night. He was maybe half a mile from his home."

"Gosh," Shane said as he began to slice up his chicken, "I knew he had some accident, but I never really asked my uncle. He was really sad about it. They were the best of friends. They met in their fraternity in college."

"It's sad," Caroline said, "He was so talented. I feel there may have been foul play just because I was one of the few that was there to see him skip out on a shoot that would have made his career even bigger. He was obviously still alive in that one-week span during his disappearance."

"Caroline," Shane began, "Do you think maybe Candy knows something. Is there a way we can contact her?"

"I don't know. She hasn't been seen in the public, and I don't see any paparazzi photos of her in the tabloids at all. She kind of just went into hiding," she said.

"Would you be interested in finding out?" Shane asked.

"Well duh, I would. After all, he was a wonderful client. He had worked for the magazine prior to Candy's shoot, but I had always been a fan of his. It's crazy that you knew him personally." Caroline looked at Shane and smiled, "Do you know something about this, though?"

"Sort of, perhaps," Shane said, "You just helped me with something."

"What?" She asked, perplexed.

"So yesterday my Uncle Robert, Derek's best friend, came over for dinner since he's in town with my aunt," Shane began, "and he gave me an audio CD with my name labeled on it that was found at Derek's house. I found it odd because it just seemed so random. I mean perhaps he was planning to give it to me when he was alive, but what was even weirder was the song burned onto the CD. It was an old sixties song that has been remade and covered over and over by several artists: "I Want Candy.""

Caroline nearly choked in her glass and gasped, "You are kidding?!"

"No!" Shane exclaimed, "And after getting your inside info, I am nearly positive that this is not a coincidence. I don't know why he wanted me to have the CD. Or what he wanted me to know—"

Just then a memory sprung into Shane's head:

Shane was thirteen years old and was at the Griffith Observatory with his cousins, aunt, and uncle. With them was Derek, who was doing family photos for the Powers' bunch.

After the shoot, Derek gave a few Polaroids he took earlier to Shane.

Derek told Shane, "There are clues within these photos. My dad always played these kind of scavenger hunt games with me.

You have to look at these three pictures to figure out what project I am going to take you on. Only catch is you have to guess right to come."

The three photos were a picture of a pretty woman (Shane now realized was Candy when she was younger) a picture of a movie studio, and a picture of stage with the number "20" on it.

Eventually, Shane figured out that it was a shoot on the set of the sitcom, "Candy's World" starring Candy Adams. The clues were easy enough for a thirteen year old, who was just getting into popular culture, to figure out. It did take him a day to think it through, as he did not want to be wrong.

Shane came back to reality and focused on Caroline who had stayed quiet noticing he went into a deep thought. Shane then thought, *What if he is playing that same game with me? But...why?*

"You ok?" Caroline asked, but without waiting for him to answer she bluntly said, "Do you think 'I Want Candy' means she is responsible for his death? I mean he was in contact with her!"

"Good theory," Shane said, but as he thought about the lyrics to the song, the only thing that came to mind was that she was something he praised. "Maybe we should find her and find out." He thought to himself, *This wouldn't be the first time he asked me to figure out who Candy was.*

"And you've met her before I take it? On that shoot?" She asked.

"Yeah, but I vaguely remember. I was very shy," Shane said.

Caroline got on her iPhone and proceeded to Google Candy Adams for any recent news articles.

"Hmm, there is nothing recent on Google for her. But I did find her Wikipedia page. It says that Candy Adams is a stage name!"

"Really?" Shane said, now even more curious about Candy. "What's her real name?"

"Mariette Polashek—No wonder she wanted to use a stage name. That doesn't role off the tongue too well, does it?" Caroline said.

"So Caroline," Shane said as he paid for the bill. Caroline was about to stop him but he said, "I got this. So Caroline…want to use your investigative skills and help me figure out what's going on? Perhaps Derek really had a message for me. It would not be the first time he sent me on a scavenger hunt, although I wonder if this was meant to happen when he was alive…"

"Yeah we may hit a dead end," Caroline added.

"Or several forks in the road…" Shane said mysteriously.

Caroline smiled, "Thank you so much for dinner. I think a second date will be in order as well as a trip to find Mariette Polashek?"

"So this was a date?" Shane asked.

"The first date, yes," She teased, "Plus you paid the bill."

They walked out of the restaurant and waited for Caroline to get her car from valet.

"Did you not valet?" Caroline asked.

"I um," Shane said.

"You had six glasses of wine and took a cab or got dropped off?" Caroline inserted.

"Cab. Yeah. Ha." Shane said bashfully.

"I'll drive you home. Aren't you on the way back to Santa Monica?"

"Yes just down the PCH," Shane said, brushing his hand through his hair.

The valet brought Caroline's Volkswagen Jetta and they got into the car. She grabbed her iPod and plugged it into the car's auxiliary port.

"I have that song, but it's a rock version cover by some band," Caroline said and she scrolled through a list of songs on the iPod screen. "Aha! Here it is, let's listen."

They played "I Want Candy" on loop over and over until they arrived at Shane's beach house.

"Wow, you live here?" Caroline said impressed.

"Well it's my parents' beach house. I am living here until I graduate. I love it. They let me stay here as long as I keep it clean," Shane said, "Do you want to come in?"

Shane blushed at his own bravery. Caroline grinned and said, "Sure."

She turned off the car, and they walked to the doorstep. Shane looked at her before he could put the key in the door, and she moved her face towards him.

They kissed. It lasted for a good minute before both of them pulled apart, their faces red.

"That was unexpected," Shane grinned.

"Was it really?" Caroline said teasingly.

Just as he opened the door a female voice called Shane from behind.

"Shane…" It was Alice.

"Alice?" Shane said in surprise. "What are you doing here?"

"Sorry. I would have called but thought you wouldn't be, um, busy," Alice said looking at Caroline and examining her, "I'm Alice by the way."

Alice reached to shake Caroline's hand. It was awkward.

"I'm Caroline," she responded, not knowing what else to say.

"Again, sorry to intrude Shane. I just wondered if you had a few minutes to talk about my photo shoot for next week?" Alice asked.

"Shane," Caroline began, "I'll text you later. I should probably go. It's late. Thanks again for dinner. Nice to meet you Alice."

"Ok, yeah I'll call you later!" Shane yelled as she headed to her car.

Caroline looked back, smiled, then looked at Alice, and then entered her car. She backed out of the driveway and headed onto the highway.

"Sorry, did I interrupt something?" Alice asked innocently.

"Um, no. She's just a friend. We, um, were discussing my new freelance gig with Fashion Rack Magazine. She's a writer there," Shane said slightly annoyed.

Shane beckoned for Alice to come in. She took a seat at his couch and pulled out a bunch of magazine cutouts of different celebrity styles.

"So these are what I'm going for," she said handing Shane the cutouts.

"Not picky at all, are we?" Shane teased.

"I need to be able to market myself and appear very, very commercial," She said.

"You are already," Shane smiled.

They spoke for about an hour, planning out the different shots and looks that Alice wanted for the photo shoot next week. Then Alice brought up Las Vegas.

"So this trip we want to plan...who else should we bring? My girls don't want to go. They are all about saving money for the 'real world' right now. Barf." Alice said.

"Me, you, and Mike for now," Shane said.

"I don't want to be the only girl either," Alice said.

"Hey, do you know much about Candy Adams?" Shane asked out of the blue.

"Um, random. But," She began, "just that she's a washed up actress and I don't want to end up like her. She's very much a hermit crab these days. Keeps to herself. I read on a blog that she doesn't leave her house much."

"Where does she live?" Shane asked.

"Actually here in Malibu somewhere. That's what it said on the blog anyways." Alice responded.

"Really? Hmm," said Shane, now even more intrigued.

"Why do you care?" Alice asked suspiciously.

"Just...she was a friend of my uncle's best friend who passed away a few years ago. He gave me a gift and I was trying to figure out what the meaning of it was and why he gave it to me," Shane said truthfully, not really sure why he divulged so much information.

"What kind of gift?" Alice asked.

"A CD. And get this, there was one song on it: 'I Want Candy!' Shane said.

"What the hell? That's so weird!" Alice said, but she didn't really seem to be interested. She was looking over her photos again.

Shane looked at her closely. Just a few days ago he would have been nervous and his heart would race being alone with her, but now she seemed just like a friend—or a sister.

"Listen, I'm tired and want to catch some Z's. I think I got the gist of what you want for the shoot. Let's talk more as the day gets closer?" Shane said, hinting for her to leave.

"You know," Alice began, "Before you would be all jittery and nervous around me. In fact, you probably would have wanted me to stay longer. I guess that girl Caroline might be more than a friend, huh?"

She looked straight into his eyes and focused all her attention on him. Shane looked at her right back, although feeling uncomfortable that she had voiced all along what he hoped she would not have noticed all those times they were alone hanging as friends.

"Well," Shane said, and he decided to use his confidence again, something that was becoming more and more easier for him to do, "I did like you. I mean, I had been crushing on you for ages..."

"Did?" she asked, and it seemed as if she were a little put out by the tone of her voice.

"I mean. I just thought you never would li—" Shane started.

"Like you?" Alice cut in, "You never even asked me out or tried."

"Well it looks as though you knew I did," Shane said, "So why didn't you just help me out?"

"No!" She exclaimed, "That would have been your job sweetie. I might have even said yes, but I guess you'll never really know."

Alice packed her magazine cutouts into her portfolio and got up from the couch. Shane reached for her arm.

"Alice, I—"

"I got to go Shane," Alice said, staring into his blue eyes. Shane stared back at her green eyes. He felt confused. He just had an amazing first date with Caroline, but the one girl he liked since high school was standing right before him, practically confessing her admiration for him. It was like one bad dream.

"Alice, wait!" Shane yelled towards her as she darted for the door to exit. She turned back to look at him and opened her mouth as if she was going to say something, but chose not to.

Shane walked over to her and touched her fingers. He had no words. She moved her hand behind her and waved with her other "goodbye." She opened the door and ran out. Shane thought about chasing her, but decided not to. He had no idea if it was appropriate.

He walked upstairs to his room and began to change into his PJs. The whole day had been so overwhelming with information. His thoughts on Alice disappeared as his mind began racing over the realization that the song he received from Derek Conrad, "I Want Candy," may have had some connection with his friend Candy Adams.

Does she have something to do with his death? Shane thought, *But no—if she did kill him he would have seen it coming. The CD was premeditative. He planned to have it fall into my hands. It was, after all, labeled with my name. I just don't get it.*

Shane walked over to his bedside table to charge his phone.

And Candy lives in this city. I'm so close to her, but yet, so far. How on Earth will I just be able to walk up to her front porch and ask for her?

Shane kept pacing back and forth thinking about his plan to find Mariette Polashek. He eventually tired himself out and decided it was best to get some rest.

After brushing his teeth and removing his contacts, he walked over to his window and opened it. The smell of the fresh breeze and ocean filled his nostrils. He took a deep breath and stared up at the sky. The moon was full and bright that evening. The sounds of the waves crashing helped ease him into a deep sleep.

What happened next, seemed to have occurred at light speed. It was early in the morning past three AM, when he was in mid-dream. His recollection of the dream was fuzzy. All of sudden he was conscious. He opened his eyes and everything was blurry since his contact lenses were off, and his vision was poor without them. However, at his window, he saw, or at least thought he saw someone peeking through the edge. It was a dark figure.

He ran to the window and squinted. There was nothing. He could no longer see the moon either, which was most likely due to the rotation of the planet, he thought.

Shane went to put his contacts back on, then walked back to the window and looked around outside. He was two stories high. There was no way anyone could be on the roof. With that in mind, he comforted himself by putting together in his mind, that he had just had a strange lucid dream. The only thing that bothered him, was he remembered a similar scenario as a child where he woke up from a dream to see a dark figure framed at his window back at his parents' house. He shrugged and then made himself comfortable in his bed.

He fell back into bed and fell asleep almost instantly. He only had one more dream that night. He was a in a dark room, and was bounded by an invisible force. He could not move. He heard strange whispers. Shane could not recognize the language the whispers were uttering. All of a sudden there was a flash of light in his dream and he saw a black shadowy figure with red eyes staring at him before flying away into darkness.

Shane's mind was at rest for the rest of his sleep, and he had no more dreams that night.

Chapter Four:

The Second Inheritance

Shane and Mike were seated in their usual spot at the 2nd Street Pub, drinking a few beers. Shane had just finishing telling Mike the story about receiving the CD from Derek and his date with Caroline and how they got into the topic of Derek and Candy.

"So what I need to do now, is find out if Derek wanted me to get in touch with her," Shane said.

"I live for this kind of stuff. I'll be happy to help you and Caroline," Mike said excitedly, "Has she found any new leads on Candy's address?"

"I spoke to her last night," Shane went on, "And she left a voicemail with Candy's former publicist. We're hoping she calls back."

"How'd she get the publicist's info?" Mike asked.

"From her boss's Fashion Rack contact book," Shane said matter-of-factly. "After all, the magazine worked with her last before she became a has-been. Remember, from the shoot before Derek disappeared that I told you about?"

"Right! Of course," Mike said defeated. "Hey, what time do you have to be at your parents' house?"

"An hour," Shane responded. "My aunt and uncle fly back to Arizona tomorrow.

"Well maybe you should head out now. You never know with L.A. traffic how long the commute will be," Mike stated.

"Yeah," Shane said, and he pulled out his wallet to leave money for the tab, "I guess I should head out now. Want to come over to my house on Tuesday? I'm shooting Caroline's headshots?"

"You mean Alice?" Mike grinned.

"Alice! Yes! Oops," Shane responded, turning slightly red.

"You are having issues, eh?" Mike asked, "You like them both, and you can't pick which one you like. Am I right?"

"The thing is, and I told you this earlier, but Alice pretty much came out to me saying she liked me," Shane brushed his hands through his hair. "I've never had to deal with two girls having a thing for me. Obviously I've gotten further with Caroline, considering we've had one date and starting Wednesday I have my first freelance gig with her. I'm going to have to pursue Caroline. She is the one that was making moves back."

"Maybe so sir, but the heart is a confusing thing," Mike said as Shane got up.

"Yeah. I'll catch you later." Shane left the pub and walked down the street to the meter where his Jeep was parked.

Shane arrived at his parents' Beverly Hills home to find his dad watering the grass outside.

"Hey dad!" Shane called as he hopped out of this Jeep.

"Shane!" Mr. Baker said, "Why don't you go keep your uncle company. Your mom and aunt are shopping on Rodeo Drive and they'll be here in maybe twenty or so."

"Sure. Where is Uncle Robert then?" Shane asked as he walked up the porch to the front entrance.

"Living room. Watching TV," Mr. Baker answered.

Shane walked into the house and put his car keys on a rack near the entrance. He went straight towards the living room and decided on something he had wanted to ask since he received the CD from Derek.

"Uncle Robert—hi. You have a minute?" Shane asked working up the courage.

"Hey Shane. Yeah. What's going on?" Uncle Robert asked.

"Well," Shane began, "I wanted to ask you if you knew a bit about what happened to Derek. You never told me how he died. I'm sorry if this is a sensitive subject."

Shane knew the story of the car crash thanks to Caroline, but he pretended he had no idea about anything.

"I thought you might ask," Uncle Robert started, "seeing as you got that CD from Derek. Did you listen to it?"

"I did," Shane said, thinking of a lie to tell him about what was on it since he did not want to go into detail about the song for it would appear random. Or so he thought.

"I Want Candy," breathed Uncle Robert, and Shane's eyes widened at the shock of this information. "Yes I lied. I did open the case and listen to it."

His uncle noticed Shane's expression and said, "I heard it before giving it to you. Forgive me, but I was curious. See, when Derek passed away—well, it was a car accident. He drove his BMW off a hill on the road about a mile from his house. I thought maybe it was a suicide, because for three years, our friendship was strained. It was mainly due his lack of communication with me. He kept to himself. The last time I saw him alive was about five years ago when your cousins, Pam, and myself came to L.A. for a bit. I met up with him, but he was not the same. He seemed disturbed and changed. I remember when we were eating at this café, he kept looking around as if expecting someone."

Uncle Robert paused and looked at Shane who was listening intently and processing.

"I've never told anyone this," Uncle Robert continued, "but I know you and him and a special bond when you were younger, and he inspired you to pursue the profession you have chosen.

Anyways, our last meeting was bittersweet. To me, it felt as though he did not want to be there with me. I paid the bill and was on my way. In the months and years to follow, I would email, call, and text him, but his answers were either one or two word responses or nothing.

I did not really understand what was going on. I'm still trying to figure out what changed him. It still hurts me that the last years of his life, he shunned me away. We were the best of friends. We were in the same fraternity. I learned about his death days after it actually happened because we didn't share any other close friends since he had written off many people in his time of seclusion.

It was Candy Adams that reached out to me. She called me to tell me what happened."

Shane's attention was now even more focused on the story. He was trying to piece together what happened, but now he knew that his uncle knew about as much as he knew.

"She seemed really depressed," Uncle Robert went on, "and she was not very detailed about his last days left before his passing. She mentioned they had contact a few days prior to the accident, but she did not tell me what it was about. I insisted she tell me, but she wouldn't budge. She proceeded to ignore me by giving me the funeral information. I did attend it, even though I was so angry with how he changed our friendship.

I never heard from Candy again. I've tried to find her and reach out, but I have no idea how. Derek was not the type to go into hiding or be secluded from friends. He was social and maybe even somewhat fame hungry. It was out of character. But maybe he was hiding some secrets? I think he went into a deep depression. That's why I think it was suicide. They found alcohol in his system so it was ruled out as a drunk driving accident. His blood alcohol level was high. There was no way he could have managed to drive up that far into the hills since they were very winding. Something doesn't fit.

Do you know what the CD means?"

"I—um," Shane said startled by the question and snapping back to reality after his mind raced to figure out more about Derek. "Well I did come to the conclusion that I need to find Candy Adams. They were lovers of some sort."

"Yes," Uncle Robert said. "Smart boy, you are. But am I wrong to think that you have no idea why he gave you this CD?"

"You are right," Shane said. "I don't know what he wants me to do."

"Derek," Uncle Robert said, now slightly smiling at a memory, "Always liked to keep secrets. His loophole was leaving clues about things so that he never did technically reveal them. He told lots of his girlfriends about our fraternity hazing rituals that way. Pissed me off, but technically the girls figured it out with some clues he gave them.

Anyways, my point is his actions were always meaningful and purposeful. There must a reason why he chose you and not me. Nothing was left for me under my name," his Uncle said.

"How did you come across this CD?" Shane asked.

"His house," Uncle Robert said, "It's still owned by him. In fact, in his will he left it to Candy, but it was stated that it would be uninhabited and left untouched. She truly honored that, which is why I thought that any theory of her being behind his death for his money could not be justified. She had her own wealth and went into hiding from a depression but never claimed any kind of ownership to his property, I think. She had one of her managers contact me about a year ago asking if I was ever in L.A., I could go into his house to perhaps take something as a keepsake since I was his best friend. I never met her face to face. This was just a few days ago when I arrived."

"Really? So you just found the CD recently?" Shane said stunned.

"Yes," he said, then he went on, "As I looked through some of his items, I saw on his desk was this CD with your name on it. It was such a shock, but I knew I had to get it to you. Especially as I would be seeing you at dinner that evening."

"So his house is still as it was when he died?" Shane asked, ideas springing into his head.

"Yeah. Eerie," Uncle Robert said. "Nobody goes in except maybe one of Candy's hired help to upkeep it. It's like some odd shrine or museum to him. Not sure why he requested it be left that way."

"We're home!" Shouted Mrs. Baker and Aunt Pam in unison.

47

Shane rolled his eyes in annoyance of the bad timing. His uncle's information was so valuable, yet the mystery just deepened.

Shane looked at his uncle and said quickly, "I live here. He wanted to tell me something. It must be important. I'll find out, and I will tell you. Where is his house? That's my next mission."

"That's why I told you all this. You will be my detective," Uncle Robert said hurriedly, "And you will call or e-mail me anything you learn. Keep me updated constantly. Also, this is our secret…"

"You boys hungry?" Aunt Pam asked Uncle Robert and Shane.

Both nodded in unison and Uncle Robert said out of the corner of his mouth, "His death may not have been an accident, and you must find out for me."

He then handed Shane a crumpled up piece of paper with an address on it. On top of the address read "Derek's place."

Shane was driving home later that evening thinking about everything his uncle told him. While the information still didn't tell him much about what happened prior to Derek's death, he did learn that he had been acting strange for at least three years before the accident. At this point, he was almost certain that Candy Adams would be able to fill in the information leading up to the accident. Still, he was unsure as to why he was involved, but he felt it was important.

The next day Shane was sitting with Mike and Caroline at the Beach Cup. Both of them had shown interest in the Derek Conrad situation. He told them everything he learned from his uncle. Caroline was writing down everything so as not to miss or forget any details. Shane looked at her curiously and she caught him doing so.

"I'm not writing a story! I'm not that kind of reporter. I write about the next best fashion or the hottest shoes celebs are wearing, remember?" She teased.

"Sorry," Shane said, "I just need you all to keep this between us. The only reason I ask is because we could learn if there was foul play involved in his death. Caroline—I know we talked about the day of the shoot he missed, but was there anything else we missed? Still think Candy—Mariette is innocent or has any involvement?

"No," Caroline said, "I know she's an actor, but she was genuinely worried about Derek. She called off the biggest photo shoot of her career—and mind you, she didn't have much of one at the time. She was going to make some nice pocket change out of it for her bank account too."

"See," Shane said enjoying how Caroline's mind worked, "That's what I was thinking too. I think there is a huge chunk of the story missing that will make things fit together easily. Mariette Polashek—Candy Adams, whatever she goes by these days—she's going to be the one to help us solve this puzzle. She must have a missing piece."

Mike seemed to be trying to process everything while he sipped on his latte. Caroline was biting on the end of her pen, while staring up at the ceiling.

"You guys are thinking hard," Shane said. "I love it."

"Heh," Mike said absentmindedly.

"Hey!" Caroline suddenly said making Mike jump and Shane turn his head too fast. "Sorry. I didn't mean to scare you guys. Shane, you have the address, right?"

Shane nodded and pulled out the piece of paper his uncle gave him.

"Well," Caroline said, "if Candy was given this house in Derek's will, then maybe we can find out where she lives if we do some real estate research?"

"Why don't we just go over to the house and stake it out. I know it's gated, but maybe we'll find something?" Mike said hopefully.

"And appear suspicious?" Caroline said.

"No word from the publicist I take it?" Shane asked.

"None," Caroline replied. "I've tried again and again. No answer, but the voicemail does confirm it's the right number."

"Can I have the number? I want try it. Maybe the publicist has recognized yours and is ignoring?" Shane added hopefully.

"Ok," Caroline said, "But she's been ignoring me since my first try. Here. Her name is Peggy Mills."

"Thanks," Shane said and he began texting the number. "I'm going to text her. Most people these days don't even check their voicemails."

"Good thinking!" Mike chimed in.

"Thanks!" Shane smiled, "Ok guys, how does this sound: Hi, Peggy. My name is Shane Baker. I am a family friend of Derek Conrad and I am under the impression he wanted me to contact Candy. Could you please contact me at your earliest convenience?"

"Sounds good," Mike and Caroline said.

"Sent," Shane said, "I guess it'll sound weird when she gets it, but it's worth a—"

Just then, Shane's phone began to ring. It was from the number Caroline gave him.

"It's Peggy Mills!" Squealed Shane.

"What?!" Mike and Caroline gasped. Caroline went on, annoyed, "She did not even call me back!"

"Hello, this is Shane Baker," he answered.

"Mr. Baker, hi, I'm not sure how you got my number or why you are supposed to contact Candy, but I do have something for you. I no longer work for Candy but we remain good friends. Your name has been mentioned before."

"By Candy?" Shane asked.

"Yes," Peggy continued. "Derek Conrad gave her a 35mm camera and specified it was to fall into the hands of a 'Shane Baker.' It was the only item he gave away a week prior to his death that was not in his will. Candy has it, but she doesn't see guests often and likes to keep to herself. I will pick up the camera from her and meet you somewhere. I can meet you at the Santa Monica Pier tomorrow at six PM."

"That works. I'll see you then," Shane said and Peggy hung up.

"Well?" Mike insisted.

Shane told them the brief conversation he had with Peggy, and Caroline began formulating ideas.

"I mean why didn't Derek just leave the camera at his house with your name labeled, if this is what he actually wanted you to have?" Caroline pondered.

"Well maybe he felt it was safer with Candy. It is, after all, a rare vintage piece of equipment," Shane added. "But you have a valid point. I mean he did always promise to give it to me, but maybe there was a reason he could not leave it at the house."

Mike jumped in, "Also, he must have really trusted Candy—Mariette—whatever you want to call her, because he left it with her. She's had it for over two years. I wonder why she didn't try to track you down or find you on Facebook or something?"

"I think we still need to find Candy," Shane said matter-of-factly. "I will talk to Peggy more in depth when I meet up with her tomorrow. I think I should go alone just to be safe."

"Yeah," Caroline said, "maybe you can figure out where Candy lives at least. Good thing you put your full name on that text. She was definitely waiting to hear from you."

"Totally." Shane said.

It took Shane nearly half an hour to find parking at the pier. Since it was summer, the beach was filled with tourists and L.A. locals looking to escape to the water. He paid ten dollars for a spot at a parking lot and darted towards the pier. Expecting that it was going to take him time to arrive at the pier, he had planned ahead and left Malibu early.

Ahead was the Santa Monica Pier. In the distance were screams of riders on the roller coaster. The Ferris wheel was revolving lazily on the pier. Shane made a mental note to bring Caroline on a date there.

As he approached the pier, he reached for his cell phone to call Peggy. She picked up right away.

"Shane?" She asked.

"Yeah. I'm just getting here. Where are you by?" Shane said.

"I'm right under the Santa Monica Pier sign at the entrance off Ocean Avenue," she responded. "I'm also wearing a red dress."

"I think I see you. I'm waving," Shane added.

He ran up to the beginning of the boardwalk and saw a woman in her fifties wave back and then put her cell phone away. A black camera case was hanging off one of her shoulders from a strap.

"Peggy, hi," Shane breathed from his run to the spot where she was at.

"Hi," she responded, and she took the camera off her shoulder and gave it to him. "Here you go. This is rightfully yours."

"Thank you," Shane said catching his breath. "Is there a way I can speak to Candy in person?"

Peggy looked at Shane through her dark rimmed glasses and brown eyes, taken aback by the request, "Why would you want to do that?"

"I just want to get a better understanding of why Derek wanted me to have this camera," Shane said truthfully. Even though Derek had promised it to him as a teenager, he was under the impression that there was something more to it.

"Look," she began, "apparently he took a liking to you when you were younger and knew you really liked it. He wanted you to inherit it."

"Did he know he was going to die? I mean did he just give this to her right before the accident? He could have easily left this at his house."

"Shane, I have no idea what his reason was. I barely knew the man. There is nothing more I can say or help you with. I'm not lying. I do not work for Candy, so I'm not obligated to her secrets anymore. She is a friend, however," Peggy exclaimed.

"Right, and friends still keep secrets," Shane said smartly with a grin.

Peggy looked at him with annoyance and chose not to answer. "I have to be on my way. I'm a mother and I have my children to attend to."

Without another word, Peggy turned and crossed the street. Shane thought about chasing her down and questioning her more, but he felt it was a lost cause. He knew it was Candy he needed to talk to. The only problem was, he was unable to divulge the information of her residence or even a phone number from Peggy. All he knew was she lived near him somewhere…in Malibu.

Shane turned back towards the parking lot where his Jeep was parked and did a double take. Caroline was sitting in a bench and staring at him.

"What are you doing here?" He asked, yet he was somewhat flattered she stalked him.

"Obviously I was curious and just wanted to make sure there was nothing shady to worry about. You are safe so that's good," she said, then she pointed to his camera, "And you got that camera. Open it!"

"Are you not going to ask what Peggy told me?" Shane said.

"Nothing," Caroline said grinning, "The conversation was short, and I could tell you were frustrated after she just turned and left. I didn't work with her much, but she was always faithful to her clients. She once lied straight to the press about this one up and coming actor's sexuality. She swore he was straight, but turns out he was gay and she kept it hush hush by setting him up with some of her other female clients. Come to think of it Candy was one of them! Ha ha."

"Damn Hollywood. It's so fake," Shane said bitterly. "But who am I to talk? I'm going to end up photoshopping Alice's headshots I take, to make her look better than she does in real life."

Caroline laughed, then reached for his camera to take a look. "Ooooooh, she's a beauty!"

It was in fact a beauty. The camera was silver and in very good shiny condition. There was not one scratch or sign of wear. Derek made sure to take good care of it.

"It looks just like it did when I last saw it several years ago," Shane admitted. He was very excited about his new toy. In his mind he was thinking about what his next photo subjects would be.

"Well it won't be useful for your gig with Fashion Rack," Caroline said after a few minutes of letting Shane feel every edge of the camera, "You know we use digital. The camera you have at home is perfect."

"Yeah I know that," Shane said. "Well stalker, now that you are here, are you up for a ride in the Ferris wheel? I'll pay."

"Let's do it!" Caroline smiled and gave Shane a quick kiss on the lips. Shane blushed but Caroline had sped ahead so fast, grabbing his hand to beckon him forward, that she missed seeing him turn red.

"Alright, next cart please," said the guy in charge of the Ferris wheel line.

"That's us two!" Shane said, pointing at himself and Caroline.

They got in the cart, and it slowly made its way to the top where it conveniently stopped. Caroline and Shane exchanged a long kiss.

After they stopped and Shane broke free, he said, "Wish I had my camera. It's beautiful out here."

"But you do have a camera! See if there's film," Caroline said, pointing to his newly acquired inheritance.

"Hmm...none in the case pockets. Let me check if there is some inside it already," Shane told her.

He opened the door where the film would be inserted and sure enough there was a roll of film.

"Bingo...oh wait. Ugh!" Shane looked defeated, "It's all used up. Damn it!"

"Well that's what cell phones are for!" Caroline said and she snapped a photo of them embracing with her hand outstretched to capture them both. "Look, it's cute! I'll upload to Facebook!"

"Nice," Shane smiled, and he went in to kiss Caroline, but as he did so, he stopped suddenly.

"What?" Caroline asked, flustered that he had stopped so quickly.

"I wonder what is in the film? I mean what were the last pictures Derek took?"

Caroline's annoyance turned to excitement, "Oh my God! You are right. Might be worth taking a look at. Maybe another message?"

"I would bet my other digital camera there is!" Shane said confidently. "I mean he already has left messages...the CD, for example. Tomorrow at work I'm going to develop them myself!"

Chapter Five:
The House on the Hill

Shane arrived at work late due to an accident on the PCH. He was already frustrated that after work he had to shoot Alice's headshots back at his house and was unable to have more free time to prepare for his first Fashion Rack freelance project.

"Sorry I'm late Bob. Accident," Shane explained, "on the PCH."

"Yeah, so I've heard. It's a slow day so don't worry. Just get behind the register," Bob replied.

After an hour into Shane's shift, Alice walked into the store. She looked really pretty with a flower in her hair and a white linen summer dress.

"Hey there Shane," she grinned. "Ready for my close up?"

"Hey Alice, of course," he lied. "Looking forward to it. I have some great ideas. Make sure you bring some wardrobe changes!"

"Done and done," she said. "I'm in the area for a while. Want to grab lunch on your break?"

"I can't," he replied, "because I have some stuff to do since I'll be busy with you tonight. I've got to take care of it during my break."

Shane's plan was to develop the roll of film from Derek's camera during his lunch break.

"I see," she said defeated. "Well if you change your mind, I'll be shopping at the Promenade."

"Ok, have fun," Shane said and waved goodbye as she left the store.

"Women," Shane sighed.

When lunchtime rolled around, Shane headed to the dark room in the back of the store, to begin developing the 35mm roll of film from Derek's camera. He began the process and left them to develop while he ran across the street to pick up a sandwich.

"The usual?" The sandwich artist from the restaurant Shane went to asked.

"You know me well Martha," Shane told the sandwich artist.

He dug through his wallet to pull a few bills to pay for his meal. Once his sandwich was ready, he grabbed it and ran back to La La Camera Co. He entered the store and went to the employee lounge in the back to eat. Bob was having his lunch too in the corner, while talking loudly to his wife on his cell phone.

Shane turned on the TV and started flipping through the channels. He stopped on CNN for a headline that caught his interest: "Strange white light spotted near Las Vegas."

Shane raised the volume on the TV and Bob shot him a dirty look.

"Sorry, this sounds interesting," Shane told his boss.

Bob walked out of the lounge and continued his loud argument with his wife.

Shane turned back to the television set. CNN was playing footage, given to them by a viewer, of this strange white light in the sky. It appeared to be moving through the clouds before it disappeared. It was rewound and played over and over about five times. The reporter added commentary:

"What started off as another late night in Las Vegas for many tourists, turned into a spectacle that was something out of a Cirque du Soleil Vegas show, except it was in the sky and disappeared into the clouds. Air Traffic Control has confirmed that there were no civilian or commercial aircraft flying in the area where the footage reveals the strange light, however it has been common knowledge that there are military bases in several areas in the Nevada desert. There has been no comment from the military on this occurrence. The videotape was taken by a family driving into Las Vegas early this morning around three in the morning.

For those of you just joining us, take a look at this footage…"

CNN began replaying the light going through the clouds. Shane was intrigued by it. It looked so magical. His first thought was that it was something out of a religious book, then the reporter said:

"Many witnesses called into the Las Vegas sheriff department claiming to have experienced a UFO sighting. What exactly was this mysterious light? Were we in fact visted by strangers from another planet? More on this, after the break."

Shane rolled his eyes and turned off the TV. He finished his sandwich, wiped his hands and mouth clean, then headed back to the dark room.

Upon entering, he noticed that the pictures were fully developed. His heart began racing. He took each photo off the hanging line they were on and stacked them together. He had ten minutes left on his break, so he ran back to the lounge and sat at the same table he ate lunch at. He began flipping through each picture. There was a time stamp on each one dated over two years back. They were taken when Derek was alive.

"Hmm…" Shane mumbled to himself.

The first few pictures were taken inside someone's home. It appeared as though the home had been burglarized. Items were thrown all over the place. Books were thrown off bookshelves and desks were over turned. Drawers were pulled out and their contents emptied onto the floor. It was a mess. The home looked very nice. It belonged to someone very well off. Shane concluded this was most likely Derek's house.

"Did he take these for insurance purposes?" Shane thought.

Most of the photos were indeed pictures of a torn apart home. Then he reached the final five photos and they were different. The first three were taken in the same home, however it looked like it had been cleaned up. Judging by the time stamp it was about a week later, and the living room looked as though it had never been touched.

The first of the five last photos showed a desk with a fancy blue pen. It was the only pen in a pencil holder on the antique brown, wooden desk, which was overturned in a previous photo.

Shane went back to the photo of the burglarized desk and saw the same pen thrown on the floor.

The next photo showed a camera case sitting on a bookshelf. It was open and empty. Next to it was a small memory card plastic case. It was propped open, and its contents were empty as well. Clearly, it was evident that they once held items that were stolen. Shane recognized the camera bag as Derek's old digital camera case.

"Someone stole his digital camera, but not the one he gave me?" Shane thought aloud, "He must have given it to Candy before this happened. Was he under the impression someone would break into his home?"

The third photo looked like it was taken by accident. It was a picture of hardwood floor and a pair of feet in flip-flops that were most likely Derek's. It appeared as though he accidently took this photo when he put his camera down and incidentally, it took a picture of his own feet.

The last two photos were exterior. The first one was a photo of a hill and several houses nestled upon it. It looked familiar to Shane. He scratched his head and racked his memory as to why it did. Shane deduced that this photo was not taken in the Hollywood Hills where Derek lived, because the house seemed spread out and not cramped together like in Hollywood.

Shane set down the photo and looked at the last one. It was a house. Shane looked back at the previous photo to realize that it was a close up shot of one the houses on the hill. It was a beautiful blue home that looked like it was built in the seventies. There was a large gate that surrounded it.

Shane went through the photos over and over, trying to piece them together. Most seemed random with no significance. He believed the only important ones were the last two: the hill and the house on the hill. The hill looked oddly familiar to Shane and he was trying to figure out where he had seen it before.

"Are you going to work or not?" Bob said walking into the lounge sounding irritated. We have customers waiting to check out!"

Shane ran back to the register to help out the queue of customers waiting to purchase their goods.

After his shift was over, Shane put the photos he developed into an envelope and headed to the parking lot outside. He got into his car and sped home. He wanted to have at least an hour of free time before Alice came over for her photo shoot to review the pictures. He called Mike and Caroline to come over. Caroline was busy on a shoot, but Mike was free.

"See you there!" Mike said to Shane over the phone.

"Great! It'll be detective work at its best!" Shane exclaimed loudly over the wind since his Jeep's top was off.

Mike arrived at Shane's beach house twenty minutes after Shane had. He barged into his house making Shane jump, sending some of his photos flying over the coffee table in front of the couch he was on.

"Dude, don't you knock?" Shane said putting himself together and gathering the pictures he dropped.

"Just excited," Mike said.

"Glad you are showing some real interest. Here, check this out," Shane told him handing him the photos.

He started off by showing him photos of the house that was ransacked, which also included items that were left in the house after it was cleaned up. Shane then showed Mike the photos of the house on the hill.

"Is that Derek's house?" Mike asked.

"See," Shane began, "I was thinking that too, but I noticed that the hills are not littered with houses. They are spread out."

"You're right," Mike said, "Actually the area looks like Malibu!"

"Mike, you are a genius!" Shane said. He looked closely and realized the landscape did in fact look familiar. The only problem was Shane did not know the exact location of where *this* specific hill was. The city of Malibu stretches out at least twenty-five miles.

"Well we have to find out who lives in this house then," Shane said, "Do you think it belongs to—"

"Candy?" Mike finished for him.

"Yeah," Shane said.

"I wouldn't doubt it," Mike said, and then the doorbell rang.

It was Alice. Shane answered the door. She looked stunning. She was hair and make-up ready.

"Wow," Shane said without thinking.

"Heh. Thanks," Alice walked into his living room, "Hey Mike! I didn't know you would be here."

"I was just visiting," Mike said. He felt he should not tell her about the photograph clues since it was Shane's business.

"Well you can watch. Ready, Shane?" Alice insisted.

"Yup. Let's do this," Shane said reaching for his digital camera on the kitchen counter.

They traveled to a park a few miles up the road, and Alice began doing several poses on the grassy lawn. Mike was rolling his eyes and yawning in boredom as Shane took shot after shot of Alice's different poses and wardrobe changes.

The sun was beginning to set over the hills and the natural lighting was waning.

"We're about to lose some really good lighting Alice," Shane said irritated, "I think we have some great shots."

"I have one more outfit. Just open the shutters!" She said in an annoyed tone. She was irritated that Shane was trying to rush and end the shoot.

She ran to her car to change inside.

"You would think she'd be more grateful considering you are doing this for free!" Mike said flabbergasted.

"She's been moody ever since she found out I was dating Caroline," Shane admitted, "It's like she's jealous, yet when I was crushing over her she never gave any indication she was interested. She never even flirted with me."

"Girls are weird," Mike said matter-of-factly.

Alice came back running barefoot in a yellow dress.

"Let's set up by that tree, Shane!" Alice called. She walked over to the tree and leaned up against it. She began contorting her face into sexy, seductive looks for the final shots. "Hurry up Baker, I have a date tonight and I don't want to be late."

Mike and Shane looked at each other. Mike grinned and Shane seemed annoyed.

"Yeah, cause I have no personal life of my own!" Shane snapped.

"What's that supposed to mean?" Alice yelled.

"I mean I'm doing this for free!" Shane retorted, "The least you can do is be thankful instead of bitching and moaning."

Shane seemed to have touched a nerve. For a second it looked like Alice was about to cry. Then, she put on her flip-flops and tore off a ribbon she had in her hair and threw it to the ground.

"Alice—wait!" Shane called after her but she ran to her car and left.

"You pissed her off," Mike said, as if this was newsworthy.

"You think?" Shane snapped turning over to Mike.

Alice took off at full speed in her car. She revved the engine and she drove up towards the hill. Shane followed her car going up the winding path with his eyes.

"Where the heck is she going? She doesn't live that way," Mike said.

"Gosh, why did she have to act that way?" Shane said irritated. "I am not going to reschedule this. She is ridiculous!"

"True that. You should not," Mike agreed. "Although, saying she was bitching might have been too harsh?"

Shane looked at Mike knowing he was right, but he proceeded to roll his eyes. He looked back at the road where Alice disappeared off to and then casually looked at the hill. He did a double take.

"Oh—my God!" Shane gasped, as the whole fight he just had slipped from his mind.

"What?" Mike said jumping.

"That's it! The hill!" Shane said.

"Are you sure?" Mike asked.

"Shane pulled the photo out from his pocket. He brought it because he knew he'd be driving through town. Any possibility of finding the hill was Shane's priority. He had the photo of the hill in case he came into familiar territory.

"Look," Shane said holding up the photo in front of him towards the hill.

"Well I'll be damned! We found that fast, didn't we?" Mike said excitedly.

"Well, I found it, but yes, it was fast!" Shane said.

Mike rolled his eyes.

"Well, it's getting dark, but I'm up for exploring! Let's go," Shane finished and they headed to his Jeep.

Once they were in the car, Shane flipped the engine on and they were off. Mike turned on the radio. The DJ was talking about the similar story on CNN Shane had heard earlier that day.

"...and there is apparently, strange lights in the sky?!", the disc jockey said with confusion. "A bird? A plane? Aliens? You be the judge! You can watch the CNN video on our website, or you can check out our Twitter or Facebook pages! Speaking of which, here's Katy Perry, 'E.T.' on JCPT 101.3." The DJ finished and Katy Perry's song began.

"Hah, nice way to make that story relevant on Top 40 radio," Shane said.

"What was he talking about? A UFO sighting?" Mike asked.

"Well there was a strange light near Vegas flying over the sky. Some family caught it on film. I haven't heard of anyone else catching those lights on film. Nobody ever sleeps in Vegas!" Shane explained, "But apparently, according to CNN, there were multiple witnesses calling the sheriff's office about it."

"I'm sure most people up at three in the morning in Vegas were drunk or on something!" Mike said, as if the statement were hard facts.

"Maybe. It's still funny to see this being reported on CNN. Some think it had something to do with the military," Shane added.

"Maybe. Hey, so where do you think Alice sped off to? What business does she have up here?"

"Nothing. She probably was going to make a scene and come back down to the park," Shane told Mike.

They continued up the path to the top of the hill.

"Mike, can you pull out the photograph of the house. It has to be here somewhere in this neighborhood. It's blue, but seeing as that it is now night time, that might be hard to tell," Shane said.

"Ok I got it. Well, the gate is very distinctive too. It's tall. Looks like wrought iron material by the looks of it. None of these other homes have a gate," Mike said looking at each and every house as they drove by them.

There were a few streetlights, but they were far and few between. They gave off an eerie orange glow.

"Looks like we are about to reach a dead end up ahead," Shane said taking one hand off the steering wheel and pointing forward.

"Dead end? More like a good start!" Mike said excitedly, "That's the gate! That's the house!"

They pulled up to the end of the road and saw a two-story home guarded by a giant metal gate. The shutters of the home were closed. There were no lights on. Judging by the growing wild bushes on the lawn—the photo showed the home looking very well kept and lively—nobody had tended to it in months. It looked uninhabited and uninviting.

"Hmmm," Shane said, "I don't think anyone lives here. Anymore."

"Good eye detective," Mike teased.

Shane turned off the Jeep but left the headlights on pointing towards the gate.

"This is creepy—don't get off!" Mike said sounding worried as Shane opened his door and walked out.

Not wanting to stay alone in the Jeep, Mike jumped out.

"Dude, it seems so dead here. Maybe we should go and come back in the daytime," Mike said with panic in his voice.

Shane walked slowly towards the gate. He examined the house. It looked as if it had been abandoned for months.

"Shane, I don't think anyone really lives here and if you are about to explore it and trespass, I will take you down. This area is creepy as hell," Mike said.

"Not a tough guy now. Are you?" Shane teased.

"Seriously man," he said.

"Candy Adams certainly is all washed up. I mean she can't even spruce up her home."

"Maybe she doesn't even live here Einstein!" Mike retorted. "Hey do you hear that? Someone is coming!"

Shane looked down the street. They could hear a car coming, but they were blinded by the Jeep's headlights. They could not see anything. Then another pair of lights entered the area they were standing in, and they were blinded even more. The car was coming at them fast.

"What the—" Shane began.

Mike ran at Shane to move him out of the way. There was a loud screeching sound of the car's breaks as it came for halt quickly, just feet away from where Mike and Shane were now standing. They could not make out the car as the lights were blazing. It had its brights on. The door opened and closed.

The silhouette of a woman was the only thing they could see. Shane's heart was racing. Mike was shaking from head to toe, but no sound escaped his throat. He looked mortified. He grabbed Shane's elbow instinctually as if beckoning him to do something.

"Wh-wh-who are you?" Shane said shivering slightly.

The figure said nothing. She pulled an object from behind her. It was long. The shape of it was obvious.

Mike gulped, "P-p-please."

Shane's eyes widened in horror, realizing what the shape was. It was an ax.

Both Shane and Mike began to back away in fear, but they were at a dead end and would be pressing up against the metal gate of the house.

"Wh-who are you?" Shane demanded again trying to sound courageous.

"Candy?" Mike said absentmindedly.

The woman inched closer to Mike and Shane. It was as if she were teasing them and testing their patience.

Mike was stiff. Shane was shaking.

The silhouetted figure of the woman raised the ax in a position of an attack. Mike let out a blood-curdling scream as she threw the ax with efficient force, as if it were made of air, straight towards Shane.

Shane's eyes widened as it came at him fast and he screamed too. His yell echoed throughout the isolated neighborhood. The nearest house was a block away. Nobody came out to see what the commotion was.

The ax hit Shane straight on the chest and he fell to the ground. Mike screamed even louder and the woman began laughing.

Confused by her laugh, Mike stopped yelling. Then he looked down at Shane. Shane was touching the ax in shock. It was fake.

Mike reached for it and examined it, "What the hell?"

"You think you are so funny, don't you?" Shane said sounding really angry.

The woman continued to laugh.

"Alice…" Shane said through gritted teeth as he got up and made his way towards her.

She moved towards them and soon they could make out that it was in fact Alice.

"BITCH!" Mike yelled and he ran towards her with the fake ax as if about to mutilate her.

"You boys scare easily. That ax is a prop." She said dodging a swipe from Mike, "I saw you drive by. I guess I needed to cool off, so I thought I'd play a little game with you. It's nice that you came to look for me."

"Alice you nearly gave me a heart attack!" Shane said.

"I nearly pissed my pants!" Mike exclaimed. "Besides we weren't looking for you."

"What are you doing all the way up here?" Alice asked.

"None of your business," Shane said deciding he was no longer going to share the real reason they were there and exclude her from any information regarding Derek Conrad.

"You dorks. Well I'm sorry I got all pissed off Shane. I can't wait to see the prints," Alice said. "Ok, I'm out. Date night!"

Shane rolled his eyes. Alice got in her car and took off.

"The nerve of her!" Mike said flabbergasted. "I mean after she nearly scared us to death, she acts like you aren't mad at her?"

"You scream like a girl," Shane laughed.

Mike jabbed Shane in the shoulder with the ax.

"Ow!" he snapped.

"Let's get the hell out of here!" Mike said ignoring Shane's dirty look.

"I just want to examine a bit more," Shane said, walking up to the gate.

The gate was maybe ten feet tall. The metal looked really thick and seemed to be in better condition than the house itself. He put his hand on the handle and attempted to twist and turn it in hopes that it would open.

"I'm pretty sure this gate is sealed shut and locked," Mike said sarcastically as Shane kept tugging and pulling.

"It was worth a try," Shane responded.

He walked to the edge of the gate where the address number was located next to an intercom. He pressed the intercom instinctively but nothing happened.

"Doesn't work," Shane breathed.

Then his eyes darted back to the address number. He moved some overgrown weeds that were covering what looked like a mail slot. Then what he saw made his heart race. He gasped so loud.

"What is it?" Mike said sounding worried.

"You will never believe who this house belongs to! It's not Candy Adams," Shane said sounding thrilled.

"Who?" Mike said running towards where he was standing.

"Take a look for yourself!" Shane said, pointing at a name in peeling silver lettering on the gate.

Mike took one look and squealed, "No way!"

"Yes way!" Shane said, a look of accomplishment in his eyes. "I guess he was trying to get us to find his house. But, still, this makes no sense. He lived in the Hollywood Hills."

Mike nodded his head in agreement, and he took his eyes off the lettering on the gate that read "D. Conrad."

Chapter Six:

The Other House

During the next few days, Shane had been distracted by the discovery of Derek Conrad's house in Malibu. He thought it would have been Candy Adams' house. He went back to visit the house during the day a few times, as the weeks passed, but there was no way of getting through the gate unless he climbed it. He decided against attempting to trespass when he spotted a neighborhood watch security vehicle patrolling the area.

Shane was under the impression one of the neighbors had called security due to suspicious activity, which was Shane visiting every so often in hopes of finding someone coming in or out of the house. Every time he visited, the house remained as empty as when he first discovered it.

It had been three weeks since the discovery of the house, and both Mike and Shane had filled in Caroline about that evening. They left out the part where Alice scared them to death out of pride for their manhood.

Caroline was using her journalistic skills to figure out who now owned the house.

"I have a friend that works in real estate. I went to college with her. She's looking into it for me. It's not an area where she has properties, but she's checking with some colleagues. If we turn up a name at least we'd have a lead right?" Caroline explained.

"Yes, true," Shane said, looking out the window of his beach house where the three were sitting around brainstorming while drinking a few beers. "So Derek wanted us to find this house? I just didn't know he owned two."

"But he does have a house in Hollywood, correct?" Mike asked.

"Yeah. I called my Uncle Robert a few days after we found his house and he explained to me that Derek owned a weekend house in Malibu. I mean the guy could afford it I guess. Anyways, I've been updating my uncle on our journey. He's intrigued by the whole camera situation and the photos that were in it. He asked me to scan and email him the photos, which I barely got around to doing yesterday."

"Did he get back to you?" Caroline asked.

"I haven't checked my e-mail today," Shane admitted. He got up and went to his bedroom. Minutes later he returned with his laptop. "I'll check now."

Shane opened up his e-mail and found a response from his uncle:

Shane-

I'm not sure what happened to his house. It appears that it was burglarized during the time I was not in contact with him. However, I recognized the photos and they were taken from his Malibu home and not his Hollywood Hills home. While the interior looks almost similar, the desk in his actual house was made of metal. The wooden one in the photo was at his weekend home. It was passed down from his father. He kept it at the weekend home. Now that I remember, I forgot to mention he had a weekend home and the address I gave you at your parent's house was to his actual house in Hollywood where I got the CD from. Keep on searching. I want you to find out all you can.

-Uncle Robert

"This is true," Shane went on, "but I have the address to his actual house in Hollywood then. My uncle gave it to me in a crumpled piece of paper when he was in town a few weeks ago. I don't see the point in going there if the pictures from the camera lead us to his second house, conveniently just a few miles from here."

"Well," Caroline jumped in, "didn't you tell us before that your uncle had said his house was inherited by Candy? Perhaps this one was too."

"So," Mike chimed in, "that means we should check out his house in Hollywood as well. It seems that Candy has abandoned taking care of the house here in Malibu."

"I'm going to call my friend in real estate and see if she's learned anything new. Maybe if I hassle her..." Caroline said, and she reached for her iPhone. She dialed a number and waited for a few rings before someone on the other end picked up. "Where are you now? Ok. Ok. OK! Yes, thank you! We should grab drinks some time girl. Ok, bye!"

"What?" Shane and Mike said in unison.

"This is too easy. The house is under Mariette Polashek's name. Candy Adams!" Caroline squealed.

"Nice. Ok, so now we know for sure," Shane said looking from Caroline to Mike, "that she owns both homes. That means she has a key. Now we got to ask her to let us into the Malibu home, because the pictures on the camera seem to be leading us into the interior!"

"Easier said that done," sighed Mike.

"Touché," breathed Caroline.

Alice was sitting outside on the balcony of her apartment. She lived close to campus. Shane had jumped out of his Jeep and waved to her. She smiled and went inside to head downstairs to let him into the complex.

"Thanks for coming by," she said, smiling as she let Shane in.

"No problem. I was worried you might ax me if I didn't," Shane teased.

She jabbed him in the shoulder playfully and let out a giggle.

"Sorry. So, you have the headshots all ready to go?" She asked excitedly.

"Yup," he said as they entered her apartment.

Alice lived alone. Her apartment was quite messy. It looked as though she had just thrown a party. There were red party cups everywhere, broken beer bottles, and beer cans on the carpet. She had empty food trays piled upon her very small kitchen trashcan.

"Looks like you had some fun last night," Shane said, eyeing the apartment's clutter with a raised eyebrow.

"Ha ha," she laughed, "It was a party for my sorority sisters. Just a girl's night. Well, it was supposed to be, but some frat guys and Jesse came over."

"Jesse?" Shane said curiously.

"Yeah—that's the guy I'm seeing now," she blushed and avoided Shane's gaze.

Shane gulped and tried to pretend he did not care.

"How's Caroline?" Alice brought up conveniently.

"She's good actually. Anyways, what do you think of the photos?" Shane said, looking at the portfolio he handed her.

Alice looked through them all without saying a word. She just stared. It was about five minutes later when she finally spoke, "They are beautiful."

"You're beautif—" Shane began, but caught himself and he turned red.

Alice looked at him and she flushed a shade of crimson. She looked into his eyes. Shane looked into hers. Then they both turned away from each other. It was an awkward minute of silence. Shane was fidgeting with his cell phone and Alice was flipping through the pictures over again.

"Listen," Alice began, "I'm sorry for everything."

"It was a joke. Maybe apologize to Mike. You scared him with the ax incident," Shane said automatically.

"No," Alice began and she put her hand on one of his shoulders without making eye contact. "I mean. The thing is…you see…well here goes. I knew you liked me. And I was scared to pursue anything because we've known each other for so long. I didn't want our friendship to be ruined. I mean we had this brother-sister thing going on. It would have been weird. That's why I might have been so cold and unassuming. I'm an actress after all."

Shane was quiet.

Alice continued, "But then I saw you with Caroline and I became jealous. Only then did I realize that I really like you. Jesse is great and all, but he's just some frat boy that likes to get drunk and make moves on me."

Alice turned red at her over share of information. Shane cringed.

"Well you should have been more upfront," Shane said.

"But I didn't realize it until after you started dating Caroline," she retorted.

Shane then began to fill her in on all the messages he received from Derek Conrad that he had purposefully chosen to not fill her in with before. The last thing she knew about was the audio CD he received.

Alice was a good listener too. She gasped and "oooohed" in all the right places. Then she smiled when she learned that during her ax prank, they had uncovered the house that Derek once owned.

Once she was up to speed, she was asking all the right questions. They were the ones Shane was trying to figure out.

"…and so you still don't know why he wanted you to have the items. Why it's you? And what does he want you to do?" she finished.

"All what I'm trying to figure out. This is no coincidence. We keep being led to something. The audio CD led to me getting that camera. It was in Candy's possession," Shane said.

"You know what I think," Alice said, "We need to find Candy. She's the key to this whole mess. She must be hiding something. Why is she hard to find?"

"Hell if I know," Shane said, "but I got a crazy idea! You free? Want to join me on a trip to the Hollywood Hills?"

"Are we going to his actual house?" Alice said sounding very interested.

"Yes!" Shane said and he pulled out the piece of paper with Derek's address on it. "I got the address. I'll drive us!"

"So we just head up this road. It'll take us into the canyon," Alice said half an hour later as they drove through the Hollywood Hills. She was using her iPhone to map their journey.

"So you said turn left?" Shane asked as they hit a fork in the road.

"Yes. Right up there onto Mulholland," Alice informed.

The roads in the area were winding and very narrow. Shane was cautiously driving slowly through every corner in case oncoming traffic was coming fast. There would be no warning with how sharp the turns were.

"It's no wonder there are so many accidents here," Shane said. "I mean that is, after all, how Derek died."

"Actually...hey stop up there!" Alice said.

"There is a sign that says 'no stopping,' Alice," Shane said.

"I know, but I think I remember from the news that this spot right there," she said pointing at the ledge before the road curved, "is where the accident was."

Up ahead by the curve, was a metal barrier that looked like it had been added and reinforced several times from perhaps several collision accidents.

"Wow, so that's," Shane said, "where he drove off the road?"

"Yeah," Alice said.

Shane parked the car and put on his hazards. They got off to look over the barrier. It was nearly a straight shot down to the bottom of the valley. Several trees and another fence a few yards below would be the only things to stop a vehicle from going over to plummet even further to the bottom of the canyon.

"Man, that is scary," Alice said, grabbing onto Shane's shoulder as if she were using it for balance to avoid falling.

"There's no way anyone could survive driving off this ledge," Shane said, trying not to picture an image of what the night Derek drove off the ledge would look like.

After a few minutes of silence, Shane gestured for Alice to head back into the jeep. They got in and continued up the hill. Alice reached for the stereo and turned it on to a pop station. She began singing along to the song playing, and Shane laughed and joined in at the chorus.

Alice looked over at Shane and smiled. Shane smiled back.

"Ah, so I think we are about to arrive," Alice said looking back at her phone's GPS.

"Yes, there it is. That's the address that's on this paper," Shane said double-checking the paper his uncle had written on.

They pulled up to the curb of a really nice two-story home. The house looked like it was still well maintained. There was a short brick fence and a small gate that bordered the home. It was a white wooden house and looked like it was built decades ago, however it appeared recently remodeled.

"There's a car parked in the driveway," Alice said pointing at an old-fashioned black convertible Jaguar.

"Someone lives here now. But who?" Shane thought out loud.

"Shall we just knock?" Alice asked Shane.

"I mean we can," Shane said, "but, like, don't you think that would be weird?"

"Maybe Candy sold it after she inherited it," Alice added smartly, "So whoever lives here may be able to give us a lead."

Shane made his way towards the gate. His heart began racing, and he was walking so briskly that he did not notice a man with thick, black eyeglasses walking his dog on the sidewalk. Shane collided straight into him knocking his glasses onto the floor and causing the small Chihuahua dog he was walking, to bark.

"Oh my God, I am so sorry," Shane said picking up the glasses for the man.

Alice was eyeing the man from head to toe. She seemed to have found him attractive and blushed in embarrassment for Shane's clumsiness.

"It's ok. Be careful though," the man said putting on his eyeglasses. Once they were on and he could see again, he stared at Shane. It looked like he wanted to say something, as his mouth opened, but no voice came out. It was a very awkward moment.

"So, once again I am sorry," Shane said not making much eye contact with the man.

"Right. I am ok and so are my glasses," the man said rearranging them again.

Alice raised her eyebrows, and then sighed with a look of defeat.

The man continued to look at Shane, and then he nodded and walked away down the sidewalk.

Alice stared at his backside and caught the man turning around and looking at Shane again, although this time he was smiling. The man turned back and bent over to pet his dog right near the Jeep. He then picked up the dog, turned back again to look over at Shane and Alice, and kept on walking. Shane was oblivious to the backward glances.

"Ha ha ha," Alice began to giggle.

"What? Accidents happen. That was awkard," Shane said rolling his eyes at Alice.

"He was cute! And I'm pretty sure he thought you were too," Alice said, fighting back more laughter, but she gave up and let it out.

"Really?" Shane said scratching his head. "What do you mean?"

"Nothing, I just saw him check you out!" Alice teased. "Anyways, are we going to knock on this door?

"Yeah. Ok," Shane said, and he opened the small brown wooden gate.

They entered the yard and walked up the cobblestone path leading to the green front door. There was a "welcome" mat at the foot of the door.

"Well, here goes," Shane said, and he rang the doorbell.

His heart began to race. He was nervous. Alice looked very excited. A minute passed and there was no answer. Alice pressed the doorbell and it chimed and echoed inside.

"Someone is home. I mean there's a car in the drive way," Alice said, impatiently trying to peak through the window on the door, but saw nobody.

"Maybe whoever lives here went for a walk," Shane said.

"Or maybe they went to walk their dog," Alice winked.

"Ha. That guy came from across the street. Not this house."

They waited another minute, then decided that perhaps nobody was home and they turned around to head back to the Jeep.

Just as they reached the brown entrance gate, they heard the door open.

"Hello," said the voice of a woman.

The lady that came out of the house stood framed in the doorway. She looked like she was in her late thirties or early forties; however it appeared she had plastic surgery in an attempt to look younger. She had dirty blonde hair. She was wearing reading glasses and had an apron over her dress. She was very curvy and stunningly pretty.

"Um, hi," Shane said, and both he and Alice walked towards the lady.

"How can I help you?" The lady said eyeing them both suspiciously.

Alice's eyes widened and her mouth flew open. It appeared as though she had seen this woman before. Shane looked at her and was about to ask her what the matter was, but Alice spoke up.

"Candy Adams?"

Chapter Seven:

The Retired Actress

"I prefer Mariette," Mariette said. "I am retired and no longer on screen. Candy is no more."

She looked sad after saying that statement. Shane felt uncomfortable and shot a glance at Alice.

"Mariette, I'm sorry. I did not mean to sound rude," Alice apologized.

"That is fine. How can I help you?" Mariette said sounding as though they were interrupting her from something more pressing.

"I'm Shane Baker," Shane said.

Mariette's look of annoyance turned into surprise. She smiled, stepped back into the house and moved aside.

"I had a feeling I would meet you soon. Come in," Mariette said and she sounded much more inviting.

They walked into the house that once belonged to Derek Conrad. There was tons of old fashioned furniture that did not look like they ever belonged to Derek. Shane assumed it was Mariette's furniture. Apparently she had moved in.

The furniture was all brown oak and it matched the hardwood floors. The place was spotless and looked well kept.

"So you moved in here?" Shane asked, then realized it sounded somewhat rude.

"Derek gave me the house in his will," Mariette said. "I moved in just recently, once I realized I could not afford my old condo. This place is paid off and Derek would have wanted me to. Besides, Derek had moved into his Malibu weekend home months prior to his death so this place was mostly empty of his belongings. He put most of it in storage. The only thing is, I have no idea what storage facility his belongings are in. I stored some of his old furniture elsewhere."

"You also own his Malibu weekend home, right?" Alice said, not realizing how odd it appeared that she knew so much about the inheritance.

"Um, yes," Mariette said, eyeing Alice suspiciously. "But I just kind of abandoned it. I have it cleaned up maybe once a year now. I know that sounds terrible, but this place is maintenance enough, and I have to be careful with money. I'm living off residuals."

"Ms. Polashek, do you know why Derek left me his 35mm camera?" Shane asked. "I have reason to believe he wanted me to contact you."

"And you are right," Mariette began, "He did want you to find me. However, due to circumstances, he couldn't tell me why or how he was going to do that. He said he could not physically ask you."

"Is that why he gave me the audio CD?" Shane asked.

Mariette gestured for them to take a seat on her velvet couch. She then sat on an armchair directly across from them.

"Derek loved scavenger hunts. When he wanted people to know his secrets, or secrets of others, he hinted them with clues. This circumstance is different. He had no choice but to create an intricate way of giving you a message. He said it could be years before you would eventually find me, but it was important that I kept what he told me a secret...for my safety."

Shane and Alice looked at each other. If there was something mysterious about Derek's gifts, it was that they seemed random. However, none of them thought that anyone's safety was at stake.

"What happened? Was his death really an accident?" Alice blurted out without stopping herself.

Mariette just stared at her. For a second her eyes glazed over. It appeared as though she was holding back tears. Alice looked uncomfortable and decided not to ask any more questions.

"I'm sorry, this is very hard for me," Mariette got up. She walked over to the blinds in the living room and closed each one shut as if she was afraid someone would be looking through.

She then walked over to the kitchen down the hallway and closed a window shut that was left open.

Shane and Alice exchanged nervous glances. Alice was holding onto her cell phone as if prepared to make a call.

"What if she killed Derek and thinks we know too much?" whispered Alice.

"Shhh," Shane said, feeling that she was overreacting.

Mariette came back into the living room and sat back down in her armchair. She crossed her hands and stared at Shane.

"Like I said," She began, "I do not know why Derek was persistent in getting you in contact with me, but I am supposed to tell you the same story he told me. It might mean something to you, or it might not."

"Do you mind also telling us a back story of the time leading up to his death? It might help me make sense of what this message is," Shane stated.

"Yeah the story I'm about to share is only part of his message," Mariette said.

She took a deep breath and looked into Shane's eyes, then she turned to make eye contact with Alice. Alice gripped her cell phone instinctively.

Mariette began:

"What I'm about to share with you is hard to believe. I'm not asking you to, but you will do what you will with the contents of this information. I also ask that you keep it to yourselves. Knowing this information has put me in danger as it did Derek. By passing it along, you will now have to be extra careful on the path you take. I was asked only to tell you, Shane, but since you are here…"

Mariette stopped and looked at Alice, and then she continued.

"…you can listen in to as you both are friends. Let me give you some back-story before I share the information Derek shared with me. It might help you understand something I might not.

Derek and I were on and off. We were more than friends, but the term dating was thrown around casually. We were very close and he trusted me and I trusted him. His whole personality changed about three years before he died. I was supposed to have a dinner date with him one night and he stood me up. He was always good at keeping appointments. He was MIA for days. I was worried, but eventually he called me and apologized. He sounded worried and stressed about something. He did not want to tell me what happened, but he said he encountered something 'big.'

For the next few months to a year, his communication with me was sparse. I eventually got upset and gave up on him. I continued to audition for roles to fix my dying career. I did not see him much. After a while, he even stopped working and began to cancel working on shoots. He pissed off big names in Hollywood.

For three years I had zero contact with him until one day, late in the summer months, he said he'd be my photographer for Fashion Rack Magazine. As part of the publicity campaign for a movie, I was set to do a photo shoot and make my comeback. But he flaked—or so I thought. He was a no-show. I was angry. He stood me up again and single handedly crushed my chances of regaining my acting career. A few days later he called me and said somebody burglarized his home. He revealed he was now living in his Malibu weekend home, which made sense as to why I never was able to find him at his Hollywood home.

He sounded scared and he was speaking quickly, but he generally sounded concerned. He asked me to meet him at his Hollywood home, which he hadn't been living at in months. And so I did."

Shane and Alice were at their edge of their seats. Shane knew he would at least get some partial answer to this mystery and urgency of Derek's message to him.

"I arrived at his house one evening. It was late. I think nearly midnight," Mariette continued, "It was the first time I saw him in three years. Any correspondence we had was via e-mail or phone."

Mariette closed her eyes and began remembering in her head every detail of that night. She began the story that Derek had wanted Shane to hear to the best of her memory. Even two years later, the memory was still vivid in her mind...

It was a dark and chilly that late July night. It had just rained that afternoon so the streets were flooded from poor draining systems and the hills left the streets muddy. Rain was uncommon for that time of the year.

Candy had just parked at Derek's old house. He was already waiting for her, leaning against the brown gate that opened to his front yard lawn.

"God! Derek!" Candy exclaimed running to hug him. He looked as if he had aged several years. He looked thinner and pale and most of his hair was practically all silver. He still had some handsome features, but there were shadows under his eyes from exhaustion.

"Candy," Derek began, "I'm so sorry for the absence. Something happened to me that night in August when I had to rush you out of my house."

"You seemed like you were in a hurry to rush me out. We made plans for dinner and then you flaked..." Candy began but Derek cut her off.

"Let's go inside," he said.

They walked into the house and Derek gave a backwards look out into the neighborhood as if expecting someone to be watching him.

"I haven't been here in months," Derek said as he turned on the living room light. "Oh God!"

While his house had obviously been emptied and practically moved out, there was still some bigger furniture, a few bookshelves, and a desk that were left behind. It appeared as if someone had been in his house recently and overturned everything. His desk had been thrown on the floor. It was metal and looked really heavy so it wasn't moved too far from its original location.

"Someone has been here too, huh?" Candy asked. "But why? What is going on with you Derek?"

"Candy," Derek began, "I'm in trouble. They are after me. I can't tell you who, so don't ask. I know some big secrets that I'm not supposed to know. They tried to use hypnosis and counseling to tap into my mind and make me forget. I caught on to their tricks and all of my memories of that one night in August, when I made you leave my house, came back to me. Candy, darling, I stayed away from friends and family in fear of them hurting the people I love. I haven't even talked to my best friend Robert in ages."

"What is going on Derek? Them?" Candy asked impatiently, yet worried.

"Sit. I have to tell you what happened that night and it won't be easy to take in," Derek said. "By telling you this, I'm putting you in danger, but they are on to me and not you."

Derek began telling Candy the story of the night in August when the military had come to his home to take him to an undisclosed location in a desert hundreds of miles away from Los Angeles.

He was as detailed as possible about everything from the plane ride to the strange military base called Sector 7. He told her he remembered how cold it was and how scared, yet intrigued he was about the whole situation.

Then, he arrived at the part of his story where he used his camera to zoom into a strange phenomenon happening miles away in the desert. Candy was completely silent and taking in everything he was saying. She felt he was somewhat deranged, but the tone of his voice was so genuine, that she felt she had to believe his story.

"And there was this white light," he began, "and out from this light a beam shot down to the ground and black figures were coming down from it to the ground. Upon zooming into the beam, I could make out silhouettes of what I believed were human children and adults. There were dozens of them. Then at one point the orb flashed and grew brighter. It gave a glowing, brilliant illumination and I was able to snap pictures of the figures. It was so quick, but I caught those moments on film, so I knew that whatever those figures or people were, I would be able to see them in the developed prints. I had inserted an extra memory card when the agents were not looking. I had been taking double photos. Without them noticing, I put one of the cards in my boot to take home with me."

Candy remained silent. Derek was quiet for a minute, but then he continued his story.

"The agents took me back to the military base, Sector 7. I was taken into a command center. They took me into an empty room with a table and two chairs. The walls were mirrored. I was positive it was a one-way mirror, and I was being watched from the other side.

Agent Green—that was the name of the head agent—told me that I was not to speak of any of these events I witnessed. I was to receive counseling every so often by one of their military personnel doctors. He told me that if I were to speak about that night's events, it would put me in danger. He was vague, but it sounded like a threat to me. He wouldn't answer any of my questions, but I overheard him throwing around the words 'third kind' to his colleagues. I was almost positive he referred to what I had just experienced as an extra terrestrial encounter of the third kind, which meant an unidentified flying object sighting."

"You are very serious about this, aren't you?" Candy said, sounding scared. She was trying to process everything she was just told.

"I have proof though," Derek continued. "I have a few photos. Remember I took double photos from that night? The reason they could not brainwash me to forget was because every time I looked at these photos, my memories would come rushing back to me. The flash from the orb that lit up the area for miles, made the dark figures' bodies visible."

Derek pulled out a few photos from his pocket. He looked at them to himself and put one back into his pocket without Candy noticing. He then handed her three photos.

What Candy saw made her clasp her hand to her mouth in shock. She let out a loud gasp, "Oh my God!"

The photos showed three short beings. They appeared to be between three and four feet judging by the size of the larger figures, which were human beings. Some of their features could be recognized. They appeared to have their eyes closed.

The short beings were slim. Their skin seemed gray or some kind of neutral tone. They had large black almond eyes and large heads. There were no visible noses, and their mouths were small, thin slits. They appeared to be wearing some kind of full body metallic suit.

They were not human by any nature.

"Aliens?" Candy asked knowing how obvious the answer was.

"Beings from another planet," Derek said.

"Why are there people with them coming from that UFO?" Candy asked, pointing at one photo that showed that humans were there.

"Humanoids," Derek said. He looked at her confused expression and explained. "I don't have much time to go into detail, but I learned—and its not important right now how—that these aliens, if you will, created beings deemed as Humanoids to live on Earth as us. To live among us, as us."

"What? Why?" Candy asked in shock.

"I only know bits and pieces, and learning this was by pure luck," Derek said. "Look, I have to leave shortly. You best keep this to yourself. The reason I told you is because I need you to relay this message to my friend Robert's nephew. His name is Shane Baker. I need you to give this audio CD to Robert. I'll e-mail you his address. I don't have it by memory and I'll have to use an e-mail address I made that is not my personal. I'm being tracked and followed by the government agency that took me to that base. Shane needs to know something for his own safety and I cannot leave that written anywhere to be found by the government. I'm leaving behind clues. He knows that I've challenged him with clues before when he was younger. Once this CD falls into his hands by his uncle, he'll know to find you and you will tell him this story and make sure he keeps it quiet. Tell nobody else, and do not speak of this until you speak of it to Shane."

"You want me to tell him the story you just shared?" Candy asked.

"Yes," Derek said, "then I want you to give him this camera."

Derek pulled a 35mm camera out of a case and passed it to her. She took hold of it.

Mariette took a deep breath and opened her eyes. Shane and Alice were dumbstruck. They had no words. Shane knew that while this sounded like something out of a science fiction film, he knew this was not the right time to be skeptical.

"Do you have those photos of the aliens?" Alice finally asked, breaking the silence.

"No. He kept them. It was too dangerous for him to leave them with me, but he said that his clues would lead you to them, Shane," Mariette told them.

"So you were supposed to give me the camera after you told me the story, but I got it before?" Shane asked confused.

"Well I gave up waiting on you to arrive. I knew it would be years. When Peggy told me you had texted her, I asked her to give you the camera. I thought it would just be easy to skip this step, but apparently this story was very new to you.

Peggy is my old publicist. She's a great friend of mine. I had her pretend that this house was still left uninhabited as per my wishes for Derek. Your uncle came over and Peggy gave him the audio CD with the song "I Want Candy" on it. It would be the first clue to get to me.

I honestly thought you would come to Derek's, I mean my house, first since your uncle had the address. You did eventually, but by getting a hold of my publicist, I thought I could avoid our meeting. I was wrong. You still came. Perhaps now the camera means something to you? What is the clue exactly?"

"There was film in the camera. I developed it," Shane said.

"Were they photos of the beings?" Mariette asked.

"No, they were pictures of his burglarized Malibu home," Shane said.

He then pulled out the photos from his jacket pocket and showed her the photos. She looked through them then looked up back to Shane.

"Yes, apparently he wants you to go inside his Malibu home. And I guess since I own it, I'm supposed to take you," Mariette said defeated. I have a key. I'd rather not go back to that house."

"Ok, that is fine. Thank you for allowing us to investigate. Listen," Shane said, "So—Derek's death—do you think it was really an accident?"

"You heard the story," Candy said. "He was in danger. He knew too much, and someone at the agency got wind of his knowledge. Maybe even those pictures he had. I think he was silenced, and it was made to look like an accident. I am not sure, but I hope you can find out."

"I will. My uncle wants to know too. And don't worry, I never thought you had anything to do with it," Shane added with a smile.

"Thank you," Mariette said. "A few people thought I knew some information about his death. I guess they were half-right, but I could not talk about it. If his death was not an accident, I knew I could be a target."

"And now I'm on the same boat," Shane added.

"We both are," Alice corrected him.

Mariette was flipping through the photos again. It looked like she was about to cry. Soon, a tear streamed down her face and she wiped it off. She reached for a tissue on the coffee table and blew her nose.

After a few silent, tense moments, Shane and Alice jumped at Mariette's surprise yelp.

"What is it?" Alice asked?

"This picture is out of place!" Mariette said.

"Which?" Shane and Alice asked at the same time.

"This one is a shot of the floor and you can see Derek's feet," She replied.

"It looks like that was taken on accident," Shane added.

"Yes," Mariette went on, "But all of the other pictures are taken in his Malibu house. Most are pictures of the burglarized scene, and a few are of his house after he cleaned it up. But this one—"

Mariette got up and showed them the picture and pointed to the hardwood floor in the picture and then back to the hardwood floor of the house they were in.

Alice and Shane looked down to their feet and realized that she was right. That picture was the only one in that roll of film that was taken inside the Hollywood house.

"You think he took this intentionally?" Alice asked Shane.

"Don't know," he said. "Mariette what part of the house was this taken?"

Mariette looked at the photo again. "It appears that it is near his desk. It was left behind."

They walked over by the gray metal desk. Shane got on his knees and brushed his hands gently on the wood floor.

"This panel here," Mariette began, pointing to a section of the floor, "always creaks. Watch."

She stepped on it, and it made a creaking sound. It also appeared to have wiggled a bit as if it were loose.

"It's loose." Alice said. She then touched the panel and wiggled it some more.

Mariette ran to the kitchen and came back with a knife. It caught Alice by surprise. Mariette apologized for scaring her and proceeded to put the knife through the crevasses of the floor panel.

After a minute she was able to pop out one end of the floor panel. She then pulled it out to reveal a hallow space beneath. It was not empty.

Chapter Eight:
The Black Car

Shane reached into the crevasse and pulled out a small bronze key. There was no key ring attached or any kind of label signifying what it opened. The only labeling was a number engraved on it that read "956."

"What do you think this opens?" Shane asked Mariette.

"No idea. I can't believe I've been standing on this for a while," she replied.

"Well he wanted me to find this," Shane said matter-of-factly. "The picture was deliberate. I'm quite impressed at the intricacy of this puzzle, really. No government agent would be able to track down whatever he's hiding."

"And wants you to know," Alice added.

"Do you think it opens something in the house? Is there a box, safe, secret room, or anything mysteriously locked here?" Shane asked Mariette.

"None that I am aware of," she replied.

"This is all just so crazy!" Alice said loudly. "I mean, aliens? E.T.? Humanoids? This is all out of some sci-fi film!"

"Alice, we can't question what we do not know," Shane said. "Mariette, any idea where we can find those photos he showed you?"

"He probably carried them around with him," She said. "He obviously didn't have them in the house when it was burglarized. My guess is after his death, they were removed from him or he hid them. However, my guess is the government agency is back in possession of them."

"So we agree," Shane began, "that there must have been foul play in his death?"

"Of course. I was one of the last to see him alive. He knew someone was after him," Mariette said looking somber.

"Mariette, I'm going to hold onto this key and the keys to the Malibu house," Shane said. "I'll go look into the house and use the photos for guidance. There are two pictures left that I am sure are clues. One is the empty camera bag with empty memory card case, and the other is a photo of a wooden desk."

He showed them to Mariette again.

"And that desk is still there as it was two years ago," Mariette assured him.

"Thank you for helping and sharing," Alice added. "Truly, we mean it. I also want to say I'm a big fan of your work."

"Thank you," Mariette said, finally smiling for the first time since they had been in her home. "I think it will be dangerous once you open a few more doors, no pun intended. I'm going to lay low…well more low than usual. Do be careful. I'll give you my cell number so that you can contact me directly. Please keep me posted, and if I can be of any assistance, I will gladly help. Talking to you all about this has taken a great weight off my shoulders."

"Thank you for trusting us," Shane said, and he gave Mariette a hug that was returned back gracefully.

Shane and Alice bid Mariette farewell and exited the house. They walked back out through the brown gate. Alice poked Shane on the shoulder all of a sudden and pointed down the street.

The man that was walking his dog earlier was across the street talking on a cell phone. He saw Shane and made quick eye contact before turning his back to them. The man continued his conversation on the phone.

"Guess he went to put his dog away. Looks like you got a stalker. He was checking you out again. I think he got shy," Alice teased.

"Shut up!" Shane exclaimed turning red. "Let's get out of here."

The next day, Shane had Mike and Caroline over to fill them in on what happened with his meeting at Mariette Polashek's. He asked Alice to come over as well to help him retell every detail of the story they were told.

Caroline was intrigued, but she began formulating ideas that Derek might have been "off his rocker" as she put it. Mike was indifferent.

"If you were there," Shane said, "you would understand how serious of a story this was. Maybe coming from me it sounds like one big joke, but there is something shady definitely going on."

Mike looked like he was thinking hard. Then he said, "What if Candy just saw those reports of mysterious lights on CNN and created this tale. To me she's a suspect in Derek's death."

"He has a good point," Caroline said.

"Cand—I mean Mariette—is not responsible. She was genuine," Shane retorted.

"She is an actress," Caroline said.

There was a very strained tension between Shane and Caroline that might have been due to the fact that Shane had taken Alice instead of Caroline, to Derek's old home. Alice seemed to be getting some satisfaction out Caroline's bitter tone towards Shane. Mike decided things were getting too awkward and cut in.

"Regardless of whatever is going on and if there is such a thing as aliens living on Earth or visiting or whatever, we know that there is in fact some sort of message that Derek had for Shane," he said.

"Still, I don't get what it could be," Shane said rubbing his forehead. "I wasn't even close to the guy after my teenage years."

"You know," Alice began, "this story can't be as farfetched as one would think. I mean are we seriously alone in the universe? Not only that, but doesn't it just give you the chills that there could potentially be beings living among us and going about their every day lives doing what we humans do?"

"So what do you think they are doing," Caroline said, giving Alice a dirty look, "trying to study us or something and then take over our planet?"

"Guys, let's not fight," Shane said trying to break the tension.

"Not sure why you didn't take me with you. I'm great at investigating and seeing through the bull crap people come up with," Caroline said still glaring at Alice.

"I'm going to head out. I need to meet up with Jesse tonight. Talk to you later Shane," Alice said and she left Shane's house.

"What's your deal?" Shane snapped.

"I mean you took her—*really*?" Caroline retorted.

"Um, should I go?" Mike asked uncomfortably.

"And are you still planning to invite her to Vegas next week?" Caroline asked Mike.

"Ok, leave me out of this. She's my friend too," Mike snarled.

"I'm sorry," Caroline said embarrassingly. She turned to Shane, "I'm sorry. I guess I just felt a little…"

"Jealous?" Shane said.

"I'm going to go too," and without a backward glance, she darted out of Shane's house.

"Women," sighed Mike.

"I'm so confused," Shane told Mike, and he sat down on his couch. "I still have feelings for Alice, but I just feel that ship has sailed."

"The ship never embarked to begin with. In fact, it never took its maiden voyage!" Mike said smartly.

"True story," Shane agreed. "So you don't believe Mariette Polashek's story?"

"Well," Mike said, "I'm just a got-to-see-it-to-believe-it type of person. I think this might be more of a sick, twisted murder mystery."

"This is not a Hollywood movie," Shane said rolling his eyes, "and we have no proof of any murder. Just Mariette's story that Derek sounded like he was in trouble."

"Well then let's go find the clues!" Mike said excitedly. "We know there is a picture of a wooden desk that is in Derek's Malibu home. You now hold the key to the front gate and door and another key that opens some unknown lock."

"When do you want to go check out the house?" Shane asked. "I'm not working today…"

"Yeah let's go now," Mike said. "And perhaps we do this without Caroline or Alice."

"Yeah," Shane agreed.

"Anyways, now that I know this super top secret alien government story, I'm pretty much a marked man. I might not be around much longer if that agency is out to get us!" Mike laughed at his own joke.

"That's not funny!" Shane said, but he couldn't help but laugh too.

They pulled up to Derek's Malibu house. It was still daylight, so it did not look as creepy as it did when they were last there. Mike was looking around as if worried they were being watched.

"Paranoid?" Shane asked grinning.

"I just don't want Alice to jump out at us again. That was so messed up," Mike said, remembering the whole ax incident.

"Ha, yeah," Shane nodded in agreement. "Let's go in."

They got off Shane's Jeep and proceeded to the large metal gate. Shane glanced at the brick pillar with the mailbox slot and Derek's name written in silver lettering. He examined the address below, which he did not pay attention to last time he was there: "1111 Ocean Hill Drive."

There was a bulky, thick padlock on the metal gate that opened easily with a few turns of the key Mariette had given them. As they pulled open the heavy gate, it made a creaking noise. It appeared as though no one had entered the home in ages.

"Spooky," Mike muttered.

They closed the gate behind them and walked up a cobblestone path to the front door.

"Watch out for snakes or something," Shane warned Mike, gesturing to the overgrown weeds and brush in the yard as they walked up to the front door. Shane used the same key that opened the padlock to easily open the front door. They walked in to see what was once a nice weekend getaway home, filled with dust and spider webs. Upon entering, a mouse darted near the foot of a staircase, making Mike jump.

"This place has gone to the rats. Literally." Mike breathed.

"Mariette couldn't keep this place in tip-top shape," Shane said. "It's sad too. This place seemed really nice. Well at least from this photo."

Shane pulled out the photo of the close-up of the very house they were in that was taken two years prior. He then flipped through the rest of the photos and pulled out two others: the photo of the wooden desk and the photo of an empty camera bag.

"I have a foreboding sense we should not be here," Mike said as they walked into the living room.

"Derek obviously wanted me to come here, remember?" Shane said, showing him the two photos he was holding.

"Right. Well there's that wooden desk!" Mike said, pointing to the dusty desk that was set against the wall near a window.

They proceeded over to it and began to examine it.

"Make sure to look through every nook, side, and crevasse of this desk. If there's one thing we learned about that floorboard at his Hollywood house, is that there could potentially be a secret door and drawer in this thing," Shane said.

"Let's just break the damn thing apart!" Mike exclaimed as he took off a pencil holder with a pen in it and moved it to the neighboring bookshelf against the wall by the desk. As he did so, he noticed the empty camera case and memory card case from one of the photos, was sitting on one of the shelves.

"Look Shane!" Mike said.

"Nice find," Shane said acknowledging the case on the shelf. "However it's completely empty. Nothing inside it. There's Derek's name written on this nametag. It also has an address. It's not his Hollywood home address though."

"310 Abbot Kinney Rd. Venice Beach." Mike read the tag. "That's not even the address of this house."

"Correct. That means we must go to this location! Next clue. That was easy!" Shane said excitedly, reminded of a clue he once had from Derek as a kid where an address on a business card marked his next clue. "Let's get out of here. I'm bringing the camera bag with us."

"What about the desk? There was a picture of it. There must be some significance…" Mike said.

"Good point," Shane began, "but we've turned that thing upside down. The drawers are empty. There's nothing!"

They looked through the desk again in hopes of finding any kind of clue.

"What if maybe there is an engraving or something on it? Maybe another address?" Mike suggested.

Shane went under the desk and examined every inch of the bottom. There was nothing.

"I don't want to leave until we find out what the message of this picture is," Shane said staring at the picture of the wooden desk. "It has to be staring right at us.

Mike took the picture from Shane to examine it. "Well the desk is empty. The only other thing that really stands out is this metal pencil holder with that blue pen in it."

Mike turned to the bookshelf where he set the pencil holder with the pen in it. He reached for it and examined the pen.

"Well there's no address on the pen," Shane said examining it from Mike's outstretched hand.

"There's a sicker on it!" Mike said pointing at a very tiny circular sticker that was peeling from near the silver pen top. "It says '1GB' on it. I think it's just a manufacturer's sicker," Shane said defeated.

"It's a really nice pen though," Mike said. "Can I keep it?"

"Sure, why not. It's just a pen," Shane said. "Shall we go?"

"Yeah," Mike agreed, putting the pen into his pocket. "Let's get out of this dump."

Shane felt that there was still some secret within the wooden desk, but they spent over half an hour painstakingly looking at ever inch of it for some kind of sign.

"We can just come back at another time," Shane said, thinking about how he would revisit the house to look over the desk again, "Preferably in the morning so it doesn't get dark on us."

The sun had already set as they locked the front door behind them. They proceeded to the main gate, and Shane locked it behind them as they exited. Once it clicked lock, Mike grabbed Shane's wrist and nodded his head towards the road ahead.

"What?" Shane said freeing himself from Mike's grip.

There was a black car parked near a house down the street. It was an Audi. The windows were tinted, but in the quiet neighborhood, it was evident that the engine was on. Shane and Mike could hear it.

"Dude it's just someone parked," Shane said, but he had a very eerie feeling about it. The headlights were off.

"It can't be Alice either," Mike said. "She drives a Volkswagen, doesn't she?"

"Yeah I guess," Shane said. "Let's just get into the Jeep."

They walked briskly towards the Jeep and got in. Shane flipped the engine on and turned on his headlights. He took out the entire set of photo clues from his jacket pocket and put them inside his Jeep middle console. The 35mm camera from Derek was also in there alongside the key labeled "956." After closing it, he took the vehicle off park, and drove down the only way they could: towards the parked black car.

They both stared at it as they drove by it. They could not tell if there was anyone inside as the windows were tinted.

"Gosh, maybe I am just paranoid," Mike said. "I mean it's probably someone just waiting to pick up one of the inhabitants of that house we just passed."

"Yeah maybe you are right," Shane said looking at the rearview mirror, only to notice the black car turned onto the street and made a u-turn.

"Oh my God!" Shane said, beginning to panic and speeding up down the street. "It's tailing us!"

"What?" Mike said, and he turned to look out the back window.

The black car was in fact following behind them.

"It doesn't have its lights on!" Shane said sounding worried. "Should I blink my hazards?"

"Screw that. Let's just cut a couple corners and turns over there!" Mike said.

Shane turned onto a street heading opposite of the direction he needed to go down to get back to his house.

"You think that's the government following us?" Shane thought out loud.

"Maybe you are paranoid," Mike spoke too soon as the car turned down the same street they did. "What the hell? And still it has its lights off."

"I don't want this car to follow me back to where I live," Shane said.

"Even if it is some alien government agency chasing you down, I'm sure they'd have other means of finding out where you live!" Mike said. "Or maybe we are being followed by a Humanoid!"

"Mike, this is not the time for sarcasm," Shane snapped. "There is something seriously suspicious going on involving

Derek's death. I doubt he was paranoid. In fact he was smart to hide his message this way so that nobody else could find out what he is hiding."

"Sorry," Mike said. "I did not mean to be sarcastic. I'm a little freaked out now. What did you get me involved with?"

"I gave you a warning before I told you this story that Mariette was too freaked out to even see me for fear of being tracked. Apparently that's what was happening with Derek!" Shane blurted.

"What if that's the killer?" Mike said pointing his thumb back towards the car that was tailing them.

Shane took another sharp turn and sped up the street.

"Trying to lose this car..." he muttered.

They started going down the hill and taking dangerous sharp turns on the winding road.

"Be careful. This Jeep can't make sharp turns at these speeds! We'll roll over!" Mike complained with a hint of panic in his voice.

"I know, but we got to lose this guy. He's still on our tail," Shane said.

"No he's not! That's a Mercedes," Mike corrected Shane.

Shane slowed down and let the car behind them pass. It wasn't the black car that was originally following them.

"I guess we lost it," Shane said.

"Yeah. Let's get back to your house," Mike said with a sigh of relief.

Minutes later they were driving down the Pacific Coast Highway and were heading towards Shane's house. Mike was fidgeting with the camera bag and opening up all the pockets over and over in case they missed something hidden. He pulled out the nametag and took the card inside it that had Derek's name and the Venice Beach address.

"Keep this in your wallet," Mike said.

"Yeah good thinking. Probably best to keep this with me on my person," Shane replied. "Think I should call Caroline? She was pretty upset earlier."

"And tell her we went to Derek's without her?" Mike said, "She'll love that, won't she?"

"Well, I can leave that part out, I suppose," Shane said.

He fumbled for his cell phone and dialed her number. He turned on his hands-free headset on and listened as she picked up.

"Hey," she said in a monotone manner over the phone.

"You ok? I'm sorry I did not bring you to Derek's Hollywood house," Shane said.

Mike was keeping himself busy with the camera case so as not to appear as if he were eavesdropping. It was pointless as he was in the car sitting next to Shane.

"I am so sorry Shane. I know she has feelings for you. It's a female intuition," Caroline answered honestly. "I shouldn't even be feeling like this. We are just dating. I don't even want to move fast." "It's fine," Shane said. "Hey want to meet up at the Beach Cup in an hour?"

"Ok," Caroline replied.

"Great, I will see you there," Shane hung up and put on his blinker to turn into the driveway of his house.

"Best of luck tonight with Caroline," Mike said as he hopped off the Jeep and put the camera case down on his seat. He waved goodbye and walked over to his car.

Shane jumped into the shower as soon as he got up to his bedroom. His phone went off twice while he was showering. It was from Mike. Mike left a voicemail then proceeded to call again immediately after doing so.

Shane entered back into his bedroom, dripping wet with a towel around his waist. He noticed his phone beep from a voicemail notification. He reached for it, but as he did so he heard a car door slam outside his window.

He looked outside and then heard another door close further in the distance. The sound of an engine starting brought his attention to the sidewalk just outside the entrance of his driveway. A black car was parked and its headlights flashed on. Moments later it drove off onto the highway.

"Crap," Shane muttered realizing that the car that took off was the black Audi that was following Mike and himself earlier.

Shane walked back to his bed and picked up his phone. He had eight missed calls from Mike and two texts, both which read "Pick up!"

Shane dialed his voicemail and listened for Mike's message, "Shane where are you? As I was leaving your house I noticed that black Audi was pulling up behind me to the sidewalk near the entrance of your driveway."

Shane dialed Mike back.

"Hey Mike, I saw the car. I was in the shower," Shane said.

"Damn, you had me worried. I almost turned back," Mike said.

"It's fine," Shane said. "When I got out of the shower, the car drove off. I'm going to go look around outside and see if I notice anything suspicious."

Shane walked downstairs to his living room. He ran to his front door. It was double locked, just as he had left it. No one had been inside his house.

"Phew," Shane sighed in relief.

He picked up a pair of sneakers lying beside his front door and took a jacket out from his utility closet to cover his chest. He walked outside in a towel and jacket. Shane walked over to his Jeep and opened the passenger side door. It was unlocked.

"I swore I locked the door," Shane said to himself.

He noticed immediately upon opening the door fully that his glove box was left open. Someone had ruffled through it.

"Damn it! Where's the camera case?" Shane yelled out loud hitting the door with his fist.

Mike had left the camera case on the seat of his Jeep when they got back. Shane had not taken the case inside with him. Then he reached for the middle center console and opened it. Shane's heart dropped. His eyes widened in horror. The photos and the 35mm camera were gone.

All the clues are gone, Shane thought as tears of anger formed in his eyes.

He looked at his stereo and pushed the eject button. Nothing came out. "And they took the 'I Want Candy' CD," Shane whispered into the quiet night.

It was the worst feeling to have spent so much time trying to figure out this mysterious message from Derek, only to have any link to them taken away.

Shane locked his doors, closed the Jeep, and walked back inside. He immediately dialed Mike and explained that someone had taken Derek's items.

"It's all gone. The CD. The camera. The photos. The camera case," Shane vented.

"Calm down man. This is serious business. It's like they knew exactly what they were looking for doesn't it?" Mike said.

"No freaking idea!" Shane said.

"Shane, I know it sucks that they took the camera. That was sentimental. And the photos. But at least you still have that address right?" Mike asked.

Shane ran upstairs and opened his desk drawer. He pulled out his wallet. The card that was inside the nametag of the camera case was still there. He had the address to the location still and whoever was in the black car did not.

"Yeah I still go it. Good thinking on making me keep it in my wallet!" Shane exclaimed, feeling like he defeated the unknown enemy at their game.

"Yeehaw! I'm brilliant, aren't I? Now we have to go there and figure out what the heck it leads to. Hey and what about the key?" Mike asked.

Shane's heart dropped again for the second time that night. "I forgot, I left it in my console as well! They took it too."

"Nooooo!" Mike yelled over the phone. "That was the one clue we had not solved."

It seemed as though they had reached a dead end.

"I am afraid to go back to Derek's Malibu weekend house, but we still don't know if that desk had any clues. I need to figure that out at some point," Shane said.

"We know we are being trailed. This is not a game. Something seriously messed up is going on. Someone does not want us to find out anything," Mike explained.

"Or someone wants to know what Derek wants me to know?" Shane added smartly.

Shane looked at the time on his cell phone.

"Damn it! I'm going be late to meet up Caroline—actually that's her on the other line. Let me connect with you later." Shane hung up and answered Caroline's call, "Hey sorry! I know I'm running la—"

Caroline cut him off, "I am too. What is on the news distracted me! Run and turn on your TV to channel five!"

Shane turned on the small TV set in his room and clicked his remote to channel five.

There was a female news reporter reporting live from a house fire in a neighborhood.

"I'm Sally King reporting live from..."

Behind her was a two-story house, or at least what was left of it, ablaze. There were police cars and fire trucks with their lights flashing. Firemen were running back and forth with hoses, attempting to stop the inferno. He could see one of the firefighters running through a familiar short brown gate into the house's lawn.

It was Derek Conrad's Hollywood Hills house that was now owned and occupied by Mariette Polashek.

Shane sat down on his bed with his hands clapped against his mouth. He dropped his phone on the bed and could hear Caroline, "Shane? Shane! You there?"

The news reporter continued her report "The home of Mariette Polashek, known to many by her stage name, Candy Adams, has been set on fire. Police are investigating the matter, however they do not suspect foul play. Officials are saying it was old electrical wiring. Well-respected photographer Derek Conrad, who passed away in a car accident, two years ago, once owned this house.

Hold on. It looks like we just got word that Ms. Adams was inside the house…"

The news headline title on the screen had read "Candy Adam's Hollywood Home on Fire." Minutes later it had changed to "Hollywood Starlet Candy Adams Killed Inside Hollywood House Fire."

Chapter Nine:

In Flames

Caroline arrived later that evening at Shane's house. Their plan to meet up at the Beach Cup was changed due to the tragic incident involving Mariette's death. They sat for hours talking about theories and their next plan. Shane had filled in Caroline about their trip to the Malibu house. To his relief, she was not upset he went without her.

"I would have been too freaked out," Caroline admitted. "This is serious. She was right. Knowing that information we received was dangerous. And apparently someone thought to silence her."

"I mean," Shane began after taking a sip of water, "You don't think it's just a mere coincidence do you?"

"She literally just told us this information. Are we next?" Caroline said looking out the window as if she were paranoid they were being watched.

"I think this proves that Derek's car accident was not an accident. Whoever did this made the house fire look like an accident. Electrical wiring? Really? Besides..." Shane said.

"You were followed by a car this evening. They know where you live!" Caroline said.

"But they took all the things I inherited from Derek. Any clue we had is gone!" Shane exclaimed.

"You still have that address though," Caroline added.

"Yes," Shane admitted, "but I've decided we need to lay low. They apparently knew we were going to Derek's Malibu home and were staking it out or following us or something. I think we need to wait this out until we feel safe to travel to this location in Venice. I don't want them to know where it is. That's the one thing we have against them."

"Do you think there is some kind of clue in that desk up at the house on the hill?" Caroline asked. "I mean, you said you looked over it closely."

"I don't know anymore really," Shane admitted. "I don't think it's even safe to go up there again. And come to think of it, staying here doesn't make me feel safe either. They invaded my property and took items from my Jeep. To top it off, they have that key with the numbers "956" on it. We'll never know what the hell it opens."

Shane and Caroline sat in silence on the couch for a while. The news was running on his living room TV on mute. The story on Mariette's death was spreading to several other news outlets.

Mike and Alice eventually called Shane asking if he had heard the news. They had just found out about Mariette's death as well. Both were shocked. Shane asked them to just stay at home and he would contact them in the morning with a new plan. "I just need to think on this," he told them.

"Want me to stay over?" Caroline asked Shane.

Shane blushed and nodded. "Sure. I don't want you driving back to West L.A. right now. We are all in this together. We can only get ourselves deeper into this mess. I don't know if there is a way out."

"Let's go to bed," Shane said.

Shane lent Caroline some shorts and a t-shirt so that she wouldn't sleep in her dress. They brushed their teeth and jumped into Shane's bed.

"Thanks for letting me stay over," Caroline said and she kissed Shane in the lips.

He smiled, "Of course. I promise I don't snore."

Shane was a little nervous. Caroline eventually fell asleep quickly and he put his arm around her. Moments later Shane was fast asleep.

They were awoken later in the early morning around three by several sirens. A sheriff's car zoomed down the highway followed by a police car.

"I guess I should have closed the window," Shane said getting up to shut it.

"It's ok," Caroline yawned.

As Shane closed the window, three fire trucks sped down in the same direction as the police and sheriff cars.

"What the hell is going on?" Caroline asked, now looking fully awake and approaching the window. She put her hand on the back of Shane's neck. He smiled at her touch.

Another police car had just zoomed by again.

"Ok, this is so out of the ordinary for Malibu," Shane said.

Just then Shane's phone rang.

"It's Alice," he said to Caroline. "Hello?"

"Shane! Sorry to wake you. You'll never believe what the hell is going on!" She said sounding as if she had ran a marathon.

"What is it?" Shane asked.

"I was woken up by the sirens of police cars and fire trucks a few minutes ago. I walked onto my balcony to see where they were headed. It looks like they were going up the road to Ocean Hill," Alice finished.

Shane's heart began to race once again.

"Coincidence?" Alice continued.

Caroline was able to hear through the speaker what Alice had just said.

"I think we learned today that there is no such thing as a coincidence," Caroline said loudly so that Alice could hear.

"Was that Caroline? Did she stay the night?" Alice asked changing her tone into surprise.

"Alice, stay put I'm going to go pick you up. Let's check this out," Shane said.

He hung up the phone and told Caroline to get dressed warmly. Once Shane had his jeans, tee, and jacket on and Caroline was back in her dress and coat, they headed out to Alice's house.

"I just figured we can pick her up since she told us where the trucks were headed," Shane said after noticing Caroline's arms were folded.

"Fine," she said. Then she changed her tone. "Sorry. This is all just starting to freak me out. Shane, what the hell did Derek do or know or want to tell you?"

"If I knew, we wouldn't be in this mess!" Shane answered back.

Alice was waiting by her apartment driveway when Shane pulled up. She got in the backseat of the Jeep and the three of them headed up towards Ocean Hill.

"I feel that something must have happened at Derek's Malibu house," Shane said, breaking up the awkward silence.

Nobody said anything. They seemed to be nervous about what they were going to find.

As soon as they got onto the street where the house was located, they saw neighbors outside of their homes walking to the end of the street. There was police tape and a barrier blocking the road up ahead. It was evident that something had occurred at the very end of Ocean Hill, which was where Derek's house stood.

"Oh my God," Alice breathed as they got closer.

There were tons of families and neighbors lined up by the police barricade. Several officers were working hard to keep them back and away from the scene. In the distance ahead, there were firefighters rushing towards the house. It was on fire. The flames were very high, and several trees in the vicinity had caught fire. It was spreading.

Shane pulled over and took off his jacket as he stepped outside. It felt as though they were in an oven. A news truck was rushing through and parked just ahead from where Shane had parked.

The news anchor Shane had seen on TV earlier that evening, came rushing out with her hair in curlers. She pulled them off and wiped her business jacket free from lint. She grabbed a microphone and the cameraman turned on his camera lights.

"In what appears to be a strange coincidence, the second home owned by Derek Conrad, Hollywood photographer that died two years ago, has been set ablaze this morning. The house was inherited by actress Candy Adams, who was killed last evening in her Hollywood Hills home, also once belonging to Mr. Conrad. Police ruled her death as accidental, but are now questioning that due to the fact that the house behind me has been set on fire. Both homes were under her name. Police believe there is a connection and are trying to figure out if this should be called a murder case."

"Dear God," Caroline said, holding Shane's hand as they walked closer to where the police barricade was set up.

They saw a police officer questioning the neighbor, "Have you noticed anything suspicious lately?"

"Well last night there was a black car staked outside this house," the neighbor said, "and there was a Jeep parked just up by the gate of the house. I didn't go outside or report it. I thought maybe it was one of Ms. Adam's people checking up on the house."

Shane gulped. He was hoping the neighbor would not recognize his Jeep parked just a few feet away. Just then another officer walked to the officer that was questioning the neighbor. He was wearing gloves and holding a gas tank.

"Arsonist," he mouthed to the other officer.

Shane, Caroline, and Alice exchanged nervous glances.

Then, another cop came up to the two officers with gloves on, holding what looked like a charred and melted...

"The camera!" Shane whispered in shock.

"Oh my God!" Alice said clasping her hand.

"Someone broke into your Jeep and decided to burn the clues—the only direction we had to finding any real evidence," Caroline whispered.

"Someone is playing a dirty game," Shane said through gritted teeth and clenched his fists. "Do you think the key was thrown in there?"

"Probably," Alice responded.

"It's metal. What would fire do to it?" Caroline asked.

"Doesn't matter. Maybe they kept it. Maybe they threw it into the ocean. But the desk—it was made of wood. It'll be long gone by the time they put this fire out!" Shane said his mouth dropping as he finished.

He felt they had reached a dead end. Without the key or the desk, there were no more clues or hints to move on with their journey to find out what Derek wanted Shane to know or do.

"To think, this all had to do with people finding out a secret that the government was hiding from the public," Alice whispered to Shane.

It was sweltering hot and the fire looked like it was finally under control. It had stopped spreading. Several on-lookers and neighbors looked relieved. The anchor continued her report on the news. Shane caught a few words of what she was saying. "Conspiracy theories...some say she was responsible for Derek Conrad's death...was she crazy?"

"Is that Peggy?" Caroline said all of a sudden bringing Shane back to reality.

Caroline pointed to a woman who was in a night shawl. It was Peggy Mills, Mariette's former publicist and friend. Peggy had noticed she was being pointed at and shot Caroline a suspicious look. Then she noticed Shane. She had a look of surprise written on her face, and walked over.

"Mr. Baker!" Peggy said, "What are you doing here?"

"We followed the commotion. I live just down the highway below the hill," he answered.

Peggy looked as if she had been crying. Her eyeliner had run down her face and her hair was disheveled.

"This has been a difficult night for me," Peggy said holding back tears. "I strongly believe Mariette's death was a murder. Someone burned her house down and burned this one too. I have no idea why someone would choose to harm a woman who has been living in sorrow at the death of her former lover and the downfall of her career. Such a tragedy."

Peggy began sobbing into her shawl. Caroline moved forward and put her arm around her. Peggy did not move her face from her shawl.

"This is all my fault," Shane said finally causing Peggy to take her face off her shawl. "If I hadn't gone to her. If I hadn't attempted to learn what Derek—"

"Don't be a fool boy!" Peggy said suddenly sounding stern and more composed, "You had no idea something like this would happen. I need to go. I can't be here anymore."

She sniffed and turned on her heel and headed away from the crowd of on-lookers. She stormed off so fast, however, that she dropped her shawl. Shane picked it up and ran after her. She was moving swiftly towards her vehicle. She took out her keys and in the distance he could make out her car. The lights had blinked as soon as she pressed the unlock button on her key.

She got into her dark-colored vehicle and closed the door. Shane was about to yell that she forgot her shawl, when he noticed the make and familiar shape of the car. It was an Audi. It was too far and too dark in the distance to tell for sure, but it looked black.

Caroline and Alice came up behind Shane.

"Are you not going to give her the shawl back?" Alice asked Shane who was staring like a deer in headlights as Peggy drove away in her car.

Both Alice and Caroline put their hands to their mouths once they realized the make of her car.

"Holy mother of—" Alice shrieked.

"Oh my God!" Caroline said.

"But she gave you the camera—and she gave your uncle the CD…" Alice added.

"Was she playing some sort of game with us? I'm so confused now!" Caroline said, theories running through her mind.

"It was her!" Shane said, convinced they had found the individual that tailed them, stole the items from his vehicle, and set both of the houses on the hills on fire.

Chapter Ten:
Fashion Rack Offices

By morning, once most of Los Angeles was awake and getting ready for another workday, the news and blogs had spread the word about the burning down of the second home belonging to Candy Adams. Her death, now being called a murder, was headlines across the country. The police had launched an investigation and were asking anyone with information, to come forward.

Shane, Mike, Caroline, and Alice were in the corner booth at the 2nd Street Pub in Santa Monica. Mike was brought up to speed with everything that had happened earlier in the morning. They all began throwing out ideas on how to find evidence to get Peggy arrested.

"I still can't believe it's her! She returned to the scene of the crime," Shane said.

"We'll nail her!" Mike said, pounding his fist to the table making some of Alice's beer splash out.

"Watch it Mike!" Alice snapped. "Ugh."

"When do you want to go check out that address that was in the camera bag?" Caroline asked.

"I don't know," Shane responded. "I think we need to lay low. Especially if Peggy is still at large. She knows where I live. She can burn down my house any minute. I think it's best if I stay at home with my parents for a bit."

"You know," Alice chimed in, "we can still do the Vegas trip we were planning. We can go for a few days until all this news just kind of settles. I mean it's all the buzz in L.A. right now."

Alice gestured over to the TV behind the bar. There was a headshot of Mariette and the title "Former Actress Dies in Burning Home."

"It'll be hard for me to get time off from work right now," Caroline said, "and you still need to do your first freelance gig, remember? The one we were going to have a few weeks ago was cancelled, but I think they want to bring in a musician for a shoot in a few days," Caroline said to Shane.

"Hmm, well I quit La La Camera Co. this morning. I called up my boss and said I had to attend to personal things. My agenda has changed in the past few days," Shane said. "As for the gig, it is freelance so I am not committed. I think maybe a few days to a week in Vegas will do me well."

"Yeah. Peggy won't find us there," Mike said.

"I thought we were dealing with the government," Caroline said.

"Thought is the key word. I wonder if Candy was deranged or something? Perhaps Peggy went along with her crazy story and finished her off," Mike said.

"Don't be so insensitive," Alice snapped. "I have a theory. I've been thinking about it since this morning. I think there is some truth to Derek's story that was told to us by Candy. There is seriously someone or some people that do not want us to uncover top-secret information. I think there is a connection with Peggy—whether she is that person or not—and I think her connection might be…"

Alice sat quietly for a second thinking over what she was about to say.

"Yes? Enlighten us," Caroline said.

"Well I was there when Candy told Shane and I the story," Alice continued. "And well, it seemed beyond real. At least she wasn't acting. I could tell. I've seen her work. She looked like it was straining her to tell us anything like it was a life and death matter if she did. I did some research on my own about UFO theories and aliens and all that jazz just to get a better understanding of the theories. Well, there are sites about these so-called Humanoids. Some theories range from aliens abducting humans at night and using them to mate to create beings that live on Earth but are incognito as humans. Look at Clark Kent. He was from Krypton!"

"So Superman is living among us, essentially? I don't see reports of anyone flying?" Caroline said.

Alice ignored her and went on, "What I'm saying is, maybe it is not the government after us. Maybe it's them: an entity from another planet outside ours that has been living on Earth as a human. What if Peggy is a Humanoid?"

Shane mulled over what Alice just said, then spoke, "I was there when Mariette told us the story. I think there is some kind of truth. At this point, we don't know much about what the hell is going on. Government or otherwise, someone or something is definitely tracking us, or at least me. Derek was being tracked too, there is no doubt now. He had to pass on a message and he had to encrypt it so that it could not be easily found. It seemed successful until my car was burglarized, and we were intercepted. Now those clues remain as charred or ash in the debris leftover from the burned down houses. And that key—we'll never know what it opens now. Right now all we can move forward with are the facts. We do have one clue that whoever is tracking us does not have. It's that address. Now yesterday we showed up at the Malibu house to recover the next clues and look what happened. The place was burned down. I do not want to go to the Venice Beach location right now in fear that something might happen there. Let's all get out of here. We have to. We all know the story about the night Derek was taken to that desert. We are all connected now."

They were all quiet. Caroline sipped on her beer and nodded. Alice shook her head in agreement. Mike winked at Shane signifying his agreement as well.

"However," Caroline said, "Do you think it wise we let her run free for another week?"

"Well, we have no proof anyways, Caroline," Shane said, "and I don't want to stick around here waiting for her to come after me and scorch my beach house.

"Where does she live?" Alice asked.

"No clue," Shane said. "I met her at the pier when she passed the camera along to me."

"Why would she want to steal it back from you though?" Mike said as if he had just discovered a new idea.

Shane thought about what Mike just said.

"Hmm," he said rubbing the temples of his head. "I have no idea how the mind of a crazy person works." Shane felt defeated. "We need to find out where she lives and investigate her."

"Well I was able to get her number in my boss's directory. I'm sure her address is listed!" Caroline said excitedly.

"Great," Shane said. "Then when you go to work tomorrow, find the address and we'll go find this psycho!"

"Ok," Caroline said. "And then I'll ask for the rest of the week off. My boss will love that…"

"So it's settled?" Mike asked. "We are really going to do this Vegas trip? Lay low. Disappear. Off the grid…"

"Why the hell not," Shane replied.

"So down," Alice said grinning.

"Well," Caroline began, "if I can get the time off."

The next day, Shane and Caroline were heading to the Fashion Rack Magazine offices in West L.A. Caroline had called Shane early that morning telling him to go with her so that he could fill out some freelancer paperwork and get his ID badge for shoots and office access.

"This is a perfect excuse to have my boss distracted as I search her Rolodex for Peggy's address," Caroline said as they walked into the offices of Fashion Rack. The offices were located in a tall, green, glass building. Fashion Rack was housed at the penthouse of the tower.

They took an elevator to the top and when the doors opened, Shane's mouth opened in awe. The entire office had a stunning view of all of L.A. and the ocean at the distance. The walls were all glass so it looked as if they were outside. There were dozens of cubicles. All were of a different color and trendy, modern furniture gave the offices a cozy feeling. People were buzzing about moving at a fast pace trying to get their work done.

"My boss's office is over here," Caroline said, grabbing Shane's wrist and leading him down a hall.

"This place is awesome!" Shane said.

As they passed a few offices he noticed pictures of Mariette. It appeared as though they were working on an article piece for the next month's issue.

"Ok, we're here," Caroline said, and she knocked on the door labeled "Stacy Wang, Editor-in-Chief."

"Come in," Stacy's voice was heard through the closed door.

"Hi Stacy!" Caroline said, "This is our new photographer, Shane."

Shane made is way to shake Stacy's hand. She looked at him for a few seconds, then her eyes moved down to his outstretched hand. She then shook it, although reluctantly. Shane felt awkward.

"Hi, I'll walk you over to HR and that way I can give you the gist of what we want and do here at FR," Stacy said in a very bored voice.

Caroline winked at Shane as Stacy took off with him. Stacy didn't even glance back or say a word to Caroline. Once they were out of sight, Caroline went through Stacy's Rolodex and found Peggy's information. She wrote down the address on a post it and put it in her jean pocket. She left Stacy's office and headed for her desk.

Stacy was showing Shane around after he had his picture taken and badge made. She seemed to have changed her tone and was much more friendly. Shane was sure her attitude changed after he showed her his portfolio of his work, which he brought.

"I still can't stop gushing over your shots, Shane," Stacy said after she gave him a quick tour of the lounge. "I mean that's some grade A work. If you can capture shots like that for F.R., you could have a really good career in this town."

"Thanks Stacy," Shane replied, blushing. "I was inspired by a family friend. I believe you know him. Derek Conrad?"

"Ah, good ole Derek," Stacy said. "It's sad about what happened to his homes. And Candy too. Scary world we live in. Derek didn't leave a good lasting impression with F.R., though. Long story. No time. Let's hop to it, I want you to meet some of our editors."

Shane knew the story behind why Derek did not leave a good impression. Caroline had explained to him, so he thought best not to ask, even though most people would.

An hour later Shane walked up to Caroline's desk.

"Nice digs," he said grinning.

"Stacy has been saying good things about you. She's usually a hard ass."

"She likes my work," Shane said, grinning even more.

"The honeymoon phase will end," Caroline teased. "This business is rough. However, Stacy will make or break you. I'm afraid to ask her for the time off. Why don't I skip out on Vegas and I'll go explore Peggy's address?"

"I really want you to come though," Shane said. "You don't want me to be alone with Alice do you?"

Apparently that was not a good joke to tease Caroline with. She gave him a dark look and opened her mouth to say something, but her expression changed instantly. Her new expression was a look of horror.

Shane turned around to notice a familiar woman with glasses walking into the offices in a navy business jacket and skirt.

"Holy sh—" Shane began, but he was drowned out by Stacy's yells of excitement.

Stacy ran towards Peggy and gave her a hug.

"It has been too long m'dear!" Stacy said, tossing her straight black hair aside.

"Stacy Wang. We meet again. It's been a while," Peggy responded.

Shane and Caroline were ducking behind the wall of Caroline's cube. They didn't want to be spotted.

"Well she wouldn't try anything here would she?" Caroline said.

Stacy was walking Peggy over to her office. Luckily when they passed Caroline's desk, none of them had noticed Shane and Caroline were crouching under cover.

Stacy left her door cracked so they could make out the entire conversation.

"Let me start off with," Peggy began, "I'm sorry. I know that it has been awkward with my PR company and F.R. Magazine ever since the whole Candy cover scandal. I'm not coming back to get some of my newer clients on the issue, but I was wondering if you could help me with something."

"Anything for you m'dear," Stacy said sweetly. "I did not take it personally. The whole Candy thing is water under the bridge."

"Yes, thank you," Peggy said. "I'm looking for an employee of yours. I actually forgot her name, but she contacted me from your office a few weeks ago. She was trying to get Candy's contact information from me. I know this might sound serious, and it is, but I need full cooperation. I need to find her."

"Um, why?" Stacy asked, not so sweetly now. "And how did my employee get your contact info. There are only a few of us that have publicists' contact information handy."

Caroline's heart began to race. She looked at Shane in horror.

"I'm screwed, if she finds out it was me! She can't see you here either Shane! Go!" Caroline said anxiously.

Shane looked at her, gave her a quick kiss, and made his way out of the office. Caroline got up and hid in an empty cubicle still within earshot of Stacy's office.

"...it's just odd that all of a sudden someone from here is looking for the contact info of a retired actress. First of all, even if she was working, no one ever asks for their direct contact information. They'd deal with the publicist!" Peggy ranted.

"Peggy, I know," Stacy said and she sounded worried. "I don't know who it was, and there is no proof. Do you have the voicemails?"

Peggy caressed her Blackberry, "Deleted. Wait, come to think of it, there was this one text from another party—I already have him looked up. He's not affiliated with F.R. Let's see..."

Peggy was looking through her old text messages. Caroline knew that Shane had texted her and was pretty sure he said her name in that text. Her heart dropped.

"Aha! Let me read it," Peggy said. "Here we go... 'Hi, Peggy. My name is Shane Baker. I am a family friend of Derek Conrad and I am under the impression he wanted me to contact Candy. Could you please contact me at your earliest convenience?' Hmm...it doesn't say the name of the female employee of yours."

Caroline sighed that her name was still clear. The only problem was...

"Shane Baker?!" Stacy exclaimed. "We just hired him as freelance!"

"What? Really?" Peggy said and there was a note of excitement in her voice.

"Yes, my former assistant, now writer, Caroline brought him in. In fact he was just here—Caroline, are you there? Is Shane?" Stacy called.

Caroline gulped and left her hiding space. The walk to her office felt like the longest walk ever. She was sure she was about to be fired when Peggy remembered her name.

Caroline walked in, and Peggy eyed her from head to toe. She had a grin. Caroline was sure it was an evil "I caught you" grin.

"Caroline, did you give Shane Baker Peggy's personal contact information?" Stacy said fuming and looking like she was about to kill.

"I-um," Caroline began.

"Oh my God!" Peggy said. "Wow this must be coming with old age. Such a strange coincidence that Shane works here actually. But I got the texts mixed up! That was not the one I meant. Shane knew Derek Conrad—that was a different situation. It was not an employee from F.R. This is so embarrassing. It was another magazine—gosh I'm such an old woman."

Both Stacy and Caroline looked very confused. Peggy just blurted out a bunch of words and not any of it made much sense or even sounded truthful.

"I must go! Let's chat soon about a model client of mine named Karin. Tootles," Peggy said and she took off.

Once Peggy had left the office Stacy turned to look at Caroline with a raised eyebrow. "What the hell?"

"I think she's off her rocker," Caroline said mustering up confidence to sound truthful. "Maybe it has to do with Candy's death and all she's going through?"

"Yeah, perhaps. Funny how Shane knows Peggy. Small world," Stacy said. "I don't have time to really process what just happened so if it makes sense to you in the future just give me the abbreviated version!" Stacy said. "That's it."

"That was a close one," Shane said, clutching his chest once Caroline filled him in on everything in the parking garage of the building.

"Yeah, but I could tell she remembered my name and put two and two together," Caroline said looking worried. "I guess she was trying to find me since she knows we are connected. And now she knows where you work!"

"This is so freaking crazy. I can't even deal with this right now," Shane said, brushing his hands through his hair.

"One thing is obvious though," Caroline said, "She's out to get us."

"Yeah," Shane agreed. "So you got the address right?"

"Yup," Caroline said. "And that will be the last time I ever try to steal information from Stacy Wang."

"Hello…" Peggy Mills said. She was walking out of an elevator and into the garage.

Shane and Caroline looked horrified. There was no one around in the garage. They were alone with her.

"I had no idea I would get you in trouble, so I made up that lie," Peggy said to Caroline.

"What do you want?" Caroline asked suspiciously.

"I just wanted to find you. Hello Shane," Peggy said acknowledging that Shane was there.

"Why?" Caroline asked, still confused.

"You worked on the shoot that Candy was on—the one Derek was to photograph—right?"

"Yeah—sort of," Caroline replied.

"I need to track down Candy's former bodyguard. I did not want to ask Stacy for her help because she won't do it, let's be honest. But you were able to get my gracious help…" Peggy then looked at Shane.

"Yeah and then you stole the camera from my Jeep!" Shane said without thinking.

"Excuse me?" Peggy said looking at him in shock. "I did no such thing!"

"You were following us that night that Candy's house was burned down. You were watching us and chased us through a neighborhood on Ocean Hill!" Shane continued.

"Chased you? What the hell?" Peggy said taken aback.

"In your black Audi!" Shane said forcefully.

"Black Audi?" Peggy said. "My Audi is bright blue!"

Peggy pulled out her keys and pressed the unlock button. A few cars behind Shane and Caroline, a bright blue Audi's lights flashed twice and in unison with a beeping sound.

Caroline and Shane exchanged confused glances. It was dark, after all, the night they saw her on Ocean Hill getting into her car, and it was at a great distance. Shane thought hard. The car that followed them and was also outside his house when his Jeep was broken into, was definitely black. They drove right by it at one point when Mike and him left the Malibu house after doing a search of it.

"Well…" Shane was at loss for words.

"Someone was chasing you in a black car then?" Peggy said.

"Yes," Caroline said, answering for Shane, as he remained quiet.

"Candy mentioned to me last week that she felt she was being watched. She noticed a black car drive by her house a few days prior to the fire. The reason I want to get her body guard's contact info is because I think he may have something to do with this."

"Why?" Caroline asked.

"She fired him without severance. It pissed him off. I was there when it happened. It was ugly. He threatened her too. He drives a black Mercedes come to think of it." Peggy said. "This is why I need your help."

Shane felt like screaming. He felt like he was hitting a dead end. He then spoke up, "Well it was an Audi that followed us."

"I don't think the bodyguard knows who you are. Why would he follow you?" Peggy asked.

"I'll get you that info by tomorrow Peggy. I should have my old notes from the shoot with a contact sheet. Come to think of it, I guess I could have got your number from there too," Caroline said.

Caroline and Shane walked across the street from the Fashion Rack offices and headed into a sandwich shop for lunch. Once they ordered their meal, they sat near a window that faced the street.

"This is one big mess," Shane said. "So Peggy isn't the person that started the fires."

"Then who is?" Caroline said. "You don't think it's the bodyguard?"

"No," Shane said and he looked up at the ceiling for a minute before saying, "It's that agency. I mean wasn't that our first thought anyways?"

"Well, yeah," Caroline admitted. "Then we saw Peggy at the scene of the crime and assumed her car was the one that was tailing you."

"It just," Shane began as he bit into his sandwich and swallowed, "seems that we are never going to get out of this dead end. Now that we know Peggy is innocent, or at least not the person that tailed me, we have no use for her address."

"But, we still have the address that was on the camera bag. There must be some significance," Caroline said.

"Yeah but even if it does, we don't have all the pieces. Remember that desk is now ash after the Malibu house burned down," Shane said, making a valid point.

"And that key. This just sucks so much," Caroline said, biting into a chip.

"I'm starting to think this Vegas trip is sounding real nice, huh?" Shane asked.

"After that awkward episode with Stacy, I do not think I want to ask for time off," Caroline stated.

"I understand," Shane replied. "So, are you going to send Peggy the bodyguard's contact info? And what do you think she'll do? Show up at his house and say, 'Hey I think you killed my friend?'"

"I think she's just really saddened by this situation," Caroline admitted. "She looked awful compared to that one time I saw her at the pier. I think she wants justice. They were best friends—the only other person still in contact with her."

"Yeah," Shane said. "I just think that the bodyguard really has nothing to do with this mess. There is something going on and we have to get to the bottom of this, but now that we don't really know who or what is after me, I think it would be safe for me to get out of town. Vegas."

"I want you to go. I'll hold down the fort here. Do you want me to go to that Venice address that was on the camera case?" Caroline insisted and she took a bite from her sandwich.

"We'll go when I get back. In case you are being tracked too, I don't want to give them any more clues to work through," Shane said. "Them. This is ridiculous. Some unknown, faceless entity is driving us crazy."

Caroline had to stay and work on a deadline assigned to her last minute by Stacy. Shane left the offices before her and headed into Hollywood. He drove up Mulholland and through the Hollywood Hills. He drove past the curve on the road with the barriers where Derek had been killed two years prior. Then he proceeded back up to where Derek's house once stood. There was police tape closing off the area. The remains of the house were nothing but debris and charred wood. There was a police car parked outside the house near the small brown gate, which had been untouched by the fire.

Shane parked his Jeep a few houses down so as not to appear suspicious. He got off and decided to take a stroll down the sidewalk opposite of where the house stood. He sat on a nearby bus bench and examined the remains from afar. The police officer was looking at him for a few seconds and then decided he was not a threat and turned away back towards the house.

After ten minutes of just staring into the sky, Shane got up and walked over the police car.

"Excuse me," he said, amazed by his courage to approach the officer.

"Yes?" the officer asked suspiciously. He had a really short mustache and was wearing aviators. He looked like a stereotypical police officer.

"I was wondering if they have any leads on Ms. Adam's killer?" Shane asked knowing that he probably went too far.

"Excuse me kid, but that is official police business," the officer said looking at Shane with curiosity.

"Candy was an acquaintance of mine and a family friend," Shane said, sounding sincere. The statement was half true.

"What are you doing here exactly?" the officer said. "This is a crime scene. Family, friend, or not...well...we just can't have anyone in this area."

Shane teetered with the idea about telling him he was being tailed by a black Audi the night of the two house fires. He wanted something to be done. He realized how foolish he looked asking these questions, let alone suspicious.

"I'm sorry to have bothered you. This whole incident has upset me," Shane said, and he nodded goodbye and took off back to his Jeep without a backward glance.

Shane got into the Jeep and said to himself, "Gosh I have no idea what I'm doing here. There's no way an answer is just going to show up and help me figure out what I must do."

Shane had the idea to go to the Venice Beach address out of desperation to get some kind of clue to move forward. He felt like he was stuck in a rut. He decided that he was going to do it.

Shane was stuck in traffic on the 405 heading to Venice. He had the radio on and the entertainment news segment was playing.

"The case of the double arsonist incident that happened on Wednesday, early in the morning to the property of actress Candy Adams, continues to baffle police. Was Candy Adam's death a murder or an accident? An electrical fire was ruled out due to the strange—coincidence or not—separate fire on her other property. Both once belonged to highly acclaimed deceased photographer Derek Conrad. Some of you might remember his death resulting from running his car off a hill about two years ago. Police are asking locals to come forward with any evidence or tips on helping solve this mystery. We'll keep you posted on JCPT 101.3"

Shane turned off the radio station and continued his slow commute through the L.A. traffic. Upon arriving at his exit, Mike called.

"Yo!" Mike said, "Alice and I set plans for Vegas."

"Oh yeah?" Shane said, half listening as he battled onto his exit with other commuters.

"I will drive since I have an SUV. We'll leave tomorrow night to avoid traffic. Pack light though! This will be fun! Can Caroline make it?" Mike continued.

"She can't. It's fine. She's got tons of work at F.R.," Shane responded. "Anyways I don't think Alice and her can be around each other every day for a week."

"That's what I thought," Mike said, "but I just did not want her to feel like she was excluded. Plus you are dating her."

"It's cool. I got to go. I'm driving and traffic blows," Shane said and he hung up the phone.

Shane arrived at Abbot Kinney Road and passed several boutique and vintage shops.

"310...310...where are you?" Shane said to himself.

He arrived at a three-story red-bricked warehouse. It looked very old an uninviting. There was a sign over an awning that read "U-Store It" with a lock design on the upper left corner. It was a self-storage facility.

"Well, this is definitely a step in the right direction!" Shane said excited. He found a vacant meter and parked. After putting in a few quarters, he walked to the entrance of the building. He was at the correct address as confirmed by the written numbers on the building glass entrance door.

He walked in and a bell chimed, getting the attention of a worker at the lobby desk.

"Good afternoon, how can I help you?" said an old woman with very thick glasses. She had really curly gray hair and had a very stern look about her.

"Hi there, my, er, uncle passed away two years ago and I think he might have had a space here. I need to be sure though. Can you look him up? Derek Conrad is the name," Shane told the woman.

"Let me see," the old woman receptionist said.

She typed into her keyboard with two fingers. After about a minute she pulled up some information.

"Derek Conrad. Yes, he does have a unit that has been purchased actually. So he owns the storage facility permanently. It's unit number 956." The old woman said, not changing her expression and still looking stern.

Shane's heart began to race. He was excited. He was one step closer to the next clue. Then his smile turned into a frown. It was obvious to him now that the key that was stolen from his car—the one found in the floorboard at Mariette's inherited home—was the key to open a storage facility in that very warehouse. Shane's mind raced to the night they found the key and how "956" was labeled on it.

"Do you have the key, sir?" the woman asked.

"Well I did. But it was lost. Is there a way to get into the storage room?" Shane asked.

"I'm afraid, for security reasons, that is not possible," the old woman said. "However every owner has two keys. Are you aware of where the spare key might be?"

"I don't," Shane said defeated.

He was so close, but so far. It appeared to be a step forward, but it ended up being a step backward. The only small glimmer of hope was the prospect that a second key existed. His hope was to open the storage before whoever stole the first key beat him to it.

"Well I'm sorry I cannot help you," the woman said. "Legally, the storage cannot be opened unless the proper key is used. Company policy."

Shane left the storage facility and walked down the street towards his Jeep. He had been so close. He was just feet away from some secret message that involved him. He knew it. A part of him also felt that he couldn't bring along his friends to this very end point. The message was just for him and already Mariette had been silenced by death. Shane did not want his friends in danger. There was something bigger than him going on. If the government agency was really involved, it was a matter of security to the country. Perhaps the world was not ready for the knowledge that intelligence from another planet or galaxy had visited Earth and the government was aware.

"What do I have to do with this?" Shane said aloud as he got into his Jeep.

Shane looked at his cell phone sitting in the cup holder. He had not realized he forgot it. There was a voicemail from Caroline.

"Shane, looks like I am going to have to work even later tonight. I'll call you at some point tomorrow night. Have a great time in Vegas with Mike and Alice. Be good...ha."

Shane grinned and put his phone back in the cup holder. He drove off back towards Malibu.

Caroline was walking back to her car in the Fashion Rack Magazine garage later that evening. She was digging through her purse for her keys.

"Damn it!" she said out loud, her voice echoing. "I must have left them back upstairs."

She turned around and was about to make her way back to the elevator, when a black SUV with dark windows and its brights on, drove up in front of her, blocking her path to the elevator.

She stepped back in shock, and the back door of the van opened to reveal a man in a suit stepping out.

"Caroline Lu, we need to ask you a few questions..."

Chapter Eleven:

What Happens in Vegas

Shane, Mike, and Alice were heading towards Las Vegas the following evening. It was nine PM when they left L.A., so as to avoid traffic. "This is going to be so much fun!" Alice yelled over Mike's really loud music. Both she and Mike were in the front seats. Mike was driving.

"What?" Mike asked stopping himself from singing the lyrics to the loud rock song blaring through the stereo of his Jeep Liberty SUV.

"Turn off the freaking music," Shane said. "I can't hear myself think!"

Shane's mind was on Caroline as he sat in the back seat. He had texted her earlier in the evening asking when he could expect her call, but he had not heard back from her.

"It's just not like her to be so unresponsive with communication. Her phone is attached to her hip!" Shane told them. He also had kept his visit to the U-Store It facility a secret. The more he thought about how dangerous this journey was becoming and how Derek had to go through lengths to make sure no one else intercepted his full message, the more Shane knew he would have to be alone on his journey once this Vegas trip ended.

Earlier that morning, Shane had decided that after the Vegas trip, he was going to find a way to break into Derek's storage facility. The building, as he remembered it, looked old. There could not possibly be high tech security. It was his only option. If there was another key, Mariette was not around to ask. She was the only person he could think of asking as to where Derek might have kept his spare key.

Then there was Uncle Robert. Shane had filled his uncle in on everything except the storage facility. Once Mariette's death made national public news, Uncle Robert had contacted Shane at once. Shane thought back to the call they had.

"Uncle Robert..." Shane answered.

"Shane, you should probably stop," Uncle Robert said. "You are digging too deep. Candy's death is all over the news. This just proves that Derek's death was not an accident."

In that last call with his uncle, Shane had told him bits and pieces about the government story leaving out any of the paranormal and abnormal parts. He made it sound as if Derek was investigating a terrorist organization and he was not supposed to know about it. His uncle bought the story—which was no surprise because the truth would have just made him think Derek was crazy.

"I know. I'm at a dead end anyways. I'm leaving to Vegas with friends. I hope this all blows over and I'll go on with my life," Shane said. "You still have no idea what this message for me could have been?"

"It was so random when Peggy let me into Derek's house. I saw the CD with your name on the desk. It was so weird. I know he really saw you as a nephew like you are to me. He never wanted to have kids himself. At least you finally got that camera too you know?"

"Yeah," Shane replied leaving out the fact that the camera was stolen and now melted and charred after the Malibu house fire. It was most likely sitting in the LAPD's evidence storage room now.

"But, I think what interested him most about you is that you and him had something more in common than just the love for photography. I never mentioned it, but Derek was adopted as a baby. Just like you were."

"Really?" Shane said surprised.

Shane never talked about it to his friends, but he was in fact adopted. He never knew who his biological parents were. All he knew was, they were a very young couple and were not ready to be parents so they gave him up when he was born.

Mr. and Mrs. Baker, Shane's foster parents, had trouble conceiving on their own child, so they decided to adopt one to raise. They adopted Shane when he was six months old. Shane thought it was funny that nobody really ever brought up how different he looked from his foster parents because he did not have their features. Shane was not ashamed of being adopted. He just wanted to fit in growing up. His parents had always been honest with him about it since he was in Elementary, but it was never really brought up. To Shane, he knew no other parents and therefore it never bothered him.

Shane was however caught by surprise because his aunt and uncle never really brought up his adoption either. It was the first time he ever heard his uncle talk about it.

"Yeah, Derek had foster parents growing up. We met in college after he had moved out from home. To me, family are the people that are there for you always," Uncle Robert said. "Anyways your aunt and I are heading out to see a movie with the kids. Just lay low. I'm probably more curious to know what my best friend wanted to tell you and not me, but that's just me being selfish. Maybe one day an answer will just come."

"Thanks for filling me in Uncle Robert. Enjoy the movie," Shane said.

Shane came back to reality. He was looking out the window of Mike's car. They were somewhere in the desert. He was not sure if he was still in California or Nevada yet. He had dozed off while daydreaming.

Thoughts began to race in his mind about his family and his adoption. His foster parents were his real parents as far as Shane was concerned. However, Shane began to think about who his biological parents were. Should he seek them out? Had they ever thought to find him?

"Earth to Shane..."Alice said, making Shane snap back into reality. "You were in another world just now."

"Sorry," Shane said. "Lots on my mind."

"We have another hour or so until we get to Vegas. We'll probably arrive around midnight or so," Alice said, checking her watch.

"Great. First slot machine I see and I'm there," Shane said with a smile.

"I'll be at the blackjack tables," Mike chimed in. "Hmm. I hope it's not going to rain. It got cloudy all of sudden."

"What? I was just looking at the stars," Shane said.

Sure enough, in the distance it appeared as though a storm was rolling in.

"This will make our travel time even longer," Alice groaned.

"Perhaps we'll beat the rain?" Shane suggested, but after taking a second glance at how threatening the clouds looked with the chance of opening up from the heavens, he knew traffic would pile up.

"I thought we were in a desert! Shouldn't it be dry?" Mike said irritated.

Mike slowed down the speed of the SUV as soon as it began to drizzle. Within seconds, it was a full-on monsoon practically. It was raining so hard, that they could only see five feet in front of them. Luckily, for the next ten or so minutes there was no on-coming traffic, nor was there anyone in front of them it seemed. The only other vehicle they saw, was one that pulled over with its hazards so as to avoid driving through the downpour.

"Hey we are being tailed!" Alice said looking at the rearview mirror.

"What?" Mike and Shane said quickly.

Shane thought she meant tailed by a black car but the headlights coming at them fast, belonged to a Hummer.

"Dude is going to hit us! Pull the hell over!" Alice said.

"God! What the hell is he thinking?" Mike said angrily as he turned the wheel to the side of the road.

It was muddy, and the SUV began to sink quickly.

"Damn it! We're stuck," Mike said even more furious than he was before.

The rain was falling hard and more large Hummers were rushing down the highway heading the direction they were going. It was a parade of military vehicles.

"What is the rush?" Alice thought aloud.

After the tenth vehicle had passed them, the only sound left was the pounding of the rain on the roof of the SUV.

"That was close. What is going on with the military? Is Vegas being attacked?" Mike said clutching his chest.

The rain began to slow down and within seconds it had completely stopped. Mike got out of the SUV to assess how stuck they were. As soon as he stepped out, his feet sunk a foot into the mud.

"UGGHHH!" Mike yelled. "My shoes!"

"I think we need to call Triple A," Alice said reaching for her cell.

As Alice dialed for assistance, Shane stepped out to help a struggling Mike. They attempted to push the vehicle from behind, but there was no luck. Alice had turned the hazards on in hopes that someone would stop by. There was no one in sight coming in either direction.

The clouds were still dark and with the threat of rain still lingering in the air. It was also very early in the morning. There were a few streetlights scattered sparsely down the highway illuminating an orange glow.

There were at least a few streetlights that Shane noticed in the distance, that were flickering. Then each one went out one by one from the distance and slowly each light closest to them was going out one after the other.

"What the hell?" Mike said, noticing that they had all of a sudden been left in nearly total darkness.

135

"They all just went out. Poof! One by one!" Shane said flabbergasted.

Then it happened. Far in the distance there was a flashing white light. It appeared as though it was in the sky, but they were unsure because they could not tell where the horizon of the desert met the sky.

"What is that? Help?" Alice said exiting the SUV.

"I don't know what that is. Looks eerie..." Mike said in awe.

"Is that the moon? Wait—it can't be," Alice said as she noticed the light appeared to be moving.

"Oh my God..." Shane said, and his heart began to race. "Is this what was on CNN? Remember the lights came from near Vegas! We're what...fifty miles from the city?"

"Forty seven," Mike corrected him.

The strange white orb was getting larger—or rather it was appearing to get closer to where they were. The next minute seemed like an eternity. The three awaited patiently as this mysterious light floated leisurely towards them.

The white-blue light that was being emitted from the orb began lighting the area for a one-mile radius. The area that Shane, Mike, and Alice stood stranded, was soon lit, and they could see their surroundings again. The SUV now shone to be dirty from the mud and stuck about a foot deep into the ground.

"What in the name of..." Shane began. He had this feeling of tranquility. It was a beautiful sight. It was like something heavenly. The orb was simply that: an orb of light.

"This isn't a UFO, is it? It's not a flying saucer of any kind..." Mike said, not taking his eyes of the orb.

Shane got a flashback of a dream he once had of the moon. This event reminded him of that dream. Although in that dream, he thought he remembered it as his dream-self being a werewolf howling at the moon.

The orb was directly above them. The light was bright and blinding. It washed out their faces. Shane looked over at Alice and saw that she appeared to look all white like an overexposed photograph. The road itself, which they were standing on, appeared white.

They stood there in silence staring up at the orb, which was making no sound either, with one hand over their eyes to minimize the shine. In the distance, a rumbling sound broke the silence. It sounded like a number of vehicles were heading towards where the three were standing.

"Someone's coming!" Alice said suddenly. "Sounds like large vehicles…"

Shane grabbed Alice's hand and called for Mike to follow them.

"Where are you going?" Mike asked.

"To that pipe!" Shane said, pointing at a pipe several yards away from where the car was. "You guys keep going!"

Shane ran towards the SUV, took out the keys and turned off the hazards, then ran back to where Alice and Mike were standing near a large metal pipe that opened near the highway and ran underground.

"Why'd you turn the car off?" Mike asked.

"I don't want anyone to know we are here. Just a gut feeling," Shane said, and he pushed them into the pipe. "Wanted to make it appear as though the car is abandoned."

"Ewww, what if this is a sewer?" Alice said in disgust, taking in the large dark hole in the pipe.

"It's not," Mike assured her. "This was probably once used for oil or gas."

They climbed in and as they did, the orb shot straight up into the sky and disappeared. Everything fell back into darkness, but moments later the streetlights turned back on.

"The clouds disappeared…" Alice breathed. "You can see the stars now!" She pointed up into the sky, revealing that the clouds had in fact vanished into thin air.

"This is so surreal," Mike said. "If I was skeptical before when I saw that CNN report…well I'm not now."

After a few minutes of the ever-growing loud noise of vehicles getting closer, the Hummers they had seen rushing by them earlier, had returned to the spot where the orb had been hovering minutes earlier. The closest army green Hummer to them had yellow words in small letters on the door. Shane could just make out what it said: "Sector 7."

"Sector 7..." Shane breathed as he peered out of the entrance to the pipe they were hiding in. "That's the name of the military base Mariette told us Derek was taken too. It must be around here!"

"And that light orb or UFO thing or whatever that was flying over us, was just like the one described in the story!" Alice said in disbelief over the realization.

"Don't you think they'll come looking for us?" Mike said. "I mean my car is just empty..."

They watched in silence as the military began doing a sweeping search of the car.

"There's no one inside," one of the men assessed.

"Are we certain there were civilians or was this car abandoned?" Another man with a low, husky voice shouted.

"We should do a search of the area to be sure," another military officer announced.

"You don't think that they were taken? If so this is a crisis and we need to alert the NHR now!" The man with the low voice said.

There was a scramble, and flashlights were vigorously being pointed all over the area around Mike's car.

"We need to move in deeper into this pipe," Shane said to Mike and Alice.

"We have no flashlights," Alice said nervously. "And this will be one of the first places they look into."

"They're coming!" Mike said, pointing at two men heading in their direction.

All three of them quickly headed deeper into the pipe on all fours. They could hear the men getting closer and the beams of the flashlights were hitting the entrance to the pipe.

"I think we are far enough," Shane said, nervous about what kind of creatures could be lurking in the pipe. "We cannot be found. We experienced something extraordinary and we already know the government agency has been tracking us."

"I don't think there's any one in there," one of the military men at the entrance of the pipe said as he flashed his light. The beam reached just a few feet ahead of where Shane, Alice, and Mike were crouching.

"It's barely missing us," Mike whispered, feeling the pounding of his own heart.

"There's no sign of life over here!" The military man called out. "This could be a case of abduction. I'm going to call Agent Green. We need to report this in the Project Moonshadow files."

"Phew," breathed Alice. "That was too close."

They sat in the pipe for ten minutes after they heard the caravan of Hummers take off, just to be safe. Shane then peered outside of the pipe. All the military men and vehicles had taken off. The Jeep Liberty was still on the side of the road but there were orange cones and reflectors propped around it.

"I think they are coming back for my car," Mike said worriedly.

"Well let's not sit here and wait for them to come back," Alice said.

"They'll have written down his plates and figured out who this vehicle belongs to by now," Shane said. "If we drive off in it we are screwed. We'll be stopped and questioned."

"I am not leaving my damn car behind!" Mike said with a look of shock in his face. "Do you propose we hitchhike? Either way they will find us and then if they connect me to you…"

"So now it's my fault?" Shane said through gritted teeth.

"Boys! Stop fighting," Alice said grabbing onto Shane's shoulders. "Seriously. It's early in the morning. I think we need to head back to L.A. If anything, they'll be looking for the car in Vegas as it's only fifty miles away."

"One problem," Mike jeered, "The car has California license plates and my address is in L.A."

Alice looked at Mike as if she wanted to slap him. He had a valid point, but she was out of fresh ideas.

"Well I'm not leaving without my car. I agree that we should just get back home. This night has freaked me the hell out!" Mike said, and he began walking towards his SUV.

Shane and Alice looked at each other. They both hesitated and realized they were stranded if they did not get in the SUV with Mike.

The sun was beginning to rise as they pulled into L.A. County later that morning. Alice and Shane had fallen asleep in the back seat. Alice's head was resting on Shane's shoulder.

"Guys, wake up. We're back in the 'Bu," Mike said. "Man I need sleep."

Shane yawned. "Thanks for driving again."

"Seriously," Alice added.

Shane was going through his cell phone. He still had not heard from Caroline. He began to worry. It was not like her to ignore his calls. She was usually prompt.

"Still no word from her?" Alice asked noticing Shane was going through his text inbox.

"None," Shane said. "I hope she's ok. I did get an e-mail about a photo shoot with a model later this week. My first official gig with F.R. Magazine!"

Shane pulled out a notepad from his luggage and asked Mike for a pen to write down the address. Mike passed him a familiar blue pen. "Hey this is the pen from Derek's, isn't it?" Shane asked.

"Huh? Oh, yes," Mike replied trying to keep his eyes open as he got onto the Pacific Coast Highway.

Shane began to examine it. The sticker that said "1GB" was still on it. The pen was nice. A thought sprung into Shane's head.

"One gigabyte. Maybe this is a clue? I mean we found nothing on that wooden desk. This pen was in the photo *and* on that desk."

"Is that literally a pen drive?" Alice asked.

"Why didn't I think of that? I must have just been too distracted to connect the dots. I sell—well sold—memory cards at the camera shop I worked at!" Shane said.

Alice reached for the pen and took it from Shane's hand. She twisted the top of it to expose the writing point of the pen. It didn't budge. She tried again with more force and then without thinking, she pulled the silver top up. It came off.

"Oh my God!" Shane said causing Mike to look back.

"It holds memory! It's literally a pen drive after all!" Alice remarked.

Shane's heart began to race. They had taken the clue from Derek's desk with them after all, and it was in Mike's possession all these weeks. At the end of the pen was a concealed USB port. The sticker signified that it held one gigabyte of memory.

"I bet we'll get some answers from this!" Shane said with glee.

Mike parked his car in Shane's carport. He was running on no sleep so Shane urged him to nap on his couch. Alice was wide-awake and ready to see what the pen drive held.

Shane walked up the stairs towards his room, dragging his luggage up the stairs. When he walked into his room, the site made him drop his luggage to floor.

"Guys! Someone's been through my room!"

Chapter Twelve:
Hidden Data

Shane's room was a mess. It looked as if someone had been looking for something. His desk drawers were open; clothes from his closet had been thrown out. His bed mattress was off its frame. It was also the only room in his house that had been searched.

"I checked the rest of the house," Mike said, looking very worn out. "All of the other rooms look untouched. Someone was in here. Someone wants answers."

"Go nap Mike. We'll handle this," Shane said.

"Ok," Mike said, and he went down to the living room.

"You think it was the government agency?" Alice said.

"Or whoever was driving the black car? They know where I live," Shane responded, in a matter-of-fact tone. This morning the military men kept saying 'NHR.' This might be the name of the agency. Ever heard of it or know what the letters could mean?"

"No. We can do some research though. What about Candy's bodyguard?" Alice said.

"I don't think the bodyguard has anything to do with this. Peggy is just paranoid and misled," Shane stated.

We have to figure out if anything is missing," Alice said, and she began to pick up articles of clothing from the floor. "Some pockets of your jeans are turned out. It's like they were looking for something in particular." "Good catch. You'd make a good detective," Shane said, impressed by her quick discovery.

"Do you think history is repeating itself? I mean we just had a paranormal encounter," Alice said, "and now you're house was broken into. This is what happened to Derek."

"So I'll be dead next week, right?" Shane said sarcastically.

"Sorry," Alice said turning red, "That is not what I meant. We need to figure out what Derek wanted you to know that he went through all these lengths to encrypt it."

"Something dangerous," Shane said. "The truth cost Derek his life and Mariette's too. They must be trying to find more clues we've gathered on Derek's behalf. They stole everything we had from my Jeep the other day; the camera, CD, key, the photos."

"But we have that address and now this pen drive!" Alice assured him.

Shane and Alice spent the morning putting away all of his belongings and cleaning up. It appeared as if nothing was missing. His computer also looked like it had been searched. Several word documents and files were open. Shane was nervous about opening the data that was hidden in the pen. He plugged in the USB port into his laptop and waited for the folder drive to appear on the desktop.

It appeared and was labeled "For Shane Baker."

"He definitely wanted you to see this," Alice said her hands clenched in anticipation.

Shane moved his mouse over the file and double clicked it. It opened up to two folders. One was labeled "photos" and the other was labeled "journal entries."

"Journal entries?" Shane said aloud. "This must be his story!"

Shane's spirits were lifted with the feeling that they were back on track and no longer at a dead end. He was sure this journal would help him make sense of what was going on.

"Let's look at the photos Shane!" Alice insisted.

He followed her request and opened the electronic file. There were fifteen photos in the folder. Shane opened them all so that he could browse through each. The photos were fascinating.

Alice's jaw dropped as they clicked through each one. There were no words. The photos just confirmed that the event from earlier that morning with the light orb, was the exact same phenomenon that Derek had experienced five years ago. The photos were the ones he took the night he was taken to that desert.

Some of the photos looked blurry and they were all grainy. It was evident that they were taken from miles away and using a very powerful zoom and night vision. In some of the photos you could see the light, which appeared to look more like a disc shaped object on film than in person. The camera somehow reduced the brightness of the light, or Derek had used photo editing to get the true image. Some of the other photos showed the beam of light coming out from the hovering disc. The close ups of that beam revealed several silhouetted figures. Some were smaller than others. They appeared to be children and adults.

However, upon going through some of the later pictures, it was revealed that the small figures were not human at all. They had very thin looking bodies, neutral in color. Shane assumed they were grey as that was how Mariette described them. The photos in the files must have been the pictures Derek showed her. The bodies were simple. It looked like they were wearing a metallic body suit. Their heads were large and seemed disproportionate to their bodies. They had large black almond eyes and a slit where a mouth would be. Their fingers were long and thin. They appeared to be fragile. Alice and Shane only counted three non-human beings. The larger figures, to Alice and Shane's shock, were humans.

"Humanoids?" Shane said as he examined some of the human looking figures. Their faces weren't very distinguishable, but they were wearing regular clothing. Their eyes were closed. All the human-looking figures had closed eyes.

The last photograph was a shot of the ground where the light beam met the surface. Congregating were the three beings all holding hands. The humans appeared to be in catatonic haze.

"Hey there's a comment attached to this file," Alice said, pointing to the sidebar of the photograph they had not noticed before. "In fact, each photo has a comment. Scroll back to the beginning."

144

Shane scrolled up and read the comment on the side of the first photo which was a far shot that showed the entire scene from the light orb to the ground. The comment read, "August 13. Undisclosed location near military base/Sector 7/Alien contact."

Most of the photos just described what the photo showed. The close up of the human-looking figures confirmed that they were Humanoids. One comment read "Humanoids being brought to the landing site by the alien beings. Each humanoid is asleep or in some sort of trance. All eyelids are closed."

The last photo, which showed the ground, read, "Some kind of ritual is taking place. The aliens, referred to by the NHR as 'Greys,' are interacting with the Humanoids on the ground."

"So that confirms it. The NHR, from what was referred to by the military this morning, is that agency. They must be tracking me," Shane said clenching his fists.

"Greys. That's what the alien beings are called. Interesting," Alice said looking closer at a picture of the alien. "Science geeks across the world would freak if they saw these. However, I wouldn't go posting them on Facebook either."

"Obviously," Shane said rolling his eyes. "This is just surreal. We really are not alone in the universe."

"Or—on Earth! The Humanoids could be living next door or in your neighborhood!" Alice said shivering at the thought.

"So Derek took these pictures without the NHR knowing, right under their noses?" Shane said, scratching his head. "If they got wind of this they'd have...well they must have. He's dead. They ransacked his house. Now mine...these pictures in my possession are putting me in danger. This is the ultimate evidence of life outside Earth."

"Smart of him to hide these in that nifty pen," Alice said, glancing at the pen plugged into the USB port of Shane's laptop. "It's something that is very easy to overlook. It was out there in the open and they never knew."

"I need to carry this pen with me everywhere," Shane said. "We cannot lose this. This must be what they want."

"What they want is the evidence under their lock and key and any civilians with this knowledge, to be silenced," Alice stated. She was most likely correct.

"A thought just struck me," Shane said jumping up from his bed. "The camera nerd side of me is coming out—but digital cameras are able to use their built-in GPS location so then when you upload pictures to your computer they appear in this world map application and you can click and see the locations around the world where you visited. Geolocation. I have this application on my laptop. I wonder if we can get the location after I drag them into the program."

"I think we can deduce," Alice said, "that the location is just outside of Vegas. Remember the 'Sector 7' stamped on those Hummers?"

"I know that, but that's not an exact location. It could be miles from that area, and we don't even know in which direction the vehicles disappeared off to," Shane argued.

"Right," Alice said, biting her lip.

Shane dragged the first photo, which was the far shot of the UFO. Within seconds, the picture appeared on a map of the U.S. within Shane's application with a pinpoint over Nevada just outside Las Vegas. Shane zoomed in on the location and saw that it was miles away from any highway in the middle of a desert. Without this exact location, they would never have had any way to find this base.

"Maybe we should go there," Shane said.

Alice looked at Shane with disbelief, "Are you kidding? Are we going to just walk up to the gate of Sector 7 and say 'hello' or what?

"Not the base! This is the location of the mountain Derek was on," Shane corrected Alice. "The alien activity seems to occur in that area. And more than once, apparently, if we just watched it happen and CNN was reporting lights a few weeks ago."

"But why must we go there? I think our encounter with E.T. this morning was enough to last me a lifetime," Alice retorted.

"We're in too deep. We know more than we should," Shane said walking up from his bed and looking outside his window. "I don't even know why Derek would give me all this information if it is at risk to my life."

Alice zoomed out of the map even more to get a larger mile radius of the area. Shane looked back at the laptop and noticed immediately that a very well known military base called Area 51 was perhaps fifty miles from Sector 7.

"Area 51. Movies, TV, science fiction in general say this is where the top-secret alien stuff is hidden. Coincidence that Sector 7 is near?" Shane said, looking at Alice straight in the eye.

"Who knows? This is all just crazy. I've never even heard of Sector 7 until Mariette told us the story," Alice replied.

Shane's ringtone began to go off. He reached for it on his desk. Caroline was calling him.

"Caroline!" Shane answered excitedly. "Why have you not been returning my texts or calls?"

"I had a long night at work and fell asleep at my desk. I just woke up here realizing I had not even left. My next shift starts in two hours! I had a deadline to finish. I'm so sorry. How's Vegas?"

"We are back in Malibu. The craziest thing happened to us. You will never believe it."

Shane spoke to Caroline for about twenty minutes giving her his account of the UFO encounter and the near run-in with the military. Caroline was silent and didn't say much. He then told her about how someone had gone through his things in his room while he was away.

"You don't sound to enthusiastic to learn about this, do you?" Shane asked her.

"I'm sorry. This is just beyond anything my human mind can comprehend. Knowing this just changes your view on the world you know. I don't know how much longer I can take of this. I don't want to be a part of it anymore."

"But Caroline…" Shane said hurt by her sudden change of mood. Just days ago she was doing her detective work to help him, and if it wasn't for her, he would never been able to contact Peggy Mills who in turn gave him the 35mm camera.

"It's just starting to freak me out," Caroline said in very somber tone.

"I didn't even tell you about the latest development of clues I found!" Shane said.

"New clues?" Caroline said and her tone began to change. She seemed intrigued.

"That's the Caroline I know," Shane said with a sigh of relief.

Shane then told her about the pen drive and how the photos Derek took five years ago, were saved digitally. He also told her that Derek left behind a journal and he had yet to begin reading them.

"And what about the address card you kept?" Caroline asked. "Did you ever find out where it leads to and what that key could open?

"No," Shane lied. He wanted to keep his visit to U-Store It a secret. He was not sure why. He just felt that it was the end of the road to this mystery and felt if the message was just for him, then only he would have to see it first before deciding it was something he could share. His greatest fear was that his friends' lives were already in danger and he did not want to be responsible in the end.

"Let's meet up soon and talk. I just think we need to talk, face-to-face," Caroline said. "I'm taking some time to myself this weekend and heading up to Sycamore Cove to camp. I do it alone once a year to collect my thoughts and write. You should join me."

"Um, sure," Shane said. "It just sounded like you wanted to break up with me, yet you want to stay alone in a tent?"

Alice looked at Shane then turned away fast, turning red. She distracted herself with a deck of cards she found on his bedside table.

"We can't break up if we never established a relationship. Maybe we can use the time to see where we are," Caroline said.

"Fine," Shane said. "I'll talk to you later then."

"Everything ok?" Alice asked looking at the confusion on Shane's face.

"She just sounded different. Like something was bugging her. I mean, she did say all this weird stuff going on with us is starting to freak her out," Shane confessed.

"Well it is freaking me out to," Alice said. "However, I'm in this with you Shane."

Shane smiled and Alice returned it.

"Thanks Alice. Honest," Shane told her. "Should we open up those journal entries?"

"I thought you'd never ask!" Alice said with a very excited expression and grin, rubbing her hands together.

Shane clicked on the folder titled "journal entries" and when it opened he noticed there were ten *Word* document entries. He opened "Journal #1" and read out loud to Alice.

"August 19,

The other day was the most amazing and scariest situation of my life. I learned that we are not alone on this planet—or universe for that matter…"

The first journal entry was very long. It described in detail the moment he was picked up by the military. It supplemented what they already knew from Mariette and it also confirmed the meaning of NHR.

"NHR!" Shane said looking at the text as he perused over the journal. "Non-Human Relations. That's the name of the agency!"

"Never heard of it. I would have thought it would be the FBI, you know?" Alice said.

Shane continued to read the journal and the first person account of the night Derek took the photos that were also in the pen drive. After reviewing the journal, it became clear that Mariette only told part of the story. They never knew in precise detail exactly what happened after Derek was taken back to Sector 7. It was left out of his re-counting of it to Mariette.

"The night was cold. I was given a jacket to keep warm, but I still felt a chill inside that cold, metal Jeep as the agents drove me back to Sector 7. Everyone was quiet. My head was still spinning with what I had just witnessed. Real life aliens were walking on our planet just miles from where I was taking the photographs. The one quote from the night that stuck in my head was, 'They live among us as us.' Not sure what that meant.

Agent Green asked for my memory card. Little did he know, I had used two memory cards to make copies of what I had snapped. The other card was safely hidden inside my boot.

We arrived at the base and were greeted by several military men. I could hear them talking about the event that just happened. I got the sense that they had protocol on how to view the site where the UFO was hovering. However, I think that the mountain we were on was the best view without being spotted. I also heard some of the military men saying words like 'communication was nonexistent' and 'we could not make contact again.' It is my belief that the NHR have been able to actually talk to the beings I witnessed. Or at least have some kind of communication.

Agent Green, who I determined was head of the NHR, walked me over to a large empty room in one of the warehouse-like offices. A one-way mirror surrounded the room. I was being watched. There was a table and two chairs. There was one for Agent Green and myself. He was about to debrief me. The other two agents, Agent Parker and Agent Ramos were most likely on the other side of the mirror. I cannot recall word for word what he said, but the conversation was very vague. He avoided certain topics. The phenomenon I witnessed was clearly abnormal. He told me that I would receive a weekly counseling session in Los Angeles that would help to 'appease' my mind. When I asked what that meant, he stated that it was a hypnosis type process the government was testing and had some success with. The hypnosis is supposedly in place for men and women in the armed forces that came back from war with coping issues and post-traumatic stress disorder. It was a way to tap into the mind and help eliminate specific events that the counselor would talk about.

"This is intense," Alice said interrupting Shane from reading the first journal entry. "It's really good. Like a good book, good."

"Yeah," Shane agreed. "Let's get through this."

Shane continued reading from his laptop screen.

"I of course argued about having this method done, but Agent Green said it was recommended. The sensitivity of the information I had obtained was dangerous. They were afraid I'd spill the beans. They were nervous that I would go out in public and tell the world that aliens existed, and the government was well aware of it. The funny thing was I didn't know too much about what the extent of their communication was. But just knowing there was communication of some sort and knowing the beings existed, was enough.

After being debriefed, I signed a non-disclosure form that stated I agree to keep silent and do the counseling sessions. Originally I was told I would not need to sign anything, but one of the agents was persistent in making sure I did. Agent Green said that the counseling would be once a week for a month. He assured me that once the counseling sessions ended, we would not see each other again. Agent Green said it would be a 'good thing' if we never crossed paths again. I felt like that was a threat.

They loaded me in a helicopter for my trip back instead of a plane, and I fell asleep on the ride back home. I was a wreck for the passed few days. I stayed at home and did not leave. I couldn't face the world or see anyone. Candy kept calling me, but I would just ignore her. I stood her up on a dinner date we planned for the following week so that I could make time for my first counseling session.

Then, there was the memory card I brought back that had the evidence of the UFO encounter I witnessed. I was too scared to even put the card in my computer. I had the feeling I was being watched, and my lines were tapped. I wasn't sure yet to the extent of how much I was being tailed, but there were several black cars with dark tinted windows that drove by my house every so often. I knew it had to be them. My counseling had just begun, so they knew they had to keep an eye on me just to be sure. They weren't trying to hide either. I'd see men in suits walking up and down my street, and when I walked outside to get my newspaper, they just stared at me. It was an unspoken acknowledgement that I was being watched.

I decided to hide the files of my memory card in a pen that had a USB and one gigabyte of memory in it so that it could be hidden discreetly on my desk. I just wanted to make sure that they could not find it if they got wind that I had created these extra photoduplicates. I told myself I would not open them until after the counseling was done. A part of me was sure I could fight this hypnosis. I was a light sleeper so I knew that I could probably fake forgetting the events of that August night on the 13th.

One final thought: At least I have this written record of my journey to Sector 7 to remind me of what happened on August 13 in case this hypnosis works. I will print a copy and leave it under my pillow.

-DEREK"

"Mind blowing!" Shane said after a minute of silence once he finished reading the first journal entry.

"This is going to help make so much sense of the events that happened from the moment Derek encountered Sector 7 and the UFO, to his death," Alice said. "Look at the date of his last entry. It's a few days before he died three years ago. It's odd that he only wrote ten entries."

"I was hoping for more," Shane said, "but judging by the dates of the rest them, they are spread out over a three year time span. They seem very detailed, so it probably covers a lot."

152

"Perhaps," Alice agreed.

"Let's read these journals together with Mike later. I promise not to read them without you guys," Shane said, closing his laptop and pulling the pen drive out. He then placed it in his jean pocket.

"What about Caroline?" Alice asked raising her eyebrow.

"Not until I get things situated with her. She sounded weird on the phone and then ignored me for nearly twenty-four hours. Something is up with her and a part me feels like she's going to end things," Shane said, not feeling as sad as he thought he would.

"But she wanted to go camping?" Alice said sarcastically.

"Ha," Shane grinned. "Well, it's a cove a few miles outside the city. She uses it to think or something like that. It could be a 'define or end the relationship thing.' Whatever. I won't lose sleep over it. This whole ordeal from the morning was nuts. I don't think I'll tell her about the journal entries just now."

"Then just keep it to yourself for now. Mike and I won't say anything," Alice assured him.

Chapter Thirteen:
The Photographer's Journal

Shane parked his car at a warehouse in downtown Los Angeles a few streets from the Fashion District. He was there to take on his first freelance job with Fashion Rack Magazine. His boss Stacy was talking to the model when he arrived. The model was a very thin Russian girl with dark straight hair and piercing green eyes. She was very pale and looked porcelain. Shane eyed a table on one end of the warehouse-turned-studio and saw a table with lots of snacks, waters, and drinks. None of it looked like the model would even touch judging by how thin she was.

"Shane, this is Karin, she'll be your subject," Stacy said, gesturing Shane to come forward.

"It is nice to meet you. I've heard much about your photography. It is good I am told," Karin said with a heavy accent.

"Thank you. I look forward to working with you," Shane replied trying not to turn red of embarrassment from her deep stare into his eyes.

"Honey, have you seen Caroline?" Stacy whispered to Shane. "She took yesterday off because she was sick, but she e-mailed me at nine last night and said she was still going to come to the shoot."

"Um, I actually haven't talked to her in two days," Shane said slightly annoyed he had to think of her.

Caroline had once again disappeared off the radar and was not returning texts or calls to Shane. He was upset to discover that she at least made an attempt to contact Stacy. He was supposed to be going to that cove with her to camp in a few days and he was not even sure if that was set in stone.

"Well I'll try her again—Oh there you are!" Stacy said looking at the entrance to the warehouse.

Caroline had walked in. She looked like she just rolled out of bed. Her hair, usually perfectly combed and straight, was frizzy and in a ponytail. She was also not wearing make up.

She made eye contact with Shane then turned away to look at Stacy. Stacy went over to talk with Caroline in private.

"So, first time?" Karin said to Shane bringing him back into focus.

"Um, yes!" Shane responded a little more loudly than he meant to. He shifted and began to take out his camera equipment so that he could set up for the shoot.

"Well I hope you make me look wonderful," Karin gushed, batting her eyelashes. "Oh! There's my publicist."

Shane nearly dropped his tripod as he saw Peggy Mills walking in. She looked quite younger than last time he met her with jeans, sneakers, and suspenders over her tank. Shane felt it was an attempt to look fashionable.

"Shane!" Peggy said flashing her white teeth, "I had no idea you would be on this shoot. Who knew I'd be working with F.R. so quickly again? Have you met my client?"

"Just did," Shane said smiling at Karin.

Peggy grabbed Shane by his arm and ushered him a few feet away from Karin to talk to him in private.

"I'm sorry about the other day. I had the police track Candy's old bodyguard, and after the investigation, it looks like he was in San Diego with his family. I was wrong to accuse him, and I feel awful for making Caroline give me his personal address."

"Oh," Shane said, thinking if that was why Caroline sounded so different lately. Perhaps she felt guilty. Shane made a mental note to ask her.

"Anyways kiddo, glad you are working on this. Sorry we got off to an awkward start. I'm sure one day we'll find out who killed Candy. I still do not believe it was an accident. The cops agree," Peggy said, still flashing her teeth and smiling wide.

Shane spent the rest of the morning taking several shots of Karin in various outfits. He really enjoyed it. At last, he felt he was closer to his dream. Derek would be proud.

When he broke for lunch, he finally spoke to Caroline. She had been working in one of the studio's offices with the door closed. Stacy had mentioned to Shane she had a deadline for five o'clock that day. Shane entered the office and made her jump, nearly spilling her latte.

"You scared me!" She said, composing herself.

"What the hell is going on? You barely have been communicating with me lately," Shane blurted.

"A lot has been on my mind Shane. A lot. Work stress..." Caroline said, then she trailed off and began to cry.

"What is going on?" Shane asked again.

"Well the reason I wanted to take my solo camping trip was to get away from the city. I wanted to take you so we can talk for sure. But, I just found out my mother has cancer. Lung cancer. She's an avid smoker." Caroline said not meeting Shane's eyes.

Shane felt his heart drop. He had no idea that this was what had been troubling her. He felt really terrible. The past two days he spent on thinking of ways he was going to call off his relationship with her since he felt that was what she was planning the same, and he wanted to beat her to the punch.

"Caroline...I am so very sorry. Is there anything I can do?" Shane said.

"Just understand that my need for space was because I had to process this," Caroline said, wiping tears from her eyes.

Shane moved in to hug her and she sobbed into his shoulder.

"I just need the next few days. Work helps me take my mind off it, but it's stressing me out at the same time. I am taking the next two days off so that I have a four-day weekend. We can meet up on Saturday evening at the cove." Caroline wiped her tears and looked at Shane. She gave a feeble smile. "I need to finish this and you need to go finish your shoot with Karin. Besides I kind of want to avoid Peggy right now."

"The bodyguard was innocent..." Shane added.

"Thankfully they found proof. The guy had a family. I feel like crap for being the reason Peggy troubled them and put them through that," Caroline said. "It just added to my grief as of late."

"Well I am here for you. Ok?" Shane said.

Caroline nodded and kissed him on the cheek. She went back to her laptop and began typing away. She looked scared.

Later that evening, Alice and Mike joined Shane at his house. He avoided talking about Caroline even though Alice attempted to ask if he talked to her earlier at his shoot.

"We were both busy. She's got a lot on her plate. Now aren't we here to talk about the journal entries? I've been holding off for two days to read entry number two. Can we move forward?" Shane insisted.

Alice nodded and folded her arms and Mike replied, "Alright Mr. Storyteller, begin."

"August 24

I arrived at the federal building in the Westwood part of town. I had received a phone call from my counselor the previous day telling me that I was to head to the 10th floor of the building where his office was. I swear everyone in that building was wearing suits. I felt underdressed in my casual clothing, but nobody really paid me much attention. When I got to the office of my counselor, Dr. Felix Morgan, a female receptionist greeted me. She then called Dr. Morgan to get me.

He was a much older balding man with oval-shaped glasses. He could pass for my grandfather. I'd say he was in his seventies. He walked me into his office, which had a nice view of Santa Monica in the distance, as well as the ocean. He sat me down in a chair and began to tell me about his work experience and what this hypnosis process would entail.

I was taken aback by how much he was telling me. My guess was since he was going to help me forget about the whole Sector 7 desert incident, he did not mind revealing much to me. He said he started working for the government in the fifties. The hypnosis process was very new and still being tested. It was merely a theory apparently, but the government was close to figuring out how to tap into the human mind. The most vivid information that I remember him telling me was that his work began with the Roswell, New Mexico UFO crash that everyone talks about in history and science fiction stories. Apparently it was real and was the beginning of the Non-Human Relations agency and their contact with them.

It still is crazy to think he was so open about this information, but then again, like I said, he was about to make me forget it all. I think he was using me as his therapist so he could talk about his secrets. It was something he must have obviously been sworn to be silent about. The story he told me is fuzzy, but I have a general idea of what happened when a rancher found the UFO in Roswell.

The police were on the scene first before the Feds showed up. The government had been tracking strange activity in the skies so they knew something abnormal was going on. They found two dead bodies of non-human beings. They were not like anything from this planet. His description of them matched what I saw in the photos—the non-human looking beings were about three feet tall and grey skinned with large dark eyes. Of course, I was silent about actually knowing that I knew how the aliens looked.

Dr. Morgan went on to say that one being had survived, however it died a week later. The government tried to keep it alive and apparently they were able to create some kind of communication method, but the doctor was not specific on how it was made. If my memory serves me right, then I can recall him saying that our government gained many technologies from the alien's spacecraft, which explains how from the 50s to the early 2000s, our technology had advanced so fast and unlike any other time in the history of mankind.

My session was definitely a very interesting adventure. I left the offices feeling as though my mind had gone through a serious work out. When I got home, I found my first journal entry under my pillow and read it. Soon memories that the hypnosis session had made me forget came rushing back, and I was aware that I was holding some intense information in the back of my mind.

-DEREK"

"That is intense information," Mike said rubbing his chin and staring out of Shane's living room window.

"No kidding," Alice agreed.

"It's all just too crazy. I mean to think that the government knew about life outside our planet for years," Shane added. "Next entry..."

The next few entries were updates on his sessions with Dr. Morgan. They were mainly written accounts to help him beat the hypnosis. There was not really any pertinent information that Shane found remotely useful. It was evident that time had passed. A year or two had gone by. His journal dates were scattered months apart. Then they reached the end where things became very interesting.

"February 17

Things have been quiet lately. Candy has stopped trying to contact me for now. I've been keeping myself out of the public because I'm so paranoid I will talk to someone about what happened last summer in the desert.

Now I have formulated a plan of what I need to do next. The pictures I took of that night near Sector 7 had one image I have been keeping guard of very closely. I need to protect someone's face. I will not write about it here in case this falls into the wrong hands, but I have devised a plan.

I have also just relocated to my Malibu weekend home. Nobody knows I've made a permanent move here. I feel like I'm being watched. I keep seeing a black car either following me or stalking outside my house. I think they want me to know their presence because they are not working hard on hiding. It's actually scaring the hell out of me.

-DEREK

June 19

I have planted my secret message for a person I need to tell about my experiences. I am finally going to see Candy tomorrow. I have a shoot with her that she begged me to do. I think I need to see her. I truly miss her, and she may be of some help with this burden. I'm getting really worried. I've been seeing NHR agents more and more lately.

I had a scare at a store I was at. I was purchasing a lock for my storage facility in Venice where I have been keeping some of my old furniture I did not bring from my Hollywood Hills home. I'm using the storage unit to leave the last piece of my message for the person I need to warn—"

"So that is what is in there," Shane said cutting himself off from the journal entry. "His old items. But the last piece of the message is there!" Shane thought about telling the others about how he already knew about the storage facility and that the address on the camera bag lead him to it. After a few seconds of mulling it over, he decided to tell them, even though in the back of his mind, he would plan to go alone. Or at least try to.

"It's the homestretch. Now we just got to get into it!" Alice said excitedly.

"Warn?" Mike said, intrigued.

"What does he need to warn me about?" Shane said. "I mean, the NHR are already doing surveillance, but it is because we've been snooping into Derek's past."

"Let's finish up the journal entries," Alice urged.

Shane continued.

"There was a black SUV that was parked next to my car in the parking lot of the store. I knew it was them. I was afraid to get into my car, but I acted oblivious to them. The windows were very tinted, but I could tell there were people in there. Once I got into my car and drove out of the lot, they began to follow me. I took some crazy turns in the Malibu hills to lose them, and after I did, I drove straight to my house on Ocean Hill. When I entered, my place was a mess. Someone had broken into it. Nothing appeared stolen, but it was as if they were looking for something. I took pictures of the mess. I didn't call the police because I knew it was the NHR. They must have known, or somehow got wind, that I had information or something that should not be in my hands. It was the pictures from the landing site, but they did not find them since I had them securely hidden in a pen that was secretly a hidden USB memory drive.

June 24

I skipped out on the shoot with Candy. I've been hiding at a hotel for now in North Hollywood, because I no longer felt safe at my Malibu house. I have also been paying for it in cash so that I don't use my credit card and get traced. I assume they have several ways to track me. I have also been drinking a lot lately due to my increased anxiety. I need to stop. It is getting dangerous. I need to find a time to explain to Candy what is going on. I also plan to tell her about my encounter three years ago. It's time she knows and hopefully she can pass along my message. With the government on my tail, I cannot contact the person I need to directly, or he will be in grave danger. His life right now is more valuable than mine. I've also had an individual come forward that has offered to help me with this task I have. I'll call him my ally.

-DEREK"

Shane looked over at Alice and Mike after reading that entry. "Intense stuff. These were his final days."

"Remember you said that Caroline thought his death was suicide because his blood alcohol levels were high?" Mike asked.

"Yeah. And?" Shane replied.

"So maybe the government didn't do him in. He was drunk driving according to reports," Mike said matter-of-factly.

"His levels were higher than the legal limit. Doesn't mean he was really drunk," Shane said.

"There is one more journal entry left in this file. This must be the one before he was killed. Let's read it," Alice urged.

Shane began.

"June 27

I finally told Candy everything and gave her the audio CD I made that begins the message process. I asked her to give it to RP ("Robert Powers," Shane muttered) at some point. I do not want her to go directly to the person that will receive the message. She will also inherit my homes should anything happen. It is the least I can do. She's genuinely scared about this and doesn't understand the information well. She did not take the proof of alien life too well. My plan is underway. Once the person learns about my warning my work is done. The ally will help him to understand more.

Sadly, I don't know how much longer I can be in hiding. I am planning to leave town. Not sure where I will go, but it won't be in this country.

-DEREK"

"I'm curious as to who this 'ally' is," Shane said mysteriously.

"Who knows? So that's it? I guess he wasn't able to leave the country then," Alice said.

"Nice work Sherlock," Mike said sarcastically.

Alice shot him a dark look and rolled her eyes.

"I want to know what this warning is and why me. I guess now we kind of understand why he couldn't tell me directly," Shane said. "We just have no way of opening that storage facility. Until we do, like I said before, we should avoid going to that area. Especially if we are being tracked."

"Yeah," Mike and Alice agreed in unison.

Mike and Alice left Shane's house an hour later. Shane hid the pen drive in his desk drawer and mixed it with his other pens. He already had his house searched once and did not want to have the journal entries taken away. His cell phone then chimed. It was a text from Caroline. "Tomorrow night I'll be at the cove I told you about. I'll have a tent. I will email you directions. See you there?"

Shane texted back, "Yes. Looking forward to seeing you."

Shane was still feeling bothered by Caroline's strange behavior the past few days. He understood she was going through a lot, but she felt like a much different person. She seemed changed, and cold even. He also had been developing stronger feelings towards Alice the more he spent time with her.

His final thought was having a romantic date with Alice before he fell asleep. A few hours into his dreamless night, and he was awoken by a knock at his door.

Shane jumped out of his bed and looked out the window where he had a perfect view of his front doorstep. There was no one there. However, an envelope was left at the doorstep. He could see it illuminated by his porch light that automatically turned on when it sensed someone.

Shane reached for a baseball bat that he had in his closet and walked downstairs slowly. He clutched his cell phone tightly in the other hand. His heart was beating as he tiptoed quietly to the front door. He peered through the peephole. There was not a single soul in sight. His porch light had gone off, meaning there was nobody around for its sensor to cause it to light up again.

He opened the door and peeked outside. After a few moments, he felt it was safe to go outside and look around.

"Hello?" he said, in more of a whisper that most people would not have been able to hear.

There was no response. Shane then bent over and reached for the envelope. It was blank but there was something metal and small inside.

He tore the envelope open and nearly dropped the contents with shock. In his hands was a brass metal key with an engraving on it.

"This is too good to be true," Shane breathed, clutching his phone and thinking about calling Alice or Mike. He then decided not to and looked at the key before him.

"956," Shane said to himself. "Someone returned the key…"

Shane went back into his house and closed the door shut. A man in the distance hiding behind a parked vehicle, began to dial into his cell phone.

"He took the bait. Now we'll know what this key opens. It's obvious what message Derek has for him, but we have to make sure that what this kid finds does not fall into the hands of the public," the man said into his receiver.

"Agent Parker," the voice on the other line responded, "Track him even more closely. Let's have him take us to the location the key opens, then we will apprehend him. I think this plan will work better than our original plan of making that girl take him outside of Malibu to the cove."

"Agent Green," Agent Parker said, "What if he goes to the cove before unlocking what the key opens? And how do we even know he knows where to go?"

"Parker," Agent Green replied, "My plan is for him to not make it to the cove. Caroline has also invited his two friends

Michael and Alison earlier this evening. I have devised a plan with her that it will be a surprise birthday bon-fire for Shane, since his actual birthday is in a few days. They know too much. The car we found abandoned at the desert belongs to his friend Michael. They've seen our visitors. We'll handle Shane Baker and others from our team will make sure the other three are..."

There was silence for a few seconds.

"...taken care of. They will think Shane is on his way to the cove."

Chapter Fourteen:
The Storage Facility

Shane had trouble sleeping. He was too excited to head straight to Venice first thing in the morning. He was however, slightly nervous about the fact that an unknown person had left the key for him. Was it Derek's ally? He was also planning to go to the U-Store It facility alone because he knew this was the end of the clues Derek had left behind.

Before he woke up, he had a dark dream. He was in some room where there were no windows or any kind of light. He woke up moments before seeing a pair of what he thought were red eyes. He shook off the dream and walked over to his desk.

"This is it," Shane said to himself after he looked up the business hours of the storage facility online. He closed his laptop and reached for his cell phone. "Let's do this Shane."

Shane got into his Jeep and drove south to Venice Beach. His heart was racing. He made sure to keep an eye out for black cars with tinted windows, just in case he had to throw them off.

It took him twenty minutes to find a parking spot in the area where the storage facility was located, but at last he found a free meter. He jumped out of his Jeep and put a few quarters into the meter.

When he arrived at the entrance of the U-Store It facility, he looked around the surrounding block. There was no black car in sight.

"Phew," Shane sighed with relief. He was paranoid that the key drop off could have been a trap, but he was not being tracked on his drive over. *Perhaps it was Derek's ally that left me the key? He must have had the spare,* he thought.

He walked into the facility and the same grumpy old woman was there. She looked annoyed at his sight.

"Find the spare key?" She said lazily.

"Actually, yes," Shane said, pulling it out of his pocket.

"The units are numbered. The 900's are back there," She said, pointing to her left down a dimly lit hall.

Shane began to make his way down the hall when he heard the woman say, "Can I help you?"

"Huh?" Shane said turning around, but he realized she was talking to a man that just walked in. Shane did a double take. He had a familiar face. Then he realized it was the man with the dog outside Candy's house that he ran into when he first went to investigate.

Shane felt his face get hot in embarrassment and he continued walking down the storage facility hallway trying to distance himself from the man.

"950, 951…" Shane said aloud reading off the numbers of the large metal doors. "Aha! 956!"

He inserted the key into the lock and took a deep breath. He was beyond excited. He took the lock off its hook and opened the metal door. He looked both ways in the hallway. It was empty. He walked in and closed the door behind him, leaving the lock back in the hook to hang.

"Wow," Shane said taking in the area. There was tons of modern-looking furniture and other personal belongings. Several large framed photographs were packed against the walls. Derek had used this place mainly to archive his original photographs judging by how they were significantly placed and labeled by date. It also appeared as though some of his original furniture from the Hollywood house that Candy inherited, was sitting in this facility collecting dust.

Nothing in the room seemed out of the ordinary.

"Derek, what did you leave behind for me?" Shane said to himself.

He then had a sudden idea come to him. He walked over the photos, which were stacked by date, and went to a section dated five years back.

"August 1...August 3..." Shane read.

Then he arrived at August 13. There was a large frame with the date labeled August 13. He pulled it out and found a picture of himself.

"What the—" Shane said out loud.

Just then, the door to the storage room snapped shut. Shane ran to it to push it open, but he heard the lock click outside. Someone had locked him in.

"Let me out! Let me out!" Shane yelled, banging on the door. He listened through the door and heard footsteps walk away. "Is somebody out there?"

He began to kick the door but it was metal and he only hurt his toes in the process. He reached for his cell, only to realize he had no service.

"Dammit!" Shane cursed under his breath.

He walked back to the photo of himself and analyzed it.

"This was taken on August 13?" He said confused.

Then it dawned on him. This photo came from the same roll as the other photos from the pen drive. The only difference was, this was developed into a portrait.

Shane still could not comprehend the photo. His face was slightly blown out due to what looked like a very bright light. His eyes were closed and he was standing up. There were other people around him and at a distance he saw a shorter figure he could not make out. He began to deduce that it was one of the aliens. The photo was from the night Derek was near Sector 7. It was the landing site of the beings.

"I...I was there?" Shane said in complete shock. "Was I abducted?"

Another frame next to where the picture frame of himself was, appeared to be misplaced. It was dated in July and three years later. The date, he realized was a day before Derek was killed.

"This was intentional," Shane said. His mind was completely disturbed by the photo of himself, that he forgot he was locked inside the room.

He pulled out the frame to find a MiniDV cassette tape. It was labeled "Shane Baker." He looked around absentmindedly and then found a digital camcorder on a shelf behind him. He hastily put the tape in and pressed play. The screen was black at first with a time code dating to the same date that was labeled on the frame. The footage was two years old.

Shane breathed in hard knowing that at last he was about to get the message from Derek that he had been seeking for the past few weeks. A message that was years in the making and cleverly hidden so that the NHR or any government agency could not intercept it.

The tape went from black to a setting of the same storage room Shane was in. Then a man walked into the frame and stood before the camera. It was Derek Conrad. He began to speak.

"Shane, if you find this, it is because I am no longer alive. By now you should have gone through my extensive scavenger hunt. You are probably wondering why I went through such lengths and risks. The reason is because what I am facing in this moment, is what could be potentially threatening to your life. The Non-Human Relations agency has been tracking me. They have realized that my hypnosis and therapy counseling sessions have not worked, and I have found a way to overcome them. They know that I have information of the existence of beings from outside our world and about Humanoids. They've been trying to track down Humanoids for years to keep tabs on them and run tests, if they were to apprehend one. They live among us as us. You would never know they were alien. The interesting thing though, is most of the Humanoids are unaware of what they truly are. It took me years of research since my fateful day in that desert, but I learned so much. A key individual became an ally of mine and helped me. He gave me lots of pertinent inside information to understand what was going on and why I was to help you discreetly. He was risking so much to help me. I cannot reveal this person, which is why I did not talk about the said individual in my journal entries or even here. This individual will know the right time to help you on your journey. You need to know who you are Shane.

By now you should have already found that photograph of yourself. You were abducted that night. However, it was part of a ritual they did with the 'Marked Ones' as you are called. Shane, you are a Humanoid..."

Shane's heart dropped. Derek's recording continued.

"The Greys, as they are referred to by the NHR, brought you here as an infant. I do not know much about your beginnings, but that is something you will learn when you complete your journey. It is my fault, however, that the government has your face. They have copies of the photographs I took from the landing site. They've been searching for you for years, but not knowing who you were and just having a photo of your face, made it impossible for them to find you. I had to tell you about what you were some how. I devised a way only you would be able to figure out because of our relationship during your youth. I left behind the clues.

Shane, this is a matter of life and death. If they find you, they will take you. If they find you, they will experiment with you. If they find you, they can potentially kill you. The NHR has been keeping tabs on the alien visitors out of worry they are hostile, but they are not. They are trying to learn our world. My ally has more information on this and once you learn more about what you are, things will fall into place.

Now here is what you must do, now that I have given you the message about your existence. You must find out what it means. Go forth to the area just outside Sector 7. My digital photos I gave you are geotagged and will give you the exact location to where the alien craft frequently lands. The closer you get to the area, the more powerful the connection between you and them becomes. They will be able to find you."

Shane began to think about the incident in Vegas. He was near Sector 7, and the site where the photos were taken. They sensed him and tried to get to him. However, they left when the military was heading towards them. Shane began to remember the feeling of serenity the bright lights gave him, putting him at ease. He tuned his attention back to the recording.

"Get to the landing site and from that point all will make sense. Lost memories will flush back to you. A new journey awaits you. Your fellow Humanoids that walk this planet are still safe. They remain anonymous. But you were unlucky to have your photo taken, by me, and shown to the government. As long as you are nameless to them, you are safe. For now you are just a face. I wish you good luck. May your journey home be prosperous."

Derek stepped out of the frame to turn off the camera. The tape then went black. Shane took a deep breath and thought, "I'm not anonymous to the NHR though…they have found me."

Just then there was a click at the door. Shane was in such shock and was processing what he just heard, that he had forgotten he was locked in. The door began to open. Shane saw a man in a dress shirt and pants enter. He was good looking and wore dark rimmed glasses and had slicked blonde hair. This was the same man he had recognized in the lobby of the storage facility. It was the man with the dog that he bumped into outside Candy's house.

"Hello Shane," the man said.

Shane's heart was beating with fear.

"I, um, why the hell did you lock me in here?" Shane stammered.

"I had to take care of the woman in the lobby to make sure she wouldn't be any trouble. I also had to put a 'closed' sign at the entrance. This business will no longer be operating today."

"What do you want?" Shane asked. "Who are you? I ran into you a few weeks ago outside a friend's house."

Shane's thoughts went to the day he ran into him and Alice was teasing him that this man was staring at him several times from afar.

"Candy Adams. Or Mariette Polashek. She inherited Derek Conrad's house. I believe Derek, even in his death, has been helping you out."

Shane gulped. "Who are you and what do you want?"

"My name is Landon Parker. Agent Landon Parker. The day we crossed paths outside Candy's house, I knew it was you. For five years I stared at your face trying to figure out a way to find where on Earth you were. It was like a needle in the haystack. What an amazing coincidence that Derek captured your image and he also knew you. He deceived us and kept a copy of the photos. We had our copy and while I was keeping an eye on Candy that day, you literally walked right into me. I couldn't act right away. I had you tracked from then on."

"Are you," Shane began, "Part of the NHR?"

"I was one of the ones that took Derek to our site five years ago," Agent Parker answered. "Apparently Derek's plan failed. We've been on to you since the day I saw you snooping around Derek's Hollywood home. You may have received his message, but it was I that planted the key at your doorstep to bring you and I here."

Shane's heart dropped. He had a feeling it might have been a trap, but he was so sure he was not being followed to the facility.

"I didn't need to drive one of our government black cars this time. I blended well with the LA traffic," Agent Parker teased as though he read Shane's mind. "It was so easy to plant that key back on your doorstep that we took from your Jeep. You took the bait and here we are. Shane, in a few minutes I will have some of my men arrive. I've summoned them to this site. We'll be taking you with us to an undisclosed location."

"Sector 7?" Shane spat.

"No, that would be risky. You would to be too close to—their—site," Agent Parker replied.

Agent Parker pulled out a tube with a needle from his pocket. It contained a clear liquid. In his other hand he had a small gun.

"This will not hurt. It will sedate you. Painless. Please oblige," Agent Parker said, inching towards Shane.

"Please leave me alone. I mean no harm. I did not even know what I am!" Shane pleaded, a tear falling down his cheek.

Just then, a man in a brown trench coat barged into the room. The door slammed open, knocking over a nearby frame and causing it to crash and shatter on the floor.

In the moments of distraction that followed, Agent Parker took his attention off Shane. When he turned to see the visitor, which was an elderly man with grey, balding hair and oval glasses, his eyes widened in shock.

"What the—" Agent Parker began, but the man had a fire extinguisher and used the end of it to hit Agent Parker on the head, knocking him out cold. He crashed to the ground falling on top of a frame, which then caused several more frames to crash down to the ground in a domino effect.

"Take whatever you found here that was for you," the man told Shane.

Shane obliged because he was very thankful this man had saved him. Shane took the tape out of the camcorder and removed the photo of himself from the picture frame and put them in his jacket pocket.

"Let's go, before his team gets here!" The man said.

They ran down the hallway and back to the lobby of U-Store It. The old woman was unconscious, but alive, at the foot of her desk. She had appeared to have been put into a deep sleep.

"Let's go out the back way. We have company," the man said pointing out the door.

Through the window two black SUVs and a black Audi had pulled up. Men in suits were getting out of the car and heading towards the entrance of the storage facility.

"Hurry!" the man said, grabbing Shane by the arm. They ran down a hall towards the back and headed to a fire emergency exit, only to find out that it was locked.

"Parker thinks of everything. We are trapped!" the man said.

"What about that vent?" Shane said, and he pulled a chair to stand on. He reached for a vent at the top of the wall near the ceiling, and pushed it open. "Do you think you can jump up here and pull yourself? We can exit out of the building this way."

"I may be old, but I'm not that incapable!" The man said taken aback.

Shane hoisted himself up and crawled into the tiny path. He felt claustrophobic. It was very dusty and there were dead roaches lying on their backs. He brushed them out of the way with a look of disgust. He crawled using his elbows to push himself forward. His allergies began to act up and he began to sneeze.

"Shh!" The old man said once he had climbed into the vent behind Shane. "They will realize you climbed up through here. They have no idea I am here. Now crawl fast!"

"Who are you?" Shane asked.

"No time for questions now. It's your life before questions at this point!" The man snarled impatiently.

Shane began to crawl forward. He could hear voices echoing through the vents.

"Parker is out cold. The boy has escaped. Search the perimeter!" one voice said.

"If we lose him we know where he will be tonight. He's meeting up that girl Caroline at a cove just outside Malibu," another harsh voice replied.

"Are they tapping my texts?" Shane thought out loud.

"The other two individuals, Michael Campbell and Alison Hastings have been invited to appear at the site as well. I need our operations team to move into position within an hour before nightfall to apprehend those kids!" One voice said.

"What? Mike and Alice were not supposed to be going to the cove. Holy crap! And Caroline!" Shane was terrified.

"It's not worth your life right now kid. You have bigger fish to fry," the man said. "Keep on moving. They will find out we are in the vents and we'll be taken by force."

They continued to travel up the vent until they finally reached the end. It led to the outside of the building.

"I can't break through," Shane called back to the older man.

He was pushing the vent with his hands and all his might, but it would not budge.

"They are in the vents!" a voice echoed through.

"Crap! They are in the room near the fire exit. Keep pushing!" the man said.

Shane began to shift himself. Never in his life would he have thought that he would be able to twist himself around in such a small space, as he did in that vent. Once his feet were now facing the vent opening, he kicked with all his strength. After three tries, he was able to knock it open. He jumped out and landed in a dumpster. The smell of garbage filled his nostrils and lungs, and he almost threw up.

Moments later, the old man fell behind him coughing for air. Shane heard rushed voices running around the building.

"We are about to be cornered. What now?" Shane said clutching onto his chest for fresh air.

"Just wait for it. I have a back up plan diversion," the man told him, and he pulled out what looked like a remote from his jacket pocket. He pressed a button and a loud explosion erupted from the front of the facility. "I set up a bomb inside my old van that I parked outside the facility. That will keep them distracted for sure. I set it off near a fire hydrant too so it'll be pouring all over the store front."

There was a ton of angry and confused voices coming from the front of U-Store It.

"Now!" The old man said and they jumped out of the dumpster and headed away from the facility. "Now they'll probably start tracking a mile radius of this place fast, so we best get away via—TAXI!"

A yellow taxi stopped at the man's summon and they got in.

"Your car will have to stay behind. They'll be tracking what you drive. This is a clean getaway. By the way, my name is Dr. Felix Morgan."

Chapter Fifteen:
Traps and Lies

"Are you Derek's ally?" Shane said very confused.

"Ally?" Dr. Morgan asked, as the taxi they were in took a turn out of the Venice Beach area. "What are you talking about?"

"Derek said, in his message I received in that storage facility, that he had an ally. Someone helping him from the inside," Shane explained.

"No," Dr. Morgan replied. "I was not helping him out...well not on purpose at least. The fact that he tapped into my hypnosis methods to overcome them to get information from me, was a complete shock. The NHR discovered this when they took the materials he left behind for you, from your vehicle. They said they were switching me to a new project in a few days, but I overheard a conversation by chance. They had a suspicion that my method did not work back then. They took Derek out because they knew he was up to something, but they never found any clues because he hid them well. Those clues were recently found a few weeks back and they wanted to apprehend you first. They are going to put me out."

"Put you out?" Shane said in shock.

"Kill me," he said. "Just like they killed Derek. Derek was at a bar. He was really drunk. One of our agents posed as a civilian and drove him to the hill near his home. Derek was unconscious, they put him in his car, and rolled it into neutral. The fence was broken to make it appear as if a car hit it at full speed. Derek's car plummeted to the bottom and he was killed instantly. Investigators ruled it out as an alcohol-related accident. That was their plan and they succeeded."

It was the first time he had heard the truth about Derek's death. Even though he was positive that Derek was taken out for knowing too much, there was finally closure on that mystery.

"And I assume Mariette's fate was the same?" Shane asked.

"Yes, but they did a sloppy job. They just wanted to get her out of the picture once they set the house on fire and also destroyed much of the evidence taken from you," Dr. Morgan said, gazing out of the taxi. They had now entered the highway.

"So now that you have me, where are we going?" Shane demanded.

"As long as I have you," Dr. Morgan began, "I live. Once they have you underneath their test tubes, they will inject me with a death serum and put me out. I know much more than most of the NHR does about the life outside Earth, but they are angry at how my epic mistakes caused this mess. If those pictures got out to the world, who knows what would happen. The government keeps this a classified to keep world order. If the world knew, there is great probability that human morality would falter."

"I need to get to where my friends are going to be tonight. The three of them are in danger!" Shane said. "Let me go."

"No," Dr. Morgan said annoyed, "You foolish boy. Don't you know that if I do, they will find and take you? They are strategically placed and ready to apprehend your friends. It's over for them."

"Can you please drop me off at that exit?" Shane told the cab driver.

"No! We need to be taken to Burbank please," Dr. Morgan said.

"No, please drop me off. I do not know this man!" Shane said angrily.

The cab driver looked confused and suspicious. He took the exit and stopped at a corner. Shane gave him a few bills and ran out before Dr. Morgan could reach for him.

"Thanks for helping me back there, but I'm on my own now. Get out of town!" Shane yelled back at a very angry looking Dr. Morgan.

Shane flagged down another cab and was soon en route to the cove where Caroline, Mike, and Alice would be meeting in about an hour. He looked out at the ocean on the drive up the Pacific Coast Highway and saw that the sun was beginning to set.

He asked the cab driver to pull into his house as it was on the way.

"Sir, just wait here. I need to get a few things. Here's a tip," Shane said, and he passed the cab driver a twenty-dollar bill.

Shane raced up the stairs to his bedroom once he was in the house. His phone began to ring. It was his mom. Shane ignored it and let it reach his voicemail. As he walked into his room, his heart sank.

It appeared as though the NHR had entered his home for a second time. His whole room was ransacked. Somebody was looking for something. Shane's laptop was left open. It appeared as though everything it ever contained had been wiped clean. Luckily, Shane had been smart and put the pen drive in a drawer with other pens. He found it and put it in his pocket. Then he reached for a small suitcase. He hastily packed in a few clothing items, phone charger, his laptop, and few toiletries. His plan was to leave town as soon as possible and go into hiding. Now that he knew he was not from Earth and was a marked man, there was no way he could stay. He was one of the "ones" among us. The new semester of school that was a few days away from beginning seemed unimportant to him now.

Shane began feverishly dialing Mike and Alice's cell phones. They both went to voicemail. He then called Caroline. Her cell appeared to be off. It went to voicemail before a single ring.

"Damn it. Where are you guys?" Shane said under his breath.

Shane concluded that nothing had been taken from his room. He felt uneasy by the invasion of his privacy.

His phone began to ring again. It was his mother. He hit ignore and sent it to voicemail.

"Sorry mom, but I do not have time right now. I'm not even your son," Shane said, feeling really sad at saying those words out loud. "I need to say goodbye to them before I leave. I can't tell them what I am going through."

The phone rang once again, but the caller ID read: "Unknown caller." Out of curiosity, Shane answered.

"Hello?"

The voice on the other line responded with a Spanish accent, "Do not go to your friends. If you are found, they will take you. You must get rid of your cell phone as well. You'll be tracked if you keep it. Check your mailbox at your house. You will find a new one along with my number and the next steps to get you home. You are no longer safe in this world."

The caller hung up, leaving Shane's mouth open in confusion. He was preparing to ask questions.

"Who was that?" he said to himself.

Shane ran downstairs, suitcase in tow, and locked his house door. He ran to his mailbox and inside was a package with Shane's name on it. He grabbed it and ran to the taxi, which was still waiting for him.

"Take me to the north cove please!" Shane requested to the cab driver.

The driver nodded and they headed off. Shane opened the box. Inside was an iPhone. There was a notification signaling a voicemail. He listened to it. He did not recognize the deep voice.

"Shane. This is a brand new phone. It is under an alias. They will not be able to find you. Use this for communication. I may be under surveillance as well, so I cannot act freely yet. I need to make sure you get to safety. If you open up the maps application, you will see that there is a pinpoint to an address located in the San Bernardino Forest. It is a house I am renting.

You will meet me there. I will arrive tomorrow at nine in the morning. I am doing this on request per Derek's ally."

That was the end of the message. Shane was beginning to believe it was a trap, but when the mysterious caller said he was working with Derek's ally, Shane began to feel a glimmer of hope. There was more than one person on his side. Shane's hope was to be able to find a way to understand what was going on.

Shane felt his phone vibrate in his pocket. He realized he needed to get rid of it. He copied down the numbers of Alice, Mike, Caroline, and his parents to the new phone he received. He then listened to the voicemail from his mother.

"Shane, where are you? We've been trying to call you. Your Uncle Robert was so generous to offer us a trip to visit them in Arizona. Your dad and I are headed to the airport now. It's for some work event at a resort just outside of their city. It'll be a nice weekend getaway. Call us back before our plane leaves."

Shane's heart sank. Knowing he would have no opportunity to say "goodbye" to the people he knew as his mom and dad, was emotionally taxing. They raised him his whole life. Even if they were not blood—or DNA related in this case—they were still his family. Just then, Shane had the thought to call his Uncle Robert. He did not keep him posted on his investigations. He was not detailed about what he was learning, but he wanted to give Robert closure and tell him that Derek's death was in fact preempted.

Shane dialed his uncle.

"Shane?" His uncle answered after a few rings.

"Uncle Rob—" Shane began but was cut off.

"Shane," His uncle began speaking really fast. "Someone called saying that I needed to get your family out of L.A. but make it look as though nothing dangerous was happening with you. I'm bringing them to Scottsdale. This person is a friend of Derek's. What exactly have you uncovered? He said this was a matter of life and death. Why does somebody want to find you?"

"Uncle Robert," Shane answered, "I cannot give you too much information. Just know that I found out who killed Derek. Yes he was killed. I am dealing with those responsible and that person that called you is helping me too. He had a Spanish kind of accent, did he not?"

"Yes!" Uncle Robert said. "Shane, be careful. I'll make sure your parents are safe. The man that called me assured me we will be ok and that you will be safe with him. Stay away from Derek's killers."

"Good. We'll talk soon," Shane hung up and then saved his uncle's number to his new cell phone.

Twenty minutes later they cab driver arrived at the cove. Shane paid him in cash. He left his old cell phone under the seat of the cab. If it was being tracked, the NHR would be chasing down the taxi, which was sure to be heading far away from where he was now.

Shane dialed Alice and Mike again first. None of them had answered. He was walking to the campsite where he was supposed to meet Caroline. He was an hour early.

He arrived at the site and saw a tent. There was a birthday cake sitting on a picnic table. Shane smiled. It was a surprise birthday party for him. There was a case of beer and a sandwich tray on the picnic table as well.

"Shane?"

Shane jumped. Caroline was behind him holding a bag of groceries that contained plastic cups and plates.

"You are early," She said. She looked pale.

"I, um. Yeah we need to get out of here. Let's pack up and go," Shane said.

"But, we planned this—" Caroline began.

"Birthday surprise. Yes I know. I also know they asked you to invite Mike and Alice. What is going on? You do not need to be a part of this," Shane said.

"How do you know…" Caroline said looking scared.

"They tried to apprehend me two hours ago. I overheard them. Why didn't you tell me? Why did you lie?" Shane said angrily.

"They threatened my life and family," she said. "My mom is not really sick with cancer. I just made that up. They apprehended me that day you came to Fashion Rack. They took me to an office and questioned me all night long. They devised this plan to use me as bait to get you when they realized I did not have as much information about what you were up to. Why do they want you Shane? It's the government for crying out loud!"

"My life is in danger. That's all I will say. Leave now. You know that Alice and Mike are in danger as well? And do you honestly think they will let you go knowing that you have been working with me?" Shane said clenching his fists.

"I should not have become involved with you!" Caroline snapped. She threw the groceries to the ground and got in her car and sped off.

Shane stared at her as she drove off in her grey Jetta. He then walked over to the table to help himself to some food. He had not eaten in hours. He set his suitcase down and opened a beer.

He heard the sound of a car hit the rocky gravel in the parking lot just near the site he was at. It was Alice's car. Her and Mike came out with grocery bags in their arms.

"Shane?" Alice said surprised. "What are you doing here?"

"I was invited, obviously!" Shane said. "We need to get out of here. Caroline set us up—although via threat. The NHR is on their way, and you are on their list too. I need you to take me to this address in San Bernardino and then you both need to skip town until I finish dealing with them."

"What the hell is going on?" Mike asked. "Caroline what?"

"That bitch!" Alice said angrily. "How? Why?"

"The NHR kidnapped her and devised this plan. They wanted a quiet area to get you guys. They tried to apprehend me at another site earlier. This place is deserted. Nobody is around. We need to go. Now." Shane headed towards Alice's car.

"So Caroline just took off?" Alice said sounding very upset.

"Yeah. I'm glad we didn't tell her much about our progress. That would have been a liability," Shane said.

"And how did you find out about this plan?" Mike asked trying to figure out what was going on.

"They tried to kidnap me at the storage facility in Venice. I came across the key. It was left at my doorstep, but one of the agents planted it at my house. It was a trap," Shane decided to be honest with them. "And Alice, you will never believe who the agent was. It was that guy you thought was checking me out outside Mariette's house the first time we went to it. He wasn't checking me out! He realized what I was up to. That's when they discovered me..."

Shane trailed off. He had not planned to tell them about discovering he was a Humanoid.

Shane continued. "Where they discovered I was trying to learn what Derek wanted me to know."

"So then you know now?" Mike asked excitedly. "Don't hold off, what was in the storage facility?"

"It was a trap," Shane began to skew the whole truth so as not to tell his friends about what he really learned. "When I arrived, this agent named Landon Parker was there. He called back up. It was by luck that Dr. Morgan, the guy that gave Derek the hypnosis treatments from his journal entries, happened to be there to help get me escape. It was by the inch of my hair I was free of the NHR. Dr. Morgan is being tracked by the them as well. They discovered that his methods had failed and now want to 'put him out' as he put it."

"Why did he help you and risk his life?" Alice asked smartly. "Is he the ally?"

"No. He helped me escape because," Shane began, "I was his collateral. He'd give me up to the NHR to save his life, I think."

"Damn," Mike said. "What time are the agents supposed to arrive here? We need to get out of here fast!"

"Get in," Alice demanded.

They all got in the car, leaving behind most of the camp items they brought as well as Caroline's.

"They might think we are still here if they see the tent," Alice said stepping on the gas pedal and peeling out south down the highway.

"So this place you need to go to in the San Bernardino Forest is where you are meeting this guy that is working with Derek's ally?" Alice asked.

Shane had left out the part where he actually did get Derek's message he had been searching for, but he did tell them how he was left with a phone at his house that had a message for him. He also explained how the NHR had gone through his room and left it in shambles.

"Here's the deal. Mike. Alice. Once you drop me off at this location, you two need to head far. I would say go south to San Diego and then cross into Mexico. Just lay low. I have your numbers and will update you. Just don't screen my calls again please.

"Sorry, I just didn't want to ruin surprise we were planning," Mike said explaining why they had not answered his calls prior to Shane's arrival at the cove.

Just then, they saw a caravan of three black SUVs with tinted windows speed by them. Shane had ducked in time, but they seemed to not have been paying attention to oncoming traffic.

"There they go," Alice said clutching at her heart.

"For you guys at least," Shane said. "I left my cell in a taxi so no doubt some of them are tracking that. The one good thing is they won't know we are together. And we won't be for long."

"I am not leaving you!" Alice said. She looked into Shane's eyes and appeared as though she was about to cry. "I know you are not telling us the full story. I know you have your reasons. But whatever it is that you have to do, just know that I am behind you and I will go with you no matter what."

"Alice. This is hard. This is my issue. I know the NHR killed Derek. I know too much. Humanoids. Aliens. Sector 7. It is my entire fault. You need not be a part this," Shane said, reaching for her warm hand.

"So they really did kill Derek?" Mike asked.

"Not surprisingly. Dr. Morgan told me," Shane assured them. "And he might be a problem too. Especially if he wants to use me to save his own ass. Anyway, the guy I'm meeting at this house in the forest will not arrive until nine tomorrow morning. I'm not sure what I'm going to do for the night. I can't go home."

"What if we get a hotel room for the night?" Alice suggested. "We can pay cash."

"Ok," Shane agreed. He wanted to spend one last evening with his friends before they parted ways.

Shane tried to call his mother, but it went straight to voicemail. She was already in flight to Arizona. Shane sighed with relief with thoughts that at least his family would be safe and far from L.A.

They arrived at a run-down motel about fifteen miles from the forest. Mike went into the lobby to pay for a room for the night. Alice and Shane stayed in the car.

"You really don't want to talk about what you found out, do you?" Alice asked Shane in a very calm voice.

"I just have to process this," he said. "I need to do this alone."

"I don't want you to though," Alice added.

"I have to," Shane insisted. "It's my fault you guys need to skip town and lay low."

"Are you not worried about who this guy is? The ally? The guy you are meeting in the forest?" Alice asked, concerned.

"No. I do not think this is a set up by any means," Shane assured her.

"This is one big mess," Alice sighed.

Mike came back to the car with a set of keys. "Guest room suite. Just kidding. This place is a shack."

They arrived in the room and washed up before getting ready for bed. Mike had fallen asleep as soon as he jumped into his twin bed. Alice and Shane shared the other bed.

Shane was lying awake, staring into the darkness. He could feel Alice staring at him. Without much thinking, he turned over to her and reached for her hand. She accepted it and with her other free hand she touched his cheeks. Moments later they were kissing feverishly for the first time. There were no words, just emotions.

"Let's go for a walk," Alice whispered, once they broke free of the kiss.

They heard Mike snoring slowly in his bed, and they quietly tiptoed out of the door, closing it softly shut.

Alice grabbed Shane by the hand and led him into the courtyard where the motel's small pool was. They grabbed a pair of chairs from a poolside table and sat down.

"We kissed," Shane stated.

"That we did," Alice smiled.

"I've always wanted to do that," Shane said. "But Caroline…"

"She sold you out," Alice said changing her tone into that of annoyance.

"She was threatened. Wouldn't you have done the same?" Shane asked.

Alice thought about it for a second. "I don't know. Maybe, maybe not."

"Regardless," Shane continued, "I still have a lot on my plate."

Shane began to think back to the video message Derek left for him.

"Get to the landing site and from that point all will make sense. Lost memories will flush back to you. A new journey awaits you."

187

Thoughts raced through his mind about what lay ahead. He was to learn about his existence. He thought back to the picture of him with his eyes closed in the desert five years ago. He felt his jacket pocket to check that the photo and tape were still safely in there. They were. What was he doing on that night Derek took those photos on August 13, five years ago, at three in the morning? He was asleep, he thought. However, the photo showed him in that Nevada desert in some sort of deep sleep or trance.

"Earth to Shane," Alice said waving her hands in front of his eyes.

"Daydream," he said, apologizing.

"I don't want to separate, Shane. I want to be with you. Like, really be with you," Alice said staring at him.

They kissed again. It was long and passionate. Shane had the sudden urge to tell her the truth, but he feared it would scare her. Then he thought maybe it would be best to scare her so that she would not head down the dangerous path he was about to embark.

They stopped kissing and looked into each other's eyes.

"You are beautiful," Shane told Alice. Alice blushed.

"You are a great guy Shane," Alice gushed. "I am sorry about my hostility with Caroline. I was obviously jealous. Do you think she will be ok?"

"I don't know," Shane said, feeling worried because she would not have been involved in this situation if it was not for him. "I want you to try to contact her. Don't let her know where you are, but make sure she also skips town too."

"Ok," Alice agreed, although reluctantly.

She then hugged Shane and they embraced for several minutes in silence while staring up at the sky. It was a full moon and the stars were much clearer in this area than in the city.

Shane and Alice got up half an hour later and walked back to the motel room.

"I'm beat," Shane yawned. "Let's hit the sack."

They walked into the room and heard Mike snoring softly still. They took off their shoes and jumped into the small twin bed. They cuddled and embraced. Shane kissed the back of Alice's neck restraining a tear. He felt sadness to leave her. He was not even sure he would ever see her again after they parted ways.

Shane dozed off into a deep sleep. He began to dream again a very familiar dream of looking out at the moon above him. People surrounded him this time, but everything seemed so fuzzy like a distant memory he could not remember. His eyes were closed but it was like he could see through his eyelids. He did not feel like he was a werewolf this time. It was apparent that the light before him was not the moon. It was an oddly familiar bright, white orb. He was unsure how he got there. His subconscious was trying to think very hard. His dream became lucid and it was as though he was really there. He felt younger too. He was eighteen years old. He was getting ready to start his first year of college at Pepperdine. His dream was rewinding, or so he felt as if it were. He was backtracking to how he arrived at the white light. Then he dreamt a familiar image of a small dark figure staring at him at his window.

Shane was staring back at the figure. He could barely make out the face. It looked like a small child framed in his window. The figure was getting closer to him. Shane's eyes darted open. He was awake, however everything was pitch black. He could not even see Alice next to him or light coming through the motel windows. *Am I blind?* He thought.

He felt a cold shiver up his spine. He began to hear a distant whisper. A strange voice was talking to him very softly. He could not understand what it was saying. It did not sound like Alice or Mike. For a split second he thought he saw a hand. Or was it a claw? He thought he saw sharp nails. Then he felt like someone was talking to him in his mind.

"*You are impenetrable. Let me out! Let me out. It hurts.*"

Shane was tossing and turning in his bed. Darkness became light in an instant, that he was nearly blinded. That same voice was heard in his head as it trailed off into nothing. "*Nooooooooo...it hurts!*"

"Shane...SHANE!"

Alice was calling his name and brought him back to reality.

"Are you ok?" She asked. Shane nodded, unsure what to think about what he just experienced. "Your phone is ringing. Should you answer it?" Alice asked.

Shane reached for the iPhone and answered. He heard the familiar Spanish accent. It was Derek's ally.

"Shane, when you get to the house in the forest, there will be a friend of mine waiting for you there with the next steps. We need to move you covertly to the desert. There is a lot of buzz within the NHR and they will stop at nothing to find you. We will connect soon."

Before Shane could say a word, there was a click and the caller had hung up.

"Was it him?" Alice asked.

"Derek's ally," Shane stated.

"This all sounds fishy," Mike said, and he took a bite out of a donut he must have picked up from the continental breakfast the motel served. "I don't think you should go. It could be a trap just like the one at the cove!"

"I have a phone that can be traced," Shane said. "If the NHR had this mysterious caller give it to me as a trick, we would have been apprehended in our sleep."

"Good point," Alice agreed.

"Even still, I do not like the sound of any of this. Plus, we're your close friends. At least throw us a bone. What is going on for real?" Mike insisted.

"There's no point in arguing," Alice said to Mike. "Shane has his reasons. He wants to protect us. Let's just help him get to this house."

"Thanks," Shane said smiling to Alice. He gave her a small nod.

Chapter Sixteen:
Another Marked One

Alice and Shane were once again in the front seats of her car, with Mike in the backseat as they drove up a winding road into the San Bernardino Forest. It was very green and the trees cut off so much sunlight, it appeared as if it were dawn instead of dusk.

"This place seems so eerie, huh?" Mike said staring out the window.

"Not so lively today," Shane added. "Mind you, it is early in the morning. Most campers are probably still asleep. How much further Alice?"

"The GPS says we'll arrive in about fifteen minutes," Alice informed him.

"Great," Shane said with knots in his stomach.

Shane had never felt so nervous. He was sure that he was doing the right thing to follow the path that Derek pointed him in the direction to. The thought of leaving Alice and Mike, however, made him feel nervous and nauseous at the same time.

Shane was half listening to the radio when he thought he heard the mention of a familiar name on it.

"Hey, guys shush," Shane ordered as Alice and Mike were exchanging a few words.

"What?" They both said in unison.

"On the radio. A news report...I could have sworn..." Shane trailed off as he raised the volume of Alice's car radio.

The DJ was going through a couple of morning stories.

"...it is thought that there might be a connection with the murder of well-known retired actress Candy Adams. She was killed in a house fire several weeks ago and the case is still under investigation. Her former bodyguard was a person of interest after Peggy Mills, her former publicist, accused him of threatening Candy in the past. After providing a credible alibi, investigators concluded Adams' bodyguard was not in the Los Angeles area or surrounding areas at the time of the former actress' death. Now, the story takes a fascinating twist. Peggy Mills is now...missing. Her family reported her disappearance just two days ago. Police have been on a citywide search trying to obtain any information that may lead to finding Peggy Mills. Just a few days ago, Peggy was seen working at a studio in downtown Los Angeles with a male client. That was the last time Peggy was seen. Vanished...without a trace. Please visit our website for recent photos of Peggy Mills. The LAPD is urging anyone with information on Peggy's whereabouts- or if you think you have seen Peggy, to call 911. You may remain anonymous. Peggy is a married mother of two. Her loved ones want her home."

Shane lowered the radio once the DJ introduced a song. "What the hell?"

"Kidnapped you think?" Alice wondered.

"You last saw her at a photo shoot too, right?" Mike asked Shane.

"Well yes, but this was obviously a different photo shoot," Shane replied.

Alice added, "She didn't even know anything about Derek or Candy's secrets."

"But she had a hand in helping," Shane said. "Although that was unintentional."

"Everything I touch," Shane began, "seems to end badly. First we met up with Can—Mariette, and now she's dead. Caroline was held hostage for a while by the NHR. Now she's on the run too."

"I texted her," Alice said making Mike and Shane look at her with curiosity. "I was just concerned since she was on our team

192

when this all began. However, I never heard back from her. I didn't tell you because I don't want you to worry."

"This is seriously all my fault," Shane said.

"I would blame Derek. He's the one that got into all this craziness of alien beings!" Mike blurted.

"Once again, that was not even his fault," Alice jumped in. "He was asked on order from the government to help in that project."

"Why does this have to be a secret? Can't the world know that we are not alone in the universe? I mean is it really that surprising considering how big it is?" Mike suggested.

"It would change many things though," Shane began thinking about what Dr. Morgan told him in the taxicab before Shane escaped from him. "Think about it. Religions. Faith. History. It could cause chaos to the world order."

"Yeah," Mike agreed. "I guess that is true. I know I would have flipped out if I didn't get this information eased in."

"We're almost there," Alice said pointing to the GPS.

They arrived at a small brown wooden house in a secluded area. They had to drive through a private gate that was left open. There was a "No Trespassing" sign that they ignored. The house had a green roof and a chimney with smoke slowly billowing out of it. It appeared to be very quaint and inviting.

"Nice little house," Alice said as they pulled up.

"Yeah. Not so scary, right?" Shane said.

His heart began to race again. It was mostly from the feeling of leaving two of his very close friends he had known for most of his teenage and adult life. He had a feeling that after he went on his journey, it would take him further than any place Alice or Mike could reach.

"When do you think you will be done with your task?" Mike asked.

Shane gave him an uncomfortable look.

"I...don't know," Shane said truthfully. "Do you two have a game plan?"

"Vegas," Alice answered.

"No!" Shane argued. "I don't want you close to Sector 7."

"I told you not to tell him Alice," Mike said nudging her. "He was going to figure it out."

"It's far enough but also close enough for us to come get you in case you get yourself into a predicament," Alice assured him. "Assuming you will be easy to contact with your new phone?"

"I think it is best we cut off communication for now. I will contact you two if and when I can," Shane said looking Alice deeply in the eyes.

Shane reached into the trunk of Alice's car and pulled out his luggage. "I have to get far from L.A. but on a different track than you guys. My life here is done."

Shane felt goose bumps rise on his arms as he uttered the word 'done.' It was like making his decision final. He knew that there was no going back to the life he had.

"Done?" Alice said curiously.

"Do you expect to be on the run forever?" Mike asked somberly.

"It's the government. We know too much. To be honest, I'm not sure how long we'll have to be on the run, but I do know that Derek pointed me on a journey that will end this. Or at least that's what is helping me sleep at night."

Shane finished with the thought on his surreal dream earlier that morning and the strange sensation of darkness.

"Should we wait until you knock?" Mike asked. "Just to make sure this isn't another trap?"

"No," Shane replied. "You two need to get a move on. Head far. Go south. I told you to go to Mexico. Lay low there. The government cannot touch you in that country."

"Why don't you just come with us?" Alice said, and tears began to slowly fall down her face.

"I will not risk your lives anymore. They want me," Shane said.

"Why do they want only you? We know as much as you do—well almost as much," Mike said.

"Trust me. That's all," Shane said.

He gave Mike an embrace. Mike looked on the edge of tears as well. He was always a very tough guy, but in that moment he was sensitive.

Shane then turned to Alice, and she ran to him, hugging him tightly. They exchanged a long passionate kiss that surprised Mike.

"What…" gasped Mike.

"Sorry, our relationships has, um, changed a bit," Alice said blushing. She then kissed Shane again.

"Oh," Mike replied leaving his mouth open.

After the public display of affection, Alice and Shane broke apart. Alice stifled her sobs and wiped her eyes clean on her blouse causing her mascara to smear.

"It will be ok," Shane said. "If all of this works out, you and I will have a picnic dinner on a sandy beach. Deal?"

"Yes. Yes of course," Alice replied smiling.

"No Vegas ok," Shane said looking at Mike and then back to Alice. "It's not safe."

"Alright. Alright," Mike responded.

They exchanged their final goodbyes. Shane knew deep down, that there would be no turning back. As he saw Alice drive away in her car with her eyes in the rearview mirror full of tears, staring back at him, he thought hard about how that moment would be the last time they locked eyes.

Shane had a flashback of the moment he met Alice in middle school. He was sitting in the back of the class when his math teacher introduced her to the class. She was new to the school. The only available desk was to Shane's right. She took it and smiled at Shane.

"Hi, I'm Alice Hastings," she said smiling and extending her hand for Shane to shake.

"I'm Shane. Shane Baker," he replied, taking Alice's hand and shaking it.

Shane could feel himself blush. Alice rummaged through her backpack for a calculator and a pencil and directed her attention to the board. She brushed her hair and put her hand against a purple butterfly sequenced clip that sat in her blonde hair.

Shane came back to the present with tears streaming his eyes. When he was just a teenager, never would he have imagined he was not even human.

He turned around and walked up to the green wooden door of the small house. He knocked twice.

Moments later a man opened the door. He was tall, muscular, and had shoulder length jet-black hair with piercing blue eyes.

"Shane?" he said in a deep voice.

"Um, yes," Shane said unsure of what else to add.

"My name is Dimitri. Come in."

Shane followed Dimitri into the small wooden house. There was only one room. On one corner was a cot that looked as if it had just been slept in. On the other side was a fireplace with a metal pot hanging over the fire, boiling water.

"So who is Derek's ally and why is he not here?" Shane said bluntly.

"In time Shane. He's risking so much to help you. We all are," Dimitri said.

"Who is 'we'? What is with all this mystery? I mean, can't I just get a straight answer?" Shane said, amazed by his own courage.

"Had you just been given all the information at once, you'd probably not be free right now. The NHR would have found you quicker. Derek's trail has given us more time. It was just the first part of the journey to help explain who you are."

"You mean what I am?" Shane responded.

"What we are," Dimitri said.

Shane opened his mouth to reply but he could not. He stared at Dimitri and analyzed him.

"I am a Humanoid as the NHR calls us," Dimitri said. We are 'Marked Ones.' We are on this planet for a purpose brought here by our Elders. I'm considered a 'Knowing.' Meaning I walk among Earth knowing what I am living a human life and hiding who I am. You are what we call an 'Unknowing.' You walk among them—humans—living unknowingly that you are a 'Humanoid.'"

"What does that mean?" Shane urged.

"In time," Dimitri said.

"You keep saying that. Who are our Elders?" Shane asked.

"You saw the photographs Derek took, correct?" Dimitri asked Shane.

"Yes," Shane replied.

"The ones the NHR calls the 'Greys' are our Elders," Dimitri said.

"The aliens?" Shane said knowing that his response may have sounded rude.

"You are an alien too, so to speak," Dimitri added matter-of-factly.

"But I do not look like them," Shane said.

"I, as a Knowing, have the knowledge you seek. However, due to rituals, you are to learn from an Elder, the information you seek. You were not supposed to learn of your true existence until your thirtieth human year. You are about six years early but due to circumstances, things are going to change. Your true identity was found out by the Earth government when they saw the pictures Derek took of you five years ago and recognized you near Derek's old home in Hollywood. My job is to get you to safety. These humans mean well, but their curiosity gets the best of them. They want to do experiments and use you to communicate and perhaps borrow more of our technologies."

Shane just stared speechless for a few moments. More and more, the reality of what he was kept sinking in, but he wished it was one big joke.

"Where is our world? Like, where do we come from?" Shane asked.

"Far. I'm not too sure myself. But it is a distance that no human here could ever reach in their lifetime," Dimitri responded.

"Why couldn't Derek's ally be here right now?" Shane asked.

"We have a new problem. Another Marked One was discovered. She was being tracked by the NHR in L.A. because of her close relations to Candy Adams. They thought she might have known something about our existence. The irony was she was one of us, although she was an Unknowing. They found out what she was because a doctor had recognized her face from a landing site ritual years ago."

"Wait who is this woman?" Shane asked feeling he knew the answer. His mind raced to the news report on the radio earlier.

"Peggy Mills. You know her," Dimitri said.

Shane's heart sank. He was oblivious to the fact that she was just like him and after all this time, he never knew. There was one point where he thought she was responsible for Candy's death.

"Was the doctor, Felix Morgan?" Shane asked.

"Yes," Dimitri said and he sounded sad. "I know he helped save you yesterday, and that was pure luck, but he had tabs on Peggy before you. He kept that tight lipped as a back up because he wanted to understand why Peggy was still on Earth passed her thirtieth human birthday."

"I was about to ask that," Shane said.

"Peggy is one of the few Marked Ones we allowed to live longer on Earth as an Unknowing. The Elders have their reasons to let a few of us go on about our existence with humans. I really never understood why. Peggy is now being held at Sector 7 according to my inside sources. She has not been told what she is by the NHR agents. All I know is she is sedated and in a deep sleep while they run tests on her. They won't really be able to find anything 'alien.'"

"So we need to get her out, don't we?" Shane said.

"Yes," Dimitri said closing his eyes. "If we do not, the NHR will figure out how to use their therapy and hypnosis methods to tap into parts of her mind that have been temporarily forgotten and she will learn much about our existences. That information in the hands of humans, is very dangerous. It could lead to the devastation of their own race if it leaks out beyond the government. We are already nervous about the government themselves knowing of us, but at least they are keeping that away from the public."

"We—the Elders—our race, whatever—do not want to take over Earth do we—they?" Shane asked.

Dimitri let out a small laugh. "No, but all will make sense when you get your time with the Elders."

"So if you have been sent to live here and know what you are and why you are here, wouldn't that make you homesick?" Shane asked.

"I came as a small child, but was filled with the knowledge when I matured enough to understand. I made a life and family here. It's pretty much how I know to live. I just have side projects that I work on for the Elders."

"And you cannot tell me what they are, right?" Shane asked knowing the answer before Dimitri nodded.

"Don't worry Shane. We will be able to get to safety," Dimitri said putting his hand on Shane's shoulder.

"Why can't the Elders just fly here and take us?" Shane said sarcastically.

"And risk attack? It would scare the humans. It would ruin their life's work," Dimitri said, and then he quickly changed the subject feeling he was close to divulging information he was forbidden to reveal.

Shane was still trying to process much of the conversation with Dimitri. Then he thought about his family.

"Will my family be safe?" Shane said.

"Yes. In Arizona they will be out of harms way. We had to make sure the NHR did not use them as bait to get you. However..." Dimitri trailed off.

"Yeah?" Shane asked.

"Your friend Caroline is also being held hostage," Dimitri said, avoiding Shane's eye contact.

"WHAT?!" Shane yelled, making Dimitri jump.

"You know they were having her work against you. However, it was through a threat. But we are working on getting her free," Dimitri said.

Shane was thinking about Mike and Alice and was hoping they were heading south towards Mexico as they spoke.

"My two friends that brought me here are in trouble too then. Can I be assured they will be safe?" Shane demanded.

"Your safety is our concern right now. And Peggy's. That is our priority. We will do our best to make sure no one else is in danger. There is a network of other Knowings that will be helping to get you to the landing site. The only difficult part is the proximity to Sector 7. It will be difficult to move covertly. The disadvantage you have is that your identity is known to the NHR. The other Knowings continue to live in anonymity."

"So what is the next step?" Shane asked.

"First," Dimitri said, "we should eat some breakfast. I'm cooking eggs. Second, we will head out around noon. I have a car and I'll drive us to a secret location where my network of local Knowings are. It's a safe underground location. We'll make further plans after our meeting with them."

As they ate breakfast, Shane's mind was racing with all the information he had to take in over the past twenty-four hours. He kept wondering what it would be like to be around the other Humanoids. He was scared for what lay ahead, but a part of him was very curious. Earth had always been his home, but to know that there was a world outside his, where he was from, was enough to make his head spin.

Mike and Alice were driving down the highway that would take them back to Las Vegas. They had decided to go against Shane's wishes in hopes that they could be of assistance to him when he arrived.

"I still wish we knew why he has to go back. Think there is something in Sector 7 he needs to get to?" Mike asked Alice.

"That place is probably full of crazy secrets. I wonder why they made that base. Isn't Area 51 not too far from that location?"

"No clue," Mike said.

"Besides, we don't even know exactly where the location is," Alice said. "This idea sounds like a suicide mission."

Mike looked at the traffic on all sides of their car.

"We aren't being tailed by a black vehicle," Mike assured her. "I'm one step ahead of you! I made copies of the pictures in Shane's pen drive. And my laptop is in my bag. We'll be able to use my geolocation software to pinpoint exactly where we need to be!"

"You are brilliant Mike!" Alice said patting him on the shoulder. "Think we'll see that UFO again?"

"I hope so!" Mike said.

"I wish he told us more. I understand it's for our own safety, but I feel like what he has to do is bigger than any of us will ever understand," Alice said, gripping her steering wheel.

"Do you think he's one of them?" Mike asked mysteriously.

"An alien?" Alice said sounding intrigued.

"I mean, why else would he not say anything? Maybe he learned he's a Humanoid? They do live among us. They've been here for years," Mike added.

"After everything we've learned the past few weeks," Alice began, "it could be possible."

"Hey pull over!" Mike said pointing at the rear view mirror.

A police car was behind them with its lights on. Alice slowed down and pulled the car to the side of the highway. The police car stopped behind them.

"I wasn't speeding, was I?" Alice asked Mike.

The cop stepped out of his car and Alice rolled down her window.

"Alison Hastings and Michael Campbell?" The officer asked.

Alice and Mike nodded.

"You are going to have to come with me. I need you both to wait in the back of my car." The officer told them.

Alice and Mike exchanged nervous looks.

Half an hour later a forest green Hummer pulled up behind the officer's car. Mike and Alice exchange shocked looks. The officer had not spoken to them and was waiting outside the car.

A man in a military uniform walked up to the car and opened their door. The officer watched from near the front of his car outside.

"My name is Lieutenant Carter. You are going to have to come with me."

"What? Where?" Mike demanded.

"You can't just take us!" Alice snapped.

"M'am, I believe you all were connected to Derek Conrad? We've had eyes on you. You possess very dangerous and confidential information. By law, you have to come with me." Lieutenant Carter ordered.

Mike and Alice were forced to get into the back seat of the Hummer by the Lieutenant and the officer.

"Hand me your phones," Lieutenant Carter told Mike and Alice. They obliged and Lieutenant Carter turned to the policeman. "Thank you for your help."

"No problem. Where are you taking them?" the officer asked.

"A base just outside of Vegas."

Alice and Mike exchanged worried looks.

Chapter Seventeen:
The Colony

Shane had taken a nap after his hearty breakfast that Dimitri cooked. He awoke with a start when Dimitri tapped his shoulder to wake up.

"Time to go kiddo," he said.

"I'm ready," Shane yawned and stretched.

He looked at his cell phone in case he had any missed calls. There were none, and he realized nobody but Derek's ally had the number to that phone. He thought about sending Alice a text, but decided to restrain. The thought of her heading south far from him, made him feel depressed.

"Ok a few things before we go," Dimitri said, pulling out a map with red markings, showing the route he was planning. "We have to travel just outside the forest to get onto the highway heading towards Las Vegas. The colony meeting of Knowings is hidden in an abandoned warehouse basement just outside of the city of Barstow. It'll probably take us an hour or so to arrive. I don't foresee us running into much traffic."

"This colony—do they all live there?" Shane asked.

"No, it's just a group of us from the west coast area that congregate and have meetings. We are all considered part of a colony," Dimitri said.

"Are there many colonies in the world?" Shane asked intrigued.

"No. We are very sporadic all over the world. I'm not one hundred percent sure what the Marked Ones' population is on Earth, but last I heard we were at three hundred. Most of those are Unknowings like yourself," Dimitri said.

"I see," Shane said, unsure of what else to ask.

"Let's get going," Dimitri added with finality, and they stepped out of the small wooden house through the back door.

Dimitri's car was a white BMW sedan. It looked polished and new.

"Nice ride," Shane said smiling at Dimitri.

"She's new. I feel so human in her," Dimitri joked.

They got in the car and sped down a narrow winding road. They did not see any campers on their way out of the forest.

Shane kept fidgeting with his phone and decided to finally text Alice, "Hey there. I hope you and Mike are almost in San Diego. I'm on my way to begin the journey back to the desert. Please keep me posted on your travels."

Shane sighed and looked out the window as they passed several pastures on the way out of the city.

"You seem very calm after all this information you've received in the last few days," Dimitri said, glancing at Shane twirling his cell in his hands.

"It is shocking. It is scary, but I have had time to process. Derek made sure I got the message, however it just was unfortunate that I ran into that Agent Parker dude back at Derek's old house," Shane vented.

"The important thing is you are safe," Dimitri said. "Derek's ally, my good friend Manuel, who you have spoken with on the phone, has been of great help. He stepped in to give Derek a hand at his time of need. Sadly, his death was something he could not stop...on time."

"So this guy is named Manuel?" Shane asked. "Who is he?"

"You'll meet him soon," Dimitri said.

Shane rolled his eyes, "At the colony?"

"No," Dimitri answered. "He has other business affairs to handle. He'll be at the landing site. Our end destination. I will tell you this, Manuel is the leader of all the Marked Ones on Earth."

"So just to make sure I am getting this right," Shane began, holding up one finger, "Unknowings—those of us who are not aware they are Humanoids—and Knowings—those that do know—are called Marked Ones?"

"Yes, but Marked Ones are all of us. It's our word for Humanoids," Dimitri said smiling. "You learn quick. And the Elders are the beings our race has evolved from. The NHR calls them Greys."

"The aliens? I mean I know we are alien, but the ones in the photos with the dark large eyes, and frail looking bodies? We've evolved from them?" Shane asked sounding confused.

"They will explain," Dimitri said sternly.

Shane decided it was best not to ask any more questions. He was distracted when his phone buzzed. It was a text reply from Alice.

"Shane, Michael and I are safe and sound. We've stopped for a bit in San Diego before we cross the border. Where are you right now?"

Shane grinned at her use of the word "Michael" then replied.

"This guy Dimitri is helping me get to a warehouse near Barstow. There will be several others there to help me get to the location Derek wanted me to go."

Seconds later Alice's reply came through.

"Where is that location? Sector 7?"

"Yes. Obviously, but just a little ways out from that base," Shane texted his reply.

Alice responded a minute later, "And when you get to the location you are going to now in that warehouse, what is your next plan?"

"Not sure yet," Shane began writing his text. "I miss you Alice."

There was a two-minute delay and she replied, "We'll be together soon. Let me know when you arrive safely at that warehouse."

"Ok," Shane replied.

"Who are you texting?" Dimitri asked suspiciously.

"This girl. This girl that's a friend," Shane said, feeling himself turn red.

"You gave your number out? Manuel just wanted this phone to be used for direct communication to him!" Dimitri said sounding worried.

"It's ok. She's almost in Mexico. The phone won't work once she crosses the border," Shane said.

"Moving forward let's just keep this phone for communication between Manuel and yourself," Dimitri said sounding stern again.

Shane nodded in agreement and reached for his laptop. He turned it on and inserted his pen drive into the USB port.

"Is that what Derek left behind?" Dimitri asked.

"Yeah. It's the photos of that night," Shane responded. He opened up the files. "I'm going to get the geolocation to help us on our journey."

"Smart boy," Dimitri said, patting Shane on the shoulders.

Shane opened the properties of each photo, then opened it on a program he had. The photo then gave a pinpoint, precise location of where it was taken. Shane did a zoom in over the Nevada desert. The map was a satellite view and he could see the base that was Sector 7 about ten miles east of it. He copied the coordinates and then input them into his map application on his iPhone.

"I just love technology," Shane said gleefully. "The only issue now, is that there are no roads that take us to this exact location. We'll have to dodge Sector 7 too. I'm sure it is heavily guarded."

"It is. The only way to the location off the highway is straight through the dirt on an all-terrain vehicle. They purposefully made it that way so civilians do not attempt to drive near it," Dimitri added.

"I hope your colony has a game plan," Shane said.

A few hours later, they were in the outskirts of Barstow in a warehouse district. Every single building looked abandoned with graffiti all over them.

They pulled into a much smaller warehouse that appeared to have been an old mill. Dimitri parked in the warehouse's small parking lot that was inhabited by a few other cars. There were people there already.

"Alright, let's head down to that door," Dimitri said, looking around before ushering Shane to move forward.

Shane walked towards the building. He pulled on the rusty door a lot harder than he needed, as it was unlocked. It opened freely and both of them walked inside.

Inside was an empty open space. There were a few old tools hanging on a wall at the side opposite the entrance, but there was nothing but endless, empty concrete space.

"The entrance is at that corner," Dimitri said, pointing to the northwest corner of the warehouse.

They proceeded to the corner. On the ground was a small metal doorknob sticking out of the ground. Dimitri reached for it, and the concrete floor opened into a small trapdoor.

"Shouldn't it be more hidden?" Shane asked?

"Nobody ever comes here," Dimitri said.

"Well there are a few cars parked outside. Doesn't that raise suspicion?" Shane replied.

"They don't live here. This is a meeting place," Dimitri said. "Ok then, let's go."

Dimitri, who was much taller than Shane, squeezed into the trapdoor with ease having apparently been experienced in entering it. Shane was not so graceful. He nearly fell onto the opening.

"Careful," Dimitri called from below.

There was a small spiral staircase that led Shane to the ground. He stepped onto the stone ground and kicked up some dust and began to cough.

"Sorry, allergies." Shane apologized.

They walked down a narrow hall until they reached a metal door. Dimitri knocked on it three times before it opened.

Inside was a small chamber lit by torches that were hanging all around the stone walls. There were a few benches and a podium where a woman was standing. In total, there were ten other individuals besides Dimitri and Shane.

"Welcome," the woman at the podium said.

She was in a bright green dress that matched her piercing green eyes. It clashed however, with her bright red hair. She looked as if she was in her fifties.

The woman continued, "Shane, my name is Agatha. Welcome to our colony gathering."

Dimitri and Shane took a seat on a bench near a very plump, balding man. They were all staring at Shane with interest. A woman on the other side of the plump man smiled at Shane. Another man with dirty blonde hair, wearing a black crystal necklace around his neck, eyed Shane with a warm interest. He gave Shane a nod. None of them spoke when Shane gave them an awkward wave and "hello."

"Agatha," Dimitri began, "Let's have this meeting. Tonight at three in the morning is when the Elders will arrive at the site. We need to be on time."

"Thank you," Agatha replied. "The most difficult part of the journey is getting through the desert. As of now our only option is on foot. We cannot arrive via air since the area is guarded by the government's helicopters. If we use an all-terrain vehicle, like an ATV—as you suggested Dimitri—our tracks will be followed."

"Are they aware that we are arriving tonight? The NHR?" a muscular man with sandy hair sitting at the end of the bench asked.

"No Devin, they are not. If they did, our insider would have informed us," Agatha replied.

Shane thought to himself, *Man, they have someone on the inside of the government—a Marked One?*

He wanted to whisper that question to Dimitri, but he looked very attentive to every word Agatha was saying. The thought of someone being on the inside however, comforted him.

Agatha continued, "So our best bet is on foot. Dimitri and Shane will travel alone. The less people involved the better."

Agatha paused for a moment and looked around at the room.

"The rest of us will wait and hope until we've been delivered the message that you are home free, Shane," She continued.

Shane began to think about heading "home" to a place he had never remembered being born in. He thought about how much he was going to miss Alice.

"Shane," Agatha continued, "I know you probably are expecting us to explain more about home and our existence here. Dimitri, from my understanding, has told you some, but it is our Elders that hold the privilege to share the information you seek. Being raised on Earth and the knowledge you have of here will make you superior in the next chapter of your life. They will explain everything tonight."

Shane was coming to terms with the fact that he was going to be whisked away to this home planet the colony was speaking of. He spoke up, making everyone in the room turn to him. "I understand. I did not realize I would be leaving today. I would love to see my family and friends before I go. I know I have no choice. I know if I stay, I am in danger."

"Darling," Agatha said in a motherly voice, "We are all your true family. Your human attachment and feelings are valuable, but you will be at ease soon. Trust me."

Everyone in the room nodded in agreement. The plump man next to Shane patted his shoulder.

"Now," Agatha continued and everyone fell silent, "we should get on to some of our items on the agenda.

Just then Shane received a text. He felt his phone vibrate in his pocket. It was from Alice. It read, "Where are you now?"

Shane looked over at Dimitri who was focused on the meeting. He typed, "Some warehouse area just north of Barstow. I'm in good hands. I thought you were going to be in Mexico already? Your roaming fees will be through the roof!"

Shane sent the text and waited for a response. In seconds Alice replied, "I'll see you soon then. We lied. We wanted to stay on your tracks."

Shane let out a loud gasp that had everyone in the room turn.

"What is it?" Agatha asked taken aback.

"I'm so sorry. It's my friends. I told them to flee to Mexico, but they lied and have been trying to find me. They are almost here!"

"What? If they are being tracked then we are not safe here!" Agatha said in panic.

Dimitri looked over at Shane and then eyed his phone with a look of frustration. "I told you, this was only for communication with Manuel!"

"I know. I am sorry."

Shane got up and headed out of the room towards the ladder that led out of the secret basement they were meeting in. Dimitri followed him out.

"You must tell them to leave now and head south like they should have," Dimitri said agitated.

"I will. I'm pissed they did this," Shane said. "It's bad enough Peggy and Caroline have been apprehended."

They climbed up the ladder and entered the spacious empty warehouse. He heard the sound of a few vehicle doors slamming outside. Then there was a series of rushed footsteps and an order from a man, but he could not make out what he was saying.

"That does not sound like them," Shane said confused.

"It's a trap!" Dimitri said, grabbing Shane by his collar and rushing him back into the secret trap door that led back to the colony meeting room. "Quick, it's the NHR!"

"Oh my God!" Shane said, and he climbed down the ladder while Dimitri followed and closed the door.

"They'll find us here. And I have no doubt they are getting every license plate from the vehicles parked outside. We are discovered. This is seriously bad," Dimitri said worried. "Our identities will now be known."

"What is going on?" Agatha demanded.

"The NHR hoodwinked Shane using his friend's cell phone," Dimitri said. "They are above us."

"Do you think they have Mike and Alice?" Shane asked knowing the answer to his question. There was no doubt they were caught since Alice's cell phone was being used to text Shane. Shane had given their location away.

"I'm sorry. We have to worry about ourselves now. We will not be held captive at Sector 7," Dimitri replied.

"I just sent a text to Manuel," Agatha began, "he is sending us a helicopter. We should all be able to fly to safety. Our agenda has changed. There is no doubt that the government will now know our identities. Manuel will communicate with the Elders of our situation and we'll wait for further instructions."

"It is not safe to travel by air Agatha," Dimitri said.

"It is our only option. We can fly straight to the landing site," Agatha replied.

"And have the military at Sector 7 shoot us down?" Dimitri said outraged.

"He's right Agatha," the plump man said. "It is not wise. The boy needs protection. The Elders need him alive."

"Fine, we'll just fly to another safe zone," Agatha said realizing her peers were correct.

"Why do I need so much protection? You all are no different than me," Shane asked with curiosity.

"Shane, you are a special Marked One," Agatha said. "Derek went through lengths to give you the message about what you are, but there is more to why we must get you home. We hoped you wouldn't be discovered soon, but the NHR is aware of your identity. You will know soon what our plans are. Now is not the time."

Shane processed what he just heard and formulated questions in his head to ask, yet he knew they would not tell him more.

"Luckily we have another exit out of here," Dimitri said to Shane. "Back there behind Agatha's podium is another secret door. There is a narrow underground path that connects to another warehouse. There we will take a van that we have parked outside and head to the location of where the helicopter will pick us up. Let's go."

The group made their way to the back of the room. Agatha pushed back a chalkboard set on wheels and moved it out of the way to reveal a blank wall. There was a very fine line that showed where the secret door was. Agatha simply pushed it and it swung open. Everyone hastily walked through with Dimitri bringing up the rear.

"Hurry," Dimitri urged the group with his hands gripping Shane's shoulder. Agatha took the lead. It was dark but she had a flashlight in front of her to help them see their way forward. Shane kept touching the sidewalls to make sure he did not run into them. He walked awkwardly in fear of stepping on someone. Dimitri kept accidently stepping on Shane's heel from behind.

After about five minutes, they reached the end of the underground path. There was another ladder they had to climb up to. Shane finally reached the top along with the others. The warehouse they were in now was full of empty aluminum barrels. He wasn't sure what they once held, but they were empty.

Agatha ran to the van and turned it on. She moved it closer to the colony and gestured for them to enter. They all climbed in. There was enough room for everyone.

Agatha's cell phone began to ring. She answered it and quickly explained the circumstances to the caller. She listened to the caller's response and nodded her head. When she hung up, she turned back to the rest of the passengers.

"That was Manuel," she said. "The NHR discovered our underground room. They've formulated that we escaped through our secret passage, which as we speak, has a few agents in there right now heading to this warehouse. We have to move fast. Shane, I am afraid they have your friends in captivity and are planning to use them as bait for you to fall into their hands. We cannot have that happen."

Shane gulped. His fear was confirmed. His friends were now being held hostage at Sector 7. Now it seemed like the only thing he wanted to do was to head over to that base and save them.

Agatha pulled the van out of the warehouse and darted straight for the nearest highway.

"I don't think anyone saw us leave. We should be good," Dimitri said, sighing deeply.

"Where are we going?" Shane asked Dimitri.

Dimitri thought hard for a minute before answering, "Brett has a ranch just outside of town here. We'll be heading there. A helicopter will be coming for us. We need to make sure we arrive at the landing site tonight."

"What if we don't make it?" Shane asked.

"Well we can try the next night, but there will be so much surveillance on all of us, that the sooner we get to the Elders, the better. We need protection," Dimitri said looking worried and tired.

"Why can't the Elders just get us from any location? Why does it have to be the landing site?" Shane asked. "I mean I was taken during the middle of the night once and brought to that ritual there five years ago."

"That is a valid question, yes," Dimitri said, "however, the reason you have to be at the landing site is because lately they've been trying to keep out of the public eye. And the government has been watching the skies as well. It's just safer for them to land in the desert."

Shane nodded his head and looked out the window. They were already outside the city and there were several fields and farms along the way. He knew there were big things going on with him, but his only priority now was to get to Mike, Alice, and Caroline. He felt at fault for their captivity. Even for Peggy. After all, it was their involvement with him that got them into this mess. He was not even sure how he would be able to tell them that he was a Humanoid.

Back at the warehouse where the colony had previously held their meeting, Agent Parker and Ramos had climbed out of the hidden trapdoor and joined some of their military forces in the empty concrete interior.

"We lost them," Agent Parker spat. "We were so close."

In his anger he threw the cell phone that belonged to Alice, and it broke into pieces a couple yards away from where he was standing.

"We will find them Parker," Agent Ramos assured him, patting his shoulder.

"We need that boy," Parker said, "Did you get the team to run records on those license plates?"

"We did," Ramos said. "We know the identity of each and every one of them. There is no doubt in my mind that they are Humanoids as well. I cannot believe that so many have been living among us all these years."

"And now we can put a face to them!" Parker said sounding slightly more relieved. "Now we have a few subjects to get answers from."

"Is the woman talking?" One of the military men said stepping up from the group of five of them that were watching Parker and Ramos converse.

"Ms. Mills?" Agent Parker asked, and the military officer nodded. "She has been useless. She claims she has no idea that she is a Humanoid. In fact she genuinely seems afraid and confused. We utilized polygraph tests and other procedures to seek the truth, but nothing. I truly believe she has been walking this planet unaware of what she really is. I believe the same has been for Shane, although Derek's message seemed to have finally clued him in."

"What is the next step?" Ramos asked curiously.

"Agent Green will not be too thrilled we failed to apprehend what could have been at least ten Humanoids," Agent Parker replied. "We will get the Humanoids and Shane at all costs. We'll have extra security around the base of and perimeter of Sector 7. Not even an ant will be able to get through."

Chapter Eighteen:
Fight or Flight

Agatha turned off of the highway onto a dirt road surrounded by farmland. On each side of the road, as they drove down the bumpy path, there were fields of vegetation. The entire colony sat in silence as they neared closer to the destination.

"I'll get off and open the gate," Brett said. "Welcome to my farm."

Brett opened the sliding door of the van and ran towards the gate to unlock it, while looking around in fear of being watched or followed.

"What time is the helicopter supposed to land?" Dimitri asked Agatha.

She gripped the wheel and turned to Dimitri. "When the sun sets, we'll have to fly far enough from Sector 7 so they cannot detect us. They have military vehicles prepared to shoot any unauthorized air craft."

"Damn," Shane sighed.

"Any word from Manuel? Does he think we'll be safe?" Dimitri asked Agatha.

"Safe or not, we have to fly there regardless. If we miss today, tomorrow will just become more difficult. There is no doubt the NHR are devising extra security and keeping more of an eyeful watch tonight."

Dimitri sat in silence thinking to himself. Brett jumped back into the van and they drove through the gate. He got back off only to close and lock it.

Brett's small farmhouse did not look as if it could temporarily house ten Marked Ones, but they had nowhere else to take shelter.

"It'll be a bit cramped, but I have plenty of floor space for everyone to sit in," Brett assured the colony after noticing their looks of uncertainty.

Everyone got off the van and made their way into the house led by Brett. Agatha put her hands on Shane and Dimitri's shoulders.

"Hang back for a second," She told them.

"What's the matter?" Dimitri asked Agatha, as the lines on her aged face twisted with concern.

"The helicopter," she began, "may not be the most stealth way to get to the landing site."

"Noisy?" Dimitri asked.

"Very," Agatha agreed. "I'm concerned for our group. It's too much to be traveling in such a large pack. There are ten of us plus you two. It's very dangerous."

"Do you think we are being tracked here?" Dimitri asked.

"No word from Manuel," Agatha said. "I have heard that their hostages—" Agatha looked over at Shane to assure him that she was talking about his friends. "—are still alive. They've been interrogated but as none of them really know about our plans or whereabouts, the NHR are beginning to find no use of them."

"Still alive?" Shane cut in. "Do you expect them to be killed?"

"I won't sugarcoat anything my dear," Agatha started, "but the government has their ways to silence humans that know about the beings from beyond this planet. Us. They silenced Derek."

Shane gulped and a tear ran down his face. "This is all my fault!"

"Nonsense," Dimitri said, brushing his dark hair back. "Manuel will make sure that no harm comes to them. He will act when the time is right. Do not worry."

Agatha looked up at the sky. The sun was beginning to slowly set on the horizon.

"We have maybe an hour before help arrives," Agatha said. "The helicopter belongs to a rich friend of mine. We will all be able to fit in it."

"Is the owner a human?" Dimitri asked.

"Yes," Agatha said. He is just under the impression that we are doing a canyon tour."

"Well then, we'll be fine. I hope," Dimitri said.

The three of them walked into the farmhouse. Everyone was sitting on the floor with pillows. A few members of the colony were taking a nap. Others were eating sandwiches that Brett had prepared.

Shane noticed a rifle against the wall near where Brett was standing.

"What's the gun for?" Shane whispered to Dimitri.

"Self-defense. Just in case the NHR put up a fight. I believe he'll be bringing that with him to the landing site," Dimitri answered.

Shane walked over to a far end of the living room that seemed empty. He took a pillow from one of the couches and used it to lay his head on while he curled up in the corner to take a quick nap. Minutes later he felt a tap on his shoulder. It was a member of the colony he had not met.

"I'm Philip," the man said. He looked very young. He had piercing blue eyes and blonde hair with reddish-blonde stubble on his face. Shane realized it was the man with the black crystal necklace he noticed earlier at the colony's meeting. It was a peculiar necklace too, Shane thought as he eyed it.

"Hello," Shane yawned.

"You are precious cargo, are you not?"

Shane was unsure if that was some type of question.

"Um…" Shane began.

"Everyone here is working hard for your safety. I mean a helicopter transfer, well, that's pretty much first class travel if you ask me."

"What do you mean?" Shane muttered in a whisper.

Philip whispered back. "They cannot tell you, neither can I, but what's an oath if they don't know I said too much? I'm not on a binding contract, just a word from my soul. I'll fill you in on as much as I feel safe. Shane, you are more than what you think you are. You are the one that will help us get back to our planet. It's been, well, taken over, so to speak."

"Excuse me?" Shane said with an eyebrow raised. "I am not understanding. I'm 'the one?'"

"Yes," Philip responded putting his hand on Shane's cheek. "You are the final evolution. Your growth, your being, what you are now is beyond valuable than any of our lives. You are what the Elders have been waiting decades for. You are the perfect being with half part Elder and half part human, evolved from decades of work and growth on Earth."

Shane looked dumbfounded. He began to open his mouth but Philip moved his hand from Shane's cheek to cover Shane's mouth.

"Shh," Philip said putting a finger to his lips. "All will make sense tonight at the landing site. But you have to understand that if you are killed, the fate of our race will be doomed. You are the key to the survival of our race."

Shane gulped. He stared back at Philip's serious expression. He knew that Philip was being very honest with his words. It seemed that he was straining to divulge more information, but he bit his lip.

"I want you to have this," Philip said, unclasping the crystal necklace from his neck. A black black crystal was hanging off a gold chain.

"What is this?" Shane said in surprise, reaching for the necklace.

"It was your father's," Philip said mysteriously. This element attached to it is a piece of our home."

"You knew my father?" Shane said in surprise. He never really thought much about who could have been his parents now that he knew he was a Humanoid. However, he must have had two biological Humanoid parents.

"I know him well," Philip winked.

"Know? He's alive?" Shane said, with peaked interest.

"The helicopter is about to arrive," Agatha called. Shane heard the sound of it in the distance.

"We'll talk later," Philip said, putting his finger on his lips to hush Shane.

Shane's brain was buzzing with questions he wanted answers to. It was beginning to get frustrating that nobody was divulging anything solid for him to better understand what was going on and why he was so important.

"Shane—with me," Dimitri ordered Shane to come to him.

He grabbed Shane by his arms and ushered him out of the farmhouse.

Once they were outside, they saw a black helicopter land in a field a couple hundred yards away from the house. The color of it made it look invisible in the night sky, however it was so loud that it could probably be heard for miles.

"Everyone in!" Agatha ordered, and the rest of the colony began to pile into the surprisingly spacious helicopter.

Brett was urging everyone to move faster with his rifle swinging in one hand absentmindedly. Philip began to go into the helicopter. He took one glance at Shane and smiled. Shane reached for his pocket and pulled out the black crystal necklace and put it on.

"Where did you get that?" Dimitri asked.

"It was my father's." Shane said closing the clasp on it and fixed it to hang center on his chest.

"He told you?" Dimitri said in shock.

"Dimitri!" Agatha yelled out from the helicopter. "Are you two coming?"

"Yes!" Dimitri called back. "We'll talk about this later, Shane." Shane raised his eyebrow.

Dimitri pulled Shane's arm and they ran towards the helicopter.

"HURRY!" Agatha screamed in a tone that sounded as though she was near the end of her life.

"Holy crap!" Dimitri said, noticing that down the farm road path that lead to the farmhouse, were a few Hummers that just drove straight through the gate causing it to break off.

"I knew they'd be able to track us if we used a helicopter. Dumb idea!" Dimitri spat angrily.

The helicopter began to lift off. Agatha looked furious and scared. She then jumped out of the helicopter's doorframe and fell a few feet to ground on the field. The helicopter took off and the sound of its propellers began to sound quieter the more distant it became.

"Why did you jump off Agatha?" Dimitri asked her helping her to her feet.

"Manuel ordered me to make sure the boy arrives at the landing site as well. The helicopter is now a target," she said getting up and brushing leaves off her skirt.

"Let's get into the fields!" Dimitri ordered.

The three of them ran into the cornfields as the Hummers pulled up to Brett's farmhouse. Military men jumped out of the vehicles with large guns and began breaking into the house in search for inhabitants.

"They probably think that we all escaped on the helicopter," Dimitri assured them.

Shane's heart was pounding so hard, he was sure Agatha and Dimitri could hear it.

"They want me. This is becoming too dangerous. I should just give myself up," Shane blurted.

"Are you mad?" Agatha said. "Do you know the kinds of tests they want to do on you? They want to utilize you as a communication tool and God knows what else!"

Dimitri held onto Shane in fear that he would run toward the NHR.

"They are tearing Brett's house apart," Agatha gasped.

The three hid in the field for what seemed like eternity. The NHR were searching the place thoroughly due to the fact that the colony was last in a location that had secret passageways.

Nearly an hour had passed since the helicopter's escape with the rest of the colony, when finally it looked as though the NHR had finished doing the search of the farmhouse. The three could hear a voice of one of the agents' carry towards them. Shane recognized it as Agent Parker.

"This site is clear. There are no individuals left. They all took off on that helicopter. I need a location of it. It may be heading towards Sector 7. Also, my team has attempted communication with the beings again, but they have continued their silence. We are unsure as to why our correspondence with them has stopped, but I have a feeling they'll be landing in their usual spot tonight. I want as much manpower surrounding the site. We fear they might be planning some kind of attack."

In the distance Agent Parker could be seen putting his cell phone in his suit pocket. He jumped into one of the Hummers and it sped off out of the farmland.

"Attack?" Shane questioned, after a few minutes of silence.

"They think we are going to attack. The Elders, I mean. They are wrong," Dimitri said.

"Our kind—well the Elders—have been in contact with the NHR for years," Agatha began. "Secretly, of course, which is why they have a department specific to the communication with us. However, recently we've stopped. I don't want to get into too much detail, but it is almost time for all of us, not just you, Shane, to leave this world."

Shane picked at a cornstalk absentmindedly as he let the information Agatha told him, mull over.

"We need to alert the colony to head far away from Sector 7," Dimitri said. "They'll be apprehended. You heard what that agent said."

"Your phone please," Agatha asked Shane, but it sounded more like an order.

Shane obliged and passed her his cell phone. She picked it up and marked the speed dial that directed her to the mysterious Manuel.

"Manuel?" Agatha spoke into the receiver. "Shane is with us. So is Dimitri. The rest of the colony is in the helicopter. I need you to tell my friend Marty, the pilot, to take them far away into hiding. Their identities are known and the landing site will be—what? Yes, of course you are already aware of the lock down at Sector 7. Ok...are you sure? Fine."

She hung up and turned towards Dimitri and Shane who were standing side-by-side. "We are to stay put here in Brett's house. This is the last place they will be coming back to."

"Good point," Dimitri agreed. "We'll be sleeping here tonight."

"We are going to have to put up a good fight if we want to escape this planet safely," Agatha said worriedly. "Humans can be fickle."

"Do we have anything else to worry about?" Dimitri whispered to Agatha even though Shane was right next to him and could hear the conversation perfectly in the still night air.

"I do not think so. We will stay here for the night and then wait for Manuel's call in the morning. We'll play this plan by ear," Agatha finished.

They set off at a slow pace back towards the farmhouse. Shane looked up at the sky and realized how clear it was. He could see all the stars, which was something he could not do living in the Los Angeles area. He began to think about Alice and the rest of his friends being held captive in that Nevada desert.

"Can we help get my friends to safety? I know that is probably not even the least of any of your worries, but they have been a part of my life longer than these Elders have been," Shane said with urgency.

"We will help them," Agatha responded. Shane was taken aback by surprise.

"Um, thank you," Shane responded with a smile.

"We've shared this planet with humans for several years. They are essentially our family. We cannot forget that. We've walked this world among them and have grown and evolved through it. It is the least we can do," Agatha said putting her hand on his shoulders and patting him.

They arrived at the house and walked into a mess. The whole place had been searched over and glass plates and vases laid in pieces on the floor.

"No point in trying to clean up. Let's go upstairs. Shane, you can take the bedroom at the end of the hall," Dimitri said.

Shane walked up in the lead and bid Dimitri and Agatha good night. He opened the door. The bedroom had been turned over as well. He picked up the pillows and mattress and placed them back on the wooden bed frame. He found blankets under a pile of clothes that were thrown out from the closet. He grabbed them and put them on top of the mattress. He opened the window to the let the cool fresh breeze enter. The sound of crickets in the distance gave him a feeling of serenity.

He rubbed his eyes and then took off the black crystal necklace he was wearing that Philip gave him earlier. He placed it on the dresser beside the bed. Questions began to formulate in his head. Who was his father? Would he get to meet him? A part of him began to dream that his father was one of the Elders.

He was walking up a large metal path that led up to a metal disc-shaped craft. In the center was a tall, thin, frail-looking being with grey skin and large almond black eyes. Shane sensed that he was related to the figure.

"Dad?" He asked the being.

It nodded its head and smiled. It reached out its long, lanky arm and fingers towards him. Shane grabbed it.

Shane woke up abruptly from his dream. One of the shutters from the window slammed against the wall from a draft that blew into the room.

He yawned, stretched, and then walked up to the window to close it shut. He looked out onto the quiet field. The cornstalks swayed peacefully in the nighttime breeze. It felt colder than usual for a summer night.

Shane shivered and searched the pile of clothes on the floor for a jacket. He found a fleece pullover and put it on.

"Toasty," Shane mumbled.

The house was quiet except for the distant snores that Shane realized were from Dimitri. He sat back on the bed and considered dialing his parents' cell phones from the phone he was given, but he realized it was two in the morning.

Shane shifted for a few minutes in bed unable to fall asleep. He twirled is fingers around the gold chain necklace and then held up the black crystal and examined it.

"This really is a piece of my home..." he thought. His mind began to wander about the world he never knew. He wondered what it would be like when he returned. There was so much to ponder. The questions that Dimitri failed to answer, made it even more difficult to concentrate on resting. He was given another day on Earth. At that very moment, had the escape panned out as planned and he was on that helicopter, he could have probably been at the landing site in the Nevada desert. It was three AM according to an alarm clock on a nightstand.

The only issue was that the NHR was on full alert and Sector 7 was on lock down. It was then that he realized that saving

Alice, Mike, Caroline, and even Peggy seemed like an impossible feat.

Finally, Shane began to fall into a daze. He experienced a series of random dreams. They seemed to have lasted only minutes and went from one dream to the next as if someone was changing a channel on TV and bored with the current program.

Shane was aware he was dreaming at one point. He knew his body was asleep but his subconscious was awake. He felt his heart beat a little harder. A strange familiar sensation swept over his body. While he felt he was awake, it truly did appear as though his body did not. He could not move his neck, arms, or legs. In fact, it was as though he was paralyzed. Shane was not even sure · his eyes were actually open or if he was still in a dream state. He tried to blink and open his eyes but nothing happened. He began to panic. It was the strangest situation he had ever encountered in his sleep. The last time something like this had happened to him, it was quick and he thought he saw a figure and claws.

In the distance he heard a creaking sound. Then the outside breeze entered the room and spread a cool chill up his body.

Then it happened. On one side of Shane's body, he could hear a whisper. It was a strange sound in a rushed voice. He was unable to understand what was being said. The whisper was in a foreign language. Shane remembered this similar feeling happening at the motel he stayed at with Alice and Mike.

Shane's heart began to race even more. A dark shadow was clouding his vision. The entire room was going out of focus. The dark shadow was becoming clearer.

The whisper continued slowly into his ear. Then, he began to hear the whisper becoming clearer and closer to him as if it was right beside him. At this point, he was not sure he was still in his bed. He knew his body was still stiff and paralyzed, but he could no longer see anything. It was as if his eyes were closed, yet he was sure they were open since he was looking at his room just moments before.

The last thing Shane remembered was seeing an outstretched hand with claws. This hand did not look human at all.

227

The fingers were long with lengthy pointed nails. Then he saw a face but it was for merely a second. His memory of it was very blurry. There were no pupils in the eyes, but they were bright red. The face was wrinkled, as if the entity was older. It had hair around its face, or at least it appeared to even though the entity was shadowy and almost ghost-like.

The entity's long outstretched fingers were reaching for Shane with its menacing bright red eyes locked into his.

Chapter Nineteen:
Shadows

"Is he breathing?" Agatha asked Dimitri in panic.

"Yes," Dimitri replied.

Dimitri and Agatha were at Shane's bedside. The sun was nearly rising over the horizon.

"Give him some water," Agatha ordered Dimitri, pointing to a pitcher of chilled water she brought up.

"Why is he not waking up?" Dimitri thought aloud.

"He looks pale," Agatha began, touching his face. "He will come around."

"What happened to him?" Dimitri asked Agatha.

"They tried to take him," Agatha said with a look of horror.

"The Elders?" Dimitri questioned.

"The Elders know better than to make an attempt anywhere that is not the landing site. This was someone—something else," Agatha said, the wrinkles around her eyes crinkling as tears began to form. A sense of fear was etched in her aged face, and she was fighting back revealing more information in fear that stating it would make it become a reality.

Dimitri put his hand on her hand that was resting on her lap.

"My dearest Dimitri," Agatha began, "Manuel and I haven't let the colony in on more than a need-to-know basis. I think now, you need to know."

"Know what?" Dimitri asked curiously.

"There's more to Shane than he may ever really know," Agatha said. "Apart from being the perfected evolution and improved form of our race to help our kind continue on back home, he is more precious than gold. Another race has learned of our project here on Earth. It is my understanding that they have been watching and hiding in the shadows. They can take many forms in the darkness. Humans call them demons. Our kind knows them as pure evil."

"Are you being serious?" Dimitri said flabbergasted.

"Very," she replied in a somber tone. "You know that our kind was forced to work on the human project due to a disturbance that nearly wiped our kind. While I have sugarcoated the story, the truth is there is a species that we call the Dark Ones. Think of them as an evil infestation that wiped out many of our people, and my family. We were unable to survive their attacks. However, human bodies, as long as they can fight the possession of the Dark Ones, can become immune to them. You've heard of demon possessions in human folklore right?"

"Yes..." Dimitri said intrigued.

"While humans think of these entities as devil or demon possessions, the truth is, they are another alien race that nearly destroyed our home. They've been rumored to have taken refuge here and hide among us as well, but I could not be sure. The Elders had their suspicions. Humans have been able to fight off possessions before. And just this morning, Shane did the same thing. He fought it off. On his own, without some kind of—"

"Exorcism?" Dimitri said.

"That's another human belief. Humans just don't know that their bodies are really strong and cannot be taken over as easily as our Elders', which is how much of our kind was killed. Shane fended off the darkness. If it took him over, we would have lost our one hope for survival and plan to avoid extinction. Us Marked Ones cannot survive being taken over. We'd die almost instantly just like the Elders would."

"Well this makes matters more serious," Dimitri said, "Why did you not inform the colony?"

"And cause a panic? Remember you are part human. It is normal for you to think like one," Agatha assured him.

Shane had been listening the entire time. He had woken up minutes ago, but heard the conversation between Agatha and Dimitri. He was in shock about the night's events. He was there on the bed trying to remember exactly everything that happened, but it was all still very fuzzy.

Dimitri looked at Agatha and realized something, "So Shane is the only Marked One that has ever been able to survive their possession? That means we can still be taken over?"

"Correct," Agatha said. "Which is why we need to get Shane to safety. That demon could have taken over you or myself last night and Shane would have been in trouble. The Dark One would have eventually killed our bodies, but not before making us attack Shane."

Shane began to shift and pretend he was waking up. The information he just heard was helping him understand more of the broad scope of this situation he was in. However, it felt as though the more he learned, the more stress he began to feel. He also realized that he had these dreams, or episodes before where there was darkness and the sense of some entity trying to overcome him. He immediately reminisced on the claw and the bright red eyes, which he had seen before.

"Shane, are you ok?" Dimitri asked.

"Yeah. A little light-headed," Shane said honestly.

"Do you know what happened to you?" Agatha asked.

"I had a strange dream. But it felt real," Shane answered.

"Lucid," Agatha said. "Just rest up. I'll go out and pick up some breakfast. Manuel has not called yet. I'm waiting for him to call to see what our next plan of action is."

"He should have called an hour ago," Dimitri said sounding worried.

"Yes, I know," Agatha said. "I'll be back. I'll have to update him on a few things." Agatha gave Dimitri a look, which

Shane understood meant that she was going to tell Manuel about the "Dark One" attack he just experienced.

Agatha left the room and went downstairs. Dimitri waited for the sound of her exiting and shutting the door before turning to Shane.

Shane looked at Dimitri and said, "I heard you all."

"I figured," Dimitri replied. "It was news to us both. I saw you shift on the bed from the corner of my eye. I could tell you were awake."

"So another alien race?" Shane asked sounding even more confused.

"Apparently they are dark shadows that possess other life forms. It's scary to think it was in our presence." Dimitri said. "Don't let Agatha know you know. She has piece of mind knowing that most of the facts have not been given to you. She leaves that upon the Elders' responsibility."

"I will keep my mouth shut. Is it true though?" Shane said.

"Is what true?" Dimitri asked, raising his eyebrow.

"That I'm the hope for our race?" Shane asked.

"It seems so," Dimitri said, not meeting Shane's eyes. "This complicates matters though, what with these demon beings and all."

"It baffles me," Shane began, "that all this time, other beings have been living among us—among the human race."

"All of this will be explained better once we get to the landing site. We need to get you out of here. I just wish the NHR were not giving us problems either," Dimitri said, and he got up from the bed and walked over to the window. "What do you remember?"

"About last night?" Shane asked.

"Yes," Dimitri said.

Shane began to think hard about the evening before. He had vague recollections of the series of random dreams he had prior to his encounter.

"I think this has happened to me before. Well, an encounter with a Dark One," Shane started. "One night a few weeks ago, I woke up to what I thought was a dark figure the size of a small child. I did not have my contacts on, so I was not sure. By the time I put on my glasses, which were at my bedside table, there was no sign of anything. I figured I was seeing things. However, a few times before, I felt that eerie, cold darkness. Last night I felt the same presence, and this time there was a shadowy figure and it got close to me. It tried to speak to me but I did not understand what it was saying."

Dimitri was staring intently at Shane with peaked interested. "Close to you?"

"Yeah," Shane continued. "I briefly saw its face. It had claw-like hands. It was whispering in a foreign language I did not recognize. Then everything went dark. I couldn't see my own body. It was like my eyes glazed over. I think it was inside me trying to control me."

As Shane was telling his story out loud, he was slowly beginning to remember. The story he was retelling was coming out of nowhere from his memory that he thought was faded or forgotten. Shane replayed the thoughts in his head and slowly, but surely, he was recalling what happened.

"It was in me," Shane went on, "and talking to me. I still could not move my body. It was a sleep paralysis or something. I think it was scared too. Inside me, I could understand its communication. It realized it could not control my body either. I think that is when I let out a scream. However, I did not feel my mouth open."

"That is what woke us up," Dimitri said. "Agatha and I ran to your aid. We saw that your eyes had rolled back, but you were stiff as a board. Your skin felt cold to the touch. But then all of a sudden you began to warm up and your body was twitching and moving. You appeared to have fallen back to sleep."

"I think," Shane added, "that it left me."

"We saw nothing though," Dimitri said.

"I think it tried to find a new body, but it was weakened by being inside me so it did not try to latch onto you or Agatha," Shane said.

"How do you know that?" Dimitri said in shock.

"I guess because it tried to take over me, therefore it could see my mind and I could see its mind. I finally woke up and could hear you all speaking. At first you sounded muffled, and then my hearing came back and your voices were clear. I felt safe at both your sides."

"Well you are," Dimitri told him. "We will make sure that no harm comes to you."

Shane smiled and reached absentmindedly for the crystal necklace that Philip gave him.

"He told you, then?" Dimitri said, shifting up from the windowsill ledge he was resting on. "Philip…"

"He said I should have it. It was my father's apparently. It is a piece of our home planet," Shane said, squeezing the black crystal.

"Shane," Dimitri began slowly, "Agatha does not want you to know yet. She will also be furious since this information was to be withheld until you were on your way home. Philip is in fact, your father."

Shane was not expecting to hear the words that had come out of Dimitri's mouth. He just stared back at Dimitri, unable to open his mouth.

Dimitri stared back at Shane uncomfortably. After a few tense minutes, Shane spoke up.

"Why didn't he tell me?"

"Hmm, I thought he had. As tiring as it must be to hear this, the time was not right. Philip's role in your new life is uncertain right now. I really can't say much more. It is not my duty," Dimitri said, looking as though he had said more than he wanted.

Agatha returned with a box of bagels and coffee. She set them on top of the kitchen table, which she had to set back up right. It had been turned over when the NHR had ransacked the house.

Shane reached for a plain bagel and began spreading cream cheese on it. Dimitri turned on the TV in the living room and was flipping through channels. He called back to Agatha.

"What did Manuel say?"

"No answer," Agatha said, trying to mask her worried tone. "I'm sure it's ok. He must have his hands full."

"When will I meet Manuel?" Shane cut in.

"As soon as we get to the site," Agatha said, pouring herself a cup of coffee.

"I also haven't heard from the rest of the colony," Agatha began. "I was supposed to get a call from the pilot once they landed, but in the haste to escape, I'm not sure where they were taken into hiding."

"Yeah, I do not think they went to Sector 7. That is, if they are smart or got the message, they would not have gone. It's going to be tricky to get back to the landing site now," Dimitri added.

"I just don't understand why they have not contacted us," Agatha continued sounding even more worried.

"Well we need to get to the desert," Dimitri ordered, "We must get there tonight. We cannot waste another minute. Last night was proof..."

Dimitri trailed off, remembering that he was pretending as though he had not told Shane about the Dark Ones.

Agatha shot Dimitri a dark look and he turned and continued flipping through the channels.

Then all of a sudden Agatha dropped her cup of coffee onto the floor and it shattered, spraying hot coffee everywhere on kitchen floor.

"You ok?" Shane said as Agatha rested her back on the counter of the kitchen sink. Her eyes began to dilate and she began shaking slightly.

Dimitri got up from his chair and ran to her aid.

"Agatha are you ok? What is going on?" He asked.

Agatha's mouth was shut and she was staring intently at Dimitri, but was unable to open her mouth and speak. For a second she had a look of terror, and then her expression went blank, almost calm.

"What's wrong with her?" Shane asked, the color from his face disappearing in shock.

"I think one of them is taking over her," Dimitri whispered, his eyes wide with fear.

"Possession by a Dark One?" Shane blurted. "Won't it kill her?"

"It can, yes," Dimitri responded automatically.

"How do we help her?" Shane asked.

"You are the only one of our kind that has a body that can free itself of this being. Humans can eventually free themselves of them as well, but last night we witnessed your survival. It must have escaped and entered Agatha."

"I thought it was too weak to take over someone else," Shane asked.

"I thought so too, from what you told me," Dimitri admitted clutching at his heart.

Agatha opened her eyes and smiled.

"Hello. I would surrender the boy if I were you," Agatha said in a hoarse, raspy voice that was not her own. "There are more of my kind lurking among this planet that are traveling to find him. You will not leave this planet."

"Give me back Agatha," Dimitri told the now possessed body of Agatha.

"Never," it continued. "I am weak. It took me long to finally take over this body, but alas, I have. However I cannot fight you. The boy has ripped my body apart. We will find a way to take him with us. We nearly destroyed your world and your people, but they sought refuge here and have slowly been planning their arrival back to your planet. My kind will not give back your world again, Dimitri, if the boy is taken back. We want a solid form. We want bodies. Our dark shadowy lives will be a thing of the past once we learn to evolve from this boy."

"You will not take me. If your kind tries to possess me, I will make sure they die like you are," Shane said with his wrists clenched.

"Boy," it continued, "You cannot fight off more than one of us. Our species will live on through you. Surrender now and I…"

Agatha's body began twitching.

"Her body is dying," Dimitri said in shock. "So is the Dark One. It can no longer survive."

"Get out of here or it'll jump into your body," Shane said.

"If it was healthy," Dimitri started, "but it is dying."

Slowly before their eyes Agatha was dying. Shane began to tear up and Dimitri began sobbing. Shane put his hands on Dimitri's shoulder. Shane closed his eyes, unable to bear witness to what was happening before him.

Agatha stopped breathing and a slight hiss that escaped her mouth just before, was proof that the Dark One inside had also died.

Chapter Twenty:
Rogue Agent

Mike, Alice, and Caroline, were locked in a cold, steel cell in the underground confines of a Sector 7 hangar. They had been grouped in together. Peggy Mills was being held in another room not too far from where they were. Peggy was strapped onto a bed and was heavily sedated with a monitor constantly checking her vitals. She was stable and looked peaceful.

Mike and Alice were sitting against the wall of their cell. Mike had his arm over Alice's shoulders. Her mascara had run since she had been crying all night. Caroline was at the opposite end avoiding eye contact with the both of them. Mike finally spoke up.

"Caroline, don't feel guilty. We've seen what these guys can do. It's not your fault you were forced to do what you did."

Alice broke in, "I would never have sold Shane out."

"Look where it brought us!" Caroline snapped. "We'll never see daylight. They'll finish us off and make it look like an accident, like they did to Derek Conrad and Candy Adams."

Alice opened her mouth as if to argue, but she decided against it. Mike continued, "I wonder what they are doing with Peggy and why she is not in this holding cell with us."

"We all know about them," Caroline began. "The Humanoids, if you will. Aliens. Whatever you want to call them. The NHR's main job is to make sure that no living civilian is aware of such classified information. But there is something special about

Peggy. I overheard the agents talking about her when I was brought in. I was sedated, but I came out of it."

"What did they say," Alice asked, still with a tone of anger in her voice.

"She's one of them. A Humanoid," Caroline said, with a tear forming in her eye. "She just had no idea. And there's something else…"

Caroline trailed off and began sobbing into her blouse.

Mike got up and sat next to her patting her shoulders awkwardly.

"Caroline, what is it?" he asked.

"It's Shane," Caroline said. "Derek was trying to protect him. That's what the message was. His final clue from Derek was the truth about who—what he is."

Alice stared into Caroline's eyes and began to sob again.

"Are you saying…?" Alice began.

"Shane's one of them," Caroline finished for her.

Mike put his hands to his mouth. "He didn't know?"

"No," Caroline said. "When they were rolling me on a wheelchair while I was supposed to be asleep, I heard the agents talking about bits and pieces of this, um, fiasco. I don't know much details, but that is what I gathered."

"No wonder Derek went through such lengths," Alice began with her hands over her mouth too, "But he's humanish right?"

"I don't know. This is the Non-Human Relations agency we are dealing with," Caroline said matter-of-factly.

"They're going to kill him and Peggy. Or worse use them as lab rats," Mike said.

"Worse?" Alice said in shock.

"I'd rather snuff it than be used for testing," Mike said, shuddering at the thought.

"Hey, I hear a voice," Caroline said, urging the others to hush.

Outside the cell, Agent Ramos and Parker were walking towards the holding cell. Their voices echoed down the hall.

"Agent Green is not pleased Ramos," Agent Parker said angrily. "You were in charge of her care."

Agent Ramos responded, sounding irritated, "She was administered the serum to keep her sedated by the doctor. She was given too much. Agent Green will handle that."

"We've lost a live specimen," Agent Parker said.

"She was a person," Agent Ramos said. "Whether born here or elsewhere, she was brought up in our world. Why must we treat them terribly? They never seemed to be of threat."

"Yet," Agent Parker interjected. "We do not know that. They've ended communications with us for a while. For all we know, they could have been building a Humanoid army to take us out!"

"We're here," Agent Ramos said pulling out a set of keys from his suit pocket.

He opened the cell and pulled out a gun. It was a silencer.

"Now, we want you to cooperate and there will be no trouble. We are moving you to another room," Agent Ramos said.

Mike, Alice, and Caroline obliged with scared looks on their faces.

"I'll handle them from here," Agent Ramos told Agent Parker.

"Don't screw this one up," Agent Parker said. "I'm off to see Green. We have some paperwork to deal with. I'll send over some of our military men to help you escort them."

Agent Parker whistled at some men down the hall, and he waved them to come over. Four men walked over with AK-47s flanked at their sides.

"Escort the kids to the interrogation room please," Agent Parker ordered.

The military men obliged and Agent Ramos led the way down another hall with Mike, Alice, and Caroline in between him and the military men who took up the rear.

"Gentlemen," Agent Ramos spoke sternly over to the military men behind him, "Any report on that helicopter from Agent Green?"

One of the men spoke up with a burly, deep voice. "Yes sir. It was shot down by military personnel about five miles from here. They tried to land on a mountain side, but they were still in our radar."

"They what?" Agent Ramos said, sounding shocked.

"The party in the helicopter are all taken care of," the officer said.

"Agent Green allowed that to happen?" Agent Ramos said with a tone that confused Mike, Alice, and Caroline. It sounded almost like sadness.

"Agent Green said it was a message for them. Perhaps they will come forward and communicate with us. Green is particularly interested in that boy Shane."

"Alright, well let's get our guests here into the interrogation room. Agent Green will want to question them," Agent Ramos said.

Mike, Alice, and Caroline were left in a room with a table and four chairs. It was cold, and the fluorescent lights above were flickering slightly. The walls were one-way mirrors. Parties on the other side could see through.

Agent Ramos left the room and so did the military men.

"What are they going to question us about?" Alice asked nervously. "This must be the room where Derek was questioned after his photograph session with the UFO, as written in one of his journals."

"No clue. We don't even know where Shane is or how to get a hold of him," Mike responded.

"I think they are going to either attempt to wipe our memories or—" Caroline stopped talking once the door opened and a man who looked very important in a suit, walked in.

"My name is Agent Green. I would like to have a conversation with you three," he said smiling.

"We do not know where he is," Mike said honestly.

"I believe you," Agent Green responded, still smiling and appearing very proper.

"I am head of the Non-Human Relations agency," Agent Green spoke as he took the last remaining seat directly in front of the three at the table. "It is my understanding that you all have been working with Shane Baker on the acquisition of very sensitive government top secret knowledge."

Agent Green placed a folder on top of the table with a photo paper clipped on top and the name "D. Conrad" in red at the top tab. The folder also had "Top Secret" and "NHR" stamped in red as well.

"We had no idea," Caroline said staring at the file that was clearly the government's tabs on Derek.

"Miss Lu," Agent Green said, meeting Caroline's eyes, "That is not of importance on whether you knew how dangerous the information you have learned these past couple of weeks was. What is important is that we work together if figuring a way to make you…forget."

"How do you propose that?" Mike asked. Alice put her hand on his knee under the table and squeezed it as to signal for him to stop talking back to the agent.

"We have used this counseling method before to help with aiding in people forgetting certain events involving Project Moonshadow, but in the past it has proved useless. As you know Derek underwent it and you are here because that procedure did not work on him," Agent Green said, putting his hands flat on the table over the file.

"What's Project Moonshadow?" Mike asked.

"Our files," Agent Green began holding up Derek's file, "on the events involving extra-terrestrial incidents and non-human relations. If these files were made public, the world would go mad."

"We heard the other agents talking," Caroline began, "You killed Peggy. You made me nearly give Shane over to you after threatening my family. You all call yourselves the government?"

The lights above kept flickering and it made the pale-blue eyes of Agent Green look empty, as if he were in a trance or thinking really hard.

He snapped out of it and spoke, "Miss Lu, this country would be in shambles if they knew that there were other beings—beings like you and I, mind you—that were walking freely and also had counterparts in other planets unknown. Religions would fall if they knew even the slightest tidbits of mankind's lies. I know things that will make you question every belief you ever had. Humanity would fall. We are an order. It took centuries and wars for humans to become civil and live by a government. We will not let something like this break us up."

"So how are you silencing us," Mike began.

Alice shivered at the questions. Agent Green was no longer smiling. He looked serious.

"That will be up to my discretion," Agent Green said, and he looked over to the mirror walls as if he could see through them.

Just then, the lights flickered vigorously as if fighting to stay lit. Consequently, the bulbs exploded, making all four in the room jump for cover under the table.

"What the hell?" Mike yelled, while Caroline let out a high pitch screech of shock.

Agent Green could be heard grunting. It sounded as if he was flailing on the ground. The table fell over as if someone had kicked it.

"Ouch!" Mike gasped. "Why the hell did you kick me?"

It had appeared as though Agent Green had kicked Mike while he was having some sort of seizure and gasping for air.

Help had come in. There were men shouting and voices ordering commands, but there was confusion everywhere.

Mike saw that light was coming out from the door that just opened so he ran towards it while grabbing Alice's hand. They ran to the door and darted out. There were five military men dead on the floor. They had been shot. There was a silencer gun on the floor.

"Oh my God," Alice gasped. "And where is Caroline."

"I think she's still in there, but we got to get the hell out of here," Mike urged Alice towards an exit.

Agent Ramos emerged from the inside of the interrogation room. Although his skin was dark, he appeared paler than he was earlier when he escorted them into the witness room.

"You two! We need to get out of here. You will follow me out this way," Agent Ramos ordered, reaching for the silencer gun on the floor.

"Caroline!" Alice shouted.

Caroline came running out of the room with a look of horror.

"He w-w-was speaking in an odd voice," She panted. "Something is wrong with him. He was clawing at me!"

"We need to get far away from him as possible," Agent Ramos said.

"Oh my God! Who killed them?" Caroline said with one of her hands to her mouth in shock and one pointing at a body.

"I did. Self defense," Agent Ramos said.

All three of them turned to look at him, not expecting that answer.

"No more questions. We need to get you out of Sector 7." Agent Ramos said with finality in his tone.

The three of them were in no place to argue with the possibility of escape.

"He was going to use a serum to put you into a sleep that you would never wake up from," Agent Ramos said. "He was playing mind games with you in hopes that maybe you had some extra crucial information from Shane that he did not already know."

"I knew he would," Mike began. "Wait, aren't you on his side?"

"I'll explain once I get you all to safety," Agent Ramos said with the gun outstretched in front of him.

Just then the Sector 7 alarms began to ring and alert the complex. A voice came over the speaker, "We have three civilians on the loose in the premises, so I need all hands on deck. Also we need to contain the interrogation room…there is a code black."

"That was Agent Parker's voice," Alice said. "What is code black?"

"It means," Agent Ramos said, "that whatever has happened to Agent Green is very serious and he needs to be quarantined. I know what the real problem with him is, and it was a close call for us to be near…it."

"*It?*" Mike asked as they ran through another corner while Agent Ramos shot his silencer at every security camera they neared.

"I'm not sure how it even got into the premises, but it latched onto Green. There is another kind of alien species that lives among Earth. They live in the shadows and have been around since the beginning of the universe. What are known as demons to the human race through religion, are actually beings from a distant world that use other bodies to live as solid, whole states. Agent Green has been possessed—taken over."

"For an agency that wants us to not know anything, you sure just divulged a lot," Alice snapped.

"I've been a spy for years, my dear," Agent Ramos said. "I am not on the NHR's side. I am merely here to make sure that our relations went smooth, but once Green and Parker's authority got too crazy and dangerous for Humanoids, I had to step in. Besides, my priority is to take Shane home with me."

"What?" Caroline said stopping in her tracks. "You are one of them?"

245

"Very observant of you," Agent Ramos smiled. "I am."

Agent Parker broke up their conversation with two military men at his side. He fixed his glasses on his face as he ran to them.

"Ahem," Agent Parker said with a murderous look, "Do I smell a traitor in our midst? I always knew you were off. You've always been so soft."

Agent Ramos raised his gun and pointed it at Agent Parker.

Both military men on Parker's side raised their guns with their fingers on the triggers.

"Hold off gents," Agent Parker said raising his own gun in defense. "He won't shoot me. He's too soft."

"There are kids in our presence, Landon," Agent Ramos said.

"They are in their twenties. Hardly kids...*Manuel*," Agent Parker sneered. "What kind of trick are you trying to pull? Definitely not that trigger."

"The work going on here needs to stop. It has become out of hand," Agent Ramos said.

"What did you do to Green? I had to get him heavily sedated to calm him down. He was attacking my men," Agent Parker asked.

"I'm afraid there is a force greater than you and I that has taken over him. He is a lost cause. If that force attacked me, it would be my death sentence," Agent Ramos said with great sadness.

"What do you mean?" Agent Parker said, lowering his gun slightly.

The speaker above them cackled. Then a microphone screeched, making everyone cover their ears.

"Code black! Total evacuation! We need everyone to head for the exits. All military personnel must be armed. Agent Green has gone mad!"

"What the hell?" Agent Parker said lowering his gun fully now.

Agent Ramos lowered his as well and spoke, "It's an alien race that has lived on this planet for a long time. It hid very well and we all know of it. Even civilians, but they know them as demons or devils or evil spirits. He's being possessed by an ancient specie. Bullets will only kill Green's body, but the Dark One will escape and latch onto the nearest living soul. The only way to kill it is if it finds a body that it cannot possess. Shane Baker is the only one that has evolved into something that can destroy this putrid, evil soul-sucking darkness."

"Are you for real?" Agent Parker said flabbergasted. "I mean I saw the look on his eyes and his voice was different. It wasn't him..."

"Parker, we are on the same side. My race and yours," Agent Ramos said.

"You mean to say…" Agent Parker began.

"I've walked among you. I am one of them. I am Humanoid. I've been placed here to keep watch and make sure your government did not do anything drastic out of panic or worry of threat. That's been starting to occur now," Agent Ramos explained. "One of my kind's goals is to keep your world order so that humans do not destroy themselves."

"This is absurd," Agent Parker gasped.

Several Sector 7 personnel came running down the hall shouting for them to move. "Ruuuuuuuuun! He's gone rogue!" An elderly scientist said, running faster than he had probably run in years.

In the distance, a figure was running behind them. Agent Ramos had a look of horror.

"My body cannot survive an encounter with the Dark One. Let's get out of here!" he said, and the he took the lead with Mike, Alice, and Caroline at his heel.

Agent Parker stood dumbfounded as his boss headed towards him. The military men had their guns pointed but awaited an order from Agent Parker.

Agent Green's eyes were dilated and he was growling. He was within a few feet from the men, when Agent Parker yelled, "Retreat. Do not shoot!"

The military men at his side turned around and ran in the direction that Agent Ramos and the others had run.

"Boss?" Agent Parker said in a terrified quiver.

"You foolish human," Agent Green's possessed body spoke, "You will never learn what lies beyond this planet."

There was a loud bang. Agent Ramos, Alice, Mike, and Caroline stopped in their tracks.
"Did they shoot Agent Green?" Mike wondered aloud.

Agent Parker stood over the dead body of Agent Green. He had shot him in the forehead. His blood began to spill out on all sides from his head, which was now facedown on the ground.

"We need to get out of here!" Agent Ramos ordered as the two military men who were at Agent Parker's side kept running towards the exit and passed them.

"Yeah, let's go," Alice agreed.

The rest of the run out of the Sector 7 building was much easier than they thought. It appeared as though most of the occupants had evacuated.

As they ran outside through an emergency exit door there were military, scientists, and confused pilots standing around in chaos. A few helicopters were hovering over the premises. The sun was beginning to set over the horizon.

"The two military men that had run out before them were addressing the crowd. Agent Parker and Agent Green are in there. Something is wrong with Green," a military officer said.

"He's dead!" shouted Agent Parker.

He had exited the building, the same way the others had, through the same emergency exit, with a gun in one of his hands and blood on his shirt.

"I'm not sure why he went rouge, but he nearly killed me. You can check the security cameras," Agent Parker told the crowd.

Everyone seemed to feel more at ease.

"What happened to him?" A scientist asked. "We saw him speaking in strange voice. His eyes were black."

"Agent Ramos here thinks he was possessed by a demon," Agent Parker laughed.

Agent Ramos shot Agent Parker a dark look.

"I need everyone to get back to work," Agent Parker ordered. "We need a clean up in there though." Agent Parker pointed at the building he had just come out of.

"Us four need to leave the premises immediately," Agent Ramos told Mike, Alice, and Caroline. "If a Dark One entered Sector 7, I wouldn't put it passed me that there are either more here or will be. They must know about Shane and that he is going to be coming to this general area."

"Won't Parker stop us?" Caroline asked.

"He's preoccupied, it seems," Agent Ramos said glancing over at Parker who was ordering some scientists around.

"I thought he was on the verge of believing you?" Alice asked.

"I thought so too," Agent Ramos said.

"Wait," Mike began. "Didn't you say that those demon things couldn't be killed by bullets?"

"I did, yes," Agent Ramos said, realizing where Mike was going with this.

"So do you think it latched onto Parker?" Mike said sounding nervous.

"It must have, but he seems so normal and doesn't sound different," Agent Ramos replied. "It confused me too. It might not have been able to latch onto a body. However, if it is hiding inside that building still, it will find a new home in someone else."

"We're lucky it's just one," Alice said.

"There are a few throughout this planet, no doubt. But I need to speak to my superiors on how we will handle them. Their threat has just come to our attention," Agent Ramos said. "I got a call from the company Shane is with that a Dark One attempted to possess him. I've just learned of this threat and now it will complicate matters. These Dark Ones are the reason my kind retreated to Earth…"

"Agent Ramos," Caroline started, "Why are you helping us humans escape?"

"You can call me Manuel," he responded. "And it is because Shane wanted you to be safe. It is the least we can do for the amount of help he will be to our people. As a matter of fact, I will call him and tell him the good news."

"You are Derek's ally, aren't you?" Alice asked Manuel and his nod signified a "yes."

Chapter Twenty-One:
Derek's Ally

Shane was sitting in the living of the farmhouse flipping through the television channels. Dimitri had taken Agatha's body to burry out in the fields. He asked that he do it alone, so Shane obliged and stayed inside.

The cell phone that Derek's ally Manuel had given him for direct contact solely between them, began to vibrate on the coffee table in front of the couch he was sitting on.

"Hello?" Shane answered.

"It's Manuel. Are you, Dimitri, and Agatha safe?" Manuel asked.

"Dimitri and I are fine, but Agatha was killed…" Shane began.

"What?!" Manuel sounded like he was on the verge of tears. "Shane what happened?"

"She was possessed by a Dark One," Shane replied.

"They've begun to attack us here at Sector 7 as well. They've been hiding from our kind and only preying on humans," Manuel said.

"Sector 7?" Shane said, astounded. "Are you actually inside?"

"Ah," Manuel said. "Your friends Mike, Caroline, and Alice are here with me."

Shane could hear them in the background yelling his name and saying that they were safe.

Shane sighed with relief at the sound of their voices and became teary eyed.

"Shane," Manuel went on, "I'm Agent Manuel Ramos. I was there the very night we took Derek to the landing site and he took those photos. I'm his ally that helped him get the message to you. I've got so much to tell you, but I would rather do that in person. I need you to get here to Sector 7. I am going to work on taking down Agent Parker in some way shape or form. I believe you and him are acquainted."

"All this time you have a been part of the NHR?" Shane said with shock.

"Only to keep an eye on them for the Elders," Manuel responded. "They were getting too nosy for their own good. I'll make sure your friends are safe. Unfortunately Peggy Mills is dead. I tried to make it stop. Agent Green, the head of the NHR, is also dead. We have reason to believe that Agent Parker might be possessed right now. One last note..."

There was silence for a few minutes before Manuel continued, sounding choked up.

"The colony that was on the chopper...they're dead. The military shot them down."

Tears flowed down Shane's face. Everyone was dying because they were trying to get him home safely. However, what was even harder for him to bear was the fact that his own father, Philip, was in that helicopter.

Shane gripped the black crystal necklace at the thought of his biological father he would never be acquainted with.

"Please explain everything to Dimitri. I must go," Manuel said, and he hung up on Shane.

Shane sat on the couch in silence going over all the information he had just learned, in his head. He pulled out the photo of himself that Derek left behind for him at the storage facility, and just analyzed it. When Dimitri walked into the house, he put the photo back in his jacket pocket. Dimitri walked to the kitchen sink without a word to Shane. He washed dirt off his hands and dried them on a kitchen towel.

He then walked into the living room and stared at Shane. Before Shane could stop himself, he was spilling out all the information about the death of the colony, Manuel's reveal of his identity, and the fact that his friends were safe.

Dimitri listened without saying a word, but his expressions gave away his feelings. His eyes widened in horror with every terrible set of news Shane had to tell.

There was a long, awkward silence before Dimitri finally spoke.

"Shane," he began, "this has all been a terrible ordeal, but do not be hard on yourself. You will be the one to ensure our kind lives on. I am sorry about your father."

"I wished he told me who he was when he gave me the necklace," Shane said while clenching the crystal tightly in his fists. "All this time I've wondered about my biological parents and, I never got to meet them."

"You will meet your mother," Dimitri said cracking a small smile.

"She's alive?" Shane said with great interest.

"Very much so," Dimitri answered. "She's an Elder."

"Is she the one that will explain everything to me?" Shane asked, now starting to understand the urgency for patience on learning about his past.

"Yes," Dimitri answered, putting his hand on Shane's shoulder. "It is her request to have the conversation with you once we get you to the landing site. Tonight will be the night Shane. I know Manuel will be able to keep Sector 7 from causing trouble for us. That is why he has been an integral part of our operation. Manuel is your mother's right hand man. He was also asked to work with Derek to leave behind a cryptic way to get the message of what you are, to you. Sadly, he was unable to prevent Derek's demise. Manuel could not give himself away. He's lived a hard life being under cover. When you meet him, you can discuss this more in detail. We need to get to the landing site. The sun is close to setting."

"How will we travel?" Shane asked.

"There's a truck we can use out back," Dimitri answered, gesturing towards the back door of the farmhouse.

Dimitri did one last sweep of the house to make sure they had not left anything behind. He took a few food items from the pantry and put them into a brown grocery bag.

"We may get hungry," Dimitri told Shane.

They walked out onto the backyard patio of the farmhouse. Near a tool shed was an old truck that was probably older than Shane.

"Can we drive that?" Shane asked with a raised eyebrow.

"It should work," Dimitri responded. "Get in. Let's high tail it out of here and head to Nevada.

It took a few tries of turning the truck's key to get the engine to start. When it finally did, they both buckled up and Dimitri drove the vehicle out of the farm and down the dirt path towards the interstate.

They drove in silence for about twenty minutes until Shane finally spoke.

"So Manuel," he began, "will be able to lead us safely to this, um, landing site?"

"I hope so," Dimitri said. "He hasn't tried calling you, correct? I mean since he last spoke to you and, uh, gave us the information about my friends."

"No," Shane replied. "Should I call him for an update?"

"No," Dimitri said. "He'll call if there is anything pertinent to be relayed to us. We have maybe another hour to go before we get near the vicinity of Sector 7. Since he's placed in the NHR he'll be able keep the military out of our way."

"It looks like it might start raining," Shane gestured towards the road ahead.

The clouds above looked threatening of a thunderstorm. There were flashes of lightning in the distance. The sun had already set and it was very dark.

"It looks too dark," Dimitri pointed out, "if you ask me."

"Yeah, I thought the sun just barely set?" Shane thought aloud.

What happened in the next moments felt like slow motion. As they sped down the highway, the clouds began to disappear. It looked as though the sky had cleared. It was pitch black, yet there were no stars visible.

"What's going on?" Dimitri mumbled.

"The streetlights have disappeared!" Shane said in shock. "In fact, I can't see anything but a few feet in front of us where the headlights of the truck end."

Shane heard a familiar whisper that appeared to be coming from his right side outside of the truck window. It was a whisper he had heard earlier that morning, however this time he was positive that he was wide-awake.

The whisper was in some language he could not understand. It gave him chills up and down his spine.

Dimitri began to slow down until the truck came to a halt. He looked over at Shane, who looked as though he was in a trance.

"Shane?" Dimitri asked shaking him. "Are you ok?"

Shane came back to his senses and the whispering stopped.

"Yeah," Shane said, sounding slightly nervous. "I think the Dark Ones are here. One was trying to possess me. I didn't think it could happen while I was awake."

"When you are asleep, you are easier to be overtaken," Dimitri said. "However, that does not mean they won't try while you are awake. They did with Agatha."

"When I was first being possessed everything went black, just like it is outside right now," Shane said.

"Holy crap!" Dimitri yelled pointing out towards Shane's passenger side window, making Shane jump.

While only visible for a few seconds, there was a shadowy frail looking figure. It was like grayish black smoke. A very distinct face was visible. It had red eyes and sharp teeth. The face looked furry, even if the figure itself was but a smoky, shadowy entity.

Shane's mind raced to the previous evening where he saw a similar face at his bedside before it attempted to overtake his body.

"Did you see that?" Dimitri said, clutching his chest. "I've never seen it reveal its face!"

The truck began to rattle and shake. Dimitri and Shane yelled in shock.

"Are we being lifted?" Shane said, noticing that the headlights ahead of them were no longer hitting pavement.

"The Dark Ones cannot lift an inanimate object like this!" Dimitri said with confusion.

Slowly, but surely, the view outside the window of the truck changed. It was no longer pitch black. They were in fact floating several feet off the ground, but now they could see the thunderstorm clouds and an empty highway below them with a row of unlit streetlights. Above them, however was a sight that Shane had only seen once.

Several more feet above them was a bright white orb floating and somehow using an invisible force to keep them afloat.

"The Elders…" Dimitri whispered, putting his hands to his mouth as tears swelled in his eyes.

"Are they taking us home?" Shane said.

"They just saved us from an attack of Dark Ones," Dimitri answered. "There must have been several."

The white orb began to raise itself higher into the sky and as it did so, the truck was slowly set on the highway below. Moments later, the orb had disappeared and the streetlights all turned back on instantaneously, leaving an orange glowing lit path ahead.

"Where did they go?" Shane asked.

"They just saved us," Dimitri assured him again. "However, they cannot risk getting overtaken by the Dark Ones. The orb is our only way home."

Shane's cell phone suddenly began to ring, making them both jump. Shane answered knowing that it would have to be Manuel on the other end.

"Shane," Manuel's voice said, "Put me on speaker."

Shane obliged.

"Dimitri...Shane. The Elders have communicated what just happened to you, to me. In order to get us out of Earth safely, we will need to fight off the Dark Ones. I am almost positive that they are on their way to Sector 7. There may be a few here already. If they are in this vicinity, the Elders will not be able to land and take us."

"Why didn't they just take me while they had us?" Shane asked.

"Because now they have to make sure that the Dark Ones do not stay on Earth to wreak havoc. They've been hiding and biding their time and now that they have realized we are almost on our way out, they may try to hitch a ride back to our world and are reveal themselves. Shane, listen carefully. You are the only being that cannot be possessed by them. If they do, they die. We need to devise a method to stop them before we can escape. The Elders will try to land again at three AM. It is just after seven PM right now. When I meet you in person we will go over a strategy. Understood?"

Shane thought about what he was just told in his head and figured there was no point to argue.

"Yes," he obliged.

Manuel hung up. There was a minute of silence before Dimitri turned the truck back on and began driving on down the interstate.

"So this was not in the plan, huh?" Shane said breaking the silence.

"I know," Dimitri responded, just staring out at the road.

"How can I single-handedly stop these shadows—the Dark Ones?" Shane asked.

Dimitri remained silent and then reached for the radio to turn it on. Shane figured he was still bothered by losing everyone from his colony and the frustration of an evil threat.

Back at Sector 7, Manuel, Mike, Caroline, and Alice were hiding in an empty conference room in one of the buildings. Manuel locked the door and then put his cell phone on the conference table. He breathed in deeply and stretched his arms.

"Is Shane ok?" Alice asked.

"He is," Manuel responded. "They were attacked by a swarm of Dark Ones. There is no doubt, now, that the entire population of Dark Ones on Earth are coming here now."

"Parker is under their powers," Mike said. "I saw his eyes. I know you are trying to deny it until he acts otherwise, but he has to be."

"I know Mike," Manuel said. "You're quite right. Parker is going to use his human influence to prepare the military to apprehend Shane. He will also make the human military start war with our kind."

"You mean we'll attack you guys?" Caroline spoke up.

"My Elders are aware that they are being mislead," Manuel said, "However this will jeopardize so much. My kind will have no choice but to fight back. Shane must not be killed. His genetic makeup has evolved from decades of generations to become what he is today. He's the only being that cannot be affected by the Dark Ones. The Dark Ones are the reason we were driven to Earth. It's a long story."

"How is Shane supposed to stop those things? How many are we up against?" Alice asked.

"Their number is unknown, but their population is definitely smaller than our Humanoid population. That reminds me. I need to get a message out to each colony of Knowings so that they can let the Unknowings know what they are," Manuel said, realizing he was saying words that left confused looks on his company. "Don't worry. This will not make much sense, but I need to make more calls. I'm going to step out to another room. Do not leave this room, please."

Manuel walked out and closed the door behind him.

Mike, Alice, and Caroline were left alone in the conference room. Caroline finally broke the silence.

"I should never have become involved with Shane."

"Really?" Alice spat. "You think it is his fault we are in this mess?"

"Well, yes," Caroline snapped.

"You dated him. You chose to help him solve the clues Derek left behind," Alice added. "You hired him as a freelancer at Fashion Rack. You—"

"Ladies!" Mike shouted. "Please, calm down. Not only are we all in jeopardy, but so is the rest of our planet. Whether we were involved or not, those demon things would have eventually attacked everyone."

"And the government? They now have tabs on us!" Caroline argued.

"The agency has fallen!" Mike retorted. "You saw that Agent Green was killed after he interrogated us. And now that other guy Parker is possessed, allegedly. And Manuel, well, he was an agent, yet a spy for the Humanoids. Right now everything is out of whack and the best you can do is shut up and stop placing the blame on Shane, because if he had it his way he would be working on a photo shoot and we could be going on with our lives!"

Alice grinned at Mike's words, and Caroline made a clicking noise with her teeth and folded her arms.

"Nothing else to add, dear?" Alice teased.

"I hope you two are happy together," Caroline said. "You and Shane."

"You tried to sell him out!" Alice yelled.

"They threatened my family!" Caroline responded through gritted teeth. "What would you have done?"

"Run away. I don't know," Alice spat back.

"Hey," Mike jumped in to stop the argument. "This place may not be safe. If those demons, or whatever they are, head this way, well, I don't want to be in their midst and find out."

"Then let's get the hell out of here," Caroline said.

Just then Manuel walked back in and put his cellphone in his pocket. He could feel the tension in the room.

"Everything alright?" He asked.

"They're just arguing," Mike said, gesturing over to Alice and Caroline who now had both their arms folded.

"You all are scared," Manuel said. "I can see it in your eyes. What you witnessed earlier with Agent Green frightened even myself. It has been decades since I came within that close proximity of a Dark One."

"Do you have any updates on Parker?" Mike asked.

"I do not," Manuel answered honestly. "I also cannot go near him. If the Dark One leaves Parker's body for mine, I will die."

"Would Parker die?" Caroline questioned. "I mean if the demon leaves him?"

"No," Manuel responded. "Humans are capable of surviving after being a host body, but mentally they could be unstable or go into shock."

"So," Alice chimed in. "You were Derek's ally? Why, if you were part of the NHR and one of the agents that brought him here five years ago to take photos of that ritual, could you not save him? Why did you use him to tell Shane a message that you could have done?"

"And blow my cover?" Manuel asked.

"You blew your cover to Derek," Alice said.

"Circumstances," Manuel said, taking a seat at the conference table. "I realized his memory had not been wiped by one of our staff doctors, and I knew he would be in danger. Derek was going through hardships resulting of the night we brought him to take photos. I confronted him one evening outside his house and explained to him who I was and that the NHR was tracking his every move. I told him to hide the photos but to make sure there was a way for Shane to get them in the future."

"But then," Mike butted in, "why couldn't you have just called Shane up and say, hey you are one of us? Isn't that what you just told your other kind to do over the phone call you stepped out to make?"

"Shane is the perfect evolution of our kind and human beings. I couldn't jeopardize him being apprehended by the government. Up until recently, I just told my colony about Shane. Now all of them, except Dimitri who is with Shane now, are dead. But a few years ago, during this fiasco with Derek, I could not tell Shane what he was by orders of my Elders. The truth is…the reason why I had Derek—and it was not mere fate he was the photographer that happened to have known Shane—scatter about these clues was not only to thwart the NHR and protect Shane's identity, but to—"

There was a series of yells coming from outside of the building they were in. Alice and Caroline jumped in shock. Mike pushed himself away from the table on his chair.

"What was that?" Caroline said, sounding nervous.

"I will go investigate. You all stay here," Manuel said.

"What do you think the reason Shane went on a wild goose chase was? We were just about to find out!" Mike said, irritated by the inconvenience of the distraction outside.

"I honestly think," Alice said, "that it is way beyond our comprehension and whatever his Elders' plans or knowledge is, I don't even think we will ever know."

"He was close to spilling the beans," Mike added.

"I say we make a run for it," Caroline blurted as she stood up from her chair. "We are humans and I do not want to be mixed with these...these aliens!"

"They are people too!" Alice snapped. "They are individuals, even if they are not from Earth. Besides the Humanoids are half-human. Are you racist now? Manuel saved us."

Mike sniggered at Alice's "racist" remark. Alice shot him a dark look. She was not in the mood.

"I'm getting out of here. Peace out," Caroline said, and without a backward glance, she ran out of the conference room and down the hall.

"Well," Alice said turning to Mike, "I won't miss her."

"You both have always had some serious tension," Mike pointed out. "But maybe she's right. We need to leave these premises."

"I'm sticking by Manuel," Alice said. "He can take care of us."

"How?" Mike asked. "If he gets possessed he's a goner. You heard him say it. We can survive on our own."

"Yeah but then we won't have free will," Alice retorted back.

Manuel came running into the room out of breath. As soon as he caught wind, he closed the door and turned to Mike and Alice.

"Wh-where's Caroline?" he panted.

"She ran out to try and escape!" Alice said, smirking.

"Foolish girl!" Manuel said reaching for the door to make an exit. Then he changed his mind midway through walking out. "Never mind. Parker is in fact possessed. He's barking orders for the military to use every weapon they have at the sight of Shane or my Elders' vessel. It also appears that a few of the bigger and stronger military men have also been possessed. More Dark Ones have arrived. There is a helicopter on top of this building. It's risky, but it might be worth a shot to escape in it. Parker will think it's the military preparing to attack. To the roof!"

Alice and Mike nodded, and they followed Manuel out of the conference room and into the hall.

"This way!" Manuel ordered and they followed him into a stairwell. "Just up a few flights and we'll be on top."

They made their way up four flights until they finally reached the top of the building.

"You didn't finish telling us the story about the clues Derek left behind for Shane," Mike panted as he closed the stairwell door behind him and walked out into the cold desert night.

"Not important right now!" Manuel yelled over the sounds of military vehicles exiting the base and Parker's voice booming from the loud speakers.

"All hands on deck," Parker's voice boomed and echoed throughout the Sector 7 base. "Shane Baker is to be taken out. He is a Humanoid. We are going to be under attack by them tonight as retaliation for taking down other Humanoids in that helicopter. I order you to use every ammo and manpower possible when you see the white light. This is my command as newly appointed Agent-In-Charge."

Manuel's eyes widened and he said, "There's no way I can communicate to the Elders now that Parker has put this base on lock down. We have a device they left for the humans which is how we have communicated, or shall I say, how humans communicated with my Elders for years. That device is in Parker's office where he is shelled up right now."

"I was curious about how you all communicated. Non-Human Relations. Those were the relations?" Alice asked.

"Yes," Manuel said. "Our kind has been in contact with the NHR agency since the Roswell crash. And I do not have time to explain more on that matter."

"Well you can communicate with Shane," Mike said pointing at Manuel's pocket. "Call him and warn him he needs to avoid this area at all costs."

"Yes, good thinking Mike," Manuel said.

He reached for his phone and then dropped it in shock. He was staring transfixed at the distance.

Even as dark as it was in the desert, it was visible ahead. A giant mass of black smoke was heading towards the base.

"The entire population of Dark Ones are before us," Manuel raised his hand to gesture towards the cloud. "They will manifest themselves on the first human they can get to. Parker will then have even more control of the military."

"He's not Parker though," Alice pointed out. "Perhaps we should refer to him as a Dark One leader or something."

"Alice, this is not time to be politically correct," Mike said finally taking his eyes off the cloud to look over at her.

"Sorry," Alice replied.

Chapter Twenty-Two:
The Tale of the Elders

Manuel bent over and reached for his cell phone. The screen had shattered and went blank. He pushed the buttons in frustration. They lit up, but the screen was still blank.

"Damn," he said in a worried tone. "I can't scroll through my contacts. I do not have Shane's number in my memory. There's no way we can communicate with him now."

"Maybe he will call us," Mike said sympathetically, however his eyes were also transfixed on the big, black smoky mass that was swirling its way like a cloud towards the base.

Dimitri was hitting over one hundred miles per hour on the interstate as they crossed into Nevada.

"We'll be there in a heartbeat," Dimitri assured Shane.

"If you don't kill us first," Shane said, grasping onto his seatbelt. "Slow down, will you? We may get pulled over."

"The law is the least of our concern. The swarm of Dark Ones nearly engulfed us whole. The Elders are obviously in the vicinity waiting for the right time to land, but noticed we were in danger and saved us," Dimitri added.

"Can they not just shoot lasers at the Dark Ones or something?" Shane asked, feeling his question was very absurd.

"You watch too many movies," Dimitri said looking over at Shane and smiling in full for the first time since Agatha had died. "Our ship is not equipped with weapons. It runs on a powerful light that protects it. The Dark Ones hide in the shadows, you see. The light weakens them, so I have been told. Our home planet had no star. We lit our planet with the elements our world is made of. That black crystal you have—the one your father gave you—well, it's really something special.

"So you are saying," Shane began, "that in order to destroy them, we need light. So why not keep them at bay until the sun rises? And what about this crystal?"

"They will hide in the corners of buildings and anywhere there are shadows. They can latch onto bodies to survive the sun, but eventually they will become weak and retreat indoors," Dimitri explained. "Your suggestion would be great, but keeping an entire population of Dark Ones at bay, is no easy feat. As for the crystal, which our planet is made up of, it is able to emit light. One wouldn't think so due to the nature of the crystal's dark color. The crystal draws energy from very distant stars, moons, and planets from hundreds of light years away through and invisible force. Once it has collected enough light it begins to glow. Our ship is powered by crystal and the power allows it to fly. Just like a humans would go to a gas station to fuel their vehicle for travel, all we need to do is fly near a star, moon, or planet to quickly make the ship glow by absorbing its light. That is how we can travel distances at light speed, because our power is, well, light. Being that the sun and Earth's moon are near, our ship has had enough power to last for now."

"So then why couldn't the light stop the Dark Ones once and for all, when they saved us?" Shane asked. "And how did they cause trouble on the home planet?"

"Your Elder mother," Dimitri went on, "will explain the history and how the Dark Ones conquered the crystal planet we lived on. I was young when it happened, so I do not remember all the details. But the reason why our ship's light can only fend off the Dark Ones, and not kill them, is because our ship's crystal is exhausted of its original power. Think of it as a light bulb. When you first screw it in, the light is very bright and powerful. As time goes by it wanes and begins to dull until it eventually burns out. Our ship is a dull bulb that will eventually stop working. Consider it a dying battery. Our Elders actually feel it will be soon and that is why they need to return to our home planet with you to undo the damage to it."

"Where are the Elders living? It sounds as if the home planet is unlivable," Shane said.

"A neighboring planet," Dimitri answered. "To keep watch on our old one. I've told you too much already, but your mother will better explain all this and the circumstances."

"Dimitri," Shane said while touching the crystal necklace, "has this ever been lit up?"

"No," Dimitri said. "Your father has kept it drawing energy from the sun and moon for years. The necklace is made of gold, which is another element we have on our planet. The gold keeps the crystal from glowing. He's been harboring its power for an emergency. My guess is that's why he gave it to you."

"So I can use it to stop the Dark Ones?" Shane said sounding like there was finally hope.

"Theoretically," Dimitri said, "But its never been tested. My hope is that since you can withstand the attacks of the Dark Ones, and now wield the only piece of crystal we have in possession that is an unused light bulb, so to speak, then perhaps you alone have a fighting chance. If I attacked a Dark One with it, I could hold them off for a bit, but eventually one will take over me and destroy it while killing my body."

"This all seems so complicated?" Shane said.

"Earth is a complicated world, Shane," Dimitri said. "Ours is just a little bit more complex."

Shane examined the crystal closely.

Could this small piece of rock actually channel a light powerful enough to destroy the demons known as the Dark Ones? He thought to himself.

"I'm ready," Shane said. "To stop them."

"I know," Dimitri smiled. "Just a few days ago we had no idea the Dark Ones had been manifesting on Earth. And by 'we' I meant us Humanoids. Manuel has communicated to me, that he has known about them as well as the Elders, but they did not want us to live in worry on Earth. The Dark Ones are weaker alone here.

However, now that they have joined together as a swarm, their power is much greater and all they have to do is take you out and their job is done."

"If that happens," Shane began, "can another Humanoid with my ability to survive them be born?"

"I do not know," Dimitri said truthfully. "I'll tell you a little bit more about our home planet. A group of Dark Ones have manifested there. I think you can figure out how you would be useful back home. Philip, your father, was planning to give you the crystal once you met with the Elders. I'm so glad he gave it to you when he did. It's almost as if he knew he would die in that crash."

Shane and Dimitri were silent for the next few minutes. It was obvious that Dimitri had revealed more about his reason for being, than Shane probably should have been given before he met the Elders. Shane felt that it would make things easier to process once he did meet them though.

"Ah, it looks cloudy again," Dimtri sighed. "It will probably rain and make things trickier."

Shane looked ahead and saw the dark thunderstorm clouds threatening to open up with rain. There was lightning streaking across the desert, revealing a marvelous view of the canyon for a second before everything went back to dark.

"Lightning," Dimitri said. "One thing we do not have back home in our planet. It's such a marvelous natural wonder that never ceases to amaze me."

"I was hoping for clear skies," Shane said defeated. "I wanted to draw more power from the full moon."

"I think you'll be ok though," Dimitri said, although he did not sound very sure of his statement.

"Hey!" Shane said so loudly, that Dimitri nearly drove off the road and onto the sand by surprise. "Look over into the clouds."

This time the light coming from the clouds was not lightning. It was a bright white orb that was floating out of it. It was zooming towards the truck Dimitri and Shane were in.

"Are they coming to get us?" Shane asked in shock.

"There's something wrong. They usually don't come here this early in the night unless of an emergency like with what happened a few hours ago," Dimitri said checking his watch. "They also have been trying to keep out of the public eye and this is a highway we are on."

"You know what," Shane said, "the light on the orb is flickering."

The orb was in fact flickering like a light bulb that was about to go out. The light the orb was emitting was much fainter than Shane remembered.

A few hours ago during the attack of the Dark Ones, the orb looked bright, but then again they were engulfed in such darkness, that any light would have looked significantly brighter.

"Just like I said earlier," Dimitri said. "Their power is running out. They must have drawn so much power to save us earlier. I don't think we'll be going home today. Or ever."

The white orb was almost directly over the truck. The light it emitted lit the area for about a mile wide. As soon as it was directly over the truck, it stopped.

"Now what?" Shane thought aloud.

His question was answered seconds later. The truck, for the second time that evening, was lifted off the ground and up into the sky. The light was so blinding that Shane had to cover his face. He closed his eyes and felt himself be lifted off the truck's seat. His seatbelt had unbuckled itself.

"Shane?" said a very soft female voice.

Shane felt as though he was dreaming. He felt awake, yet his body seemed to have still been asleep. He could not move it. He told his brain that he needed to get up, but his legs were still on the floor, which was pearly white.

"Shane, wake up," said the same soft-spoken voice.

Shane opened his eyes and first noticed he was in an area that had no walls, floor, or roof. Everything was bright white. There was not a speck of dirt or anything to disturb the perfect whiteness of the area he was in.

Dimitri was sitting next to him, wide-awake and smiling. He nodded his head towards the direction that was behind Shane.

The next sight surprised him so much, he let out an inaudible gasp of surprise. Before him were three slim figures. They were small, perhaps the size of children. Their skin looked smooth. It was a whitish grey. Shane's first thought was their skin looked whiter due to the room they were in.

The three thin figures all looked alike with metallic silver suits that covered the torso and legs and just the shoulders. The sleeves cut off at the shoulders and arched into a shoulder pad-like shape. They had peaceful looking faces, but they were not human or like anything he had seen in real life. He had, however, seen these faces in photographs. Although, in the photographs, the beings before him had a greenish tinge due to the night vision settings of the camera they were taken with.

Their faces were oval and looked bigger as if not proportional to their bodies. They had large black almond eyes with eyelids that would occasionally blink. They had no definable nose, just two small slits. Their mouths were a thin line with no noticeable lips.

The figure in the middle had stretched out its hand to Shane. Shane reached for it instinctively. The creature was warm. He could feel a pulse through the hand as if somewhere in its frail-looking body, was a heart.

"Are you…" Shane began staring at the creature of the hand he was holding.

"I am," the creature nodded. "I am your mother. I go by the name Genesis."

For years Shane had always wondered who his biological mother was. However, looking at the alien before him, he was skeptical that she could even remotely be related to him. She was nowhere near close to looking human.

"There's so much I want to ask," Shane said.

"I know. And I owe it to you to finally tell you. Dimitri has told me that he has filled you in a bit about where you are from and the circumstances regarding it, but I will give you the full story. It is, I, as an Elder, and as your mother, who has the privilege to share this in full. I will begin from the beginning and you will listen. Then we can talk about the next steps. Unfortunately, when we saved you earlier this evening from the swarm of Dark Ones, we used up most of our left over power. Our ship is no longer fit to travel back to Threa, our home planet. It is uncertain how much longer we will be able to hover, but we are slowly heading towards the landing site. We will not be able to get too close, since the Earth military is preparing to attack. The Dark Ones have entered the premises of that base and have begun to prey on human souls. I have not heard from Manuel. I fear the worst."

Shane swallowed hard thinking about his friends that were still trapped at Sector 7.

"I'm ready to learn," Shane said, finally deciding it was time for answers.

"I will tell you the tale," Genesis spoke. She began the story:

"In the entire wide universe, it would be unwise to think that solely only one race of species exists in its vast expanse. Millions of years ago there were more different civilizations scattered across the cosmos. Some planets hosted animals, like those here on Earth, and other planets hosted intelligent beings capable of creating a civilization. Of course, the universe is very large and as time passed, species died out.

The planet Earth was a rare case of a planet that was inhabitable for millions of years. Most planets are not able to keep life because they became too cold and eventually became a dying rock.

271

Our kind discovered Earth millions of years ago. My ancestors found the planet inhabited by giant reptiles. Humans today call them dinosaurs. The creatures were primitive and just too large. They were unable to live in harmony, as some of the different species would fight each other. Consider modern human history where different races faced segregation and wars. The same was true for the dinosaurs, however it was much more vicious with them.

Our ancestors wanted to inhabit the planet, but it was not safe because the wild creatures were a danger to our lives. Eventually our government decided that they were undeserving, due to lack of intelligence, of ruling the planet, so we sent a meteor to crash onto Earth to wipe them out into extinction.

Please understand that my ancestors, although intelligent, did not hone the morals our people do now. It was a terrible decision they made, but it did eventually benefit for the birth of human life.

Human beings came to existence on Earth many, many years ago. When we came back to visit Earth, after hearing about how it was wiped out by our ancestors, we were surprised to find that more life had sprung up. To this day we do not know if it was something in the meteor that caused humans and life to spawn after the extinction of the dinosaurs, or something even more powerful than us that once visited Earth. Perhaps there is a higher power that human religion speaks of, although we do not understand. That mystery is unanswered to humans and ourselves.

Regardless, we studied the humans. The 'cavemen' as they are called in human history, were very primitive and barbaric. They were not very intelligent. For years, we visited them and brought them gifts. We gave them fire, the Pyramids of Egypt, Stonehenge, crop circles, the belief in Gods, and so much of early human history. We slowly shaped them. With time, they began to advance and grow. They had their own wars, and slowly began to invent their own means of travel across the oceans. They domesticated animals and harvested crops. These traits were a natural cause and effect from our small push in human history.

We loved the human race. They were becoming intelligent, but they were so behind in technology that our race has had for millions of years. We are a very old civilization, mind you, therefore we did have a large head start.

Humans started to become smarter and their technologies grew. They'd see us flying in the skies. We've always been the very silent brothers to humans. We were just watching over them, because their planet was full of resources. Of course, none of them were useful to us, but in case other species came to harvest on Earth, we knew we could protect them.

Then, tragedy happened. Back at our home planet, Threa, we had been noticing that several of our kind were dying of unexplained reasons. Slowly, our numbers were being wiped out until, a few of us, myself included, witnessed what we now call the Dark Ones.

The Dark Ones are the oldest species of the universe that existed at a time when there was nothing but darkness. As the universe grew they began to feast on newly formed beings. They avoided the light though, so they were never seen.

However, one night I saw them. The Dark Ones killed my parents...your grandparents. They showed their faces for the first time to us and I knew what we were dealing with. The Dark Ones were a legend told by our ancestors who had faced them in another galaxy millions of years ago. Somehow, they found their way into our world and realized that we were a very intelligent group of beings that they could feed on. However, when they possessed our kind, our bodies would die quickly. The Dark Ones grew strong from us, but they had no bodies.

Threa is made of a black crystal element. Its only known existence is on Threa. The Dark Ones realized how powerful it was when I, myself, used a crystal sword I once owned, to push them away with the light of the distant stars. The light could kill them. Thus, they disappeared into nothing. They ceased to be, when a powerful light hit them.

The Dark Ones realized how much of a threat the crystal was, and they created a giant shadow of their bodies all around Threa. It blocked off any light from the distance, which would normally penetrate into our crystals, making the crystals useless rocks. Within days, most of our population had died out, except five of us."

Genesis turned around and pointed at the two other Elders. Then continued.

"Behind me are Renner and Starro. My younger brothers. Your uncles. I had two other brothers, Jax and Steg, whom eventually died later. Since I was the only female of our kind left, I knew my responsibility to reproduce was necessary if we were to get our numbers back up. The only issue was that we could not mate with blood family. The same applies for humans. We'd be defected.

Us five escaped Threa and hid on a planet in a nearby galaxy. Our ship, thankfully was able to soak in light from distant sources, however, it would be no match for the Dark Ones. They would eventually be able to penetrate our ship and destroy us. We would be extinct and the Dark Ones would forever continue their travels of taking out species across the galaxies.

Almost every single species that ever existed in the galaxy has died because of the Dark Ones. We are not sure who or what else is left out there except humans.

The Dark Ones had eventually found their way to Earth, but they were not able to overtake human bodies. They could possess and control them, but not much else. Plus, they were weak during the daylight as the sun is really close to planet Earth. Only a small number of them roamed Earth for years to come.

Most of the Dark Ones stayed on Threa to guard the crystal because they were aware that five of us had escaped and did not want to risk becoming extinct, in case we found a way to stop them.

Finally, I had an idea. I figured that we should study humans. Over time in the early 1940s in human years, we began to 'abduct' humans for testing purposes to see what it was about them that made them immune to the possession of a Dark One.

We could never find the answer. Starro theorized that it was something to do with the human belief in religion. Whether there is such a thing as a human God or something more powerful

274

and spiritual, we do not know, nor do we question it anymore. We accept that while humans have been much more primitive than us, they have strengths that we will never have.

Well, I had the idea to use the human DNA and mix it with a piece of our DNA. All five of us mixed five different human DNAs in a test tube, if you will, with ours.

Humanoids were created. They came out looking like humans and had every characteristic and trait. The only thing was, they could not withstand a Dark One attack.

For years we had created our Humanoids to slowly develop and walk among humans as humans. We were among them living and learning their ways. Blending in. We knew that after years of walking among humans, one child Humanoid would be born that would posses both our genes and also the human gene to survive a Dark One attack. Our theory was that this Humanoid would be able to kill the Dark Ones. Our plan was to have an army of this Humanoid race to bring back to Threa to fend of the Dark Ones that currently have taken over our home.

Sadly, on a trip to visit Earth, Jax and Steg's ship ran out of light and crashed in what is called Roswell, New Mexico. The mini ship was just a smaller ship that was an emergency pod for our current vessel, which you are in now.

Both of them were killed, although Jax lived a week after. The human government was all over the wreckage and our technology, which eventually helped human technology advance tenfold. Before we knew it, humans were already traveling to space. But just barely.

Us three final Elders eventually chose Manuel, one of our current Humanoids, to join forces with the government agency to create the Non-Human Relations agency. He was our spy to make sure humans did not overreact after this entire mess. We eventually got them to keep everything quiet and out of the public knowledge so as not to cause chaos with our Humanoid population. Most Humanoids, however, did not even know they, themselves, were of alien decent.

As the years would go by, we communicated with the NHR occasionally. We shared technology and knowledge. They used the information for their own scientific purposes. Only a handful of agents were in the know. Sector 7 was built so that we could visit in private with them and have talks out in the desert. We gave them a communication tool to keep in contact with them."

Genesis pointed to a metallic silver cone object with a point that was about one foot tall. Shane wanted to ask how it worked, but Genesis pressed on with her story.

"The humans were so curious about us, and we knew they were also scared. We were not a threat, but human nature told them to keep the peace, as we were way more advanced in technology. I never told the NHR the part where our kind was nearly extinct and if they wiped us three out, we'd all be gone.

So Shane, I've told you a bit about our history. Now comes a little fast forward into your history."

Shane shifted a bit. He was still sitting on the ground. All the information he heard made the beginning of his summer feel like a fairytale. It was almost as if his part time job at the camera shop or his Malibu house were just a made up dream.

"Go on," Shane said, nodding.

"I will," Genesis said, "So on Earth, we finally grew to a very good size population of Humanoids. We selected some of the older Humanoids to gather colonies of the over thirty year old Humanoids to prep them for their departure to the planet where we hid before coming to Earth after fleeing Threa. These groups called themselves Knowings.

We would slowly take a few back so that they could begin growing a community outside Earth and get used to life away from humans.

Any Humanoid under thirty was an Unknowing, and did not know they were walking among humans as being something other than human, so that they could grow in human culture and adaptation, thereby enabling them to bring those traits with them to our temporary planet outside of Earth. Once an Unknowing reached thirty, their colony master Knowing would bring them to us and we would tell them all, just like we are doing with you. However, at twenty three human years, you are an exception to our normal operations and we'll get into that next."

276

"Why was Peggy still an Unknowing?" Shane asked. He had a million questions, but for some reason this was the first that popped into his head.

"An experiment to see if after fifty human years, she would be more useful and wiser to the Humanoid Knowings. We'll never know now that she has been killed and had to find out what she was before we could tell her."

Shane nodded that he understood, and he looked over at Dimitri who put his finger to his mouth to signal for Shane to stop asking questions and listen. He obliged.

"You were born on this ship," Genesis continued her story. "And when you were, we knew you were different. You had Philip's genes and mine. My understanding is that you briefly met him yesterday. We are sad about his loss.

It took several generations of Humanoids for the perfected evolution, which is you, to be born. I could sense that your body was much stronger than mine. A mother would know. I knew that if a Dark One attacked you, you would be unharmed. We sent you off into the world as an Unknowing child, where you were adopted into your human family. You would grow into an adult and eventually when you were old enough, be our warrior against the Dark Ones."

"You were discovered, however, by a Dark One, one night. It sensed your Humanoid presence and went to your window one night, as a kid. You may or may not remember. I know you do remember when it came back to see you as an adult not too long ago from today. You were confused by it. You just saw a dark figure at your window and it was gone before you could put on your glasses. It never attacked because it was fearful and unsure what would happen. Of course, we learned yesterday, that when it finally did try to possess you, you weakened it so much that it had to latch onto Agatha. Both died.

Now it is my understanding that, that very Dark One had told its population about you just recently, which is why we are in a predicament. But I'm getting ahead of myself with that story.

Five years ago we took you to do a ritual at the landing site near that military base. The ritual was to test you out among a few other Unknowings and see if you were the one that we've been waiting for. Our tests proved you were.

Meanwhile, Manuel was with the other agents and Derek. We Elders were not aware of this at the time, but Manuel was devising a plan that was dangerous and rebellious, yet to this day I am thankful he took this risk that we otherwise would have turned our shoulders to.

It was obvious that you, Shane, were immune to Dark Ones after the testing, but we still would have twelve years before we would come to tell you who you are. Manuel wanted to expedite the process on the suspicion that the Dark Ones were aware of you as well. Which they were since they had visited you as a child. Manuel did not alert us, in fear that we would abandon Earth and leave them behind. It was a mistake in his thinking as that was not what we would have done.

Manuel is bound by our code. If he were to directly tell you what you were, we would find out and he would have been punished. His punishment would have been the end of his Humanoid life. We live by code just as we had when we all thrived on Threa.

He eventually met up with Derek when he found out Derek still knew about that night he took those photographs. He had actually chosen Derek as the government's photographer since he was a friend of your human family. He knew he would recognize you from the photos.

Derek eventually became paranoid and scared. Manuel revealed himself to Derek and after Derek calmed down and soaked in the information, he told him to create a set of clues to leave for you, so that he could communicate what you are, without Manuel, technically revealing that information. A nice loophole he found.

The other part of the clues and that scavenger hunt you went through, was because it would keep you safe from the NHR, but unfortunately they became aware of you after being recognized one day, and Manuel came forward with what he had done.

We nearly punished him, but he then revealed to us the Dark Ones were also aware of you. However, they were keeping their distance for now."

"So that is why I had to go find all these clues left behind for me? It was not just to thwart the NHR, but it was to thwart you, the Elders, as well."

Shane finally had the answers he had been pondering since the day he had been given that audio CD, or just the other day when he saw the picture of himself in that ritual when he was eighteen.

"Yes," Genesis replied, "Manuel made a decision for your safety that we would have easily overlooked and ignored. Now that you are aware of what you are and the importance of your existence to our kind, we have to prepare for a fight with the Dark Ones."

"Genesis," Dimitri chimed in. "But this ship. It cannot be powerful enough to get to Threa."

"This is true," Genesis said. "However, Philip's crystal, which Shane now has, may be our only hope. My theory is that it will wield enough light to destroy the Dark Ones, if used correctly, and restore power to our ship for one last spark, to get us back to Threa."

"Risky," Dimitri mumbled.

"Anyways," Genesis continued, "Manuel tried to keep Derek safe, but it would involve giving himself away as a Humanoid to the NHR, and we could not afford to blow our cover. They knew there were Humanoids that lived on Earth, but they had no names or faces of who they were. The NHR had been trying for years to find at least one, and once they saw that photo of you that Derek took, they had a face. It was unfortunate that Agent Parker saw you when you were investigating Derek's friend Candy's home. That is when Manuel came forward and told us. I let you go on with your journey to learn who you were on your own as another experiment of wit, courage, and intelligence. You succeeded. This gave me great happiness because I knew you would be able to take on the mission that lies before you. We must—"

Genesis stopped talking abruptly. Renner and Starro exchanged looks with Genesis, but they had no distinguishable facial features like humans or Humanoids. Shane could not figure out what the looks were. He guessed they were worried glances.

"What's happening?" Dimitri asked.

"Our light has run out," Genesis said, clasping her hands together.

There was a humming sound that Shane had just noticed. Within seconds the humming ceased. The white room's walls became a dull grey and transparent. He could see through the walls outside and saw they were high above the canyons and below was the vast desert.

The ground was slowly getting closer and closer. The Elder's ship was plummeting towards the Nevada desert.

"We're going to crash!" Shane shrieked.

Chapter Twenty-Three:
The Landing Site

Manuel, Mike, and Alice were being held in a cell just below Agent Parker's office. Parker was pacing up and down the cell outside with an evil grin on his face. There were several military men standing still just up and down and the hall flanking their large guns.

Half an hour earlier the entire base of Sector 7 had been taken over by the entire population of Dark Ones. They flew onto the base, showing their ugly furry-looking, smoky faces and sharp fangs. Several military and scientist personnel had been taken over. Their eyes had a dark glazed look due to dilated pupils.

The rest of the people that had not been possessed, because the Sector 7 personnel population had outnumbered the Dark Ones, were being attacked by their possessed colleagues and killed.

It was a dark sight on the base. Bodies were slain everywhere. Those that were possessed were picking up weapons and heading to every corner and wall of the complex to prepare for an attack and a word from Parker, who was being possessed by the Dark One leader.

Back in Parker's holding cell a girl walked in to greet Parker.

"Master," she said. "All the humans that were not taken over, have been killed. The only ones remaining are those two and that Humanoid."

She turned and pointed at Manuel, Alice, and Mike. To their shock, they realized that Caroline had been possessed and that girl that walked in, was her.

"Oh my God," Alice gasped.

"She should have stayed with us," Mike said.

"If she did," Alice responded, "she would have ended up in this prison cell with us."

"Hope is not lost as long as Shane stands his ground," Manuel hoped, but he sounded defeated.

Agent Parker thanked Caroline and walked over to their cell.

"I am the leader of the Dark Ones," Agent Parker announced. "I go by Noom. Thought we were a legend, did you Humanoid?"

Manuel gave him a dark look and responded, "You can kill me now, but you do not stand a chance."

"Ha!" Noom laughed. "Your silly experiment on Earth with these humans? I admit the human's bodies are quite strong. I enjoy the fact that I can possess this one and it won't die."

"Savages," Manuel spat.

Noom just grinned and winked back at Manuel. Caroline walked up to him and said, "Master, we found another human trying to enter our premises. They are bringing him now. You might wish to speak to him."

Just then, a few guards were dragging in an older man in a lab coat. It was Dr. Felix Morgan.

"Ah," Noom said. "What is his purpose?"

One of the guards answered, "He worked here. He said he would tell us where to find the boy Shane if we spare his life. He saw him not too long ago."

Mike and Alice exchanged nervous looks.

"Nep, possess him for the truth!" Noom ordered.

Caroline's body went rigid and began to shake. For a second a black shadow escaped her mouth and went straight into

Dr. Morgan's mouth. Caroline's body fell to the ground, quivering. She opened her eyes in shock.

Dr. Morgan was released by the guards and stood up. "Master, his mind tells me he was lying."

Noom turned over to Manuel, Alice, and Mike. "One of our gifts is that we hold the knowledge and language of the individuals we take over. That is how we can speak this human tongue. English. We also get to know their minds and histories so that if we ever need to live their lives as a spy or for secret missions, we can. Isn't that what you did, pretending to be part of this U.S. government agency for several years? We've lived among humans too, Humanoid. And to think, humans thought they needed to be exercised due to demonic possession! If only they knew that the oldest living creatures of the universe were taking over them. Not some demon."

"Posses me now," Manuel said. "I know you want to kill me like you did my colony."

"I want to keep you around as bait," Noom responded. "Besides, I find it interesting to speak with you. Do tell me, Manuel. Where are the other colonies around this planet? We will eventually find them and terminate their existence."

"They are aware and will formulate a plan to fight your population!" Manuel snapped.

"Sir!" One of the guards that brought in Dr. Morgan yelled.

"Yes?" Noom said, turning to face him.

"We just got word that the Elder's ship is crashing into the desert from the sky. They've ran out of power."

Manuel's eyes widened in horror.

Noom turned to face Manuel, "Looks like the final three Elders will become extinct."

Noom turned to face his guards. "Let me know when the ship has hit the ground. We'll gather the remains. I still want to make sure we keep an eye out for the boy." Noom walked into a nearby room and carried out a metallic silver cone. "I'm unable to contact their vessel. They really did lose power."

Shane was gripping the crystal necklace as the ship plummeted down towards the desert. From his point of view, it seemed the sand below would be soft enough to cushion the fall, but it was wishful thinking.

The three Elders embraced each other in preparation for their demise. It felt as though everything was moving in slow motion. There must have been some kind of gravitational force that was keeping each individual inside the ship from sliding to the side of the ship that was pointing towards the ground.

In fact, Shane was able to stand up. It did not feel like they were falling. All was still inside, but the view through the transparent walls contradicted that feeling. The ship fell through some clouds. Shane noticed in the distance on the ground, was a lit area. It was Sector 7. Just beyond that were more clouds and lightning.

Dimitri closed his eyes and gripped the air, as there was nothing else to grab in the empty room. Shane looked above him and through the transparent roof he could see the sky. The moon was peaking through the clouds. Below him, he saw that there was a large canyon getting closer and closer. They would crash into a mountainous area.

"That's where Derek took the pictures, huh?" Shane said aloud. "Just like in the story I heard about that night. How ironic that we are about to crash into it."

Dimitri opened his eyes to look and Shane. He nodded in agreement.

Shane continued to grip his necklace. Without thinking about what he was doing, he ripped the gold chain off his neck. The crystal was freed from the golden clasp.

The Elders opened their eyes and all looked at Shane, then at the black crystal. The most beautiful moment that Shane had ever experienced in his life happened next.

The crystal began to glow white. It became brighter and brighter. A stream of light was coming from the moon and causing the crystal to glow so bright that it looked as though a small orb of light was in Shane's hands. It felt warm to the touch.

The Elders put their hands to their mouths in surprise.

"Of course...the crystal!" Genesis said, apparently having forgotten that Shane had the last free piece of crystal from their planet.

The orb in Shane's hand grew bigger. The descent of the ship to the ground began to slow. Genesis spoke up again.

"Shane, allow me."

Genesis reached for the crystal. Shane handed it over. Within seconds of her touching it, the ship had stopped falling and was floating a hundred feet above the canyon where it nearly crashed.

"You use your mind to control the crystal technology," Genesis continued. "I'm having it guide us to the landing site where you were supposed to meet us the other evening. It is also the place where you had the ritual done to you that proved to us that you were in fact the one."

The ship was slowly lighting back up, but it was still much duller than Shane had remembered it the first time he saw it on his road trip to Las Vegas.

Finally, they were in an open area of the desert. Below was a large crater. The ship landed softly in the middle of it. Shane looked just beyond the stretch of land and could see the lit area that was Sector 7.

"Here," Genesis said handing Shane the black crystal back. The light had disappeared. "I want to conserve its power. It used the light from the moon to save us and give us power to land safely. I want to focus the rest of the power on stopping the Dark Ones. You will have to do it. If I wielded this crystal, I would eventually be overcome by their darkness...the Dark Ones' darkness."

"Shane has managed to overcome a lot," Dimitri said. "I know he can do it.

"You are our hope," the Elder named Starro spoke for the first time. He sounded much older than Genesis.

285

"Yes, nephew," the other Elder named Renner spoke too. "You are our last and only hope."

"Can we get you to fly far from here?" Shane asked. "If you three are the only original inhabitants of Threa left, then I don't want you to be in harms way here. There is no doubt they realized we are here now." Shane looked over to where Sector 7 was nestled just a few miles away in the desert.

"No doubt at all," Dimitri agreed. "I was wondering why they weren't already here waiting for us, but we were about to crash so they must have been shocked that we managed to get out of a Roswell-like situation."

Genesis walked towards one of the walls of the ship. She touched it and an arch exit appeared with a small slanted walkway that led to the ground. She gestured for everyone to follow her out.

Once everyone was out of the ship, Genesis turned to face them and spoke with great dignity.

"Whatever happens on this night, do know that we have marveled in our sciences since we have been away from Threa. The Humanoids have been a wonderful way to keep our genes alive and to make us stronger. This is our fight too, and I will have us stand our ground on this ship. It is because of us, that Earth is threatened. Starro, Renner, and myself will be inside of the ship. The light will guard us, but it will run out eventually. Do not use the power of the crystal on us. As long as the Dark Ones are destroyed on Earth, Earth can continue to revolve for years to come."

Genesis walked up towards Shane and put her hand on his forehead. His eyes flashed and he was looking at a memory as seen through the eyes of Genesis. He was looking at himself, five years younger in the exact same spot he was standing now…

He heard several voices. Each of the entranced Humanoids were speaking in whispers. He saw himself just as he looked in the photograph Derek took.

Shane turned away and looked for the mountain where they almost crashed on, and while he could not see anything, he knew Derek was there taking the photos.

Genesis spoke to Renner and Starro, "He is the one. He will be able to fight off the Dark Ones that are blocking our return to Threa. Once he's grown more, we can bring him home with us. We can return, at last. My son will save us."

Shane stood transfixed as the Elders and all the Humanoids were transported into the ship. It then flew away up into the sky.

Shane opened his eyes and saw the present day Genesis staring back at him. He was reflected in her large black eyes. Shane opened his jacket pocket and pulled out the photo of himself that Derek left for him. In the photo, he was standing in the exact same area he was in now. After a few seconds of examining the photograph, he placed it back inside his jacket pocket.

"That's the moment I knew it was you, son," Genesis told Shane. "Our vessel flashed and lit the area for miles signaling our success in the perfected one…you."

"Now you understand everything," Starro spoke. "The challenges you faced the last few months, and the secrets we have kept until now—the right moment. I hope you are ready."

"Be brave," Renner added. "The Dark Ones are strong inside the human bodies, but you are the warrior that will stop these legendary creatures. They have overstayed their welcome in the universe. Most species do not get the chance to live so long. Today we will give them a taste of what they have done to our civilization and several civilizations before us."

Shane clenched the crystal in his hands and looked over towards Sector 7. In the distance, he saw headlights belonging to military vehicles heading towards the landing site.

"They are coming," Dimitri announced.

Shane looked over at Dimitri but saw that he was looking up at the sky and not towards the war zone heading their way from Sector 7. Shane followed his gaze up to the sky and saw a ball of light heading towards them.

"Just before we landed, I used some of the light you gave our ship to transport the entire population of our Humanoids," Genesis informed the group. "This is how we got you out of your bed that night you were brought here to the ritual. Think of it as a kind of teleportation. The Knowings have already schooled the Unknowings. While our Humanoid group cannot survive a possession of a Dark One, I wanted us all to be here as one and a family. Shane, you are our leader now."

The ball of white land landed behind the ship and it lit the area for miles. The light faded and a crowd of over one hundred people appeared. Some looked determined, others appeared scared or out of their minds in confusion.

Shane turned his back on them to face the oncoming Sector 7 camp that was now being controlled by the Dark Ones. He looked at the crystal and glanced towards the moon.

Tonight, he thought, everything will end. One way or the other.

More thunderclouds began to form above them and Shane began to worry that they would cover the moon. A strike of lightning and a clasp of thunder later, the clouds had swept over, hiding the moon from sight.

Chapter Twenty-Four:
Darkness and Light

Inside one of the Sector 7 Hummers was Noom, Nep, Manuel, Alice, Mike, and Caroline. The driver was one of the military guards.

"Faster!" Noom ordered to the driver. "I can see their ship glowing just ahead. We have our powers and human weapons. They have nothing but a dying ship.

"There are more Humanoids," Nep said.

"It looks like they brought their entire population," Noom said smiling. "We can kill them all in one go. Bring on the tanks!"

Alice had tears strolling down her face. Caroline patted her shoulder and Mike tried to calm Manuel down, who was shivering with fear because at any moment he could be possessed and would die almost instantly.

"Manuel," Noom said turning to him. "Afraid, are you?"

"You will pay," Manuel said, not making eye contact with Noom.

Noom laughed and said, "You will be my first example."

"What does that mean?" Mike spoke up.

"You will see," Noom teased.

Genesis was addressing the Humanoids about the situation that was taking place. Shane was not really paying attention to her words of comfort and hope. He was more preoccupied and scared with the scenario he was in. Thoughts kept racing in his mind. He wondered what would happen to his human parents or his Uncle Robert. He thought about his job at Fashion Rack and how they were probably wondering where he disappeared off to as well as Caroline. His mind rested on Alice, who he finally professed his feelings for, yet they could not be together.

When this is over, Shane thought, *I have to go back to this place that is supposed to be home. I don't event know Threa.*

Shane looked over at the mountains where they almost crashed earlier and imagined that Derek was there looking at him and taking photos. Shane did not know whether it was his imagination, or a trick of light, but he could have sworn he saw two small lights on the side of the mountain pointed at his direction. They appeared to have flickered on and of, then dimmed and got brighter before they turned off.

It appeared as though Shane was the only one who noticed the strange lights. He rested his thoughts on the fact that there was lightning in the sky as well that may have caused the strange flicker.

He turned back towards in the incoming military vehicles in the distance. He noticed there were several Hummers and two large tanks with threatening looking guns pointed towards them.

"Shane," Dimitri whispered, "You can do this. I know your father believed you could as well."

Shane did not answer. His mind was focused on the danger before him.

"Our population will be inside the ship for protection," Genesis said, gesturing to the large group of Humanoids slowly walking into the ship. "As long as the ship's light is emitting, they will be safe in there. Myself, Renner, and Starro will stand by your side. We've decided not to take refuge in the ship."

"I will too," Dimitri stated.

"And Dimitri," Genesis said patting Dimitri's shoulders.

"What if the light stops," Shane said, staring at the dull light glowing around the ship. "It appears as if it's losing power."

"It is," Genesis said, "but should its power fail, you can recharge it with the crystal on my command. I want this power used to stop the Dark Ones."

"Isn't our population important though," Starro questioned.

"Yes," Genesis replied, not taking her eyes off the incoming vehicles. "But I need to gauge how strong the Dark Ones are. This crystal is the only piece of Threa we have to stop the oldest creatures of the universe. For years they have wiped out other civilizations. I will not let them harm Earth as they have Threa. If this does not stop here, the humans will be in for an unexpected attack."

A few Hummers had stopped several hundred yards away from where Shane, Dimitri, and the Elders were standing. The door opened on one of them and Shane was surprised to see it was Dr. Morgan.

"You!" Shane yelled in surprise.

"Ah," Dr. Morgan said. "This doctor has met you before."

"He's possessed, Shane," Dimitri said through the corner of his mouth.

"Call me Nep," Dr. Morgan's possessor said. "I believe I have a few friends of yours."

The Hummer opened again with each of his friends flanked by a military officer. Agent Parker came out of the vehicle as well, and escorted out another man that Shane had never met before.

The man looked straight at Shane and mouthed, "I'm Derek's ally Manuel."

Shane nodded his understanding. He did not think he would first meet Manuel in this type of situation.

"Call me Noom," the possessed Agent Parker said in an evil, raspy voice.

"Noom," Genesis said. "We meet again."

"You escaped last time, Elder," Noom hissed. "However, your ship looks like it is about to die. How did your ship get saved when you were falling down to Earth moments ago?"

"You will soon learn," Genesis teased. "My people live on with the help of the human body. This time, we are prepared for your attacks."

Noom looked up into the cloudy sky. The moon was barely visible through a small opening in them.

"If it was a clear night," Noom said, "I would point out that your planet's light does not reach Earth. Earth would be in well range to see your planet as a star, but my sons are shadowing your planet and have kept it in darkness for many years."

"You are afraid that the elements of Threa will destroy you," Genesis said. "Our crystals absorb the lights of the universe that have allowed us to travel faster than its speed. It has allowed us to brighten your darkness and destroy you. If I am not mistaken, we are the only civilization that has ever been a threat."

"Well," Noom said. "You are no longer a threat. There are only three Elders left." Noom made eye contact with Starro and Renner.

Nep moved closer towards Shane. Shane moved backwards a bit to keep his distance.

"What makes him so special?" Nep asked Noom.

"Try him out and see!" Noom hissed.

Dr. Morgan's body began to shake and then went rigid. His eyes turned back into their green color and a black shadowy figure escaped his mouth and headed towards Shane.

Dimitri moved towards Shane, but Genesis held him back. She looked over at him and told him, "Stand back."

Nep eyed Shane up and down in his true form. He was a shadow, but his limbs could be made out. He had sharp toes and fingers signifying claws. His face had two pinpricks of red, which were his eyes. It gave Shane chills up his spine. His first thought was that he was standing before an entity that was as old as the beginning of time. Shane thought back to the several nights he had dreams of the Dark Ones. The more Shane thought about it, he realized they were not really dreams, but an actual Dark One trying to possess him or keep an eye on him as he slept.

"The Elders," Nep whispered so that only Shane could hear, "have been trying to create a being that could withstand us. They found the human race and created Humanoids. Half-breeds. Disgusting."

Caroline and Mike reached for each other's hands in the distance in fear. Alice was sobbing quietly. Manuel was transfixed on the floating Nep and Shane's interaction.

Nep hissed and his shadowy figure wisped into Shane's mouth. Shane fell backward into the sand with the pressure of the entity entering him.

He felt the same feeling he had felt the night before when one of the Dark Ones first attempted to possess him. Everything around Shane went black. He no longer could feel the sand under the back of his head. The military vehicles and the Elders' ship vanished from sight. It was quiet. He could not even see his own hands.

Shane could hear a whisper in a foreign tongue. He was not sure if it was speaking to him or to itself. Shane then began to see images of a purple-black orb. A blanket of darkness then encompassed the orb. He heard distant yells and hisses. Then he saw a small white light shoot out of the orb just before it all became black.

Threa, Shane's mind thought.

"Yes," said the voice of Nep.

Shane realized he was looking into Nep's memory of the world they had taken over. He saw the escape of the five Elders. This was Shane's home that he was to return to. The mission would be to destroy that blanket of darkness that was the power of the Dark Ones' overtaking it.

"How are you still able to think and see my own mind?," Nep's voice said, sounding very worried.

Shane began to think about his friends that were in danger because of the mission he was set on. Something from deep down inside him came alive. He kept on thinking about his life, his Earth parents, his job, his Malibu home, Derek, Candy, Peggy, and everything that had happened to him within the last few months.

The more his mind was working, the lighter the darkness became. Soon, his world began to materialize before him. He could see figures appearing before him. He felt the desert sand beneath him and he could move his fingers and touch their grains.

Shane turned his neck to see the Elders staring at him with Dimitri at their side. He could still feel coldness inside him. Nep was still in him, but he was trapped.

"What..." Noom said, his eyes widening at the shock of Shane standing up and looking normal.

"Shane, he's still inside you, isn't he?" Genesis asked him.

"Yes," Shane said, smiling. "He is afraid to escape me now. But I can push him out of me. I just know I can."

"Use your thoughts," Genesis said.

Shane focused on Nep. He could feel Nep's fear, and Nep was unable to feel Shane's emotions or see his memories. Nep had no control.

"Leave me!" Shane yelled to himself.

Shane's body shook for a second and out of his mouth, a dark shadow escaped and floated before Shane for a second before dissipating into nothing.

Dr. Morgan was on the ground, still unconscious, but he was alive. Noom walked over to his body and pointed his gun over Dr. Morgan.

"NO!" Shane shouted.

"His human body lives," Noom began gesturing the gun over the unconscious Dr. Morgan. "Yet, when we possess a Humanoid or an Elder, they die within minutes as they are unable to withstand our grasp. And you...you are of the Elders' decent...you are a Humanoid. You survived and killed one of my kind before my eyes. That has never been done. The Elders have in fact created a perfect evolution. Well, I'm afraid you are outnumbered and since you are part human, you will be able to die like a human."

Noom shot Dr. Morgan with the pistol. Alice, Mike, and Caroline looked away, with Alice's sobs becoming audible.

Manuel shifted uncomfortably under the grasp of one of the possessed military guards that was holding him. The Elders stood still, unwavering to what had just occurred.

Shane had been yelling as a lifeless Dr. Morgan lay before him, blood spilling onto the cold desert sand.

The thunder from the storm clouds cracked loud and echoed throughout the canyon. Lightning was flashing across the sky, illuminating the clouds.

"Your body, however, is still human," Noom whispered into the night at a moment when the thunder had subsided. His voice carried over to Shane.

Noom raised the gun towards Shane and he could hear Manuel and Alice scream. At the exact same moment that Noom pulled the trigger, Shane had raised his hand in the air with the crystal pointed to the sky, clasped by his fingers.

There was a loud bang and a roll of thunder. The heavens above appeared to have opened up. The entire landing site had been lit. Shane's first thought was that the clouds had cleared and light was coming from the moon, however the blinding light was lightning striking onto the crystal and him.

There were yells from the possessed Dark Ones and their human hostages. The Elders closed their eyes.

Like veins, the lightning in the clouds spread to the middle just above Shane and flowed down into his crystal. The bullet that Noom shot had turned to dust after coming within feet of Shane's body. Three military men had ran towards Shane at Noom's command and their bodies were electrocuted by the lightning entering the crystal. Dark shadows escaped their mouths as their human bodies fell to the ground, lifeless. The dark shadows turned into wisps of nothing and let out soft hisses that faded into the night.

"Noooooooo!" Noom shrieked in anger.

"That has never been done before," Genesis said in wonder. "We have never had lightning in our planet. It is a light source of course. I've never seen the crystal defend itself so strongly. The lightning is more powerful than the light from the moon!"

The lightning storm ended. It was as if Shane had stolen it all from the sky. The clouds above them began to disappear too leaving a clear sky above them splattered with many stars and the full moon.

The crystal, still in Shane's fingers, was now consistently glowing bright white. It felt warm to the touch and slightly static.

"Attack! Fire!" Noom ordered to the nearest tank and group of military men.

The men opened fire and began shooting towards the ship. The tank shot a missile from its large gun. Before any of the firepower could come near the ship or the Elders, the crystal emitted a glowing shockwave that created a small barrier around them. The bullets and missiles turned to dust upon coming contact with the barrier.

"That is amazing power," Genesis said. "I never even thought we could harvest the power of Earth's natural lightning."

Manuel spoke up, and it was quiet due to the shock of what just happened. "It worked for Ben Franklin. He used the power of lightning to learn about electricity, which runs light for humans."

"That is correct," Renner said. "We did push humans a bit in the advancement of their technologies, but electricity is one they learned themselves."

"Shane has tapped into Earth's light," Genesis said. "Remarkable. May I hold the crystal?"

Shane handed over the crystal to his mother. She held it tightly for a few seconds before returning it back to Shane's hands.

"Give the ship power now," She asked him.

Shane pointed the crystal to the ship and it became brighter than it had ever been. The orb was so bright that the entire canyon became lit for miles. It looked as though morning had come early.

"They'll be protected. You all should go in there too," Shane said to Genesis and the other Elders as he pointed the crystal in the direction of the ship.

Noom whispered a command to two of the guards next to him. One was holding Manuel and the other, Caroline. He gave them a signal and seconds later shadows shot out of the mouths of Parker, and the two military guards.

The shadows headed straight at the three Elders, all of whom had their backs to the Dark Ones.

"Noooo!" Shane yelled and he aimed the crystal at the Elders.

The shadows had entered the bodies of the three Elders. He heard them shriek in what sounded like horrifying, wall-climbing pain. Shane never heard a noise like that in his life.

Caroline and Parker covered their ears. They were confused about the scenario they were in, having just come back to consciousness after being possessed.

Manuel closed his eyes and tears streamed down his face. Dimitri retreated back and fell to the ground. He screamed at the top of his lungs as well.

The shadow that was inside Genesis had escaped before the crystal's light hit the three Elders in an attempt to protect them.

Starro and Renner fell to the ground and writhed for a few seconds before their bodies became still. They were dead.

Shane ran towards Genesis's body and fell to his knees sobbing. He put his hands on her forehead and held her small frame in his arms like a baby.

"I am here because of you," Shane sobbed. "You gave me a life. I will make the sure Marked Ones return home and that the Dark Ones that have created a barrier around Threa, are destroyed."

"Son," Genesis whispered. "You posses the light. It will guide you to where you want it. My child, do not let our extinction scare you. We live on within you, Manuel, Dimitri, and our population. You will make sure the Humanoid civilization will thrive on Threa for us. Thank you Shane for all you have done. Use Earth as a map...an example"

Shane cried and tears fell onto the smooth grey skin of his mother. Genesis closed her eyes and that was the last time she would ever open them.

297

Noom had repossessed Agent Parker and was standing right behind Shane. Dimitri backed away sobbing.

"See how easy that was for us," Noom said, catching Shane by surprise. "They cannot withstand us even for a few seconds. Yet, you can."

"You will pay for this," Shane muttered.

Noom backed away and raised his hands. Every single military official and scientist that were possessed, were falling to the ground as the culprits escaped through their mouths and floated above the landing site.

Noom spoke to the shadowy dark cloud above them, "My family...all of you enter the boy!"

The military officers freed Manuel, Mike, and Alice since they were no longer possessed. They all stood up and ran toward Shane instinctively.

Shane saw Noom laughing, but everything around him turned to darkness as the swarm of Dark Ones swirled around him, creating a wall.

Shane yelled out into the darkness, "Manuel and Dimitri! Get into the ship and take everyone home! Do not turn back. Do not worry about me!"

Shane figured that if they left in the powered ship, they could escape and their civilization could continue...his civilization.

Manuel and Dimitri heard Shane. They could not see him because the Dark Ones were swirling around him creating a barrier funnel that looked like a tornado.

"We must go," Manuel told Dimitri. He then looked over to Alice, Mike, and Caroline. "You three...get into one of the Hummers and drive off. Noom is distracted and only concerned with Shane right now. Go!"

"But..." Alice began.

"Do not come back here. I will leave a signal with you if everything is safe and they are stopped. I promise," Manuel said with finality.

Manuel hugged Alice, Caroline, and Mike. Then he turned and embraced Dimitri.

"Let's go," Manuel said to Dimitri.

Both Humanoids ran to the ship. When they got closer, the arch appeared. Dimitri picked up Starro and Renner's bodies and brought them into the ship. Manuel lifted Genesis's body and also made his way in where they were greeted by their fellow Humanoids.

The arch door closed and the orb glowed even brighter and began to float up into the sky. Alice, Mike, and Caroline stared at it as it elevated into the sky where it remained shining and stable.

"Are they not leaving?" Mike asked as they got into the Hummer, holding Caroline's hand.

"Probably not without Shane," Alice sniffled a sob.

Mike turned on the Hummer and he drove it off through the rough desert sand, putting a large distance between the landing site and Sector 7 far away behind them.

"Stop," Alice ordered Mike who instinctively stepped on the breaks.

"Why are we stopping?" Caroline asked. We need to get out of here."

"I just want to say goodbye," Alice sobbed.

Shane was standing still inside the shadowy funnel created by the Dark Ones' bodies. They were not attempting to posses him. It felt as though they were biding their time. Then, the body of Agent Parker walked through the shadow barrier and was now inside with Shane.

"It ends here," Noom hissed. He pulled out a gun from his suit jacket pocked and pointed it at Shane.

"You are right, it does end here," Shane smiled while rubbing the crystal behind his back. "The moon derives its light from the sun."

In the sky, there were hundreds of distant stars stamped across the ink-black heavens. The only other light was the bright, white orb, that was the ship hovering silently above the landing site, and the full moon.

Shane's crystal emitted another shockwave of light and then a large beam of light was streaming from the moon.

In the far distances across the country, one would be able see a huge beam of light shooting up into space. It was a miraculous view. The far reaches of the universe were very dark, but for that instant, it was as if the entire universe lit up. Everything went white for one second.

Shane saw the swirling smoky shadows dissipate before him with hisses of agony that faded into the air. He saw the look of horror on Noom's face through the body of Agent Parker.

Agent Parker's body fell to the ground and writhed until it was silent. He appeared dead at first, but Shane saw that his chest was moving up and down. He was still alive.

Noom had appeared before Shane in his true figure. His red eyes stared into Shane's blue eyes.

"You will now be extinct as well," Shane whispered into the night. He aimed the crystal at Noom, who did not move, and light emitted from the point of the crystal and hit the shadowy figure with such a force, that Shane fell backwards to the ground.

There was a small hiss and Noom's shadowy body disappeared into nothingness. Once Shane had got back up to his feet, he stopped the crystal from lighting up. Everything went slightly dark except for the bluish light from the moon and ship. Shane looked at the crystal in the palm of his hand. It still felt warm to the touch. It was glowing slightly, still showing signs that its power was still intact.

In the distance, Shane heard the sound of a vehicle heading his way. He grasped the crystal instinctively as to protect himself. He saw a green Hummer pull up and recognized its occupants.

"Guys!" Shane said, tears streaming down his face.

"You did it Shane!" Alice called out and she ran towards him and gave him a tight hug and a passionate kiss.

"Well done," Mike smiled.

"I am so glad this is over," Caroline sighed. "To think, we were just on a scavenger hunt with you and now you just battled these evil beings."

Shane smiled at Caroline's words. She seemed a little off, which may have been a side effect of her possession.

"You all helped me discover who I was in some way, shape, or form. I'm glad you are accepting of the truth," Shane said.

"She was your real mother, right?" Alice asked.

"Genesis? Yeah," Shane said quietly.

They stood there embracing each other in silence. The glowing orb of the ship hovering above them lit up the landing site again. It grew bright and dim as if signaling something.

"That must be Manuel's sign," Alice said. "That all is safe."

"Yeah," Shane agreed.

"Are you..." Alice began.

Shane looked at the crystal and then back into Alice's eyes.

"I have to," Shane said. "There's a cloud that is full of darkness in it and we have the only light that will change that darkness. I need to finish off the last remaining Dark Ones."

Alice nodded her understanding and began to tear up again. Shane gave her another kiss then pulled out the photograph of himself that Derek left behind for him. He gave it to Alice who took it with fresh tears streaming down her cheeks. Shane turned and walked towards the ship, which shot a beam of light to the ground.

Shane turned back to Alice, Mike, and Caroline and gave them a wave goodbye. He then continued to walk in the direction of the glowing ship wishing he could have said goodbye to his Earth family as well. He knew it was better this way. Manuel and Dimitri needed him on the ship.

Shane looked down at the sand and wondered if he would ever step foot on Earth again. He turned over to the canyon and thought about how much Derek played a role in preparing him for his mission. Shane even saw a few flashes from far away, but he figured he imagined it.

Shane walked into the beam of light and began to float up towards the ship. A rush of memories came flooding into his mind that may have been an effect of the light. It was as if he was learning about himself and what was to come.

The figures of Alice, Mike, and Caroline grew smaller. In the distance, he could see Sector 7 still standing there. Several of the military personnel and scientists that had been previously possessed were staring up at Shane from below with shocked looks on their faces. Shane wondered if Sector 7 would be closed for good after this evening. Dimitri and Manuel were waiting for him once he was back on the ship.

"It's time to go home," Dimitri said smiling. "You did well."

"Yes," Manuel added. "Your mother and father would be proud. Now let's go take care of the Dark Ones at Threa."

Shane nodded, clenched the crystal in his hand and entered the ship. He took one last glance at his friends below him. Manuel patted his shoulder and then took a glance towards the canyon ahead. He smiled at it.

The arch door closed after Shane entered. The bright ball of light floated up into the air. It hovered for a few seconds. Mike and Caroline waved. Alice stared at it crying. Agent Parker began to stir and became conscious. He looked at the orb in surprise and fell back to the ground.

The orb became so bright, it was nearly blinding. It then raced into the sky, and the light dissipated out of Earth's atmosphere.

"What happened?" Agent Parker asked Alice, Mike, and Caroline.

"They are no longer among us," Mike said. "They've left."

They all looked up into the star encrusted sky. Years later, a new star would appear in the constellation that would offer a radiant glow.

Chapter Twenty-Five:
Fifteen Years

It was a late summer night in Los Angeles. A man, in his fifties was walking up a flight of stairs with a bag of groceries. He had sandy blonde hair that was graying and he wore black square-framed glasses. He reached the floor of his condo and made his way to his unit.

He arrived at his door and saw that another man, wearing a baseball cap, was waiting outside.

"Can I help you," the man with the groceries asked of the strange guest who was waiting outside his door.

"Landon Parker?" the man with the baseball cap asked.

"Yes," Landon responded with suspicion.

"My name is Robert Powers," the man in the baseball cap said, extending his hand to shake Landon's.

Landon put his grocery bags down and accepted it. He then put his key into his door to unlock it.

"Come in," Landon told Robert. "I know you."

Robert followed Landon into his condo. Landon lived alone in a very modern and expensive looking condo. His dog ran up to him and began barking at the new guest. Landon told his dog to hush and he obliged. The living room had a spectacular view of downtown Los Angeles, as it was perched on a hill.

"Nice place you have here," Robert said as Landon set his bags on the kitchen counter.

"I had a nice retirement," Landon responded. "Thank you."

"You are probably wondering why I am here," Robert said.

"I have an idea," Landon replied. "You know it is not safe to be here. I may be retired, but what makes you think I won't make a few calls?"

"Because I know you do not want to get involved on this issue anymore," Robert explained. "I have emailed you many times and tried calling you and have received no reply back from you. I'm sorry I've showed up uninvited, but a little digging around and I found your residency."

"Yes," Landon replied. "Very foolish to do that. I read and heard your messages. I will speak to you here, off the record and I must ask you that you never contact me or see me again after today's meeting."

"Understood," Robert nodded.

Landon closed the blinds to every window in the living room and invited Robert to take a seat on the couch. Robert accepted the offer and sat down. He looked around the apartment, taking in the fascinating items that were on one of Landon's bookshelves. Apart from books, there were awards, medals, trophies, and a peculiar, shiny silver cone ornately placed on the shelves.

Landon took a seat across from Robert in a recliner and waited for Robert's attention to focus back on him.

"So," Robert began. "I'm here to speak about my nephew. He went missing fifteen years ago. My sister-in-law, his mother, never got closure. She passed away a few months ago."

"I'm sorry to hear that," Landon said. He genuinely sounded sympathetic. "I know that your family has been through so much. You were very smart to take your sister-in-law and her husband with you to Arizona during the time my agency was looking for Shane."

"A man named Manuel called and told me something was happening and asked me to leave," Robert said. "His father is still alive though. He is depressed and alone, but still living in Beverly

Hills. Mr. Parker, I want answers. I've kept quiet for so long and I just want closure for myself. My friend Derek was killed in an accident twenty years ago. I know it was not really an accident."

Landon shifted uncomfortably in his chair. He looked into Robert's eyes and said, "You are right. It was not an accident. He knew too much. And from the e-mail you sent, so do you."

"I was there that night," Robert said. "I was in that mountain that night in the same place Derek was. That man, Manuel, told me the whole story when he called, but I kept it quiet. I knew the story but I did not know much about what Shane was facing. But that summer night, fifteen years ago, I was taking pictures like Derek was from that desert canyon."

Robert pulled a few photos from his jacket pocket and showed them to Landon. Landon looked through them and saw himself standing and facing Shane.

Landon's mind flashed back to that night. He had no recollection of what happened up until he was freed from his possessor. When he came around, Shane had left Earth.

"You tried to kill him," Robert said as he noticed Landon staring at a photo of himself pointing a gun towards Shane.

"I was possessed," Landon said. "By an entity that had been living on Earth unnoticed for years."

"I flashed my vehicle headlights at one point," Robert recounted. "I tried to be noticed and perhaps cause a distraction. Not really sure what I was thinking, but nobody ever noticed. At least I do not think anyone did."

"So you were there and not in Arizona? You saw the lights then?" Landon asked.

"Yes," Robert said, racking through his memory. "There was a huge stream of light that was coming from the moon and it saved Shane and stopped whatever that dark cloud was. That same light was seen for miles. It was on the news. Of course the government said it was an experiment they were working on."

"A cover up," Landon said. "Right before I was discharged from the government, I worked on tying up those loose ends and putting closure to the Non-Human Relations agency. The agency would no longer exist and every file we had was burned. Our base camp, once known was Sector 7, was burned down. Every person that was possessed or worked at Sector 7 was discharged too, but are bound to secrecy."

"The government's plan?" Robert said with resentment in his voice.

"Yes. People, myself included, that worked for Sector 7 were in fear to ever speak of those events. Our world is better off not knowing *the truth*; that life outside of our planet exists and we were in contact with them. I actually wanted to be 'silenced' myself. The memories are painful. The world will never know that alien beings once walked among us. That chapter has ended. Ever since the evil was destroyed, thanks to your nephew, there have been no reports or sightings of unidentified flying objects or anything paranormal for that matter. I imagine that Shane's kind are now living in their world—millions and millions of miles away. Only we know that there is another civilization out there of people that look like us. They have never returned since they left. I can only imagine that their civilization lives on."

"Only we know?" Robert questioned. "What does that mean?"

"Well you were there," Landon said. "You saw Shane left at will with them. Everyone else that was there that night is not talking. Shane's friends Mike, Alice, and Caroline never spoke about that night publically either. Before they drove off, I told them I would not let the government know about them as long as they kept quiet. They obliged. I do not know what happened to them. I do not even know if they are still alive. I never tried to find them."

"I do not know where they are either," Robert replied. "So Shane went back to where his ancestors are from?"

"Yes," Landon said. "I hope you have closure now. I'm sure you've wanted to talk about this with someone for so long, but you kept quiet because of what happened to Derek, is that not true?"

"Yeah, that's true," Robert admitted. "Why are you not going to report me then?"

"To be honest," Landon responded, "because it would endanger me too. I do not want to let the cat out of the bag. This is a case that remains closed forever. Shane was reported 'missing' by his parents and believed him to be dead." Landon's dog jumped onto his lap and he began to pet him absentmindedly.

Landon told Robert more details of that night that he learned from Alice, Mike, and Caroline as they witnessed it first hand. Robert finally understood much of what happened and why Derek left his message to Shane.

"It's funny," Robert said. "He was my best friend and he never told me anything. I guess he was worried that since I was Shane's family, he did not want me to be involved. In the end, I guess I somewhat did get involved."

"Things are better left unsaid though," Landon told Robert, signaling the end of their conversation. "We live in a world that is not the only one that holds life in this universe. We may never be able to visit the planet that Shane lives on now, but I leave you with this thought, Mr. Powers. If our population knew the truth or if they learned that the human race was used in an experiment to help an alien population live on and avoid extinction, there would be chaos. Religions and social order would be challenged. Our government was right to go through the lengths it did, if it meant keeping world order with seven billion people. I'm not saying they were moral, I am just saying they were smart. It would have been dangerous. Earth is no longer threatened and communication with Shane's kind ended years and years ago. The best thing we can do is live on. We have been left alone to go about living the way we always have."

Robert nodded in agreement. In retrospect, he thought, world order was very important and he knew that Earth's best-kept secret would forever have to remain a secret.

Robert stood up from the couch and walked over to the fireplace that was lit with a very warm fire. He threw the photos he took into it and they burned to ash before him.

Landon stood up and walked next to Robert, shaking his hand. Without saying anything, there was an understanding between the two men.

"Thank you for talking to me," Robert said. "I'll be off."

"One second," Landon called to Robert has he made his way to the door, "My team never gave this to Derek after he took those photos for us. I want you to have it. You are the only living person left that was close to him."

Robert reached out for an envelope that Landon handed to him. Robert opened it to find its contents. It was a check for twenty-five thousand dollars.

"Have a nice life sir. We speak of this no more moving forward," Landon said, and smiled saying nothing more.

Robert shook his head, still awestruck by the money, and made his way out of Landon's condo. His last words to him were, "Thanks."

Landon locked his door once Robert left. He walked over to his kitchen counter and pulled out a letter from his drawer. It was addressed to him. He read the letter many times, but kept it to re-read whenever he thought about that night when light saved the world. He read it aloud in a whisper to himself.

Dear Landon,

It was nice to hear from you. I'm doing well. I will not say where I am in case this letter falls into the wrong hands, but the new house is gorgeous. We are near the beach. I miss California though, but we feel safer out here. M and C are our neighbors. Can you believe those two ended up married? I did not see that one coming. My fiancé and M have become great friends too. I hope that we cross paths again. I appreciate all you have done for us and keeping us off the radar.

I saw that special on TV again about unsolved mysteries and S's disappearance. I miss him so much. I wonder sometimes, what life would have been if he stayed? Sometimes I feel like he's watching me from up there beyond the stars.

Let's plan to meet up soon, whenever we visit California.

Sincerely,

A

      Robert got into his car after walking out of Landon's complex. He drove off down the winding hill roads. He eventually reached a sharp turn in the road and parked his car. There was a metal barrier that was built so that any oncoming vehicles that crashed would hit the barrier and not drive off the edge. Robert took a bouquet of flowers from the backseat of his car and set them on the ground.

      "Go in peace, Derek," Robert said, while looking up at the starry sky. "You are up there somewhere. And so is Shane."

About The Author

A.J. Mayers was born and raised in Laredo, TX. At 6 years old, he had a dream to one day be a published author inspired by his passion for writing. Years later he also became interested in the entertainment industry in Hollywood. He attended the University of Texas at Austin, and moved to Los Angeles, CA after graduation where he currently works in the film industry.

This novel is a childhood dream come true.

www.aj-mayers.com/amongus

8032529R00185

Made in the USA
San Bernardino, CA
26 January 2014